**Nick Ford's record with the federal government is spotless. He's on the fast track to success—and running for his life. . . .**

Accountants lead straightforward, conventional lives, or so Nick always believed, until the day he began his audit of the Yünnan Project.

Soon Nick's every move is shadowed by a boss of the Chinese underworld, his best friend and colleague is brutally murdered, and he's accused by a leading U.S. senator of a crime he didn't commit.

Alone, discredited, Nick must choose: hide from his problems as he has all his life, or fight back with the help of the one woman willing to stand by his side. His decision thrusts him into a deadly realm of plots and counterplots where things are not always what they seem and even his own gover...

To survive, Nick ... ...les, because when the ... ...ot be trusted, only a ... . . . .

Trust no one or be ...

# DECEIVED

# DECEIVED

## James Koeper

A SIGNET BOOK

SIGNET
Published by the Penguin Group
Penguin Putnam Inc., 375 Hudson Street,
New York, New York 10014, U.S.A.
Penguin Books Ltd, 27 Wrights Lane,
London W8 5TZ, England
Penguin Books Australia Ltd, Ringwood,
Victoria, Australia
Penguin Books Canada Ltd, 10 Alcorn Avenue,
Toronto, Ontario, Canada M4V 3B2
Penguin Books (N.Z.) Ltd, 182–190 Wairau Road,
Auckland 10, New Zealand

Penguin Books Ltd, Registered Offices:
Harmondsworth, Middlesex, England

First published by Signet, an imprint of Dutton NAL,
a member of Penguin Putnam Inc.

First Printing, May, 1999
10  9  8  7  6  5  4  3  2  1

PUBLISHER'S NOTE
This is a work of fiction. Names, characters, places, and incidents either are
the product of the author's imagination or are used fictitiously, and any resemblance to actual persons, living or dead, events, or locales is entirely
coincidental.

*For my parents,*
*whose love of the printed word*
*opened the world to me*

## ACKNOWLEDGMENTS

I would like to acknowledge Pat Maloney, Adriene Clifford, Curtis Mo, Carl Haberly, Hans Klijnsmit, Joe Pittman, and Mel Berger for their invaluable assistance, and offer a special thanks to my wife, Lorraine, whose counsel and support I treasure.

# 1

Nick Ford thumbed the contents of his briefcase a last
time, added a notepad and two pens, then snapped its
cover shut. A quick inspection followed: he smoothed
the front of his dark blue suit coat, straightened his
rep tie, and pulled at the cuffs of his white oxford
shirt. The standard Washington, D.C. uniform—no
spots, no wrinkles, no risks.

He caught his reflection in the frame of a photo set
on his desk. A strong face, light brown hair parted on
the side, beginning to show gray above the temples.
A competent, reliable image. He approved.

"All right, Scott, you ready to go?" he asked, rising
from behind the desk.

In response Scott Johnson groaned and rolled his
head backward, letting his neck go limp.

"Scott," Nick tried again.

"But lunch hour's almost over. We'll miss her."

Nick closed his eyes and sighed. They were the same
age, thirty-five, but Scott still acted like a college kid.
Almost looked the part too with his lanky build, tousled black hair, and deep tan.

Scott put his palms together as if to pray. "Just a
few more minutes, huh, chief? Word running around
the office is she's dynamite."

"She" referred to the new staff auditor down the
hall, and yes, Nick had heard the same. "If I had any
brains, I'd make you pick up the office manual and
read the chapter on sexual harassment." As if he, boss
or not, could *make* Scott do anything.

Scott grinned. "You think I need some how-to
instructions?"

Nick chuckled in exasperation, then shook his head.
"Someday your big mouth is going to land you in one

hell of a mess. And I suppose you'll look to me to bail you out, won't you?" And if Nick could, he would—both knew that.

Scott's grin only broadened. "C'mon, Nick, screw 'em if they can't take a joke. What happened to people's sense of humor?"

"Just rein it in, okay?" Nick employed an authoritative tone, but it rang hollow. "Oh, hell," Nick said, falling back into his seat, "dig your own grave. Just remember not everybody knows you as well as I do. Some might even take you seriously. You're going to be working with this new auditor, and I'd like to avoid any problems."

Scott's eyes lit up. "Working with her?"

Nick nodded. "Starting this afternoon, she's part of the team. I'm staffing her on the Yünnan Project audit. I thought it would be a good introduction for her." Nick didn't add: "and you would be a good teacher," though he thought it. When Scott focused on work, he was a damn good auditor. Gifted, really, if you could apply that term to an accountant.

"That means late nights . . . weekends . . ." Scott stiffened ramrod straight and made a show of crossing his heart. "I'll be on my best behavior. Just one peek, though, huh?"

Nick glanced at his watch. Forty-five minutes to the start of the Senate hearing—time enough to drive the dozen or so blocks, park, and review his notes a last time, not much else. Certainly no time for games. "Two months riding on these hearings, and what're you interested in . . . ?"

Nothing new there. Scott hadn't changed since they started at the General Accounting Office, the GAO, eleven years ago. In many ways Nick admired Scott's ability to so easily divorce work from play.

Scott ripped a sheet from a yellow legal pad on Nick's desk, crumpled it into a ball, and tossed it from hand to hand. "Let's make a deal. One shot." Scott pointed toward the wastepaper basket. "From the outside. I make it, we stay five minutes; I miss, we leave."

Nick shook his head.

"*C'mon,* I'll make it easy for you," Scott persisted. "Two in a row or we vamoose. Here's the first." Scott arched a long shot over a make-believe defender; it fell cleanly through the rim of the wastebasket. "Bango! All net. Just tickled the twine."

Scott beamed, arms in the air. "Do you realize I've got all my college eligibility left? It's just a matter of time before some Georgetown scout catches my game, then *boom,* I say good-bye to all this"—Scott gestured to the office—"and hello to big-time hoops. Man, I'm going to rake in some coin then."

Nick smiled despite himself. "Right, a lot of Georgetown scouts hang out at the Y, watching the over-thirty league."

Scott studiously ignored the comment. He retrieved the paper ball and ran back across the office. "Down by two. Six seconds left. Only a *miracle* can save Georgetown now. St. John's brings it up the court. Johnson moves in to take the foul, but wait! He *steals the ball.* Dribbles up court." Scott conscientiously acted out his part. "The clock shows one. He stops, sets, two defenders on him, but he's going to go up! He launches a long desperation shot from three-point range!"

Nick tracked the paper ball's arc and, at the last moment, a foot above the wastebasket, swung out his arm and intercepted it. He imitated Scott's voice while trying hard to keep a straight face: "Ford from St. John's blocks the shot! The crowd goes wild, carries Ford off the court on their shoulders!" Nick lifted his briefcase and started for the office door. "Georgetown loses, Scott. Now, let's get going."

Scott's protests—"unfair, goal tending"—fell deafly. Swearing under his breath, he grabbed a briefcase full of documents and followed.

The Energy and Commerce subcommittee filed in late, as a doctor might to an appointment, a habit refined to make clear who was in control and who had to answer to whom. Their posturing dovetailed nicely with the raised bench behind which they sat, two, maybe three feet higher than the table from where the witnesses testified, allowing the senators to peer down on their prey.

Charles Whitford III, seventy-eight, senator from the great state of Alabama since the Civil War—at least it seemed he'd been in office that long—led the group of six, walking briskly with the aid of a cane. He wore a khaki summer suit offset by a pale blue tie. The tip of the reading glasses he wore to such good effect during his famed inquisitions showed from above his suit pocket. Above average height. Not yet infirm, but definitely bowed by age. His white hair, worn long for a man of his age, was combed straight back and, after a few waves, curled at the nape of his neck: the mane of an old lion.

It took several minutes for the senators to find their seats. In the interim, at the witness table, Nick busied himself reviewing his notes while Scott calmly shuffled papers, arranging four neat piles of material. Nick was to be examined; Scott was there for support if needed, both technical and moral. In front of Nick, at the table's midpoint, three light bulbs were affixed—one green, one yellow, and one red—to apportion questioning.

Two cameras, from C-Span and CNN, stood to their left, tucked in a small balcony built especially for that purpose. The hearing was news, maybe of a back-page business section variety, but news just the same.

Nick noticed the CNN camera had swung in his direction. Testifying in front of a Senate subcommittee, especially in front of cameras, would once have set Nick's heart racing and turned his palms moist, but no longer. After eleven years with the GAO, all of it in the Division of Special Investigations, testifying before Congress had become, if not an everyday occurrence, at least a common one. As the chief auditor on the case before the subcommittee, Nick would be questioned, give answers, then head back to the office to divide his time among a dozen other similar investigations. A cut-and-dried case of overbilling.

Routine.

Beneath the seal of the United States imbedded in the white marble wall, the six senators spread out along a curved bench of dark mahogany. They sat in high-backed leather chairs, microphones set on the bench in front of them. Behind the senators, in simple wooden chairs, sat the senators' aides: young men and women in their twenties, all freshly scrubbed, all conservatively dressed in dark gray or blue, all intelligent if somewhat naive, and all particularly eager to please their bosses.

Nick let his eyes travel from committee member to committee member. A couple approving looks, a couple disapproving, the balance bored. Senator Whitford clapped his hand on the back of a fellow senator and laughed. Probably at one of his own jokes, Nick guessed.

Nick had testified in front of Whitford twice in the past, each time before the Senate Armed Services committee, which Whitford chaired. Rarely was there a doubt what position Whitford would adopt during an Armed Services hearing—it was said, with some justification, that the senator had never met a defense appropriation he didn't approve of. Whitford had only recently joined the Energy and Commerce committee, however, and so far his loyalties were less apparent.

The strong voice of the chairman of the committee, Senator Callahan of Texas, silenced the gallery. He called the hearing to order, then began his brief introductory remarks.

Nick took a drink of water and a deep breath, his nerves steady. Learn your material, deliberate before each answer, stay poised, never show nerves: Nick mentally reviewed the preflight checklist for giving testimony.

Chairman Callahan concluded with time-honored puffery: "Today, our first day of direct testimony, it will be our honor to hear from a most esteemed witness: Mr. Nicholas Ford of the General Accounting Office's Division of Special Investigations. Mr. Ford, if you will please rise, raise your right hand, and repeat after me. . . ."

Nick rose, straight-backed, and parroted the chairman's words, swearing the testimony he was about to give would be truthful. He then sat, the floor his. He mustered a confident voice and plunged headlong into a short written statement.

"Mr. Chairman, members of the committee, as you know, two months ago the ranking minority member of the Energy and Commerce committee asked me to undertake an audit of the contract between Smith Pettit, Inc., and the People's Republic of China for the design and construction of a pair of hydroelectric dams along the upper Yangtzee River in China's Yünnan Province . . . the so-called Yünnan Project. My staff and I began our investigations immediately, and those investigations are ongoing.

"I must stress that the testimony I give today is based on a preliminary review; I offer it only in the interest of furthering the subcommittee's goal of fact finding. At this stage in our investigation we have uncovered evidence of unallowable charges by Smith Pettit in excess of twenty-eight million dollars. Evidence, in my opinion, sufficient to warrant a referral to the Justice Department for possible criminal sanctions."

Nick looked up from the paper and said, "I am open to your questions."

Senator Raine from New Hampshire jumped in first, as Nick hoped she would. A vocal advocate of budgetary constraint and the GAO's firmest ally on the subcommittee, she had first called for the audit. Chairman Callahan recognized her.

"Mr. Ford, on behalf of the entire committee I thank you for taking time from your busy schedule to appear before us today. I'd like to start today's questioning by tracing the investigation's time line . . ."

And so it began, Senator Raine lobbing softball after softball, enabling Nick to present the GAO's findings in the best possible light.

It had started in the spring of that year, as Nick explained. Senator Raine, upset the Yünnan Project had ballooned two hundred million dollars over budget, had requested a GAO audit. The GAO honored her request, as protocol demanded of all requests from ranking minority committee members. A preliminary review found multiple instances of duplicate billing. That triggered a fuller audit, and revealed evidence of widespread billing irregularities.

When Nick finished his summary, Senator Raine asked, "Mr. Ford, can you explain why the GAO, or the Senate of the United States for that matter, has any interest whatsoever in billing irregularities between a U.S. company and the People's Republic of China?"

"Although Smith Pettit contracted with the People's Republic of China for the construction of the hydroelectric dams, a portion of the estimated one point eight billion dollar project cost, ten percent to be exact, will be paid from the general revenues of the United States pursuant to the Alternative Energy Assistance Program."

"Can you explain to the subcommittee the purpose of the Alternative Energy Assistance Program?"

Nick nodded. "The program seeks to encourage foreign nations to develop environmentally friendly forms of power—hydroelectric, wind, geothermal, and solar—and specifically seeks to discourage the construction of nuclear power plants which could be used to refine weapons-grade plutonium."

"Encourage and discourage how?"

In the present case, the United States has agreed to fund ten percent of the dams' construction costs, and in return China has agreed to abandon all plans for nuclear power plants in the Yünnan Province. The program requires the host nation to employ an American company as general contractor—in essence a means for the United States to indirectly recoup much of its outlay—in this instance China chose Smith Pettit."

"All right, so the taxpayers' money is on the line, and you say it's been misspent."

"We have found numerous cases of unallowable billing, that is correct."

"Can you share any specifics with us?"

"I'd be happy to, Senator. The subcommittee members have my interim audit report in front of them; it itemizes the twenty-eight million dollars in overbilling we have documented to date. Let me touch on them briefly. . . ."

Nick mentioned the fictitious overtime costs, the inflated construction costs, and the improperly allocated overhead costs. He cited the unallowable expense-account items, including charges for liquor and golf junkets to Thailand. Then Nick hit the numbers and concurrently his stride. That was his domain: estimated costs, depreciation allowances, material price variances, projected cost overruns. To him they made the case plainly: the GAO has caught Smith Pettit playing a dirty game.

When Nick finished, Senator Raine paused, letting Nick's statement settle. Obviously pleased, she let the panel know it by her silence.

"Is the senator from Maine prepared to yield?" Chairman Callahan asked after a few moments.

Senator Raine shook her head, "Mr. Ford, this is a one point eight *billion* dollar project. Surely in a contract of that magnitude we have to expect some billing irregularities?"

Nick smiled to himself—Senator Raine played the game well: first dispense with the objections, then drive the point home. He dove gladly into his appointed role. "Let me make myself clear. In the course of our investigations we uncovered many examples of clerical errors. I am *not* faulting anybody for such errors. Far from it. I'm quite sympathetic to bureaucratic inefficiency, but that is not the problem in this case.

The reason I'm here before you today has nothing to do with simple mistakes. It has to do with gross improprieties bordering on fraud. Inflating actual costs, creating fictitious costs, treating the Yünnan Project as a cash cow."

"You estimate, Mr. Ford, that Smith Pettit was unjustly enriched by in excess of twenty-eight million dollars. Can you be more exact?"

"At this point, no. There are tens of millions of dollars in questionable charges we have yet to review. In addition, given the magnitude of improprieties we have uncovered, I have come to the conclusion that examinations of the subcontractors are warranted to verify their fees and expenses are appropriate and reasonable. If we do in fact discover similar billing irregularities in the subcontracts, we can expect total—"

A voice exploded in anger. *"Point of order, Mr. Chairman. Point of order!"*

Eyes flipped in the sound's direction, toward Senator Charles Whitford III, who glared a long moment at Nick before speaking, his voice resonating in the now still chamber. "If I may remind our *esteemed* witness, we have convened here today to hear the results of an audit, not to engage in unsubstantiated and inflammatory *speculation.* Unless the witness has hard *facts* to place before us in evidence, I insist the chair instruct him to limit his speech accordingly."

Chairman Callahan nodded deferentially in Senator Whitford's direction, then turned to Nick. "Mr. Ford, Senator Whitford's point is well taken. You mentioned subcontracts. Have you evidence of billing irregularities in any subcontracts?"

"Not at this time, Mr. Chairman," Nick said, chastened. "We did not originally intend to include a review of the subcontracts within the scope of our audit."

"Then I suggest, until such time as you can produce evidence, you limit your testimony to facts on hand."

"Yes, Mr. Chairman."

Chairman Callahan turned to Senator Raine. "Senator, do you wish to continue?"

"I do, Mr. Chairman. A few more questions."

Senator Raine spent the next few minutes rehabilitating Nick; when she finished the questions from the other subcommittee members began.

The senator from Kentucky asked technical questions, the senator from Oregon insisted on making speeches that weren't questions at all, and the senator from Florida made mild, noncommittal statements, waiting for Senator Whitford, the big gun, to join the battle.

Nick risked a few glances at Whitford, each time to find the senator glowering in his direction. Whitford, however, seemed content to let the other members carry the questioning; he sat sternly, his hands folded in front of him and his famous glasses parked in his suit pocket.

The hour of testimony ended with just the one outburst from Senator Whitford—for that Nick was grateful.

Scott leaned into Nick when Senator Callahan declared the short afternoon session closed. "Man-o-man," he whispered, "you really hit some kind of major nerve with Whitford. I've never seen anybody turn so red. What the hell was that all about?"

Nick shook his head; Whitford was about the last person he wanted as an enemy. "I wish I knew, Scott. I really wish I knew."

# 2

The curtains parted and the waiter reappeared. In his right hand, by a bamboo handle, he carried what looked like a box cloaked by an embroidered red silk cloth. He set it gently on the table in front of Pu-Yi.

Pu-Yi eyed the silk-covered box for a moment, then continued with his meal. He left the waiter standing uneasily, hands folded in front of him, head and eyes to the ground.

From the plate before him Pu-Yi used chopsticks to pinch the last piece of roasted eel. The few bones he encountered on chewing he spat onto the tablecloth to the side of the plate—a small mound of bones which joined a half dozen other mounds.

If the waiter or Pu-Yi's eating companion gave the action a second thought, they did not show it. Spitting—of food, of phlegm, of almost anything—was not only accepted but common throughout China, though rarely at the dinner table. However, in Huizhou it was unwise to remark upon anyone's manners. The city, a rapidly expanding metropolis of luxury hotels and skyscrapers seventy miles north of Hong Kong, catered to the triads, the Chinese criminal syndicates. China's Las Vegas, though Pu-Yi had a much more interesting diversion than gambling in mind tonight.

He examined the young woman sitting beside him—sixteen, maybe seventeen—dressed in a dark blue *cheongsam*, a silk dress with high slits up the sides, worn tight and form-fitting. A traditional costume long in disfavor except at houses such as this one. Pu-Yi caught the hint of fear and embarrassment in the girl's eyes. The job was still new to her, Pu-Yi guessed; catering to the sexual whims of a stranger still shocking.

What would those eyes hold, he wondered, when he had her pinned beneath him? When she bucked at the pleasure, and at the pain?

The proprietor had offered her to him. A gift. Pu-Yi, after all, was a man of importance—he worked for John Li—and John Li's reach stretched all the way to Beijing. A favor to one of John Li's men, especially his *hung kwan,* chief lieutenant, might be repaid many times over. A good investment.

Pu-Yi finished his soup, and only then acknowledged the waiter with a curt nod. On signal the waiter gripped a corner of the silk cloth and jerked it to the air.

Underneath was not a box but a metal mesh cage. In its bottom a snake, dusty colored and mottled, lay coiled and unmoving.

Pu-Yi considered the animal dispassionately for a moment, then reached for his plate and banged it against the side of the cage.

The snake's coils tightened slightly, the only movement.

The waiter's lips trembled as Pu-Yi raised his eyes and glared—the instructions had been clear: price was no object, but quality was.

Pu-Yi lifted a chopstick from the table and poked it through the half-inch mesh, prodding the snake. It unwound quickly, fluidly. Against the far side of the cage the snake reared up and revealed itself. Its hood flared, four inches or more across—a cobra.

Pu-Yi looked again at the girl beside him. She shivered, but also grinned crookedly, both apprehensive and fascinated, it seemed. Pu-Yi gently intertwined his hand with hers. His fingers caressed for a moment, then found and encircled her index finger, and suddenly, like a different type of snake, constricted sharply, clamping vice-like.

The girl's eyes widened in surprise, but just as quickly relaxed as Pu-Yi drew her finger to his lips. Gently, he kissed its tip—so delicate and pink.

Pu-Yi's eyes jumped, from snake to woman and

back, as he turned the girl's finger from his lips and redirected it at the cage. He monitored her expression closely as he forced her finger forward.

The girl's smile held steady for a moment, and Pu-Yi imagined her thoughts: *a game, a joke to make me squeal like a schoolgirl, but I will do nothing and call his bluff.*

Another foot forward and the girl's smile broke. It turned flat—a sharp red gash—as her face grew taught. Then, when her fingertip was but a few inches from the cage, the girl screamed. "Bu xing. *Bu xing.*" No, *no.* She turned her free hand to a fist and thumped it against Pu-Yi's shoulder.

As if gnat bites, Pu-Yi ignored the blows; he poked the girl's fingertip through the mesh of the cage.

The tongue of the cobra shot out, three times in quick succession. With a hiss its hood flared wider, a final warning before it launched itself forward, mouth gaping, led by the fangs of its upper jaw. In that instant Pu-Yi jerked back the girl's finger.

The snake hit steel mesh, nothing more.

Pu-Yi returned the girl's finger to his mouth, again kissed its tip gently. He laughed then, loudly, amused and pleased. The waiter joined him after a moment, nervously. The girl, her face white, eyes completely taken by fear, did not.

Pu-Yi looked at the waiter. "The snake will do," he said in Cantonese.

The waiter nodded and produced a Y-shaped utensil from his cadre jacket. He fit it between the mesh of the cage and expertly pinned the head of the cobra to the cage floor. He then opened a trapdoor on the top of the cage, reached in, and took hold of the snake just behind its head. He released the Y-shaped utensil and lifted the snake from the cage, his other, now free hand stretching the snake its full length, almost three feet.

One outside corner of the cage hosted a short, razor-sharp blade. The waiter turned the snake upside down and with a quick motion sliced open the snake's underside just below its head. From the horizontal wound the blood of the snake flowed freely into a waiting bowl.

When the last drops had fallen from the snake's now limp body, Pu-Yi pulled the bowl toward him. The drink would make him strong, and hard, ensuring a lengthy and enjoyable night.

Pu-Yi stared at the girl. She lowered her eyes, her cheeks still white. It was good to be home where the women knew their place, not like the American cows who so often had to be reminded.

He lifted the bowl in two hands, prepared to raise it to his lips, when the curtains again parted and another waiter entered carrying a telephone. The waiter bowed low and held the phone out to Pu-Yi.

"Who is it?" Pu-Yi barked angrily.

"Mr. John Li," the waiter said, and Pu-Yi's annoyance left him instantly.

"Bring the phone here," Pu-Yi demanded, and then, after the waiter had set the phone on the table: "Out." He looked at the girl and pointed at the exit. *"All of you."*

All three scrambled for the exit. When they were gone, Pu-Yi lifted the receiver. "Hello," he said.

The gruff and familiar voice on the other end of the line was all business; Pu-Yi expected nothing more. "Be in front of my hotel. Two hours."

"Yes, sir."

"We leave again. A two a.m. flight. Out of Hong Kong."

Pu-Yi looked after the departed girl, disappointed. "Tonight?" he confirmed.

"There have been certain developments—unfortunate developments—in Washington concerning the Yünnan dams. My presence is required."

"Yes, sir," Pu-Yi said again. He did not ask for a fuller explanation. In John Li's eyes he was a soldier, a trained weapon, nothing more, certainly not one with whom to discuss developments or strategy, and frankly Pu-Yi preferred it that way.

"Call Chen Tao-tzi," Li ordered. "Have him place another call to Ford. Immediately."

"The amount?" Pu-Yi asked.

"Eighty thousand. Tell him the money will be wired to his account within the hour."

The line went dead, their discussion terminated with no exchange of pleasantries.

Pu-Yi looked from the bowl in front of him to his watch. Two hours. It would take him close to an hour to collect his things and drive to John Li's hotel, another quarter hour to contact Chen Tao-tzi. That left only forty-five minutes, little time for the diversions he had so eagerly anticipated.

The girl did not know how lucky she was. Tonight Pu-Yi would satisfy himself, nothing more. Sometime in the future, however, when he had the luxury of time, he would return and ask for the girl. On that day her luck would run out.

Pu-Yi called impatiently for the girl, then raised the bowl to his lips.

# 3

"Nick?"

Though the voice registered dimly in Nick Ford's consciousness, he had no visible reaction—he kept his back to the door, eyes fixed on the papers splayed over his office's work table.

Judy, his secretary, tried again, a little louder this time. "Nick?"

Scott, standing to Nick's side, nudged him in the ribs. "Earth to chief. Earth to chief."

Nick raised an index finger, then shut his eyes, a column of figures running in his head. Point seven six-two, point seven five-four, point seven six, point seven four-eight, point seven five-eight, on an on—all well within the range of historical variance. The standard deviation would be harder to check. He reached for a manila folder. Over a hundred pages of computer printout inside—his calculator wasn't going to cut it on this one. He'd have to assign someone to run a regression analysis. Input all the numbers, or at least a sampling sufficiently large to reduce the probability of error to plus or minus—

Judy interrupted his thoughts. "Nick," she said impatiently, "Meg Taylor's here."

Nick turned, then jogged his head as if to clear it. "Sorry, Judy, what was that?"

"I said the fire alarm went off, we have to evacuate the building."

He lifted his head, suddenly alert. "I don't hear anything."

She rocked her head slowly and smiled. "I was kidding, Nick. Meg Taylor's here to see you."

Nick nodded, finally understanding—the new auditor.

"And a few messages." Judy laid three yellow memos on Nick's desk. "One from overseas . . . a Chen Tao-tzi?"

Nick shook his head, the name failing to register.

"Hong Kong," Judy added.

Nick nodded this time. "Right." He remembered now and picked up Chen Tao-tzi's message. The man had first called a month or so back, claiming firsthand knowledge of billing fraud in the Yünnan Project. In two subsequent calls he had reasserted his claims but had yet to share any specifics, and Nick's patience was beginning to wear. Still, Nick would return the call, at least one more time.

Nick dropped the message on his desk—he would deal with it later. He faced Scott and pointed at the door. "Out," he whispered. "I want to talk to her alone."

Scott shook his head slowly and deliberately, then flopped into a side chair next to Nick's desk, kicking one of his legs over the chair's arm.

Nick rolled his eyes, then circled his desk and sat down, establishing a formality to the meeting. "All right, send her in, Judy."

Judy sidestepped toward the door and gestured to the outer office. Meg Taylor appeared, walked past Judy into the room.

The buzz around the office had done her an injustice, Nick couldn't help thinking. Five-six, five-seven. Dark brown hair, cut above the shoulders. Great eyes, also brown. Professional dress—not flashy, but fashionable and well tailored. A good smile, genuine. Nick hoped she had a sense of humor to match.

Nick stood and reached his hand over his desk. "Meg. I'm Nick Ford, and this is Scott Johnson." On the mention of his name, Scott saluted crisply from his chair and said, "Nice to meet you."

Meg returned the greeting, her voice deeper and richer than Nick expected.

Nick pointed at the chair in front of his desk. "Have a seat."

"Thank you, sir."

"Please, let's forget formalities. Why don't you call me Nick, and him"—Nick pointed at Scott with his thumb—"you can call anything you want."

Scott piped up at the jab. "Scott will be fine," he said.

"All right . . . Nick, Scott."

Nick smiled. "I've read your résumé. Impressive." It was.

"Thank you."

"NYU undergrad. Combined finance and accounting degree from Wharton. Top ten percent of your class."

"What the heck are you doing here?" Scott interrupted.

"Sir?"

"Scott, remember."

Meg nodded, clearly embarrassed.

"Forget the big five accounting firms," Scott went on. "I can understand how you could pass that up, but with that finance degree you have your ticket to the big leagues. You must know what investment bankers are making on Wall Street."

"Believe me, I'm painfully aware of government versus private-sector pay disparities."

"But?" Nick prompted.

"Truthfully, I don't know. Let's just say the investment-banking path seemed too pat. That's the way some of my friends are going. I suppose I might be jealous in a few years when they all own beach homes in the Hamptons, but . . . it just didn't seem right for me. This does."

Nick nodded. "I'm glad you feel that way. Almost makes me doubt your sanity, but I'm glad just the same."

Meg smiled. Nice, Nick couldn't help thinking.

"We do take some pride in what we do around here," Nick continued. "Sometimes we even feel like we're making a difference. I emphasize sometimes.

Other times it feels like we're knocking our heads against a brick wall."

"I'm pretty much an optimist."

"We need more of those around here. Do you have any questions."

"The personnel director answered most of them over lunch. General type of work, pay, benefits, that sort of thing."

"Good. All I can add is that we're pretty informal around here. Anything we can do to make a tough job easier, we do. Scott can vouch for that; he's an expert at finding the easiest way to do something."

Scott nodded vigorously. "My first piece of advice: don't fall into the clutches of Dennis. Avoid him like the plague."

"Dennis?" Meg asked.

Dennis Lindsay, the head of Special Investigations, and Nick's direct supervisor. Disliked almost universally, Nick included. "And *my* first piece of advice," Nick said, "unless Scott's talking accounting, one of the only things he knows anything about, don't pay any attention to him."

Meg appeared bewildered, uncertain of the correct reaction.

"We like to kid each other," Scott explained. "Actually, I know something about"—he counted off on his fingers—"at least eight things, which puts me two or three ahead of Nick."

Nick steered the conversation in a new direction. "Meg, take this as a compliment, because that's how it's intended. You seem a bit more mature than most of the recruits we get out of grad school."

"You mean older," Meg said.

Nick hadn't, though clearly Meg wasn't in her mid-twenties. Perhaps thirty, thirty-one, he guessed. "No, I didn't mean it like that. . . ."

"It's okay. I won't be filing an age-discrimination suit. I worked for a few years after undergrad. Got involved in a start-up company—computer software.

We busted, no public offering, no big bucks. That's when I decided money wasn't worth chasing. So I went back to school—Wharton. Applied my computer skills to accounting."

"Well, I'm happy to have you on board. And we're going to have you jump right in. There's a case we're working on: overbilling by the contractor of a hydro-electric project in China. I'm going to have Scott get you up to speed on it. His speciality is computer-aided forensic accounting . . . I thought the two of you might make a good team."

Nick knew firsthand of Scott's conquests, knew how attractive women found him. Suddenly it seemed almost inevitable that a relationship would develop between Meg and Scott. Did that bother him somehow?

Scott, sporting a huge smile, said, "I could use your help around here, Meg. Ask Nick to use anything more complicated than an adding machine, and he gets the jitters."

Nick shrugged. "Scott's exaggerating, though not as much as I wish." He turned to Scott. "Could you get Meg a copy of the files . . . my testimony, our interim report? Forget the minutiae for the moment."

Scott nodded.

Nick turned back to Meg. "Specifically, I'm going to have you two focus on subcontracts." He began to explain what he wanted them to look for, lapsed almost immediately into details, and noticed Meg's face had gone blank. "Don't worry, you'll catch on quick enough," he assured her. "Believe it or not, Scott knows his stuff and is an excellent teacher. . . . Any questions?"

Meg shook her head. "No, not at this point."

"You find a nice place to live in the city?"

"I found a place; I wouldn't call it nice. Small is actually the first word to come to mind."

"In D.C. we say cozy, never small. But don't worry, we'll keep you working so hard you won't have any time to spend there."

Meg gave a short laugh. "Great. I'd really appreciate that."

She was warming up, relaxing, Nick could see. He found himself staring into her eyes a bit too long and looked away abruptly. Suddenly tongue-tied, he left Scott to make the rejoinder. "Least we can do," Scott said.

"All right, then," Nick said finally. "I'll let you two get started. We'll get together again shortly to discuss specifics."

At that signal, Scott jumped to his feet. "C'mon, Meg," he said eagerly. He started toward Nick's door, but stopped when he got there. "Your office is right down the hall, to the left?"

Meg nodded. "Twenty-five-oh-eight."

"Okay, I'll meet you there in a moment."

She nodded again and left. Scott returned to the chair by Nick's desk, trailed a second later by Judy, who had left her station outside Nick's office.

Scott whistled, and Judy's eyebrows immediately sank. "I'd almost consider pulling Ms. Taylor aside for a little bit of womanly advice," Judy said, "if I didn't know you were actually a big pussycat."

"And I," Scott countered, "would most certainly consider pulling you aside if you weren't married."

Judy shook her head, her lips pursed to keep from smiling.

Nick raised a hand in the air. "All right, all right, enough. Am I the only person around here with work to do? You"—he pointed at Judy—"are supposed to be typing my comment letter. And you"—he pointed at Scott—"try and keep it professional. Use your judgment. . . . Nix that. Use *good* judgment. And I want a preliminary report on the subcontracts, top priority. Next time I go in front of Whitford, I want facts."

"How about lunch tomorrow?" Scott suggested. "The Pig and Whistle. I'll give you a rundown on my ideas so far."

"How about tomorrow night instead? We still on?"

For years Nick and Scott had met once a week or so for a pizza and a few beers at a local sports bar.

"Yeah."

"Good, you can fill me in then."

Judy cut in proudly. "Nick's already booked for lunch tomorrow. Carolyn Reed. She called Nick after the hearing."

Scott's eyes arched. *"Carolyn?"*

Nick nodded slowly, embarrassed. "Yeah."

Carolyn Reed, the comptroller general. The head of the GAO. Nick had worked under her back when she headed up Special Investigations. Considering their age difference, they'd become surprisingly close, although business strictly delineated their continuing friendship.

"Where?" Scott asked.

"Lunch? Top of the Royce building."

Judy's voice took on an air. "Her private dining club."

"Swanky. You know what's up?"

Nick shrugged, and Judy answered for him. "I'm guessing she's thinking of stepping down . . . probably wants to interview her successor."

"Uh-huh," Scott said sarcastically, and then, when Nick wasn't more forthcoming, added, "Really, you have any idea?"

Nick didn't. "I assume I'll find out tomorrow," he answered.

"Maybe she's thinking of taking a lover."

Nick shook his head in exasperation. "Right."

"Hey," Judy said, "Scott could be on to something. There's plenty of sixty-five-year-old men around here who aren't shy about making passes at women half their age, believe me. Maybe Carolyn believes in putting the shoe on the other foot."

Scott nodded. "You're single, she's single. And you both spend all your time at the office, so you'd certainly see enough of each other."

"Consider the consolidated balance sheet," Judy added, laughing now.

"Exactly," Scott agreed. "On a pro forma basis, the synergy of such a merger would—"

Nick looked to heaven, then herded the two toward his office door. "Okay, okay, enough. Both of you, out now. I've got phone calls to return, work to do."

The two left smiling and whispering conspiratorially.

# 4

Though Nick passed it every day on the way to work, he had never before entered the Royce building. Its lobby met his expectations: marble floor, marble walls, marble colonnades, ceiling frescos. The lobby, like the exterior, was an anachronism, a hold-out against the sleek mirror-sided buildings that had claimed much of the neighborhood.

Nick's footsteps echoed as he crossed to the elevator bank. He pushed the Up button, and instantly pulleys whirred as a gold dial above the doors tracked the elevator's slow descent.

The doors opened on a proper white-haired man in uniform. "What floor, sir?" he asked as Nick entered.

Nick shrugged. "The Stanton Club.".

"That would be the top floor, sir."

No button, not even a number, marked the floor, just a keyhole the operator accessed with a key fished from his pocket. When was the last time he had seen an elevator operator? Nick wondered. He realized, with the exception of old movies, he probably never had.

An anteroom with dark paneling and overstuffed leather chairs grouped in tight circles around tables laden with carefully folded copies of the *Wall Street Journal* and the *London Financial Times* preceded the dining room proper. It looked out of the 1920s, just as Nick imagined it would. The dining room itself, on the other hand, surprised him—not its decor, as staid and sober as the anteroom, but the diners themselves: all women. A mix, from their sixties to their thirties, some dressed conservatively, some dressed not so conservatively, but all dressed expensively.

A white-haired man, a twin of the elevator operator

but for the uniform, in this case a black tux, intercepted him before he could enter the dining room. "May I help you, sir?"

"I'm meeting Carolyn Reed for lunch."

The man bowed his head slightly. "This way, sir."

Nick wondered if a few heads might turn, if he'd garner a scathing look or two; he was strangely disappointed that the women, engrossed in discussions, paid him no attention whatsoever.

The maître d' led him toward a circular table fronting a large window overlooking the city. Carolyn sat there, a cup of tea in front of her, a newspaper open in her hands. She looked as she always looked: a leanness born of activity, auburn hair given over almost completely to gray. She was sixty-four, sixty-five, something like that, but people rarely took note of her age—her mind was timeless. Smart and savvy, she never took a back seat to anybody. A woman who had established her career at the GAO at a time when *Father Knows Best* topped the television ratings.

Carolyn saw him approach, dropped the newspaper, and stood, *"Nick,"* she said, clearly happy to see him.

He returned the greeting using her given name, a habit carried forward from when they worked together. She gripped his hand warmly before gesturing to a chair. "Sit. Sit," she said.

Was he the only man who liked lines on a woman's face? Deep lines, radiating from the eyes, across the brow, bracketing the mouth. Character lines, they said of men. Carolyn Reed had them, and they added character and more: thoughtfulness, intelligence, experience. The ones around her eyes deepened as her mouth broke into a broad smile. "I'm so glad you could make it."

"Thank you for the invitation." He scanned the dining room. "Nice place."

Carolyn leaned toward him across the table. "Pretentious is the word," she whispered, "but useful. Of course you've noticed it's all women. . . ."

Nick nodded. "Hard to miss."

"I hope you don't mind; I had to see someone else here earlier. Besides, I thought you'd get a kick out of it. It's really not fair, is it? Women have screamed for years that men's clubs are exclusionary, then the first chance we get, out with the men. Personally, I couldn't give a damn one way or the other. I belong to three different clubs . . . there aren't more than a half dozen women in one of them . . . but as I said, this club serves its purpose. Every woman here, it's almost as if they're on a mission to out-network their male peers. That has its advantages."

Carolyn's famous logic: advantages, disadvantages, everything a cost-benefit analysis. Nick said, "I'm not the least bit offended."

"Good. . . . How's everybody in Special Investigations?"

"Just fine. Scott and Judy send their best. We all still miss you."

Carolyn looked down, obviously embarrassed.

It had been four years since Carolyn had jumped from the directorship of the Special Investigations Division to deputy comptroller general, and two since her presidential appointment to comptroller general. The staff of Special Investigations still remembered her fondly not because she used to pat them on the back or go easy on them, but because she was fair, honest, and damn good at her job.

Nick remembered her fondly for an additional reason: as director of the Special Investigations Division she had appointed him her senior aide. He had leapfrogged a dozen and a half more experienced staffers in taking the position, but Carolyn's judgment was sacrosanct. She backed Nick to assume the responsibility and, young as he was, that sufficed for most people. Carolyn had never made a secret of the respect she had for Nick professionally. The respect was mutual, though from Nick's perspective it bordered on awe.

Unfortunately, Carolyn had moved on not long after, and Nick didn't get along nearly as well with her successor, Dennis Lindsay. Then again, who did?

By mutual assent, Dennis was a jerk and, in comparison to Carolyn, a disaster.

As they ordered and then ate their lunch, they talked office gossip. Not that either of them cared overly much for the subject, but protocol demanded light conversation before moving on to business. And there *was*, Nick knew, a business purpose behind the lunch—Carolyn had a reason for everything she did.

They discussed staff, who had retired, who had married, who had had children.

"So Michelle had twins," Carolyn exclaimed at one point. "Does that make three?"

"Four. Real cute kids."

"I'd love to see them."

A lie, Nick knew, unless things had changed dramatically. Carolyn and Jack, her husband, who had died of cancer a few years back, had no children—whether by choice or circumstance Nick didn't know. That might explain why Carolyn had never been comfortable around kids, but Nick had developed his own theory: if a child wasn't old enough to reason logically, the child didn't rate Carolyn's time. That, in Nick's mind, wasn't a criticism of Carolyn, almost the opposite. It was just the way she was—she took life seriously and, perhaps because of it, was always treated seriously.

When their plates had been cleared, Carolyn shifted into more familiar territory.

"Nick, it's a pleasure catching up on old times, but I do have something else on my mind."

Nick nodded, expecting as much.

Carolyn dropped her eyes and played with her teaspoon. "I believe I've always made it clear I thought you had a great future in Special Investigations. That's why this is sort of hard for me."

Nick's chest tightened. *Hard for her? What the hell did that mean?*

Carolyn left Nick's stare unmet. "I'm not happy with the way things are going . . . in Special Investigations, I mean."

Nick racked his brain. Hadn't he done a good job, *at least* a proficient job?

"I know," Carolyn went on, "that you and Dennis have had your run-ins over the years."

*Dennis,* that explained a lot.

"I thought maybe, given time, you two would work out your differences. I no longer believe that's possible. The problem is, Dennis, for all of his . . . let's call them idiosyncrasies . . . is an extremely valuable employee. Bottom line, he's a loyal assistant who's done an admirable job in a tough position; I don't care to lose him, not right now."

*But you, Nick, I can afford to lose*—Nick imagined her thoughts. "Carolyn," Nick started, then swallowed involuntarily, "are you about to ask me to quit Special Investigations?"

"Yes, Nick. Yes, I am. . . ."

*Yes?* Just like that. Nick thought too highly of Carolyn's judgment to object. She had her reasons—she always did. Instead, he hung his head and bit his lower lip.

"Of course," Carolyn said, "I do have something, another position, that I think you might be interested in."

*Another position?* Great. He'd have to start over, prove himself to new people, climb the ladder all over again—

"In fact," Carolyn added, "I think you might be *very* interested."

Nick looked up to see a grin steal Carolyn's face. She said, "As you've probably heard, Burt Knowles had a heart attack a few months ago. What you've probably *not* heard is Burt plans on announcing his retirement by the end of the year. I've got six months to find his replacement."

Burt Knowles, assistant comptroller general for the General Government Division—Carolyn was looking to fill *that* position? And she was talking to him? Nick's mouth gaped open, his emotions flipping a hundred and eighty degrees.

Carolyn continued to grin. "I think, maybe, I've found a way to replace Burt and keep two young men from wasting effort butting heads."

Nick wasn't sure what to say. "Are you offering me Burt's position?"

She nodded. "I take it you're interested?"

"Are you kidding? For a second I thought . . ."

"I apologize . . . it was a dirty trick. Seriously, are you interested?"

"Of course I am."

Carolyn held up her hand. "Okay, but before you say any more, I want to provide full disclosure. For six months, until he retires, you'll do Burt's work but won't have his title—you'll keep your own. After the first of the year that'll change, *if* you work out, that is. No promises: you prove your worth and you're in; you wash out and I pick someone else. Anytime in that six months the work gets too tough, you find the position isn't what you hoped, you can have your old job back. That's the deal. You understand?"

Nick, in shock at his good fortune, nodded dumbly.

"Another thing, if and when you officially become an assistant comptroller, your salary will go up significantly, not before. And Nick, you're going to earn every damn cent. Being the head of a division is a lot harder than it may sound, and Burt hasn't done a thing since his heart attack. I don't even expect him to set foot in the office for the rest of the year, his condition is that serious. The backlog is incredible."

"I've never been afraid of hard work, Carolyn." Of course she knew that; the whole GAO knew that.

"Good, because that's what you'll get. All the assistant comptroller positions demand long hours, but the Government Division—well, just don't expect to have much of a personal life anytime soon. Republicans *and* Democrats, everybody, is pushing the government to do more with less. Developing, implementing, and reviewing efficiency plans, that would be your department. There, now you know the downside as well as the up. Still interested?"

"I can't believe it."

"I'm guessing that's a long form of yes."

"Yes. I don't know what to say . . . I'm honored . . . surprised."

"You shouldn't be. You've done a great job in Special Investigations. Your co-workers agree. No one's had anything but glowing praise, and that *includes* Dennis."

Nick raised his eyebrows, and Carolyn nodded, reading his mind. "That's right," she repeated, "*including* Dennis. In fact, he first brought up your name when the position opened . . . couldn't have given you a better recommendation. We had a few people in mind, but frankly, you grabbed the best reviews by far. My decision became quite easy. You have talent, Nick. Nobody seems to have any doubt on that score."

Nick felt his face go red. He bowed his head modestly. "Thank you."

"We'll see if you're still thanking me six months from now." Carolyn glanced at her watch, then signaled to the waiter who hovered near the table. The waiter took a slip of paper from his pocket and set it on the table in front of Carolyn and offered her a gold pen. She signed the slip and he took it away; neither spoke to the other.

"Unfortunately," Carolyn said as she dabbed her mouth with a napkin, "I'm late for another meeting and have to run. Tomorrow and the next day I'm out of the office. That means we can't meet until Friday. I'll give you a call to set a time—we'll go over job responsibilities. In the meantime, I'm going to need you to hit the ground running. Burt had been reviewing the National Direct Student Loan Program. The Department of Education had asked us to do an evaluation with a view toward streamlining overhead expenses. Burt's deputy has been pinch-hitting, but frankly, the guy just doesn't have what it takes. I'm going to have him stop by your office; he'll brief you." She paused for a moment, then said, "I'm afraid I've promised the Department of Education a preliminary report by the twenty-seventh. That's the Friday after this."

"How far along is Burt's deputy?"

"From what I've looked at, my guess is you'll be starting pretty much from scratch."

Nick's mind whirled. A report, *by a week from Friday? From scratch?* That could take months of solid work, and Carolyn wanted it completed in a week and a half?

She evidently read his mind, or more likely his sinking face. "I know the time frame's tight, Nick. Like I said, the backlog's incredible. Do you think you can handle it?"

"How preliminary?"

"The report to the Department of Education? You know the procedure. Every footnote doesn't have to be in place, but it's got to take the reader from A to B in a logical and convincing manner."

Not very preliminary, Nick realized. "What about my current assignments?"

"This report has to take precedence over everything. I repeat, everything. The Secretary of Education has been looking for an excuse to jump down my throat ever since we ripped him over procedures last year. I don't want to give him that excuse."

Nick nodded.

"After the report's done," Carolyn continued, "it's up to you. Your plate will still be more than full, but if you can find time to clean up some of your Special Investigations work, more power to you. I talked to Dennis this morning; he knows about your . . . hell, it's a promotion, official or not, and let's call it that. Stop by his office when you get back—he's expecting you. Whatever you work out with him is fine with me."

Carolyn slapped the table lightly with both her palms. "Good, I think we're all set."

Carolyn stood, then put her arm out as Nick began to rise. "Please, Nick, don't rush on my account. Anything else you want, coffee, dessert, just signal the waiter. Everything's taken care of. Enjoy your last minutes of freedom. They may be your last for quite some time."

Nick remained in his seat, his eyes trained on Carolyn's departing figure but his mind locked on a title: assistant comptroller. Assistant comptroller. At thirty-five. He'd hoped, even planned, to reach the position someday, but to have it actually happen, and so soon—

He took a large swallow of water. God, he felt high.

The waiter, now by his side, interrupted his thoughts. "Sir, would you care for anything more?"

"A cup of coffee, black."

The waiter nodded. "Anything else?"

Nick started to shake his head, then stopped himself. Why not? "I saw some kind of cake on the dessert menu?"

"Flourless chocolate cake, sir."

"How about a big slice with the coffee?" It was, after all, a celebration.

# 5

Dennis Lindsay actually smiled, something Nick had rarely seen. It didn't seem to fit him, not with that severe face and almost nonexistent chin. It made Nick uncomfortable somehow.

Dennis pointed at the empty chair opposite his oversized desk. "Take a seat, Nick."

Nick did, surprised for the second time. Dennis had a reputation for making people stand, making them summarize reports while he gazed out one of his corner windows, perhaps listening but more likely not.

"Coffee, anything?"

Nick shook his head. "No, thanks."

Dennis waved off his secretary, who stood waiting in the doorway, then rolled up his sleeves, ignoring Nick as he did so. "Damn air conditioning's gone nuts," he said when finished. "Your office okay?"

Nick shrugged. "If anything, it's a bit too cold."

"Figures. Nothing fucking works around this place." Dennis placed his arms—long and all bone—flat on the desk and eyed Nick slyly. "I understand you and Carolyn met for lunch today?"

"That's right."

Dennis smirked. "Enjoy it?"

Nick nodded once without explanation. He hadn't intended to be short, but something about Dennis demanded it.

"You accepted, I assume."

Nick nodded again.

"Congratulations, you deserve it." Dennis offered his hand over the desk; Nick hesitated a moment before taking it. He held the clasp only as long as politeness dictated, then shrugged modestly.

Dennis pulled open the top drawer of his desk and

threw a pack of cigarettes on the desk. "Hey, take the praise," he said as he searched further and found a book of matches. "The praise is the good part. The rest of it, the baggage, can suck." He struck a match and lit a cigarette, then puffed three times in quick succession. He held out the pack to Nick.

"No, thanks."

Dennis set the pack back on the desktop. "Head-aches, all the time goddamn headaches. You just wait, you'll have a million deadlines to meet, you'll be running on nothing but caffeine, and suddenly you'll have to deal with some dumb-ass personnel problem. It sends me through the fucking roof." He puffed again. "Managing personnel, that's the worst part of the job."

Not exactly a news flash, Nick thought, considering Dennis's personality.

As if reading Nick's mind, Dennis said, "Hell, maybe I've lost patience with people . . . I don't know. But give it another ten years, until you're my age, and see if the same doesn't happen to you. There's so much incompetence, it drives me up the goddamn wall." Dennis paused, giving Nick the opportunity to agree.

*You're a saint, Dennis; people just don't understand you.* Nick neither believed it nor said it.

Dennis looked down, softened the tone of his voice. "Nick, I know we've had our differences in the past. Maybe my fault, I don't know. Anyway, I hope we can put that behind us."

*Dennis, humble?* An act, it had to be; Nick had experienced too much at Dennis's hands to think otherwise. He remained expressionless.

"I hope," Dennis went on, "you'll believe me when I say I've nothing but the highest regard for your professional abilities."

Carolyn had said Dennis pushed Nick for the job. Why? Nick couldn't help wondering. Generous? Self-effacing? *Dennis?* Despite himself, Nick acknowledged the olive branch. "Carolyn said you recommended me for the job . . . first brought up my name. Thanks."

"You're an A-1 accountant, Nick. I'd never tell anyone otherwise."

With some effort, Nick managed a smile. "After a few sleepless nights I might regret your recommendation. I get the feeling Carolyn's planning to work me till I drop."

"So she told me. Well, don't worry, as far as I'm concerned you're cut free from all your assignments in Special Investigations."

"Thanks." Nick had thanked Dennis twice now, that had to be some sort of record. "Frankly, I hate to leave any investigation unfinished, but—" He shrugged. "I figure I can find time to shepherd a few sensitive cases through."

Dennis knocked the ashes from his cigarette into an ashtray. "Really, don't worry about it. You're going to have enough on your plate."

"Just a few. Hydro-safe, the Florida FICA case, the export control board, and the Yünnan Project, I think I can handle those."

Dennis leaned across the desk; he had stopped smiling. "Nick, each of those cases is going to require an intensive time commitment. I really don't think you'll find room in your schedule."

"Who needs sleep?" Nick joked. "Besides, I've got too much history in those cases. Bringing someone else up to speed, that could take a heck of a long time."

"You didn't work those investigations solo, remember?" Dennis said, an edge to his voice for the first time. "When . . . if . . . we need you, we'll know where to find you."

"You don't understand, Dennis. I *want* to see some of these investigations through to their conclusion. I'll *make* the necessary time."

Dennis shook his head. "I don't think that will be possible."

"What do you mean, you don't think that will be possible?"

"What aren't you understanding?" Dennis asked stiffly. "What good are you to me if I only have a fraction of your attention? In the long run it's gonna be more efficient to have a clean hand-off."

Nick paused, taking time for a deep breath, working hard to keep his voice in check. He noticed how Dennis's body position had changed: hunched forward now, hands in fists—the old Dennis.

"Look," Nick said calmly, "these are my cases. My investigations. I'm not giving them up."

The muscles on Dennis's face bunched. "And if you don't have a choice?"

With Dennis you had to draw lines and stick to them, Nick had learned. "You'd have a fight on your hands."

Dennis opened his mouth to say something, evidently thought better of it, and sank back into his chair. He took a long draw on his cigarette. "Okay," he said finally, "in the spirit of compromise, let's split the difference. Keep a couple of the cases and drop a couple. Let's say . . . oh, how about you let the FICA case and the Yünnan Project go. Both are time-consuming . . . neither's all that sexy."

Nick considered the suggestion. "Two cases. All right. I can do that. But it's going to have to be Hydrosafe or the export control board, not the Yünnan Project."

Dennis's face turned ugly. "Why?"

"You know the history of the investigation. Senator Raine personally requested I head up the audit. She's going to want me to see things through—I think it's important I do." Nick didn't have to explain, Dennis knew. Senator Raine was one of the GAO's chief allies in the Senate—a powerful, outspoken senator with a couple of crucial committee seats. You accommodated her, if at all possible, and certainly didn't run out on her two-thirds of the way through an investigation.

"I don't think—"

Nick interrupted. "Two cases, Dennis. Your suggestion."

Dennis stubbed his cigarette out in the ashtray. "Okay," he said coolly, "so you want to keep your finger in the goddamn pie. You want a piece of the glory."

"It's not a matter of glory. Like I said, it's seeing something through."

"Whatever," Dennis said impatiently. "Bottom line, you think you'll have free time. . . ."

"I'll make time, yes."

Dennis threw his hands in the air, not bothering to hide his displeasure. "All right. You say you can handle it, take all *four* fucking cases. But this is my department. Ultimately, my butt's on the line—if something goes wrong, something gets ignored, I take the heat. So this is the deal. You keep me abreast of all developments. To the extent you have free time, can do the necessary work, you remain in charge. But if you fall at all behind, I reassign the cases as I see fit. Agreed?"

Nick shrugged. "I can live with that."

Dennis's face relaxed. "And if you aren't keeping up, Nick, I don't want any argument. I take over the cases . . . no argument, no interference."

"If I'm not doing my job, you're not going to have to call me on it. I'll call you."

Dennis tipped his head. "Fair enough." He offered a strained smile. "Again, Nick, congratulations."

For the third time that afternoon, Nick found himself thanking Dennis Lindsay.

# 6

Tracked by three independent surveillance cameras, the Mercedes limousine rolled to a stop just short of a retractable metal barrier fronting a heavy iron gate. The driver lowered his window. Immediately a voice squawked over the square speaker attached to the metal pole to his side.

"May I help you?" the voice asked in a monotone flavored by a Chinese accent.

The driver responded, "Mr. John Li to see the deputy ambassador."

The gate opened and the barricade sank flush to the pavement. The limo then started forward, the gate closing behind it. A small square building with darkened windows and curved mirrors at its corners stood beyond the gate. A soldier in a crisp tan uniform exited. He approached the driver's-side window, one hand restraining the automatic weapon slung over his shoulder, and peered into the backseat. The driver handed him two business cards and a letter.

The soldier examined the material, then said sternly, "Wait here a moment, please." He returned to the guard house, leaving the limo idling.

John Li, above average size for an Asian in height as well as girth, reflecting his mixed Chinese and British blood, sat in the backseat. He watched his fellow passenger wring his hands. The American headed a major circuit board manufacturer based in Champagne, Illinois—very little else about the man mattered to Li. A rich man looking to get richer—in Li's eyes just another in a long series of easy marks.

"Kind of a strange feeling, driving through this gate," the American said, his eyes following the guard nervously.

"You'll get used to it," Li assured him, his voice hinting only slightly of his ancestry. "Forget the label 'free enterprise zone.' If you want your business to run smoothly, you must rely on *guanxi*"—Li interlaced his fingers—"the web of obligations that tie the Chinese business world together. At the center of that web you'll find the government."

The American nodded. "Not all that different than business in the good old U.S.A."

"Just a much better return."

The American slapped Li lightly on the thigh. "That's why I like you, Mr. Li—we both understand the bottom line."

Li feigned a smile. It was so easy; the Western appetite to reach the billion-plus Chinese consumers made it so.

China meant money, a lot of money—it always had in the eyes of the West. In the 1700s it was the tea and silk trade, in the 1800s, Chinese silver, paid over by the ton to feed an opium habit the British first cultivated, then supplied. Now it was two things: access to her market, the largest on earth, and to her cheap but skilled labor pool.

The American next to him, like all *guai lou*—foreign devils—saw only what Li wished him to see: the glorious profits to come. Dollars. The American's greed blinded him to Li's purpose. Simple subterfuge, a high Chinese art form from before the time of Sun Tzu.

Fool, Li thought as he broadened his smile.

The American had hired him three months ago to act as liaison. The result: today's meeting to explore the possibility of a joint venture—a state-of-the-art circuit board assembly plant north of Guangzhou. The American had only to front two-thirds of the plant's cost and all technical expertise, and in return reap half of the profits. Of course, once his manufacturing techniques had been learned, the Chinese government would establish a competing factory, ignoring the niceties of international patent law. Soon thereafter, finding land, labor, and material costs—all controlled by the Chinese government—rising exponentially, the American would be driven from business.

Li expected a sizable commission on completion of the transaction. There would, however, be no profits for the American.

The soldier returned to the limo's window. "You may proceed," he announced formally.

Deputy Ambassador Jiang, built in the same proportions as Li but close to four inches shorter and a decade older, greeted Li with a bow on the front steps of the embassy. "My friend, it is good to see you."

"And you, Deputy Ambassador," Li lied. He had cared little for Jiang on meeting him five years ago, and the deputy ambassador's dull mind had done little to win him over in the interim. Business was business, however, and he smiled politely.

Li introduced the American, who fumbled a greeting in Mandarin, eliciting an appreciative nod from Jiang. "I applaud your keen sense of language," Jiang said, "but it is not necessary. You have come to talk business, and the language of business, we know, is English . . . I am most proficient in it."

Deputy Ambassador Jiang shuttled his guests inside the embassy. The American seemed noticeably impressed by the collection of Chinese pottery and calligraphy; his head swung from side to side as if cataloguing.

"Deputy Ambassador, are our other guests here?" Li asked, referring to the four men who were to meet with the American, each a member of the new capitalist class in China, a class that had first taken root in the era of openness which followed Mao's death.

"Yes, in the conference room," Deputy Ambassador Jiang answered. "This way."

Li motioned for Jiang to proceed without them. "We'll be just a moment."

Li waited until the deputy ambassador entered the conference room, then pulled the American aside. "When you enter the room, the four may stand and applaud; you should politely return the applause. Take

note of how the four have lined up—their positions
reflect their rank. First in line, the most powerful, so
on to the rear. Introductions will be made . . . remember the family name comes first in China, the given
second. It was Mr. Mao, not Mr. Zedong. Given
names are used only between the best of friends."

The American nodded, and Li continued with his
canned speech. "When the businessmen bow, bow
back. *Don't* bow from the waist like the Japanese.
Bow from the shoulders."

Li demonstrated, and the American imitated him
poorly.

"*Never* refer to anyone as comrade," Li warned
sternly. " 'Comrade' recalls the Cultural Revolution, a
time most Chinese would rather forget. And it is
China or the People's Republic of China, not Red
China, and *never* Mainland China. If you must refer
to Taiwan, say the *Province* of Taiwan. Remember
our discussions of face and loss of face. Remember
also that to the Chinese, 'maybe' and 'we'll see' invariably mean no."

The American nodded again, now perceptively nervous. Good, Li thought. The American would think
Li an indispensable guide through a maze of strange
customs. That Li played both sides of the field, that
he intended to funnel the American's negotiating positions to Jiang and the Chinese businessmen, would
never cross the American's mind—dependence would
drive out suspicion.

"Okay, then," Li said, his face reassuring, "let's go."

Li led the American to a large, narrow room dominated by a conference table at which Jiang, the four
businessmen, and an interpreter sat. Introductions
were made, business cards and gifts exchanged, small
talk begun. Li then pulled the American aside. "The
deputy ambassador and I need to discuss governmen-
tal approvals. May I leave you for a short time?"

The American nodded. "I can handle myself."

Li laughed to himself at the absurdity of the statement. No matter, this day's visit to the embassy had

little to do with the American. The CIA monitored visitors to the Chinese embassy less diligently than they once had; nonetheless it was best not to take chances. If the CIA checked, the American would bear unimpeachable witness to the visit's supposed purpose.

A perfect front.

Li and Deputy Ambassador Jiang excused themselves. Once in the hall, their smiles vanished and the language changed to Mandarin.

"How long do we have?" Jiang asked anxiously.

"The American is a fool, and of no concern. We shall return when our business is over, not before."

"Good," Jiang said, and pointed down the hall. "General Soong arrived an hour ago; he's waiting in the ambassador's office."

General Soong was not an imposing man—short, five-five, overweight, balding, narrow shoulders—until he opened his mouth. Then he turned formidable. His speech came low, guttural, and steeped in authority.

General Soong rose from his chair and bowed as Li entered the ambassador's ornate office. "Li Xiansheng. It is, as always, an honor."

Li took quiet satisfaction in the suffix General Soong had attached to his family name—"Xiansheng"—a term of respect. For much of his youth Li had endured a baser mix of suffixes. In China, a country which prized purity of race, foreign blood meant ostracism or worse.

"I am the one who is honored, General," Li responded.

General Soong bowed again. "Please take a seat," he said, indicating a chair across the desk from him.

Deputy Ambassador Jiang received only a curt nod with no verbal recognition. Chastened from the start, he sat to the side of Li and General Soong in a chair against the wall.

General Soong moved immediately to business. "I have heard rumors, Jiang," he snapped. "Some most disturbing rumors."

The deputy ambassador shifted uneasily in his chair. "General?"

"I do not have to stress the importance Beijing places on her dealings with Mr. Li. And yet I understand those dealings now stand in jeopardy. Is my information correct?"

Deputy Ambassador Jiang's lips paled; he glanced quickly at Li, a plea for help that wasn't forthcoming. Li had decided to let Jiang twist in the wind—the trouble was, after all, of Jiang's own making.

After a moment Jiang answered weakly, "It is true, General, that the audit has taken a regrettable turn, but—"

*"Regrettable?"* General Soong interrupted. "A minor bureaucrat, this Ford, threatens a project vital to our national security, and you call it *regrettable?* What I find regrettable, Deputy Ambassador, is that I placed any faith in your ideas in the first place."

Jiang, white now, fumbled out a hurried answer, "I assure you, General, I can . . . I will . . . handle the present situation."

"How?" General Soong asked sharply.

"At this time I'm not . . . fully prepared . . . that is . . ."

General Soong cut off the deputy ambassador with a wave of his hand. "This trouble lies at your door, Jiang. And like dung, it attracts flies. You structured the flow of moneys, promised we would all profit as a result. Instead, Mr. Li's operation is now vulnerable." He shook his head in disgust.

"We never imagined—"

*"You* never imagined," General Soong corrected Jiang heatedly.

The deputy ambassador's shoulders dropped. "Yes, General."

"The view of Beijing is you should have stopped this Ford long ago. The situation must not, *will not,* be allowed to deteriorate further."

"Of course not, General," Jiang said. "However, our options at this point are limited. Ford suspects nothing . . . he wanders like a blind man. In a few weeks the hearings will end without incident."

"I have your oath on that?"

Jiang shrank further in his chair. "I am confident, General."

General Soong frowned. *"Confident?"* His eyes bore into Jiang's. "Confident enough to accept the full consequences of failure?"

Jiang's face drained. "The full . . . I . . ." He stammered to a halt.

Li had so far watched without speaking, taking pleasure in Jiang's predicament. The deputy ambassador was an ineffective fool; General Soong, it was clear, had finally reached the same conclusion. Li cleared his voice, deciding the time had come to intercede. "I offer you *my* word, General." His voice came measured and strong.

General Soong swung his head in Li's direction. *"Your* word, Li Xiansheng?"

Li raised an arm in the air, palm forward. "The hearings will turn up nothing—an irrelevant annoyance. I would swear as much to our ultimate leader in Beijing."

Surprise took General Soong's face. Li could feel himself being appraised as he continued. "As you are aware, I voiced reservations to Deputy Ambassador Jiang's plan from the start. The risks always outweighed the benefits, in my opinion. However, I am a servant to our leaders' wishes, and followed orders, although I felt it wise to take certain precautions. Insurance policies, if you will. As of today Ford is no longer of concern. The matter *has* been taken care of."

General Soong cocked his head, then rose and silently paced the room. He stopped by the window, peered through the blinds to the street below. "Deputy Ambassador Jiang, please leave us," he said at last.

"But, General—" Jiang started, caught off guard.

"I said, *please leave us now,*" General Soong demanded. He waved his hand dismissively.

The deputy ambassador's face reddened. He started to object, thought better of it, and summoning what dignity he could, stormed from the room.

Li settled deeply into his chair. Deputy Ambassador Jiang's comfortable days in the United States had most probably come to an end, Li knew, but he had little sympathy for men in general and none for men like Jiang.

General Soong adjusted the wand to the blinds, widening the gap between the slats. Light fell in harsh stripes across his face. "You say you have dealt with the situation?"

"Yes, General. I apologize for not informing the deputy ambassador of my plans, but I felt it in our benefit to act quickly and decisively. I am happy to report success. Of course, I have incurred certain expenses. . . ."

General Soong nodded. "Your expenses will be taken care of." His voice turned reflective. "Deputy Ambassador Jiang is a product of the new openness. He does not see, the leaders in Beijing do not always see, that sometimes the old ways are best. Sometimes we must take matters into our own hands."

Li had taken matters into hand for the benefit of General Soong many times, within the last few months, in fact. When more subtle forms of persuasion failed, Li had dispatched his lieutenant, Pu-Yi, to convince a reluctant Hong Kong businessman to sell a minority stake in his aeronautics firm to a front corporation owned by General Soong. Pu-Yi, as always, had been very direct and very persuasive. The businessman lost the use of a hand, but gained a silent partner.

"You and I," General Soong continued, "we are very much alike."

Li bowed his head. "You honor me, General."

"If things are as you say, you've honored yourself."

General Soong circled the ambassador's desk. He opened the liquor cabinet and removed a bottle of cognac, a favorite drink among the Chinese elite. He poured a splash in two glasses and held one out to Li. "Now tell me, my friend," General Soong said, "what exactly have you done to Mr. Ford?"

"Done to him? Done for him would perhaps be better phrasing. Hopefully, he will have the sense to accept his good fortune, or"—Li shrugged—"as you say, I am not afraid to employ the old ways." Li drained his glass before explaining.

# 7

"I really don't need another shot," Nick repeated as Scott Johnson waved a twenty in the direction of the bartender, ignoring Nick's protests.

"It's a party in your honor," Scott insisted, his voice slurred. "Participation is required." He reached for the knot in Nick's tie and pulled down. "Loosen up, huh? Here, maybe this will help. You ever hear the one about the constipated accountant?"

"No," Nick dead-panned.

"He worked it out with a pencil."

Nick looked to Meg and made a face. "That's a little sick, Scott."

"No, that's humor." The twenty finally caught the bartender's attention. "Jack Daniel's," Scott said, then looked at Meg. "Will you be joining us?"

She looked at her watch. "I should be getting home."

Scott let his head fall to the bar. "*Two* of you. Where do you people come from? No one's going home until I say so." He lifted his eyes to the bartender and held up three fingers. "Make it three, to the brim."

The bartender set a shot glass in front of each of them; Nick and Meg both grimaced.

The party had started at seven—a Friday night get-together with three dozen or so GAO employees to celebrate Nick's promotion. By ten-thirty only a dozen remained, by eleven, when Meg arrived after a late night at the office, only a handful. It was now eleven-thirty, and all but Nick, Scott, and Meg had filtered home.

There had been plenty of pats on the back, a jealous face or two, and numerous rounds in Nick's honor.

Too numerous, in Nick's opinion—he felt sloppy. Time to pack it in for the night; he faced a long weekend of work.

Scott raised his glass. Nick and Meg reluctantly followed suit.

"To Nick," Scott said, weaving slightly on the bar stool. "Whenever the occasion arose, he rose to the occasion. Congratulations."

Meg chuckled, then added, "Here, here."

All three emptied their glasses. Meg's face soured on swallowing.

"That was really good," Nick commented sarcastically, eliciting a cough, then a laugh from Meg.

Scott's eyes lit up. "Another?"

"No. There's such a thing as work, remember?"

Scott motioned again for the bartender, pointed at their glasses. "For you, Nick, work comes around an average of six point five days a week, but a promotion to assistant comptroller, that's a bit rarer."

"So is a liver," Nick said, cupping the top of his shot glass. "One a life, that's the allotment. Besides, for the foreseeable future my work week's gonna be an even *seven* days, dusk to dawn—a hangover won't help." He turned to the bartender. "Make it three light beers."

Scott puckered his face in distaste. "*Light* beer?"

Nick nodded, then draped an arm over Scott's shoulder. "And then, regardless of how much I enjoy your company, buddy, I'm out of here."

Scott sulked for a moment, then stuck a thumb in Nick's direction. "You know, I've *seen* this man loaded," he said to Meg. "When we first started with the GAO, I got him to close up a few bars with me. Believe it or not, the guy's a pretty damn good drunk. He can actually be funny."

"Hey," Nick said, feigning offense, "I'm funny all the time."

"Right. You've been cracking us up so far tonight." Scott imitated Nick's voice. " 'Have to go now. Gotta work tomorrow, dawn to dusk.' I don't know about

Meg, but it was all I could do to keep from rolling on the floor. Could you tell us another one?" Scott put his hands together in prayer. "Please."

Nick laughed as the bartender set three beers on the bar. "Okay," he said, accepting the challenge and instantly regretting the decision—his repertoire of jokes was thin; his delivery weak at best. "Let's see, I must know a couple of— Okay, here's one. Ready? How can you tell you're talking to an extroverted accountant?"

Scott drummed his fingers on the bar, leaving Meg to ask, "How?"

"They'll be staring at your shoes instead of their own."

Scott's reaction was a half chuckle, half snort; Meg, on the other hand, rewarded Nick with a hearty laugh. "That's cute," she said. "I like that one."

Nick smiled. "Unlike you," he said, pointing at Scott, "this woman appreciates real humor. Now, on a high note, I'll excuse myself for a moment. Carolyn said she might call . . . better check my messages." He picked some change off the bar and headed for a pay phone in the room's far corner.

"Carolyn *Reed*?" Meg guessed, watching Nick's retreating figure.

"Yep," Scott confirmed. "You're looking at her protégé." Scott took a long chug from his beer bottle. "You want a prediction. Write it down. That man"— he gestured in the direction Nick had disappeared— "is gonna take Carolyn's job someday."

"Might you be a bit biased?"

Scott nodded emphatically. "Hell, yes, I'm biased. Nick and I started at the GAO the same year . . . the same week. We shared an office for two years. He doesn't have any siblings; I don't either. We've sort of adopted each other. But forget all that . . . I stand by my prediction. He's that good at what he does."

"You make him sound like Superman."

Scott paused for a moment, then shook his head. "Hey, we all have problems, right?"

Meg raised her eyes; in response Scott leaned into her, lowered his voice. "C'mon. You can see it. Everybody sees it. The guy's got to get away from work more. He's been living in a land of spread sheets, balance sheets, and income statements for so long that if you make him smell the air, kick the tires—he's a lost soul. That's the one thing—the *only* thing—I've got over Nick. I can find my way through most accounting thickets, but I know the whole thing's a lot of bullshit make-believe. You know what I mean?"

Meg nodded uncertainly, and Scott continued.

"He almost broke out of his shell those first couple of years here. Then Carolyn got her hooks into him, and you see the results." Scott shrugged. "It was like he just quit trying. The job became everything to him. Not that it was all for the worst—look where he is now. Heck, maybe I'm the one who needs the counseling."

"You both seem like pretty stable individuals to me."

Scott sat up straight and frowned. "I haven't been called stable in years. . . . I'm not sure I like it."

"It was meant as a compliment."

"Hmm. Stable a compliment? I'd have to get used to that. Nick, on the other hand—" Scott coughed, clearing his throat. "Would you look at me? About to start on Nick again. I must be more loaded than I thought. Here I am talking about him when what I really want to do is learn more about you. Now tell me, how long has it been since—"

Meg caught Nick's approaching figure from the corner of her eye. She called out to him interrupting Scott. "Any messages, Nick?"

Nick nodded glumly as he approached the bar. "But I'm not going to worry about them tonight." He looked at the beer in Meg's hand. "I thought Scott would have talked you into another shot by now."

Meg grinned. "If you hadn't reappeared soon, I think he might have tried to talk me into any number of things."

Scott dropped from his bar stool, hands in the air showing surrender. "Hey, I know when I'm not appreciated. You two want to nurse your beers, that's fine with me. She's all yours, Nick. My turn to make a quick detour—I have to piss so bad my back teeth are starting to float."

"Nice," Nick called after Scott. "Real nice."

Meg watched Scott disappear into a rest room, then remarked, smiling, "He's fired up tonight."

"This?" Nick shook his head. "This is nothing. Give him a crowd and watch him take center stage. Truthfully, sometimes I envy him the talent."

Meg turned to her beer and took a sip. "Scott tells me you two started with the GAO at the same time?"

"Uh-huh. Eleven years ago. Surprised?"

She bobbed her head. "Scott seems . . . younger, I guess."

"Thanks," Nick said in mock annoyance.

"No, I didn't mean it like that. It's just that you seem more . . . Who knows, I'm surprised, that's all."

Serious was the word she thought but didn't say, Nick knew. He'd heard the word often, always, it seemed to him, said with an edge to it—part accusation. *What was wrong with serious, anyway?*

"It must be sort of strange," Meg went on, "you two started out together, now you're his boss."

"Whatever you do, don't let Scott hear you say that. As far as he's concerned, I make suggestions, that's all."

Meg grinned, then said earnestly, "You two make an odd pair."

Nick hunched his shoulders. "Maybe, but . . . I don't know, we agree on most things. We just have slightly different . . . styles is the best word, I guess."

"Slightly different," Meg agreed sarcastically.

Nick looked at his beer. Suddenly uncomfortable with the direction of conversation, he jumped subjects. "So, how do you like the GAO so far?"

"To be honest, right now it's sort of overwhelming. Less than a week and already I'm staffed on four different projects. I thought government work was supposed to be easy."

"Everybody feels a bit overwhelmed at first. You're doing a great job, don't worry about it. After a couple of years you'll be amazed how many things you can keep up in the air at the same time."

Nick's eyes, as if on their own, ran quickly down the length of Meg's body—toned, slim—and for the first time in a very long time he wondered if it was worth it. Juggling a couple of dozen projects but no personal life. He turned from her and pushed his beer away across the bar—he'd definitely had enough.

They sat a few moments in awkward silence until Scott reappeared.

"Meg's been telling me how hard you've been working her," Nick said.

Scott ignored his stool and leaned heavily against the bar. "Can't help it. It's the curse, Meg. You have it, Nick has it. Not to brag, but I do too. You're smart, logical, you use common sense. The makings of a good accountant. But you know what your reward is going to be? More fucking work, that's what your reward will be. There's so much deadwood in our department that when someone comes along who can actually think, they get one hell of a lot loaded on their shoulders."

"Lucky me," Meg said.

"That's not the worst of it. Maybe if they left it at that, dumped the work on your shoulders and let you go about business, you could live with it. But they won't do that. Control, egos, and politics—they get in the way every time. Nick here is an exception. Want to take a look at the mold? Set up an appointment to see Dennis."

Nick frowned, indicating Meg's presence with a quick glance. "C'mon, Scott."

"The hell with it, Nick. Dennis's an asshole—she's going to find that out soon enough. We've got the

Monday meeting with him on the Yünnan Project audit—if I know Dennis, he's not going to disappoint."

"Maybe you don't know Dennis as well as you think. According to Carolyn, Dennis pushed me for the promotion. Gave a great recommendation."

Scott's eyes widened. "No offense, Nick, but if Dennis did that, he's got a reason, and it has everything to do with helping Dennis-fucking-Lindsay."

Nick shrugged, not altogether in disagreement. "Maybe. . . . Hey, look it, I've reached my limit for tonight. Time for me to crawl under the covers."

Scott looked at Meg expectantly. "What do you say, Meg, want me to introduce you to the late-night haunts? Turn it up a notch or two?"

Nick felt strangely pleased when Meg shook her head. "I don't think so."

"All right, you're all party poopers," Scott complained. "I'll be a good boy and head on home. Where do you live, Meg . . . want to share a cab?"

"Georgetown. Off Wisconsin and O."

Nick and Scott looked at each other. Scott lived to the west of Dupont Circle, not exactly on the other end of town, but hardly close to Meg's. Nick, on the other hand, lived just off O, within three blocks of Wisconsin.

On the ride to Meg's apartment, the cab's windshield wipers kept a rapid beat, as if to compensate for the lack of activity within. The driver, stiff and impassive, guided the vehicle smoothly. In the backseat Nick and Meg sat silently side by side, her face turned to the window and the dappled world passing beyond.

Meg's breath had fogged the window, and she wiped it clear with her fingertips. "City looks pretty when it rains," she said.

Nick nodded, then realized she wasn't looking his way. "Yeah," he said finally. He inhaled, surrounded by her scent—a light perfume. His heart began to pound strongly, and he worried he'd never be able to say anything intelligible now, even if he wanted to.

Meg turned to him. "You like Georgetown?"

"Yeah." He looked out the window, finding it easier to talk with her out of his field of vision. *Why was she having this effect on him?* "You get onto the back streets, walk by some of the old houses . . . they're beautiful. The red brick, the landscaping. I almost bought a few times, but . . ." He kicked himself. *You started it, now finish it.* ". . . But it seems sort of wasteful somehow: a house, a yard, when there's only me."

*God, what a sap.* Must be the drinks, he lied to himself.

"You go to school here?" Meg asked.

"No. Michigan. Yourself?"

"NYU undergrad, Wharton grad, remember?"

The résumé. "Oh . . . yeah." *Good, Nick. Real good.*

They rode in silence, both staring straight ahead, as if mesmerized by the rhythm of the wiper blades, until Nick said, "I'm sorry I won't get much of a chance to work with you . . . after the Yünnan Project audit, I mean." *That didn't sound like a come-on, did it?* The way she looked at him, he wondered.

"Me too," Meg said.

Nick's mind whirred, but he could think of no follow-up. His foot began to tap rapidly of its own accord. Finally the cab pulled onto Wisconsin.

"Driver," Meg said after a couple of minutes, "could you drop me off over on the right . . . end of the block."

Meg reached for her purse as the cab pulled to the side of the street.

"Forget it, Meg, I've got it."

She removed a few crumpled bills, but Nick held out a hand to block her. Their hands brushed briefly— electric. "Really," he insisted, "it wasn't out of my way."

Meg tipped her head. "Thanks." She opened the

door and popped her umbrella. From the street she yelled a last "thanks," then shut the door.

Nick had the cab wait a few moments, until Meg entered the apartment house, then slumped back in his seat, intoxicated and knowing it was more than the alcohol after all.

# 8

Nick's eyes opened, just a slit, long enough to catch an irritating flash of light from the bedroom window. He clamped his eyelids quickly shut against the cruel invasion.

*Morning already.* It seemed he'd just gone to sleep. He moaned, then pressed the heels of his hands hard against his eye sockets. Suddenly he bolted upright and reached for the alarm clock.

Five-forty. Five minutes left to sleep. Not a crisis.

Nick snapped off the alarm, circumventing the impending irritation, then relaxed and let his head sink back to the pillow, shut his eyes. He groaned once, for nobody's benefit but his own.

It had been a crazy three weeks. Carolyn had warned him, but— He had had no idea. Meetings took up most of his day, then, finally at six when the bulk of the employees left for home, he would begin his real work—the pile in his in-box that just kept growing and growing throughout the day.

He had finished, on schedule, the report to the Department of Education on the National Direct Student Loan Program. It had meant working through that first weekend and a string of near all-nighters, but he flopped the report on Carolyn's desk the morning it was due. She called him that afternoon, extremely complimentary. Nick remembered her words: "You deserve the rest of the day, and the weekend, off, you really do. Unfortunately, some things have come up. . . ."

More projects, more impossible deadlines, always a staffing shortage. Four hours of sleep a night, if he was lucky.

Funny, tired as he was, once at work he'd take that

first phone call or start in on that first report and the sleepless nights seemed to fade in memory, like an annoying background noise one gradually became conditioned to. Judy, his secretary, had warned him he couldn't maintain the pace he had set for himself, but so far he had kept his head above water, if only barely, and would continue to. And if a few things went by the wayside in the meantime—he had not done his laundry since the promotion, or met Scott for their weekly outings, or paid his bills—that was the price he had to pay.

When people doubted him, when impossible deadlines loomed, that's when he had always been at his best. Things would settle down, it would just take time. No way was he giving up. Not even Carolyn had made assistant comptroller at thirty-five.

Nick grabbed the corner of the covers and threw them toward his feet. He forced himself to a sitting position, poised on the edge of the bed, head cradled in hands. The fatigue held him from deep inside, but had started showing itself in his washed-out complexion and the dark circles forming around his eyes.

He felt like absolute crap, and chastised himself for acknowledging as much.

Nick looked down at his slowly spreading waist and, to no great effect, tried to suck in his gut. What had happened? In his twenties, even early thirties, he couldn't eat enough, showed off a washboard stomach, now—

An exercise program. He really needed to get on an exercise program before he lost control of the situation, before he was just another stout middle-aged accountant. Just as soon as he got the new job under control, he would begin taking care of himself. Three healthy meals and regular trips to the weight room.

Why had he started to think about exercise and his waistline? He knew the answer, and only half-successfully pushed the image of Meg Taylor from his mind. How was she doing? he wondered.

Nick made a beeline for the coffee machine in the

kitchen, taking in his functional but cold apartment. Empty walls, shelves stacked with case work.

He poured himself a cup of coffee—already made, set on a timer. He started toward the bathroom, but his mind shifted to work, to the quarterly reports, and the fisheries audit, and the food stamp restructuring, and the dozen other similar crises that would demand his time within the hour. He hoisted his briefcase onto the kitchen table, snapped the lock open. Just a few things to look at before his shower.

A half hour later, he looked to the wall clock and jumped to his feet. Great, he thought, now I'll be late. He started to the bathroom, but on the way veered to the coffeepot and refilled his cup.

"Judy?" Nick called.

She appeared at his office door.

"What time is my meeting with Carolyn?"

"Four."

Nick checked his watch. "Okay, can you make sure Greg will be there? Oh, and I left the Jenkins file on your desk. Could you make copies and distribute them to the working team? Come up with the usual cover memo and I'll sign it."

"Anything else?"

Nick snapped his finger. "Yeah, I need the new draft of the food stamp recommendations. You finish the changes yet?"

"Hours ago," Judy said sarcastically, hands on hip. "I managed to finish it in between running to the copy machine, making a dozen odd phone calls, preparing—"

Nick held up his hand, recognizing his blunder. "Sorry, Judy. As soon as you can get to it, okay?"

Judy glared at him, arms now crossed in disapproval. "Why did I ever agree to transfer departments with you?"

Nick adopted a hopeful grin. "Because we're a team?"

"My husband is starting to think so—I spend more time here than at home."

No return smile, Nick noticed. "I appreciate all you've been doing, Judy. You know I do."

Judy shook her head slowly. "I saw Scott in the cafeteria last week. He said he hasn't seen much of you."

In answer, Nick gestured at the papers on his desk.

"He looked a little down," Judy continued. "You know Scott, that's not like him."

Nick nodded. "It's the Yünnan Project audit."

"What about it?"

"Dennis is calling the shots now." Dennis had been right all along. Since his promotion Nick, always desperate to meet some deadline or called away to some meeting, had found no time to devote to his old cases, including the Yünnan Project audit. Dennis, as agreed, had stepped into his shoes.

"Evidently," Nick went on, "Dennis has been telling Scott how to conduct the audit—what to look at, what not to. You know Scott, he doesn't think much of authority and thinks even less of Dennis. Pissed him off. He thinks Dennis is glossing over the whole case, missing the boat. He started telling me about the things he'd found but . . ."

"But you didn't have time for him, right?"

Nick sighed. Couldn't people understand that with his promotion had come greater obligations? Sacrifices came with the territory, and that meant he hadn't seen as much of Scott or, for that matter, Meg, as he would have hoped. "Judy, I don't even have time for myself right now. Things will change, I promise."

Her face didn't soften. "Can't you do anything?"

"About Dennis and the Yünnan Project? If I can clone myself, yes, otherwise no. Right now my primary responsibilities are to the Government Division. I can't turn my back on those responsibilities. I just can't."

Judy frowned. "You're supposed to be best

friends." She started to leave, and Nick finally set down his pen.

"C'mon, Judy," he pleaded, "we are, but . . . I've got less than six months to prove myself to Carolyn. She expects a lot, and I'm going to give it to her. Scott understands that; I know he does." He tried another smile. "I just think you miss his obnoxious voice."

Judy looked out the office door, then answered wistfully, "Honestly, I do. Everyone in this division is so . . . so stuffy."

"Like me, huh?"

"No, you're not actually stuffy. You just act that way most of the time."

*Was that supposed to be a compliment?* Nick threw up his arms. "Okay, okay, the hell with it. The work goes to the side for a while. Get Scott on the line. I'll invite him down and we'll . . . I don't know . . . play hooky. Go to lunch, all three of us. How's that?"

"Now?"

Nick nodded. "Let's do it. To tell you the truth, I sort of miss his obnoxious voice too."

Judy ran eagerly to her desk. Nick heard her voice, muffled from the other room. He reached for his phone on her return a few minutes later. "Is he on the line?" Nick asked.

Judy shook her head, crestfallen. "No. . . . He's on vacation—two weeks."

"Two weeks?" Nick repeated. Scott's usual m.o. was a long weekend in the Caribbean, time enough to check out the local watering holes and catch a nice hangover. "Where'd he go?"

"His secretary doesn't know. He didn't leave a number and he hasn't called in."

Nick scratched the side of his face with his knuckles. It surprised him, even bothered him a bit, that Scott hadn't filled him in on his plans. Then again, he hadn't made time for Scott lately. Why should he expect Scott to make time for him? "Maybe something came up, some emergency."

"And he didn't tell us?"

Nick hit on the answer. "He probably met some girl. Flew her off somewhere on the spur of the moment."

Judy's face brightened. "You might be right."

"Sure," Nick said, his thoughts already veering back to work. "He didn't tell us because he didn't want to get ribbed. When he gets back, I'm sure we'll be treated to all the juicy details. In the meantime, I have a pile of work to finish. I've got to get back at it."

Judy watched him for a few moments, until she saw that his mind had returned to the world of figures, then slipped from his office.

# 9

The silver BMW slowed, then angled to the right into a parking space. Scott Johnson did the same, four spaces back. Three days of surveillance had emboldened him: he didn't bother circling the block.

The BMW's door opened, and Andrew McKenzie—early forties, average height, athletic and well dressed—got out. Scott watched him disappear into a bar across the street.

Scott monitored his wristwatch. He let five minutes pass, then exited his car and started for the same bar. A stream of guys and girls, all twenty-something, hit the entrance a few steps before him; he joined them, losing himself in the group.

On entering, Scott spotted McKenzie almost immediately, his back to a wall, a drink in hand, his gold Rolex set off by a deep tan. By himself, for now. McKenzie looked in Scott's direction, but only for a split second—checking out the women that had entered with him, Scott guessed. Only an idle glance, nothing more.

A stool stood empty on the opposite end of the bar from McKenzie, and Scott claimed it. On the neighboring stool, a rail-thin kid with a sparse red goatee did nothing to acknowledge his presence. Scott ordered a bottle of Miller from the curly-haired bartender, then arranged it and a fold of currency on the bar, staking out his territory.

He took a sip of beer while appreciating his surroundings: a popular place in the Five Points area of Birmingham, but with some history, as evidenced by the wood bar stained dark by beer and time. A world apart from D.C.—not a blue blazer in sight. Only a few blocks from UAB, the University of Alabama-

Birmingham, the bar was loaded with co-eds, McKenzie the exception.

All and all, not the worst place to blow a few days of vacation.

Scott had latched on to McKenzie three days earlier and had stuck with him ever since. The guy was amazing. He had an office downtown, but since Scott had begun following him, he had visited it only once, and then for all of about thirty minutes. McKenzie slept late, till almost noon, then played tennis or lounged by the pool. The nights he spent in places like this, working the co-eds, trying to cut one from the pack. A big-time sleaze. Even worse, a successful sleaze, two times in as many nights.

So far Scott had little to show for his surveillance. Just two mornings of hangovers and a rudimentary knowledge of Birmingham.

*Maybe I'm wasting my time. Maybe I'd be better off forgetting McKenzie and making my own play for one of the college girls at the bar.*

Patience, Scott scolded himself. Remember what brought you here: evidence. Maybe not concrete evidence, but certainly enough to raise a host of suspicions.

Things would have been easier if Dennis had given him a free hand to investigate the Yünnan Project subcontracts, but that hadn't happened. "Extraneous to the investigation," Dennis had stated, and thereafter cut off all debate. Extraneous, hell. Scott investigated on his own, and it wasn't long before he stumbled across McKenzie. The man smelled dirty; his company smelled dirty; his subcontract with Smith Pettit smelled dirty. And if Scott was right, more than overbilling was involved. McKenzie never seemed to work, his few employees seemed idle, yet they supposedly toiled on a significant subcontract under the Yünnan Project? Something didn't add up. Scott just needed answers, and if he got lucky he would have them by the end of the night.

Scott wished he could have confided his plans to

Nick, but why put Nick's career on the line as well as his own? Just being here under guise of a vacation was a gross act of insubordination, and tonight he intended a far riskier act. If things blew up in his face, at least Nick could plead ignorance. Better to keep Nick in the dark, at least for now.

As Scott watched, McKenzie scanned the bar, lingering over a table of women well on their way to inebriation. McKenzie then motioned to the bartender.

Scott had seen this before, the last two nights. McKenzie would send over a round, and then another, and another. As long as the women kept accepting, he would keep buying. Sooner or later they would ask him to sit down.

Tonight it took only two rounds. McKenzie pulled up a chair between the two prettiest girls. Within twenty minutes his hand had crept to one's thigh, and when she didn't object, crept higher.

Scott fingered the shiny new key in his breast pocket. A locksmith had cut it for him earlier in the day. Simple: you gave him the master key code, he gave you a key, no questions asked.

Getting the key code had been easy. Scott had accessed a national registry of phone numbers over the Internet; it listed two numbers for the company that managed the apartment complex where McKenzie lived. The second of the numbers connected him to the management company's computer. There had been no security procedures, no pin numbers to enter, nothing. He had gained access in a matter of minutes. A simple search had lead him to McKenzie's name under the heading "Apartment 8E." A quarter page of information had followed: McKenzie's lease term; his monthly rent; his place of employment; the cost and date of apartment repairs; the age, make, and model number of the refrigerator, the stove, and the dishwasher; and finally, sandwiched between a bank account number for McKenzie's security deposit and a parking spot number, the master key code to his apartment door.

When would people learn that a file cabinet guarded by a two dollar lock was safer than an unprotected computer system?

Scott finished his drink, laid a dollar on the bar, and started for the door. By the looks of things, McKenzie would be busy here, at least for an hour or two—enough time for Scott to enter McKenzie's apartment and conduct a thorough search. Illegal, but if he found nothing in McKenzie's apartment, what harm had been done?

That he could be arrested and unceremoniously expelled from the GAO if caught, for some reason didn't seem to worry Scott. He had no second thoughts—unorthodox measures were called for. Truth be known, the danger excited him.

As Scott started to his car, the lyrics from a classic Lou Reed song began circling through his mind. He started quietly singing along: "Hey, babe, take a walk on the wild side." A particularly fitting song, he decided.

# 10

Meg did a quick computer search of the GAO's form files and found exactly what she wanted: a document request list from a prior GAO audit: cost overruns in construction of the Seawolf submarine. She copied the list from the network to her computer, relabeled it, and began marking it to reflect her current assignment: investigating cost overruns on a new-generation armored personnel carrier.

The senior auditor on the investigation had asked her to "try her hand" at the request list. "We'll go over it together when you're finished to see what you missed," he had said.

*See what you missed?* Meg didn't intend to miss a thing.

The pace of work over the last week had slowed since Scott had gone on vacation. She still put in ten-hour days, but found time to hit the gym in the mornings and managed a few nights out with a group of younger GAO accountants. Though at seven or eight years their senior; she didn't exactly feel one of the crowd.

Funny thing was, Meg didn't mind the long hours all that much. Maybe the challenge of a new skill to master kept her interest focused, or maybe it was the piecing together of a puzzle from a financial trail. She had no regrets so far, other than Dennis Lindsay. Scott had been right about him. A jerk. Condescending with an undeserved superiority complex. It would have been nice to have had a chance to work under Nick a bit longer. He seemed . . . well, different. Straightforward, kind, a bit shy, obviously talented.

She found herself starting to blush.

Over the last two weeks she'd made a point of visiting some of the coffee shops close to his apartment. She shook her head, embarrassed at the thought, knowing she'd been hoping to run into him but refusing to admit it to herself.

Stupid, she thought. This wasn't a school, and she wasn't a schoolgirl. She shook Nick from her mind and returned to work.

The phone rang a few minutes later, and Meg reached out absently for the receiver. "Hello," she said.

"Meg? It's Scott."

Scott's voice came gravelly and hoarse; he'd obviously been drinking the night before—hardly shocking. "Hi, Scott. How's your vacation going?"

"Vacation . . . right. Let's just say I've been keeping pretty busy. I—" A knock sounded over the receiver, and Scott paused. "Hold on a second, will you?" he said, and the line went silent.

Meg could hear a door open, then unintelligible conversation. "I'm back," Scott announced finally. "Just having my morning java redelivered. They gave me decaf the first time . . . you shouldn't even be able to call that crap coffee. Do you think we'd have any luck getting the FDA to review that? Fair labeling law or something."

Meg laughed, then asked, "Where are you?"

"A hotel, pretty grimy one if you want to know the truth."

"Sounds like a pleasant place to spend two weeks."

"Oh, I haven't limited myself to just *one* grimy hotel room—I've been spreading myself around. In a few minutes I'm off to the coast. Sort of a tour of Southern cities, one grimy hotel after another."

Meg set down her pen and leaned back in her chair. "Wish I were there," she said sarcastically, then instantly regretted her words, knowing what would come. Scott didn't disappoint.

"I'd be happy to fly you down . . . twin grimy beds, of course."

Meg liked Scott, but her interest didn't extend beyond friendship. She chose her tone carefully. "Thanks for the offer."

"That sounds like a no. Oh, well, on to more mundane matters in that case. Business. My secretary told me you called."

"Right. I finished the draft report for Dennis. The one he asked for: a summary of the Yünnan Project investigation to date. I wanted to know if I should send it to him, or hold off until you get back and have a chance to review it."

"Why don't you hold off?" Scott said after a moment. "I happen to know that report is going to need some updating. Besides, if everything goes well, I'll be back by the end of the week."

Meg glanced at her calendar. Scott had scheduled vacation through next Tuesday. "Huh? If your vacation goes well, you're going to cut it *short*?"

"Yeah, well, vacation might be a bit of a misnomer. Actually, it's more of a working vacation."

"What are you working on?"

After another pause Scott whispered conspiratorially, "I didn't plan to tell anyone but now . . . If you want to know the truth, I'm busting to tell somebody."

"I'm somebody. Shoot."

"I've been looking into something on my own."

Meg waited for Scott to explain, and when he didn't, she said, "Job related?"

"Put it this way: Dennis has his ideas about how thoroughly we investigate the Yünnan Project subcontracts, and I have mine."

Meg left her chair. The phone cord was just long enough for her to reach the office door. She shut it. "Scott, I don't really know how things work around here, but is that . . ."

Scott finished her question. "Smart? To ignore direct and unambiguous instructions from your boss? Probably not. Then again, unless I found something, I didn't intend to tell Dennis or anyone else what I'd been doing."

"Which means you have . . . found something, I mean?"

"I sure did," Scott said proudly. "I won't go into specifics now, but get ready, Meg. When I get back, if everything pans out the way I think, I'm going to light off some fireworks."

"Have you told Nick?"

"I just tried his line, but he's tied up in a meeting."

"I can pass on a message if you want."

"No. It can wait till I get back. I'll tell him in person, see his mouth drop for myself. . . . Meg, in the meantime, could you keep this conversation our little secret?"

"Great," Meg said stiffly. "First you involve me in your little intrigue, then you won't allow me to cover myself." Being blunt with Scott somehow came easily.

Scott laughed. "You're disappointing me. I pegged you for an independent streak."

"Accountants follow set accounting rules and standards—it's not exactly the career of choice for thrill seekers."

"Yeah, job can suck, can't it? I'll tell you what. Forget I even opened my mouth. It wasn't fair to say anything. As far as you know, I'm doing the typical vacation thing: sunscreen, lounge chairs, margaritas. Okay?"

Meg closed her eyes and shook her head. "It's your funeral."

"Fair enough. I'll see you in a few days, Meg. And you'll see, ol' Scott's not about to get in any trouble."

Meg heard a click, and was left holding a dead line.

# 11

Nick stopped for a moment at the entrance. He hated these things.

Everybody in Washington, it seemed, insisted on throwing a banquet. To raise money for a candidate, to celebrate a campaign victory, or for a popular charity, it didn't matter. As long as the women got a chance to hang jewelry around their necks and men got to compare the size of their wallets, everybody seemed happy. Peacocks, strutting and showing off, and Nick wanted no part of it.

Of course, he went just the same. Someone called you up—a friend, or person you owed a favor—and said they had bought a table at such and such a function, and what choice did you have? It is for a very good cause, they'd say, and guess who will be there? Nick never cared, but they were sure to tell him anyway. A TV anchor, or movie star, always a senator or two.

Tonight's cause was as good as any, Nick supposed. And more important, the call had come from a friend in the Office of Special Investigations desperate to fill a table for ten.

Nick would make an appearance, have a drink or two, force down the dry, warmed-over chicken, laugh a bit too hard at the celebrity speaker, then head home. All in all, considering it was his first night off work early in almost four weeks, he would have preferred to spend it at home vegged out in front of the TV.

Nick walked into the hotel ballroom. Two women stationed behind a long table handed him a name tag. He pinned it to his tux, unconcerned with pin holes—the tux was cheap to begin with, bought a decade earlier when he was poorer and a size smaller. During Nick's first year with the GAO, Scott had dragged him to a half dozen of these things in pursuit of daughters of high-placed government officials.

Nick peered down at the tag, his assigned table number printed in the lower left-hand corner. Twenty-two. He looked over the maze of tables, all empty, the attendees bunched around the bars ringing the ballroom.

A drink would help, Nick decided, and headed off for a gin and tonic.

One tour around the ballroom, drink in hand, brought him to the klatch of GAO employees—a tight circle of eight, most younger than he, who seemed to be enjoying themselves and their drinks. He joined the circle, and discussion halted abruptly as a flurry of hands shot toward him, acknowledging his unofficial position as assistant comptroller.

Talk shifted to work, as it often did around Nick, and soon he debated proposed GASB rules with two of the group while the remainder sealed themselves off in a new circle, relieved, Nick guessed, to have cut him from their number.

Over the crowd noise Nick heard a name—"Meg" —called across the floor.

He turned and spotted her almost immediately: dark blue dress, graceful.

Meg smiled and waved, and Nick was about to do the same when he noticed her eyes were directed to his left, to the group of six standing apart. He lowered his hand self-consciously.

Only when Meg drew closer did she notice Nick and call out his name.

"Meg, how are you?"

"Fine." She started to swerve in his direction, but one of the younger accountants intercepted her and led her away by the elbow. Meg looked back to Nick over her shoulder and mouthed "Sorry" to him apologetically.

Meg joined the group of six, and Nick resumed the

discussion of GASB rules, hoping his embarrassment did not show.

Periodically, his eyes jumped to Meg's back, to the slim waist and bare shoulders.

He dismissed any thought of detouring to her side. She was, after all, a co-worker. He'd seen enough relationships between co-workers go bad, heard the resulting gossip, saw the lines drawn between opposing camps, witnessed the effect on people's careers. Not for him.

*As if he had a chance.*

He knew himself well enough to predict the outcome of any conversation. He would have nothing to say to her, then the talk would necessarily drift to work, and that would be worse than saying nothing at all.

Rationalizations maybe, but each made perfect sense. Everybody had their element, and his was work. Issues, logic, reasoning. Accept that, he told himself.

Assistant comptroller at thirty-five. An important, demanding job, a bright future—the glass was more than half full.

Nick started toward the bar for another drink, wishing he had never come.

# 12

Scott waited until the gates had closed and the van had pulled to an empty bay, then slid the transmission into gear and allowed the car to roll slowly forward for a better view. The port warehouse was large, square, undistinguished—its windows high and gated. He counted eight truck bays, three of them full, including the one the van now occupied.

Scott reached for the small duffel bag set on the passenger's seat beside him and removed a Nikon automatic camera. He pointed it at the warehouse gate; the attached 200mm lens magnified the weather-beaten sign affixed there. Kiajong Shipping, it read. He snapped a photo.

Panning with the lens, he snapped a shot of the van and the camera whirred loudly—the automatic rewind—signifying the end of the roll. He extracted the film and set it in the duffel with the other three rolls he had shot earlier in the day. Then he loaded in a fresh roll and took another series of shots, of the van, the workers, and the other trucks in the lot.

His hands shook with excitement. The search of Andrew McKenzie's apartment had yielded much more than he ever dreamed: a computer disk that, with the help of a friend in the Federal Reserve, had led him from Birmingham to Raleigh and finally here to Norfolk, the trail complete. By tomorrow he would be back in D.C. with an incredible story and evidence to back it up.

He couldn't wait to see the look on Nick's face.

Scott looked again at the warehouse. A series of piers jutted from its rear, each crowned by a massive crane for loading and unloading freight. One ship lay in dock. Scott pointed the camera at the ship's masts.

A flag flew there, but he couldn't make it out. The same with the name of the vessel—he couldn't quite read the white lettering on the hull.

If he could get closer, just another couple of hundred yards—

A cyclone fence circled the warehouse lot sixty yards or so from him. No more than seven feet high, free of barbed wire. Easy enough to jump.

Tugging at his chin, both excited and nervous, Scott monitored the warehouse lot, camera ready. Within a quarter hour the van left, and he fired off another half dozen shots as it passed. The last two trucks followed shortly after, and then all activity in the lot died. Scott checked his watch: 6:32 P.M. He set the car radio to a rock channel and waited.

By seven not a truck had entered the warehouse lot; he hadn't seen a soul.

Needing no further invitation, Scott exited the car, duffel bag slung over his shoulder with camera inside. He made his way to the cyclone fence.

Climbing the fence proved easy, but Scott went over its top less than gracefully. He hit the ground hard and fell to his side; simultaneously metal tinkled against asphalt. He jumped quickly to his feet. His hand went to his pocket—empty—and he scanned the ground unsuccessfully for his car keys and motel key.

A nervous glance at the warehouse showed all remained still, no one had heard him.

Glints of silver caught Scott's eye, a coin, a screw, and there, against the fence, his car keys. He scooped them up and ran for cover behind the nearest tractor trailer. The lost motel key did not concern him—it was easily replaceable.

From around the trailer's corner, he looked at the ship, and instantly realized his mistake. In the car he had been elevated, parked on a slight hill overlooking the warehouse. From where he now stood, the warehouse obscured the ship entirely.

Scott had come this far, and didn't hesitate. A quick

sprint brought him to the warehouse itself. He would circle it to get his photos.

Adrenaline coursed his bloodstream. He felt high, exhilarated. Field work appealed to him; he seemed to have an aptitude for it.

The side of the warehouse served as a convenient dump. Old tires, twisted bits of metal, odd lengths of pipe and coils of cable lined the narrow passage between warehouse and fence. The only windows were ten feet or more overhead. Scott moved carefully but confidently to the far side of the building.

As he neared the edge of the warehouse he heard voices, a number of them, speaking an Asian tongue—Chinese, he thought. A stack of pallets marked the warehouse's corner. He took cover behind them, risking only a quick glance around the stack to identify the voices' source: a group of dockworkers another fifteen yards farther on, their backs to him, resting on crates with lunch boxes at their sides. He also saw the ship, an unobstructed view.

Scott unslung the duffel bag, removed the Nikon, and directed it at the ship. The name first, the *Shansi,* and then the flag. A cluster of five yellow stars marked the upper left-hand corner of the red flag, one larger than the others. The flag of the People's Republic of China, Scott realized. *Jesus.*

His finger hesitated over the shutter button.

*How loud was the camera's shutter? Loud enough to alert the men to his presence?*

He wiped the back of his hand quickly across his forehead. How much could the dockworkers hear, fifteen yards distant, with their talking and the sound of forklifts in the distance? Not much, he decided.

Scott offered a quick prayer, then pushed the shutter button. The shutter fired with a soft click, no dockhand turned.

Confident now, Scott snapped another photo of the flag. Just a photo of the ship name, and he would be done.

He framed the name, then pushed the shutter button, only to be greeted by a whirring noise.

The automatic rewind—*dammit*—impossibly loud, it seemed.

A dockworker turned, caught Scott's eye a fraction of a second before Scott managed to duck behind the pallets.

Scott didn't wait to see what the man's reaction was; he ran. Six strides, and a coil of wire caught his left ankle and left him sprawling. Before he could regain his feet, both of his arms were pinioned behind his back. Then a face filled his vision, screaming loudly in a language he could not understand.

Scott scanned his surroundings: the hold of the *Shansi*, cramped with crates and dark, lit only dimly with safety lamps protected by heavy-gauge wire. He inhaled and tasted a mustiness born of oil, rust, and sweat.

Eight men surrounded the wooden crate on which he sat, all Asian, most a full head shorter than he but all lean and fit, some in stained T-shirts, others in khaki work shirts with the arms cut off.

They had given up screaming at him finally, and seemed to be waiting for something or someone. In a moment Scott saw who.

A man dressed in white pants and a black silk shirt approached. Asian. Large, nearing six feet, with a wrestler's upper body and torso. Scott tried, but could not read the dark eyes set in the broad, flat face. A dangerous face, all the more so because he carried a three-foot length of steel bar.

One of the dockworkers bowed and said, "Pu-Yi." Scott made note of the name.

The man, Pu-Yi, stopped in front of Scott, looked him up and down with distaste. "What are you doing here?" Pu-Yi snapped in heavily accented English.

Scott rose from the wooden crate. "Nothing," he said, adopting an indignant tone. "I was just out for a walk."

"This is private property."

"I didn't know that."

"There is a fence, all around the yard."

Scott conceded as much with a nod. "Look, I'm sorry about that. I jumped the fence. I just wanted to get a good view of the ship in port. I'm nuts about ships. A hobby of mine. I didn't think anybody would mind if I took a look." He tried his most endearing smile, but Pu-Yi continued to scowl.

Pu-Yi pointed at the camera in Scott's right hand. "You have a camera?"

"Like I said, I like ships. Sort of a hobby of mine to take photos of them."

Pu-Yi scratched his fingers in the air, palm up, a clear order to hand over the camera. Given the circumstances, Scott thought it best to cooperate. Pu-Yi examined the camera quickly, then pointed at the small duffel bag slung over Scott's shoulders. "What do you have in the bag?"

"Just a few personal things."

Pu-Yi reached for the bag, and again Scott chose not to object. Pu-Yi unzipped it, rummaged inside. His hand came out holding three rolls of spent film. He held them up to Scott's face accusingly.

"Some of those have been in there for . . . I don't know . . . weeks, I think," Scott lied. "I just haven't got around to getting them developed."

Pu-Yi placed the three rolls in his pants pocket, then studied Scott's face intently. "You ran."

Scott nodded, trying to appear embarrassed. "Hey, no one ever accused me of being smart. I reacted without thinking. I guess I knew I shouldn't really have jumped the fence, so, yes, I ran . . . like a little kid."

One of the dockworkers to the side of Pu-Yi said something in Chinese. A short conversation between the two followed, the dockworker pointing at Scott repeatedly.

Scott waited until they had finished before speaking again. "Hey, look, I apologize. Really. I've learned my lesson, and I'll never do it again. Okay? Now, I really have to get going or I'll miss an appointment."

Scott began to walk confidently toward the one called Pu-Yi and the wall of men to each side of him. *Keep your head high, your eyes unblinking, and the wall of men would part.* He'd go over the fence, get back in his car, and head back to D.C. Just another scrape he would extract himself from with a little charm, a little self-deprecating humor, and a bit of cool. That easy.

Pu-Yi turned his back as if to make way. The beginnings of a smile showed on Scott's face, then froze there as his eyes went round. Pu-Yi continued to spin, and when he again faced Scott, the steel bar, held like a bat, led his body.

Scott had no time to react. He took the blow in the chest, at the sternum, and dropped immediately to the ground in a fetal position, hands clutched in fists and folded over his heart.

He tried to suck in air, but none would come. His eyes bulged, and only with great effort did he eventually manage a series of quick and shallow gasps.

Above him, the dockworkers had closed. A flurry of Chinese followed that Scott barely heard as he focused on regaining control of his lungs.

At last the muscles constricting his chest loosened. His lungs filled deeply, though the sharp pain localized about his sternum remained. He stayed on the ground, breathing labored, as one of the dockworkers bent and reached for his wallet. The dockworker extracted it from Scott's back pocket and handed it to Pu-Yi.

Another flurry of Chinese followed. Then Pu-Yi walked away, leaving Scott on the floor, surrounded.

Scott struggled to all fours, then to his knees.

*God, that hurt.*

He looked up, at the dockworkers; blank faces stared back.

*Keep your head high, your eyes unblinking, and the wall would part?* Hell of an idea, Scott. One hell of an idea.

For the first time an edge of real fear tinged his thinking, but he banished it quickly. *Nothing to worry about, Scott. You just misjudged the situation.* Plan two: sit tight, don't make a sound unless spoken to. They were probably holding him for the police, and willing to use force to ensure he remained. Fine. The police would come, they'd take him away, and as soon as he was safely in the squad car he'd tell them who he was and what he was doing there.

You wanted field work, Scott, well, here is the baggage. At least he'd have a good story to tell around the GAO, and a nasty bruise, perhaps a few cracked ribs, to prove it.

Suddenly a day spent reviewing financials seemed refreshingly boring.

After a few minutes the circle of dockworkers parted again; Pu-Yi had returned. He squatted next to Scott. "You will tell me the truth now."

"There was no reason to hit me."

"What are you doing here?" Pu-Yi barked, ignoring Scott's complaint.

*What the hell was this?* This was America, where people had rights. "I told you already," Scott replied angrily. "I just wanted to look at the ships."

Pu-Yi spat at Scott's feet, then stood and reached out his hand. One of the dockworkers handed him a handkerchief. For a moment Scott thought Pu-Yi intended to offer help, then Scott noticed there was something within the handkerchief, and an alarm sounded in his head.

Pu-Yi unwrapped a blue-steel handgun. He gripped it and held it pointed at the sky as he circled Scott. "You wanted to look at ships?" he said.

"Yes," Scott said, his voice breaking.

"You are lying."

*"No."*

Behind Scott now, Pu-Yi raised his eyes slowly to a pair of dockworkers, and nodded. The dockworkers leaned over Scott and grabbed his right arm by the wrist. They then pressed Scott's right hand flat against the top of a wooden crate.

Pu-Yi bent from the waist and rammed the handgun's barrel against the index finger of Scott's right hand, just above the first knuckle. Scott tried to jerk his hand back, but the dockworkers held it firmly planted in place.

Scott swallowed hard; blood rushed loudly in his ears. *Time to tell the truth?*

Pu-Yi looked into Scott's eyes, but did not repeat his questioning. Instead he smiled and tightened his finger on the trigger.

Scott's eardrums exploded; the muzzle flash clouded his eyes. He felt nothing for a moment, then he looked at his hand. From the stump where his finger was once attached, blood spurted rhythmically in time with his now racing pulse, forming a growing pool of blood. He saw what remained of his index finger—small and white—curled a half foot from his hand.

*Blood?*

*His blood? His finger? His hand?*

*Jesus.*

The two dockworkers released Scott's hand, and he reached instantly for the severed finger, tried to refit it to the raw flap of flesh and shattered bone that once held it. Rationality deserted him, replaced by horror and an odd fascination as the futility of his attempts sank in. He clutched his mutilated hand to his breast as pain hammered him in waves.

*"Motherfucker,"* Scott screamed, rocking back and forth, blood streaming down his arm, staining his shirtsleeve crimson. *"I'm a federal agent, do you understand?"* He choked on the words and then vomited.

*"A fed,"* he yelled again after recovering his voice.

Scott collapsed to a sitting position, his eyes right, as if to wipe out the reality of the last few moments.

He sobbed, "Why'd you do this? Why the hell did you do this?" He looked at Pu-Yi, fought to control his voice. "I'm a federal agent, do you understand?

I'm not a thief. I'm not going to run. I want the police here, and I want them here *now*."

"The police will not be coming," Pu-Yi said coolly, lifting up Scott's face by his chin. "No one will be coming. You can leave when you tell me what you are doing here."

Sitting in his blood, in his vomit, Scott felt tears building in his eyes.

Two dockworkers again leaned over Scott, this time grabbing his left arm by the wrist. "You will tell me now," Pu-Yi yelled, brandishing the handgun.

The world around Scott fell away, all but the gun and a throbbing hand. When Pu-Yi asked his next question, Scott answered honestly, prepared to trade the truth as needed to stay alive. Even then, however, his anger gave him the strength to withhold certain things—McKenzie, the disk. He wanted that evidence, wanted to be able to track down this Pu-Yi and all who worked with him and see them rot in jail.

Perhaps it had been a mistake to take Johnson's second index finger, Pu-Yi thought. Afterward, his answers had quickly turned disjointed, rambling. Pu-Yi convinced himself he would get little else of use from Johnson—in truth, he tired of the pathetic whimpering.

Pu-Yi uncorked a bottle of whiskey and held it out with a simple order, *"Drink."* He slapped Johnson hard to convince him the order wasn't open for negotiation. Johnson drank then, with the aid of a dockworker.

When Johnson had finished almost half the bottle, Pu-Yi pulled it away. He then pointed the handgun squarely at Johnson's chest. Johnson's eyebrows shot up; he struggled to gain his feet.

Pu-Yi tightened his finger—this man deserved to die on all fours, like a dog, not a man.

He smiled broadly, the only warning before pulling the trigger. Multiple explosions knocked Johnson back against a shipping crate.

Johnson looked down at his shirt, at the holes ripped neatly across his chest and stomach. Three, rimmed in expanding red. He then looked up at Pu-Yi, standing over him, still holding the gun outstretched, and shook his head slightly, as if to wake himself from a bad dream.

Pu-Yi watched the life drain rapidly from the body, fascinated as always by death. So satisfying to have the power to condemn at a whim, to snuff out an existence on impulse.

Johnson's head listed, then fell to the side, unmoving. Pu-Yi turned from the body; there were other important matters to attend to. John Li must be informed, and of course there was the matter of disposing of the body.

# 13

As soon as the door swung shut behind him, Nick relaxed. The air tasted almost cool; a light breeze took the edge off the humidity. A beautiful night.

He sat in the dark, on one of the hotel's balconies overlooking a small courtyard, the tip of the Washington Monument visible in the distance, glowing white.

At dinner Meg had sat across the circular table from him; a tall centerpiece separated them. She had attempted to start up a conversation, but all Nick caught was his name—the rest came garbled. He had pointed at his ear, and called back, "What?" A few more "whats" voiced by each and both had given up. After dinner, after the guest speakers, the dance floor had opened—Meg was quickly monopolized. Too self-conscious to cut in, Nick had remained seated, enduring periodic bouts of strained small talk until he had sought refuge here.

In the context of work or debate, Nick considered himself almost dynamic, but at a cocktail party or an event such as this one— A room full of people, and yet he had never felt so alone.

He sipped his gin and tonic, listening to the car horns and far-off sirens, wrapped in a strangely comforting blanket of melancholy.

His mind drifted, as it often did when he was alone, with a drink in his hand.

Second grade, Woodhill Elementary School. The school bus ride in, friends sliding over on their seats to make room for him. He could not remember names, not even faces, just blurred snapshots of isolated incidents. Catching a garter snake in the schoolyard; a stack of valentine cards; a chicken fight on the jungle gym.

Surrounded by friends. At ease. A very different time.

Nick shut his eyes hard, but could not keep his mind from finishing the school day and heading home. He saw his parents then, as he always saw them: smiling, locked hand in hand in perpetuity, changing only as the photo tucked in his wallet yellowed.

Thirty-one and twenty-nine, just kids, with a son, and a new home, and so many dreams. Funny that he still subscribed to them the wisdom and experience of parents, when both, in the photo, were younger than he was now.

The door to the balcony opened, pulling Nick's mind to the present. He twisted but caught only a silhouette before the pie slice of light pinched to nothingness with the closing door.

"Nick?" the figure said.

"Yeah," Nick answered as the figure approached, and then, "Meg, is that you?"

"Yes."

Nick could just make out her features in the ambient light. She stopped a few feet from him.

"I was just catching some air," he said, embarrassed to be found here in the dark, alone.

Her head turned up. "It's a beautiful night."

"It is," Nick agreed.

"Tom thought he saw you come out here. I just wanted to say hi before I left—I didn't get much of a chance before."

"You're leaving?"

She nodded. "Everybody is moving on . . . The Tower, I think they said."

"Should be fun," Nick said, at once sarcastic and jealous.

"You can still join everybody if you hurry."

"You're not going?"

"No. It's late and I'm not really up for bar hopping. . . . I think maybe I'm getting old or something."

Nick chuckled. "I know the feeling."

A long pause followed; Nick searched for words to fill the vacuum but found none.

"Well, I'm off," Meg said finally. "Good night."

Meg started to turn, and Nick, too urgently, said, "I checked before, there was a backup for cabs."

She shrugged. "I planned to walk."

"Home?"

"It's only a couple of miles." She lifted one of her feet and pointed. "These heels aren't bad—I'll make it. . . . Have a good night."

Meg's hand had reached the balcony door before Nick spoke again. "Meg?"

She turned. "Hmm?"

So easy to say nothing. To stay here alone with his drink, with no risk. *Remember, work is your element. You don't have the capacity to connect on a different level. You've tried, and always failed.*

Nick forced the thoughts from his mind and said, the darkness somehow making it easier, "I don't really feel like waiting for a cab either. Would you mind if I walked along?"

She shook her head. "I'd enjoy the company."


North, then west, then north again—they agreed on direction, then started side by side, his long strides setting the pace. Was she nervous too? Nick wondered, and stole a quick glance.

No, he decided. Her hair swung in an easy rhythm; her lips curled just at the corners, but not self-consciously. She seemed cool, relaxed.

It was not a race, Nick reminded himself, and slowed his gait, falling in step behind another couple who shuffled slowly arm in arm.

*Another* couple? He stole one more glance at Meg, finding the idea not unappealing.

Nick began on his prepared list of questions: How's the job going? Are the hours long? Tell me what you're working on? Obvious, work-related questions— pro forma and uninteresting—but a start nonetheless.

"You're still working primarily with Scott?" Nick asked.

"Until his vacation I was. Since then it seems I've been pulled in a couple of different directions. Binley's just pulled me in on the Riegle-Neal Interstate Banking Act."

"Interesting project. I've talked to him about it. Of course, there were always inherent limitations in measuring loan and deposit activity on a state-by-state basis. Still, with call reports encompassing multi-state transactions, their utility will . . ." *What the hell was he saying?* His voice dropped off as he finished the sentence: ". . . necessarily diminish."

"I suppose," Meg said, sounding disengaged.

Nick's insides twisted. *Idiot.* He had spotted shelter—an issue he could examine and dissect—and, unthinking, had run for it. What did she think of him now? Characterless, bookish, boring—a few possibilities jumped to mind.

They walked on in near silence, and Nick glanced again at Meg's face. Did she now appear ill at ease or was it his imagination? He ran his tongue nervously about the inside of his mouth, as if searching for dialogue.

Soon nothing marked their passage but the click of heels on concrete.

What did Nick have to look forward to now? Two wordless miles? How long would that take? Nick did a quick calculation in his head: at two and a half miles an hour, two miles would take . . . Forty-eight minutes. Over three-quarters of an hour.

Meg glanced up and said, "It feels like rain."

Nick followed her line of sight, saw the stars were now invisible, blotted out by unseen clouds. He agreed—it did feel like rain—and used the comment as an excuse to resume a quicker pace. Meg's long strides barely matched his own.

Suddenly Meg jumped sidewise with a short yelp, bumping up lightly against Nick's shoulder.

"What is it?" he asked, steadying her with two hands.

She shook her head, embarrassed. "Something moved, hopped by my foot. Just surprised me, that's all."

Nick investigated, expecting to see a squirrel, or more likely a rat, scurry off into the bushes. Instead he spotted the culprit in a tuft of tall grass bordering the sidewalk. He pointed it out to Meg.

"A toad. Big one." He bent over it. "I don't think I've ever seen one in the city."

Meg squatted next to him. "Ugly," she commented, but without distaste.

"In a way."

"I had a book of fairy tales, growing up," Meg said. "Grimm's or Aesop's, I suppose. It had ink illustrations. I remember one of them vividly: a toad, sitting on a throne, with a scepter in its hand and a crown on its head. When I see a toad, for some reason I always see that drawing in my head."

Different pictures came to Nick, as his memory stirred as well. He tore a single blade of grass, used it to gently stroke the toad's back as he considered the images. Things he had not thought of for a long time. The toad sat unmoving, either unconcerned or grateful for the attention.

"My family had a cottage," Nick said finally, tentatively, in a reflective tone, "on a lake. A point." How long since he had mentioned the cottage to anyone?

"At night, in the summer, we'd go swimming . . . my parents and I. We made it a race. Cottage door to the pier." He paused, the smell of water, sand, and pine needles filling his nostrils. "First one in the water earned bragging rights. There were toads all over the place. In my mom's rock garden, along the shore. I was always so afraid of stepping on one. At the same time I wasn't about to lose the race. I'd fly down the path barefoot, my fingers crossed."

The toad along the sidewalk, evidently bored with

its back rub, hopped once, twice, to the security of a low-hanging bush.

"Looks like he's taking no chances," Meg said, pointing.

Nick looked at her; they shared a smile. "You ever step on one?" she asked.

"Nope. Never."

Nick stood; Meg did the same.

"And the races?" Meg asked.

"Never lost one of those either. Of course, it didn't occur to me that Mom and Dad let me win. . . . Funny, I used to think Dad could do about anything in the world—anything—and yet I thought I could outrun him. And at what? Seven, eight years old?"

Meg laughed. "I was the same way. My mom, she was prettier than any of my friends' mothers, as beautiful as anyone on TV—that's what I thought. But for a few years there, around twelve, thirteen . . . a competitive age, I guess . . . I convinced myself . . ." She regarded him suspiciously. "Don't laugh, okay?"

"Of course not," Nick lied.

"I convinced myself . . . that I had a more regal face."

A wide grin took Nick's face, and Meg swatted him lightly on the shoulder. "You said you wouldn't laugh."

"I'm not," Nick protested. "Let's see, give me a profile." Meg played along, and Nick said, "Yes, I can definitely see the royal lineage . . . it's the cheekbones, I think."

"All right, all right," Meg said, swatting him once more. "In reality I was a snot-nosed little kid with acne—I know that. I was just sharing a story."

Nick could not hold back a laugh any longer. "And now?"

"Am I still a snot-nosed little kid?"

"No." Nick smiled. "With the perspective of age, were you right? Was your mom as beautiful as anyone on TV?"

"No, I suppose not, but . . . A few months ago I

went through some of the old black-and-whites my parents have up in their attic. From the fifties, early sixties. I found a photo of her in a dinner dress: poof dress, pillbox hat. She looked . . . elegant best describes it, I guess."

Nick nodded. "Those were elegant times." He started down the sidewalk again, Meg at his side.

"Do you think we've lost something, our culture, I mean?" Meg asked. "I'm all for blue jeans and sweatshirts, don't get me wrong, but did we throw out some of the romance along the way? I mean, once in a while dressing up and going out, it must have been fun."

"Meg?"

"Hmm?"

Nick pointed at her. "What do you think you have on?"

She laughed shortly. "But tonight was different. A charity event someone had to twist our arms to attend. I mean throwing a dinner party, not because you have to, but because you want to."

"I think I'd hate it. Playing Ward Cleaver, dressing in a suit for meals."

"I know." Meg bobbed her head in agreement. "I would too. And that's sort of the problem, isn't it? It's as if our generation can't be bothered . . . dressing up, manners, all sorts of things."

"The danger of a revolution—if that's what the country went through in the sixties—is that revolutionaries often tear down the good institutions along with the bad. Maybe the pendulum has swung too far . . . maybe we're just coming to grips with that."

"I feel that way . . . sometimes," Meg concurred. "Like maybe we're all starting to grow up a bit after indulging ourselves for so long. You know, when I was in high school . . ."

Nick listened, and laughed, and shared a story of his own. Time no longer dragged. Twenty blocks shrank to ten, then to three, and what a short time ago seemed like much too long a walk now seemed much too short.

"Once, when Scott and I were—" Nick stopped himself. "Did you feel that?"

Meg held out a hand, palm up. "Rain?" she asked.

"A few drops." Nick gauged the sky. "I think we better hurry," he said.

A block and the scattered drops turned to a steady drizzle. Nick tugged Meg urgently by the elbow, pointing at a doorway a few yards farther on. They jumped under its cover just as the sidewalk ahead erupted in a torrent of falling raindrops.

The doorway was small, much smaller than Nick had realized. They stood side by side facing the street, backs up against the doorway, shoulders nearly touching.

Nick looked at Meg. Hair damp, flattened in a few places to her scalp. She grinned wildly. "Just made it," she said.

"What?" Nick cupped his ear.

"Just made it," she repeated, shouting to be heard over the downpour.

Nick leaned toward her for his reply. "Just made it? I'd say we were two blocks short."

"It'll let up soon."

Nick poked his head out from the doorway for a quick glance upward. Welcomed with a face full of water for his trouble, he looked to Meg and sputtered in mock annoyance.

"I said soon," she chuckled.

He wiped his face with his hand. "You remember the party for my promotion? We shared a taxi home."

"Uh-huh."

"It rained that night too, didn't it?"

She nodded.

"Think somebody is trying to tell us something?" Nick asked.

"Like wear a raincoat?"

"Something like that." He laughed again; it felt good.

Meg inhaled deeply. "Doesn't it smell great?"

Nick nodded. "I love rainstorms. Always have."

Lightning cut the sky, and Nick began counting out loud. ". . . Two, three, four, five, six, seven, eight, nine, ten," then the thunder rolled overhead.

"A little more than two miles away," Meg announced.

Nick stared at her, surprised.

"Sound travels at a bit more than one-fifth of a mile per second . . . that's the rule of thumb, isn't it?" Meg asked. "Ten seconds since the lightning times one-fifth equals two miles."

Nick rolled his eyes. "Don't ever try to impress an accountant with trivia."

A stream of water, thin but steady, started suddenly from above the doorway, falling on Meg's left shoulder. She squeezed against Nick to avoid it. Feeling the length of her, he froze, as if to move might send her into retreat. Another stream started a second later, this one falling squarely on her head. Over Meg's complaints, Nick switched places with her.

He looked again at the sky. "All right, I see three choices. One: we stay here. Since we're starting to spring leaks, I don't see much advantage to that. Two: we try and grab a cab. Problem is, I've been watching—they've all been full. Besides, we'd have to leave this doorway to flag one down. That leaves three. My apartment's two blocks up the street. I run for an umbrella, come back and get you."

"You'd get soaked."

Nick smiled. "Just a moment ago you were bemoaning the end of chivalry."

"Not chivalry. Romance. There's a difference. I'm just as capable of getting wet as you."

Nick pointed at Meg's dress. "You'd ruin your outfit."

"Cotton. It'll be fine."

Nick shook his head, then pointed down the street. "Look, you can see the awning to my building. I'll be back in—"

"Nick," Meg said, interrupting him.

"Hmm?"

*"Watch out for toads."*

Meg jumped from the doorway and took off down the street, melding with the rain after only a few yards. Nick started after her.

Two blocks or ten miles, it wouldn't have made any difference, because after twenty yards Nick's clothes were soaked through. He started with his hands protecting his tie, but as the water streamed from his head and shoulders to his chest, he soon abandoned the effort.

He caught up with Meg after a half block. They ran side by side, first avoiding, then purposefully splashing through puddles.

Meg reached the awning to Nick's apartment first, a half step ahead of him. Laughing uncontrollably, she clutched an awning pole for support as he bent at the waist, hands on knees.

"I'm the winner," she choked out, and raised one hand triumphantly.

"Unfair head start," he retorted.

Their laughs died out eventually, and he looked at her then, and his face went blank. The blue dress clung to her, showing off the lines of her body. Her legs. Her waist. Her breasts. Suddenly embarrassed, he averted his eyes and dug into his front pocket for the lobby door key.

"You cold?" he asked as he busied himself with the lock.

Meg shook her head. "I'm fine."

He held the door to the lobby open. "Come in. But no way am I letting you up to my apartment—it's way too much of a mess. I'll run up, grab an umbrella, and get you home. Okay?"

She did not argue. "Okay."

Too excited and full of energy to wait on the elevator, he took the stairs, two at a time, to the fifth floor. Once in his apartment, he went immediately to the closet and grabbed the umbrella that hung there. As an afterthought he made for the bathroom, deciding to strip his tie and suit jacket and leave them to dry from the shower curtain rod.

As Nick passed through the kitchen, he noticed his answering machine, the numeral two by its message button glowing red. He pressed the button, then continued on to the bathroom as the tape rewound.

"Mr. Ford," the tape played after a moment, "this is Inspector Madison of the D.C. police department. Could you give me a call as soon as possible?" The inspector went on to leave his number; the answering machine clocked the call at 11:18.

Drawn from the bathroom by the message, Nick started slowly back toward the kitchen as the second message began.

"Nick . . . it's Judy. I . . . Call me, just as soon as you get in. It's important." Then the metallic voice of the machine took over. "Eleven thirty-four," it said.

Nick looked at his watch. Only a few minutes ago. He didn't like the sound of her voice—angst displaced the joy he had felt only a moment earlier. He lifted the phone and punched in Judy's number from memory.

"Judy, it's Nick," he said, recognizing her hello.

"Oh, Nick," she said, her voice flat.

"What's wrong?"

". . . Judy?" Nick tried again, after a long couple of seconds.

"You haven't heard?"

"Heard what? Has something happened?"

Something had.

Nick's vision blurred as Judy gave him the news. He placed a hand against the wall to steady himself.

A few minutes later, he let the receiver fall to its cradle, saying almost nothing in the interim. *What was there to say?*

Nick slumped to a chair, dazed. *Christ, it couldn't be true.* Tears welled in his eyes. He clamped his eyelids fiercely shut.

*Why?* he asked himself, and tears eventually came,

even through the clamped lids. They mixed with the rainwater on his face and diffused.

It was another two minutes—maybe ten, Nick could not be sure—before he looked at the umbrella in his hand and remembered Meg. He forced himself to the front door then, shuffling, each step an effort, his suit and tie still on, the idea of leaving them to dry forgotten.

The elevator ride down took forever. Eyes closed, hands clenched, he repeated a mantra to himself, over and over. *Keep it together, Nick. Keep it together.*

Meg stood in the lobby; her face turned down when she saw his expression. "Is everything okay?"

"No," he managed. He handed her the umbrella. "Could . . . could I ask you to walk yourself home. I have to get back upstairs and return a call . . . the police."

"What is it, Nick?"

"Judy left a message. . . ." His voice wandered off.

"And?"

"They found Scott, in an alleyway. . . ." In halting words Nick repeated Judy's words as Meg, eyes full, whispered, "Oh, my God," over and over. Finally Nick handed her the umbrella. "I'm sorry. I have to get upstairs. . . . I'm sorry."

Nick turned his back on Meg and started back to the elevator, blind to her desire to comfort him, blind to her own suffering, knowing only that the demons had returned and he would not be able to keep it together for very much longer.

# 14

Dressed in a charcoal gray suit and burgundy tie, Nick sat motionless on his couch. The apartment was dark. A dim, diffuse glow from the closed window blinds and a single slice of light which fell across Nick's left leg from an ill-fitting blind provided the only illumination. With time the stripe of light on Nick's leg advanced from his knee to his thigh and finally to the fingers of his left hand. He jerked his hand back as if burned, buffeting the dust flakes floating in the sun's rays.

Nick looked at the clock. Barely able to make out its face, he squinted: 1:21 P.M. If he left immediately, he would still have time to make the funeral. If traffic ran smoothly, that is.

Nick didn't move.

Turning his gaze from the clock to the bare wall, he rubbed his palms together. His breath came shallow.

They would expect him. Associates from the office, Scott's parents. As Scott's best friend, they would look for him and wonder why he didn't show. Is he sick? Caught in traffic? Is he all right? Nick could hear the questions.

His eyes wandered back to the clock; he watched the minute hand fall toward the six. So slowly, it seemed.

Come Monday, he would have no explanation, certainly none he wished to share. He would have to lie: his car would not start, a flat, something. Time enough to think of that later. Now he wanted only for his mind to remain blank, to keep the images and memories locked behind the walls he had so carefully erected over the many years.

Since Scott's death—two days now—he had man-

aged only a few hours of fitful sleep. Last night he
had not slept at all. Still, until a short time ago he had
coped and accepted Scott's death, accepted the loss of
a friend. But to see Scott's body laid out, face white,
eyes closed and lifeless, that was something else entirely. Would the walls hold then?

The minute hand passed six and inched upward.

Inaction was action. In a few more minutes Nick
would not be able to make Scott's funeral if he tried.
What anybody thought, he didn't care. He sat motionless because he no longer could command his body
to do otherwise. Voices convoluted his thoughts; he
could hear them now. *See what happens when you get
close to someone, when you let someone get close to
you? See how much safer life is alone?*

Scott was dead, and there was nothing but a deep
and growing pain. Again.

He had thought he would be okay. Through the
morning, during his shower, as he got dressed. Then
it had hit him. Memories. A flood of images: the
knock on the door. His aunt standing there. And her
words, "Are you ready, Nickie? It's time to say
good-bye."

He retreated behind his walls and waited, as he had
waited more than a quarter century earlier in a closet
smelling of suits and shoes and dresses and perfume.

# 15

"Nick . . ."

Meg stood at his office doorway, eyes puffy and darkly lined. Instantly Nick's mind flashed back to the two of them under his apartment building's awning, drenched and laughing. Before his face could warm, before he could rise and put an arm on her shoulder, he pushed the image from his mind. *And if he seemed cold to her as a result, maybe that was for the best.*

He labored to strip emotion from his voice. "Meg," he answered evenly.

Whatever Meg had been expecting, it was clearly not this controlled response. She stammered through a response: "I left a message . . . with Judy . . . earlier."

Nick indicated a stack of yellow notepaper by his phone. "Sorry, Meg." He grimaced. "I haven't felt like going through them."

A lie. He'd been through every one, but had no desire to return most of the calls. Why should he? He knew what they'd say: isn't it terrible . . . he was such a good guy . . . I'm so sorry. And then the inevitable question: we missed you at the funeral, where were you?

He would pass on his lies soon enough.

Meg's message sat on the top of the stack. Twice that morning he had picked up the phone to call her and twice had set the receiver back on its cradle. *The other night, in the rain, was a mistake—an error that must not be compounded. That had to be made plain to her.*

"Did you need something?" Nick continued, affecting indifference.

Meg picked at the eraser of the pencil she held. "If you have a moment. . . ."

"Right now I've got a lot—" Nick paused as Meg's face fell. He saw her again, huddled against him in the doorway, smiling wildly, and tempered his tone. "Of course, Meg, I've got a moment." He pushed aside the pile of documents he was working on. "Come in." And when she hesitated: "Really, come in."

She took a seat across from him, but paused before speaking. "I'm so sorry about Scott," she said softly after a few seconds.

Nick shut his eyes and nodded shortly. "I am too." His hands started trembling, and he hid them behind his desk, out of her view.

"I . . . We knew each other for only a short time, but . . . I don't know, I was comfortable around him. He made work . . . interesting . . . fun."

Did it really make things better to dwell on all that had been lost? To raise memories that burned and haunted? From necessity he had spent a lifetime doing just the opposite, and he offered Meg no words of empathy.

*Understand, Meg, it's not you, it's me. It's the way I am. The only way I can survive.*

Meg shifted uneasily in her chair. "There's something you should know. I wanted to tell you before, at the funeral, but . . ."

*But you weren't there. . . .* Nick pushed beyond the unstated question. "What is it?"

"Scott's vacation."

Nick's eyes arched at the reply—not what he expected. "What about it?"

"He told me . . ." Meg started, but took a deep breath before continuing. "Told me it wasn't a vacation at all, Nick. He was working on something."

"Working on something? What?"

Meg didn't answer immediately; she resumed picking at the pencil's eraser.

"Meg?" Nick prompted as the pause lingered.

"The Yünnan Project audit."

Nick's mouth dropped slightly. "I don't understand.

Why would Scott say he was on vacation if he was working on an audit?''

Meg sat mutely until Nick reached for the phone, then said, "If you're calling Dennis, he didn't know."

Nick lowered the receiver. "Dennis is heading the audit. He'd have to know."

Meg shook her head. "Scott was investigating on his own."

*Investigating on his own?* "Why would Scott do that? Keep it from Dennis?"

"Because. He was looking into things Dennis instructed him not to."

Nick's brow furrowed as he considered the information. Knowing Scott, it wasn't all that hard to believe. How often had Scott disregarded Nick's orders? Nick stood, went to the door, and shut it. He then sat on the edge of the desk and encouraged Meg to go on.

"After you dropped off the audit, we started reporting to Dennis. He had his own ideas about the investigation: what we should focus on, what he considered a waste of time. He reassigned us accordingly. Scott . . . well, he wasn't too complementary of Dennis or his decisions."

Nick could guess the rest. "So he ignored him?"

Meg nodded. "He covered himself by taking a vacation. No one knew what he was doing."

Nick's eyes narrowed. "Except you?"

Meg wouldn't meet Nick's gaze.

"Meg?"

"I didn't know anything until last Wednesday. He called me. Said he tried to reach you first, but you were busy."

Nick exhaled slowly, remembering. He had been in a settlement conference. Judy had interrupted, said Scott was on the phone, but Nick had brushed her off. Brushed Scott off too. "Why didn't you come to me earlier?" Nick asked.

"Scott asked me not to. Made me promise. He said he'd be in the office to tell you himself in a few days, and . . ." Meg hung her head. "I don't have a good excuse."

And what was Nick's excuse for ignoring a friend? He lowered his voice. "Meg."

She raised her eyes.

"Don't beat yourself up—I know what dealing with Scott could be like. Did he tell you what he was investigating, specifically?"

"No. But he said he'd found something, said he was going to . . . I think he said 'light off some fireworks.' "

*Scott investigated on his own, found something explosive, and then was killed?* More than a coincidence? His gut tightened at the thought.

Evidently reading his mind, Meg said, "Nick, Scott's death . . . The police, everyone, assumes it was a mugger, but . . . Could it have been something else?"

"Don't know." He swung his head slowly from side to side.

"I can't get the thought out of my mind. . . . Maybe if I had told you about Scott's call immediately . . ."

*Or maybe,* Nick thought, *if I had taken Scott's call last week . . .*

Nick chewed the nail of his index finger, lost in thought. When he finally looked up, he said, "Tell me *exactly* what Scott said, Meg. As much as you can remember. Word for word."

# 16

A secretary escorted Nick and Meg into Carolyn's corner office. Impressive, both its size and furnishings. A couch, a worktable, nice artwork. Neither feminine nor masculine.

Carolyn sat behind a leather-topped desk, arms folded in front of her, Dennis seated beside her. She rose from her chair immediately on their entry, and Dennis followed suit.

Meg and Carolyn had not met, and Nick made the introduction. "Carolyn, this is Meg Taylor . . . she's new as of last month."

Carolyn tipped her head. "Meg."

"A pleasure to meet you, Ms. Reed." Meg's tone, Carolyn's tone, were both befittingly somber.

The four took chairs, in Nick's and Meg's case two black leather library chairs facing Carolyn's desk. Nick noticed Carolyn's eyes—bloodshot—and imagined his must appear many times worse.

Nick had requested the meeting; he asked the first question. "Do you have an update on Scott's death?"

Carolyn shook her head sadly. "All I know is what I told you yesterday. A boy came across Scott's body in a D.C. alley. A high-crime area—mostly black, Hispanic. Death occurred early evening. Scott had been beaten and . . . well, you know about his hands. He'd been shot three times in the chest."

Carolyn had recounted the police findings dispassionately, and Nick struggled to analyze them with the same sense of detachment. Just details—items on an account ledger. "Do the police have any leads?"

"Not of any substance. They've interviewed the residents of the apartments fronting the alley. No one heard or saw a thing. Not too surprising, since the police think the body was moved to the alley after death. There wasn't much blood at the scene, and they didn't recover any bullets."

The *body?* This was Scott they were talking about. He took a deep breath and asked, "What do the police think?"

"The obvious: Scott strayed into a bad neighborhood and got mugged. He'd been drinking . . . a lot. His blood-alcohol level was extremely high. That probably made him an attractive target."

"They think they'll turn up anything?"

"Without any leads?" Carolyn's shrug did not indicate confidence. "Odds aren't good, I wouldn't think."

"And if there *was* a lead?"

Carolyn's eyes went to slits. "You know something, Nick?"

Nick turned to his right, to Meg. "Why don't you tell Carolyn and Dennis what you just told me?"

Meg nodded and then did.

Carolyn's face, almost always unreadable, sank as Meg proceeded, while Dennis's went from white to dark red. When Meg finished, Dennis slapped his hand on his thigh for emphasis and exclaimed, "This is inexcusable. *Inexcusable.*"

"Scott's dead, Dennis," Nick reminded him.

"I'm not talking about Scott; I'm talking about Miss Taylor." Dennis turned on her. "Scott was disobeying my explicit instructions. You *knew* it, and you *didn't* feel it necessary to notify me?"

"I . . ." Meg began. "Scott was of the opinion that there was more to the case—"

"*Scott* was of the opinion?" Dennis objected sharply. "I don't give a holy crap about *Scott's* opinion. Who's in charge of the Office of Special Investigations?"

Meg fumbled with her fingers while Dennis's face turned a brighter red. "Who is in charge of the Office of Special Investigations, Miss Taylor?" he repeated.

"You are," Meg said, her voice faltering.

"Damn right. So why in hell would I care about Scott's opinion? Huh?"

Meg looked down, saying nothing.

*"Answer me."*

Annoyed at Dennis and annoyed at himself for allowing the cross-examination to go on as long as it had, Nick cut in heatedly. "Hey, settle down, Dennis."

"You have nothing to do with this, Ford," Dennis spat in Nick's direction before turning back on Meg. "I'm waiting for an answer, Miss Taylor."

Nick's fingers dug into the arms of the chair. If he had thought, even for a moment, that Dennis's reaction would be so hostile, he wouldn't have brought Meg to the meeting. Now all he could do was try and defend her. "It's not her fault."

"Then whose the hell is it?" Dennis asked.

Nick bit his tongue. *Take a moment; compose yourself.* He counted to three before speaking. "Scott's dead. Whoever killed him—that's who's at fault. I don't think it really matters any more what Meg did or did not do."

Dennis sneered at him. "And what about you, Ford? Did you know about this?"

"As of a half hour ago. Not before."

Dennis spun in his chair, pleaded his case directly to Carolyn. "The hell he didn't."

"Are you saying I'm *lying,* Dennis?" Nick asked, surrendering to anger. "Why would I do that?"

"Because you're a—"

*"All right,* both of you," Carolyn interceded, patting the air with open palms. "Calm down. . . . Nick, you started the conversation by saying you had a lead in Scott's death. Let's ignore the rest of this for now and get to that."

Nick's heart still beat wildly, but he managed to calm his voice. "I thought I'd already made myself clear." He counted off the time line of events on his fingers. "Scott was investigating the Yünnan Project. He found something. We don't know what, but evidently Scott thought it significant. He told Meg he was heading for the coast to continue his investigations. Two days later he's found in a D.C. alley. Dead."

"And you think there is a connection?" Carolyn asked, clearly incredulous. "You actually think his death is tied in some way to the Yünnan Project audit?"

"That's crazy, Ford," Dennis broke in before Nick could answer.

Nick continued to direct his speech toward Carolyn. "I admit it's unlikely, but no, not crazy."

Dennis shook his head and laughed mockingly. "We're talking minor billing irregularities in an almost two-billion-dollar contract. I'm sorry, but no one gets killed on account of that. Let's be honest. Scott had a drinking problem, we all know that. He was loaded . . . hell, he was *crocked.* An easy target. He walked into a bad neighborhood—a stupid mistake he paid for. End of story."

"And what makes you so sure that's what happened?" Nick demanded.

"Common fucking sense."

Carolyn's mouthed turned down. "Sit *down,* Dennis," she ordered and pointed at his chair. Dennis hesitated, then sat with arms folded across his chest, unchastised. Carolyn turned to Meg. "Meg, did Scott tell you anything else? Anything that could help us figure out exactly what he was looking into, what he might have found?"

Meg shook her head. "No. Not that I can think of."

Carolyn leaned back in her chair. Her index fingers tested the limits of a rubber band as she stared at the ceiling. "Okay, Dennis," she said, after a long silence, "I want you to pass this information on to the police and the FBI."

Dennis rolled his eyes. "Can I tell them what *I* think of the story?"

*"No,"* Carolyn reproached him sternly. "You tell them the facts, just as Meg told us."

Dennis nodded, smoldering, and Nick pressed his advantage. "Carolyn . . . the Yünnan Project audit. I want it back. If there's a connection between Scott's death and the audit, I want a chance to uncover it."

Dennis shook his head, as if the request had been put to him. "You're in another division now, Ford, if you haven't forgotten. I'm in charge; I'll stay in charge."

Carolyn pressed her fingertips together, then said, "Nick, as far as I see it, Dennis is right on this one. You're not in Special Investigations anymore. He is. That makes it his call."

Dennis adopted a self-satisfied smirk, one Nick looked forward to wiping from his face. "Carolyn," Nick said after only a moment's hesitation, "when we talked, when you offered me the promotion, you said if it wasn't working out, I could take back my old position anytime—take over right where I left off. That was the deal."

Carolyn stared at him in astonishment. "I remember, but—"

"Well, it's not working out."

"Nick—"

He left his chair. "I'll be resuming my old responsibilities immediately. Of course, I'll be available to aid whoever you choose to replace me as assistant comptroller."

"No way," Dennis barked, jumping to his feet as well. "I'm director of Special Investigations, and *I'm* going to see the Yünnan Project audit through. That's the way it's going to be."

"You making decisions for Carolyn now, Dennis?"

"Fuck you," Dennis growled. "It's *my* audit. And I'm not giving it up to some—"

"Dennis," Carolyn interrupted angrily, "that's enough. You may leave. Meg, thank you for coming up, telling us what you know. I would like to speak to Nick now. Alone."

"Carolyn—" Dennis began, before Carolyn repeated herself. *"Alone."*

Meg left quickly, Dennis reluctantly and with a parting scowl.

"Please take a seat, Nick," Carolyn said once Meg and Dennis had left the office. "I'm sorry that got so heated. It wasn't necessary."

Nick sat. "I'm sorry too."

Carolyn nodded. "Everyone's a bit on edge today . . . with what happened to Scott. But I think we have to guard against saying things we might regret."

"I meant what I said." He had, and stood prepared to sacrifice his job, the promotion, everything he had worked for.

"Nick . . ." Carolyn paused. When she went on, her voice caressed softly. "I know what good friends you and Scott were—he was my friend too—but what you're doing . . . I think you're too emotionally caught up in the audit to oversee it."

Of course he was, but the fact remained he *had* to resume control of the case. He owed Scott at least that much. "I don't," Nick lied. "I'll do my job professionally, as always."

"And if I asked you to leave the investigation to Dennis?"

"I'd refuse."

Carolyn put her fingertips together. "And if I made it an order?"

"I'd fight your order if I had to." The words came without deliberation and shocked Nick almost as much as Carolyn. Fight *Carolyn's* order? If a day ago someone had told him he would make such a statement, he would have laughed. Absurd, and yet he knew he would not retract the words.

Carolyn's face turned hard. "And how would you do that?"

"Senator Raine has let me know in no uncertain terms that she isn't happy with the way Dennis has conducted the audit since I left. I was just as plain—I told her my new duties precluded me from reassuming control of the audit. But if I went to Senator Raine now, voiced my concerns, and asked her to appoint a Senate panel to conduct an independent investigation— Well, you know the senator. What do you think she would do?"

Carolyn's eyebrows sank. "You'd actually attempt to force my hand?"

"We made a deal, and I'm asking you to stick to it. That's all."

"I'm sorry to hear that," Carolyn said bitterly.

He had hurt her, Nick knew. And if a special bond existed between them, he had damaged that too, perhaps irreparably. He tried to make her understand. "I owe Scott, Carolyn. For . . . for all sorts of things. And I have no faith in Dennis. None. I have to do this myself. I have to."

If the emotional plea had any effect on Carolyn, she didn't show it. She appraised him for a long moment. When she spoke again she was all business. "All right. If tomorrow morning you still want your old post back, it's yours. That's the deal I offered, and I won't go back on my word. But I won't change the deal either. You take the position, you resume control of the Yünnan Project audit, you give up the position of assistant comptroller."

"I assumed as much."

"You understand, Nick, your future with the GAO—what looked to be a very bright future—could be severely damaged by your actions here today?"

Nick nodded. "I do."

Carolyn clenched her teeth together. "Okay. Then I don't see that there's anything left to discuss. I'll expect your answer in the morning."

Their conversation over, Nick started for the office door, but Carolyn stopped him at the threshold. "Nick?"

He turned. "Yes?"

"You can't bring Scott back. No matter what you do, you can't bring him back."

Nick looked through Carolyn. *She's right, you know, he's not coming back.* Finally he bobbed his head once and walked silently from the office.

# 17

Head down, knees slightly bent, weight on the heels, left arm straight, John Li ran down the checklist. Then he swung, a fluid, powerful stroke—surprising given his stout figure, bulging in the waist and the seat. The club head connected solidly, sending the golf ball two hundred and thirty yards down the driving range, where it landed to roll another twenty-five.

Li used the club head to pull another ball toward him from those fanned out from the overturned bucket. A voice stopped him before he could swing.

"Li."

He looked up to see who he expected: J. T. Frasier. A tall, slender man. Usually the picture of corporate decorum befitting his position, but not today. Dark hollows underscored his eyes, his mouth was caught in a frown, and his graying hair, usually neatly styled, lay tousled.

That was one of the things Li liked about dealing with Americans: they were so easy to read. Not like Asians, or the Arabs, or even the French, who made an art of subterfuge. In America, where society chastised men for having even one mistress, the straight shooter had become the ideal. John Wayne, Jimmy Stewart, Gary Cooper, men who didn't lie and therefore were transparent. So much easier to manipulate a man when you knew his thoughts in advance.

Things had gone wrong, Frasier had clearly learned that. But his reaction— So unlike Li's own. In written Chinese one symbol stood for both change and opportunity. The first you accepted, the latter you seized. And there *were* opportunities to grasp, even now.

Li nodded in recognition, then turned back to the golf ball lying at his feet and readjusted his grip. Head down, knees slightly bent, weight on the heels, left arm straight. Again he swung, smoothly and powerfully, with the same result.

Another thing Li liked about America: golf, a game he could not have imagined growing up in China, working a five-acre rice paddy. How could he? Acres and acres of prime land devoted to nothing but a game? Unthinkable. But he'd grown to love it, the necessity of controlling one's emotions and ignoring pressures, so much like his profession.

Li watched the ball until it stopped rolling, then smiled broadly at Frasier. "Mr. Frasier, so good to see you again."

"Yeah," J. T. Frasier answered, distracted as he checked the faces of the others lined up at the driving range.

They shook hands, a cold, indifferent grasp. Frasier didn't bother hiding a frown as he gestured toward the first tee. "Let's tee off."

"You don't want to hit some balls first?"

"What I want to do is get this meeting over with. The tee's empty, let's go."

Li shrugged and returned his three wood to the bag. "As you wish."

Frasier had parked an electric golf cart near the range; he took the driver's side, Li the passenger's. They started toward the first tee.

"I really don't like being here," Frasier said, plainly irritated.

Nor did Frasier like him, Li knew, and for obvious reasons. Frasier cooperated for only one reason: hooks were buried deep in his side. Li himself felt neither like nor dislike. J. T. Frasier had been and would continue to be useful to him—those were the standards by which he judged the relationship.

Li said, "Excuse me if I'm wrong, but if I remember correctly, you were the one who called me."

"I called because something's come up. But you chose this spot—a public spot—where we can be seen together. I don't like it, not a fucking bit."

Li smiled thinly. "I suppose I should be insulted. Come now, Mr. Frasier, I'm just a Hong Kong businessman enjoying a round of golf with a corporate executive. Nothing unusual about that."

Frasier's eyes continued to sweep the course. "It's too public."

"Mr. Frasier, let me ask you this: if someone saw you sneak off to meet me in a back alley, they'd wonder what we were up to, right? But meeting here, on a golf course? They're not going to give it a second thought."

Frasier stopped the cart by the first tee. "Let's just play the damn game."

After two practice swings Frasier lined up for his tee shot on the first hole, a 395-yard par four with a dogleg to the left. Li noted Frasier's technical proficiencies—good grip, good body turn, good transfer of weight, good form—but Frasier nonetheless hurried his down swing. Another sign the man hadn't complete control of his emotions.

The ball sliced off the club's head and one hundred and seventy yards later disappeared into the heavy rough on the right of the fairway.

"Shit." Frasier's only comment.

"Feel free to take another shot, Mr. Frasier, penalty free," Li offered.

"The hell with it," Frasier said as he cleared the tee.

Li wasted no time lining up his own shot. No practice swings. No show of nerves. He swung and the mechanics, as always, were there. The ball traveled ninety yards beyond Frasier's and rolled to a stop in the middle of the fairway.

Li smiled to himself. The tone had been set.

Golf: the modern-day equivalent of a royal hunt—at least that's the way Li always thought of it. In the 1500s it was boars and stags. Next, with the rise of the British empire, came partridge and fox. Then the Americans' turn and golf. It required different weapons, clubs, and different prey, pars and birdies, but the goal was the same: an outing for the elite, often with caddies in tow like gun bearers of old. A pretext for negotiating business, plain and simple.

Frasier came out of the rough badly, his ball traveling less than a hundred yards. He exploded on returning to the cart. "Dammit, Li, I don't have all day to ride around a fucking golf course. . . . We've got problems."

Li nodded. "I assumed as much from your call. And you need my help?"

Frasier rubbed his forehead. "Your help? You got me into this mess in the first place."

"Then perhaps this meeting serves no purpose." Li pointed toward his ball; Frasier stopped the cart ten yards to its side. Li selected an eight iron. A deep bunker protected the front of the green; he decided to aim long and draw the ball back to the hole. He could tell by the clean click of club head meeting ball that the shot would unfold as planned.

His golf ball landed on the green; backspin brought it within twelve feet of the cup.

The two carried out the rest of the hole in silence, Li finishing with a tap in par, Frasier swearing, having missed a short double-bogey putt. They reentered the cart, but Frasier did not start it toward the second tee.

"I've had enough of this, Li. You screwed up."

"Explain?"

"I hold you to blame for it. God damn you for what's you did, and God damn you for getting me involved."

"Calmly," Li urged. "Tell me what's happened."

"What's happened? You know exactly what's happened."

"I appreciate your faith in my sources of information. However, in the present case, specifics would help."

Frasier ran his free hand through his hair. "The GAO investigator, Scott Johnson. *Now* tell me you don't know why I called."

"I'm sorry, Mr. Frasier . . . Johnson?"

"No more games, Li. Scott Johnson was killed last week—shot and left in a D.C. alley."

"That is unfortunate."

"That's unfortunate? *That's unfortunate?* Hell, Li, it's a fucking nightmare, that's what it is. I haven't had a decent night sleep since the audit of the Yünnan Project began . . . then the hearings, now this . . ."

"People die. America is a very violent place, especially her capital city."

"I learned yesterday that Johnson was investigating the Yünnan Project. I want to know if there is a connection."

"Between his investigation and his death?"

Frasier stared at him without answering.

Li left the cart, went to his golf bag secured to its rear, and returned with two cigars. He offered one to Frasier.

"No, thanks."

"It's Cuban."

*"No."*

Li shrugged, then lit one for himself. He puffed a half dozen times, appreciating the cigar's rich flavor and aroma, before Frasier, eyes narrowed, his face a deep red, spoke again. "I want an answer."

Li pulled the cigar from his mouth. "My people came across Mr. Johnson in a very sensitive area, with a camera. They did not know who he was, or what his purpose was. Unfortunately, by the time they found out, Mr. Johnson was in no condition to be released."

*"You son of a bitch."*

"Calm down."

*"The hell I will."* Frasier added barely above a whisper, "Johnson was a GAO employee. You've tied me to a murder of a federal agent."

"You are *tied* to *me,* Mr. Frasier—I wouldn't forget that," Li said icily. "My people reacted to circumstances, appropriately, in my estimation."

"They *over*reacted, and I don't want any part of it."

"You are a part of it, whether you like it or not. If you had done your job, if the investigation of the Yünnan Project had dried up as you assured me it would, we wouldn't have had this incident. And if you had informed me of Johnson's actions, we would have been forewarned, could have avoided the unpleasantness."

"I didn't know."

"Well, then, perhaps you better improve your sources of information."

"I . . ." Frasier started, then stopped. He stuttered out a response finally. "I . . . I didn't sign on to be a party to murder."

"May I remind you, Mr. Frasier, you corrupted yourself. We all want to avoid . . . unpleasantness. However, there are realities which must be faced and dealt with. Mr. Johnson had learned quite a bit about us, including *your* involvement—does that change your opinion?"

Frasier's face went momentarily blank, and Li continued. "I can see that it does. Remember, there's no way out for either of us now except one: make sure the truth stays buried. Whatever it takes, Mr. Frasier. *Whatever it takes.* No one will trace his death to us."

Frasier wiped a fist across his forehead. "Listen to me, you son of a bitch," he said in an acerbic whisper, "I don't want it ever to happen again. Do you understand me? It can never happen again, or I stop playing ball. Do you understand? Everything stops."

Li tapped an ash from the tip of his cigar, then ground it underfoot. "Do not threaten me, Mr. Frasier," he said, unrattled. "You'll continue to cooperate, because you have no choice. Consider your position; consider what you have to lose if you turn your back on me. Do *you* understand? If you don't like my methods, stop the investigation as you promised. Stop it cold. Otherwise I cannot guarantee there will be no further unfortunate incidents."

Li climbed back into the golf car and pointed at the second tee. "Now, shall we continue?"

In response, Frasier ripped the golf glove from his left hand, then started the golf cart back to the clubhouse.

# 18

The conference room was cluttered with papers, some neatly stacked in front of the room's occupants, others, earlier, now obsolete drafts, pushed to one end of the table or onto the floor. Bunched in the center of the table lay remnants of a working lunch: paper soda cups, styrofoam coffee cups, crusts of cafeteria sandwiches on paper plates.

Nick, for the fourth time, prepared to repeat the GAO's position. "Look, all your client has to do—" he started.

The door to the conference room swung open cautiously, just a foot. All heads turned, including Nick's. Judy peered through the opening, searching for Nick's face. He waved her in.

"What's up?" Nick whispered to Judy, who bent to his side.

"Sorry to bother you, Nick. It's Meg. She's on the line for you. Extension 662."

Nick gestured at the table. "I'm in the middle of things here."

"She said it was important."

Nick nodded and said to the other men in the room, "Excuse me, this should just be a second." He reached for the phone on the table. "Hello?"

"Nick, it's Meg."

They last spoke yesterday afternoon, after the meeting with Carolyn and Dennis. "What's up?"

"I'm outside Scott's office. The FBI's in there. They're cleaning it out. . . . I thought you'd want to know."

"Cleaning what out?"

"Scott's office," Meg repeated. "Three agents,

they're boxing everything up. Emptying his desk, his shelves, his file cabinets."

*Boxing up his office?* "Okay, I'm tied up in conference for another . . ." He appraised the lawyer across the room—reaching a settlement with him would be like pulling teeth. "Another half hour, at least. You stop them until I get there."

"I already tried that. They barred me from the office."

"Do they have a warrant?" Nick asked.

"No."

"Then get them the heck out of there. Without a warrant they have no authority to conduct a search, no authority to seize anything."

"They don't need a warrant, Nick. They have permission."

"Who gave it to them?" Nick asked, and somehow knew the answer before Meg gave it to him.

"Dennis."

"Dammit." Nick drummed his fingers on the table. "Okay, I'll be right down."

Nick spotted Dennis on the far side of the cafeteria, sitting with two other auditors. "Dennis," he called when still a dozen feet away.

Dennis swung his head in the direction of the sound, just long enough to identify its source and display annoyance, then turned back to his food.

Nick advanced on Dennis's table, set his palms flat on its surface. "I was just down at Scott's office," he said, voice harsh.

"I'm eating now, Ford," Dennis replied, biting off a corner of his sandwich to emphasize the point.

"I don't give a damn. What the hell is going on down there?"

Dennis glanced at Nick from the corner of his eye as he chewed, his face expressionless. Finally, his mouth clear, he said, "I take it you're referring to the FBI?"

"You called them in?"

Dennis nodded. "Of course."

"Gave them permission to seal Scott's office?"

Dennis took a sip from a Coke can, then reached for his napkin. He dabbed his mouth quickly. "You seem upset, Ford, and frankly I don't see why. If I may remind you, *you* were the one who thought Scott's death might relate in some manner to his official duties. As preposterous as that claim may be, I followed Carolyn's instructions. I acted on your suspicions and called in the appropriate law enforcement agency, in this case the FBI, to investigate."

"Do you know what they're doing down there?" Nick demanded.

"I assume they're doing their job." Dennis reached for a French fry and shoved its full length in his mouth.

The two auditors seated with Dennis looked at each other, then pushed back their chairs. "We'll catch you later, Dennis, Nick," they said before leaving.

Nick claimed one of the abandoned chairs. "They're boxing up Scott's papers, his files. Everything."

"I'll go way out on a limb here, Ford, and guess they consider it potential evidence."

"But I haven't been given the chance to review anything. To make copies. The Yünnan Project is my audit again, remember? How can I do my job if I can't retrace Scott's steps? How am I supposed to dig up leads?"

"I'll remind you you're investigating an alleged case of overbilling, not a murder. If there are *leads* to follow in Scott's papers, the FBI will follow them."

"But I know the case."

Dennis slid his plate forward. "French fry?"

*"Dammit,* I don't want a French fry." At the outburst, heads swung in Nick's and Dennis's direction, and Nick lowered his voice. "I might be able to spot something in Scott's papers the FBI'd overlook."

"You'll have a chance to brief them on your investigations."

"C'mon, Dennis, they're not accountants, that's not their area of expertise."

"Expertise?" Dennis said sarcastically. "What about your area of expertise? You're not authorized or equipped to undertake a murder investigation, and that's the last time I'm going to make the point. The FBI has accountants on staff . . . let them do their job. Now, can I get back to enjoying my lunch?" Dennis picked up his sandwich and held it in front of him, as if waiting for Nick to excuse himself.

Nick did not accommodate. "I'd like the chance to read Scott's files," he persisted.

"After the FBI has inventoried and reviewed them, I'm sure they'll make them available to you."

"You know the FBI . . . that could be weeks, months."

Dennis shrugged. "A thorough review might well take that long, correct. Is there some reason you don't want a thorough review?"

Nick hung his head, exasperated. "C'mon, Dennis."

Dennis put down the half-eaten sandwich, wiped his hands with the napkin. "C'mon, nothing. You seem awful anxious about those files falling into the hands of an independent law enforcement agency."

"That's bull, and you know it. I'm interested for one reason: Scott was a friend."

"Which would lead me to believe you'd want to support the FBI in finding his killer."

At that moment Nick would have taken great pleasure in shoving Dennis's sandwich down his throat. "With or without your help, I plan to find out what Scott was on to."

"You obstruct a federal investigation, and I'll see you're suspended."

"I'm charged with investigating billing irregularities in the construction of two hydroelectric dams in China." Nick kicked back his chair and stood. "That's my job, and I intend to do it."

Nick had turned his back, prepared to leave, when

Dennis said, "Hey, Ford." And then, just loud enough for Nick to hear, "You screw her yet?"

Nick jerked his head toward Dennis, teeth clenched.

"I figured," Dennis said, grinning, "the way you stood up for her in Carolyn's office, you must have. Was she as good as she looks?"

Nick leaned over the table, a violent rage taking hold of him from deep within. "I've never punched anybody before; until now I've never wanted to. You stay out of Meg's way, you stay out of my way. You understand, Dennis? I'm through with pretensions—you're an asshole, and it's about time someone said it to your face." Not until Dennis lowered his eyes did Nick turn and head for the cafeteria exit.

# 19

Nick stopped outside Meg's office door and peered in. A typical first year's office—desk crammed, overflowing. Stacks of paper everywhere. Against the wall, lining the radiator, blanketing the shelves.

A poster hung from the wall: a photo of a man in a white oxford shirt with pocket protector and glasses. Its caption read: "It Took an Accountant to Catch Al Capone." Cute.

He started back to his office, planning to call and leave a message for her. That wasn't necessary, as it turned out. He rounded a corner, mind lost in thought, and almost ran Meg over.

As she jumped back, the coffee in the mug she carried rode up its side and over. A dollop fell to the carpet.

"Sorry, Meg," Nick apologized, reaching out to steady her.

"Don't worry, you didn't get me." Meg transferred the mug to the other hand and wiped its bottom clean with a napkin. "You find Dennis?" she inquired when finished.

Nick nodded. "We'll have a chance to review Scott's files."

"Really?" Meg said, eyebrows arching.

"Yeah. Just as soon as the FBI finishes with them." Meg made a face. "Oh."

"Have a minute?" Nick pointed toward her office.

Meg nodded, and led the way. Once behind her desk, she cleared a swath of documents so they could look across at each other unimpeded.

"Meg," Nick started, "I've been out of the loop on the Yünnan Project for a while now. You know that. Scott's not here to fill me in, and now it seems I won't even have access to his files. That means I'm going to have to rely on you. . . . We'll be working together." Nick paused, self-conscious and uncertain how to continue. One of his feet tapped nervously against the floor.

Meg looked at him, clearly puzzled at his discomfort.

*Why did you start this?* Nick asked himself, though the answer was obvious. He had to. He could not just keep avoiding Meg, not any longer. "The other night . . . after the charity event," Nick started before swallowing, "I want to apologize."

If Meg seemed puzzled before, she seemed doubly puzzled now. "For what?"

"It's just . . . well, I know I probably was a little out of line and want to let you know it won't happen again. If . . . since . . . we'll be working together, I think it's best that we keep things on a business level. That's what the department recommends."

*There, he had said it. It was out.*

She reddened; her gaze sank to her feet. "Of course."

Seeing Meg's reaction, Nick didn't feel nearly the relief he expected. He had wanted distance between them, for reasons only he could understand, and now he had it. What was said could not be unsaid. Mission accomplished, so why had his stomach soured?

"Good. . . . That's good. Again I apologize." Nick swallowed, then cleared his throat, preparing to shift gears quickly to more comfortable territory. "The Yünnan Project audit. I need to know where the investigation's gone. Everything you can remember."

Meg stared to her right while answering, at the office's one small window. "Since you left? There's not much to tell. Almost nothing's happened."

"Nothing?" Nick repeated, surprised. "It's been . . . what . . . four weeks? You must have made some progress."

Meg shook her head. "That's what got Scott so down. All we've done is rehash old evidence, write memos, and summarize testimony. A waste of time, Scott thought."

Meg still would not look at him; that made it easier, somehow, to concentrate on business. "Why didn't you move the investigation forward, then?" Nick asked.

"Couldn't. Dennis's orders. He wanted to reassess the audit's status before, in his words, we wasted any more of our time."

"What about the undocumented billing?"

Meg shook her head again. "Never got to it."

"And the subcontracts?" Nick rattled off the questions, his mind now shifting fully into work mode, the previous subject not forgotten but subsumed.

"We'd started, but Dennis pulled the plug. He said there were other more fruitful avenues of investigation he wanted us to pursue."

"Like?"

Meg shrugged. "Your guess is as good as mine. As I said, all we did was rehash."

"You say you had started reviewing the subcontracts?"

"Yes. Scott had me read the principal documents. I summarized them for him. Dates, dollar amounts, material terms. And some other information: principal place of each subcontractor's business, the names of the key officers, addresses too if I could find them."

*Addresses of key officers?* "Scott asked for addresses?"

"Actually, he emphasized the point—said he would need them."

Nick had a hunch why. "Do you still have that summary?"

Meg nodded.

"Okay, I've got to get to a meeting." Nick checked his watch. "I'm already late. Do you have some time this afternoon?"

"I can make some."

"Good. This is what I want you to do. . . ."

Meg wrote down Nick's instructions on a legal

pad—three bullet points. "Anything else?" she asked when Nick finished.

"No. That should keep you busy. Leave whatever you come up with on my desk before you head home. I'll be in early tomorrow morning to look it over." He stood, about to put a halt to the conversation, but hesitated. Meg deserved something more than cold indifference—if not a hint of his feelings, at least a touch of humanity. She had done nothing wrong; the problem was his.

Nick softened his voice and said, "Meg, working with me on this, I'm afraid it's going to put you on Dennis's bad side permanently."

"Don't worry about it." She smiled, thin-lipped, finally gazing directly into his eyes. "I'm guessing that's the right side to be on."

# 20

It was well after midnight, long past working hours. The two cleaning women worked as a team, each responsible for one side of the hallway. They were new to the building, hired only that Monday, but both had been employed by one janitorial service or another for all of their adult lives. Or so their résumés said.

Fifty offices lined the floor, and though only one of the fifty interested the women, their profession demanded patience, and so they entered each of the darkened offices in turn, flicked on the lights, and proceeded with a thorough cleaning. They collected styrofoam cups, emptied wastebaskets, vacuumed carpets. "Diligent and hardworking," their supervisor had written on their initial review.

Two-thirty brought them to their goal. One of the women—black hair streaked with gray, medium height, and, as with so many in her profession, unexceptional-looking, tending toward plain—nodded quickly in the direction of her partner, then disappeared into the office marked NICK FORD wheeling a garbage bin before her. Her partner remained in the hall, vacuuming in place, eyes flicking side to side, ready to snap the vacuum off, then on again—the prearranged signal.

The dark-haired woman moved quickly. She reached into the bin and withdrew a small, dented cardboard box, by all appearances just another piece of trash. She opened the box and removed a small leather wallet which she unfolded to reveal a set of jeweler's tools, a small wire cutter, and a loop of wire.

She started with the phone. The bug, voice-activated and state-of-the-art, fit neatly into the receiver. It transmitted on the same frequency as a popular local radio program. If anyone scanned for bugs, an unlikely prospect, the radio broadcast would mask its signal.

Ford's computer came next. Unlike Scott Johnson and Meg Taylor, whose offices another cleaning woman had bugged a couple of weeks ago, Ford did not use a laptop. That made the job simpler; there was only one computer to deal with. She opened the system case—not locked, though she carried a duplicate key if necessary—and found what she was looking for in the second expansion slot: the U.S. Robotics fax/modem. All GAO computers, of Nick's year and make, were similarly equipped, the woman knew.

The dented cardboard box provided what looked to be an identical fax/modem card protected by bubble wrap. The woman switched them, expertly, quickly, snapping the new card in place, then resealing the system case. They'd have access to Nick's computer now, whenever, and from wherever, they desired.

Last, she powered up Ford's computer and installed a short program—a hidden file unlikely to be detected and seemingly innocuous if it was.

The woman stood and checked her watch. Seven minutes and twenty seconds. A full thirty seconds less than in the practice sessions. Good.

She scanned Ford's desk, and two stacks of papers caught her eye. More exactly, the heading of the cover memo of one caught her eye:

To: Nick Ford
From: Meg Taylor
Re: Yünnan Project Audit/Subcontracts

She flipped through each stack quickly, but the papers meant nothing to her. Others, however, might find the information valuable. It was her call, and she made it. For seven minutes she laid herself open to exposure as she ran both stacks through the copy machine down the hall. Then she returned, and replaced the papers on Ford's desk.

The woman signaled to her partner in the hall, who

nodded perfunctorily before disappearing into another office. Back to their routine—they had another twenty offices to clean before their shift ended at four.

The dark-haired woman emptied Ford's wastebasket, then began on the carpet. She reached for the cleanser at one point, spotting a dark stain at the front of Ford's desk. Ground-in soil, probably from a mishandled plant.

The woman scrubbed diligently at the stain, until it disappeared, taking satisfaction in a job well done.

# 21

Nick flipped the light switch. The fluorescent tubes mounted in the ceiling flickered twice, then caught, bathing his office in a harsh white light.

It was five a.m., early even for Nick, but these first few hours in the morning were his most efficient of the day, when he could focus on selected projects without the maddening interruptions that frequented business hours. This morning he had set aside for the Yünnan Project.

Two stacks of paper sat on his office desk. The first, the shorter stack of the two, each page perforated along the left-hand side, came from the records department. The taller stack was from Meg; Nick flipped through it with his thumb. By the look of things she'd put in some long hours last night.

Nick stowed his briefcase behind the office door, then left for the coffee machine down the hall. He returned with two cups, black, a long-running ritual, and settled into his chair.

He started on Meg's papers first, laboriously examined the summary of subcontracts she had previously prepared for Scott. Nothing unusual jumped out at him; frankly, he had not expected anything to.

He sent the last of the first cup of coffee down his throat.

Next came a table—a couple of dozen pages long— what he had asked Meg to construct when they spoke yesterday afternoon. "Meg," he had said, "I've got maybe fifteen file folders full of construction bids for hydroelectric dams down in storage. Dams that were built, dams that weren't built, winning bids, losing bids. Ask Judy to pull the files. I want you to go through them."

"What am I looking for?" Meg had asked.

"Itemized costs. I want to determine if the payments called for under the Yünnan Project subcontracts are reasonable in comparison to similar projects. Make a table. Yünnan costs in column one, itemized, other corresponding project costs to its side."

From the looks of it, Meg had done a thorough job. He started his review, and, simultaneously, his second cup of coffee.

Nick compared itemized costs—any Yünnan subcontract payment that seemed wildly out of step with the norm he marked with a paper clip.

An hour brought him to the end of the table and the end of coffee number two. Four paper clips were affixed to the table. Each indicated a subcontract that was now, in Nick's mind, suspect.

Before turning to the second, shorter stack of documents, the sheets with the perforated edges, Nick rubbed his eyes. He had started at five-fifteen. It was past seven now, and the coffee did not seem to be doing the trick. What he needed was a solid night of sleep, an impossibility since Scott's death. What rest he had managed was short, fitful, and uneasy. When he had answers he would sleep soundly, not before.

He stretched his arms wide, groaned, and started in again. He lifted the first document from the stack and examined it.

Kautza, Norman C., and wife, Emma. Three late payments on a joint Visa card within the last year. Credit line of ten thousand dollars. Five other credit cards, three of which carried a substantial balance. A $190,000 mortgage. Two outstanding car loans.

The finances of an upper-middle-class American couple living slightly beyond their means with the help of credit cards, the ballooning balances at eighteen and nineteen percent hanging over their heads. Nothing of interest.

He turned to the next, squelching a yawn. There were almost three dozen credit reports to check, and the start of office hours—eight o'clock—was quickly approaching.

Meg stood in front of Nick's desk, bleary-eyed. She must have worked extremely late last night, Nick thought, to look so tired at ten in the morning.

"I got your message," Meg said anxiously. Nick had left the message at eight-thirty, asking her to call. "Sorry I got in so late, but—"

Nick held up his hand. "No need to explain." He pointed at the stack of papers on his desk. "You did a good job."

Meg visibly relaxed. "Thanks."

"I've made eleven-thirty reservations on a flight to Pittsburgh, for both of us." Nick did not ask if her schedule was clear. If it wasn't, she would have to clear it—he needed her.

"Smith Pettit's headquarters?"

Nick nodded. "I called their general counsel earlier. Tom Morgan, the CEO, has agreed to make himself available to us."

The sleep began to clear from Meg's eyes. "You found something?"

Nick nodded.

"The payments under some of the subcontracts?" she guessed.

Nick nodded again. "Four of them seemed way out of line."

Meg allowed herself a self-congratulatory smile. "I saw that."

"Well, you didn't see this." Nick shot a sheet of paper, its left edge perforated, across the desk at Meg.

"What is it?" she asked as she reached for it.

"A credit report. I had records pull one on each of the subcontractors' key officers under our blanket subpoena. I'm just guessing, but Scott may have done the same thing. It would explain why he wanted you to dig up the officers' addresses—you don't want a credit report on John Smith of Main Street if you're investigating John Smith of Second Avenue."

Meg started to read from the report. "Andrew McKenzie?" she said, frowning, obviously unable to place the name.

"President of Tremont Engineering. One of the subcontractors whose payments seemed out of line. Not too long ago, McKenzie had at best a spotty credit history. Late payments, many over ninety days. All sorts of late charges. Then suddenly things changed. Turned rosy. He started paying everything on time. Bought a new BMW. Loan went through no problem after he put forty percent down in cash."

"Wouldn't a large subcontract from Smith Pettit explain the improvement in his financial condition?"

"It would," Nick agreed, "if the improvement had occurred *after* the subcontract was signed. Interesting thing is, Mr. McKenzie's credit rating turned around more than four months *prior* to signing the contract. Could all be on the up and up . . . maybe he got a bank loan, who knows? But an inflated contract *and* personal enrichment, that calls to mind all sorts of questions I'd like answered."

"And you think Smith Pettit has the answers?"

Nick shrugged. "Let's just say I'm going to throw a few theories at the CEO and see if anything sticks."

# 22

The elevator opened on a floor-to-ceiling glass wall, clear except for gold and black lettering which read, "SMITH PETTIT, Building a Better World since 1848."

Nick strode purposefully to the double doors set in the center of the glass wall. The doors were propped open, and he passed through to the reception area; Meg followed.

Her eyes jumped to the burnished wood walls, to the impossibly large Oriental rug, to the half dozen oil paintings. Nick remained focused on the receptionist, unwilling to be awed by his surroundings.

"May I help you?" the female receptionist, attractive and professionally attired, asked.

Nick made the introduction. "Nick Ford and Meg Taylor to see Mr. Morgan."

"Just a moment, please." The woman picked up the phone and punched in a number. "There's a Mr. Ford and a Ms. Taylor here to see Mr. Morgan," she said, and then: "All right, I'll tell them." The woman hung up the phone and smiled. "Mr. Morgan's secretary will be right out to escort you to his office. If you'd care to take a seat . . ." She gestured to the waiting area to her rear.

Nick bypassed the grouping of four couches—the sitting area—drawn instead to the bank of windows. Predictably, the view was tremendous. He could see most of the western tip of downtown Pittsburgh—similar to the tip of Manhattan, though in miniature—including Three Rivers Stadium, where the Pittsburgh Steelers played.

Nick could have pointed out the stadium and a few of the other sights to Meg, but didn't care to. He had set the tone on the plane ride by burying himself in documents, and Meg had soon done the same. They had discussed, and would discuss, business, nothing more.

*Did it bother him that Meg now seemed to accept this?*

A voice pulled Nick from the window. "Mr. Ford, Ms. Taylor." Nick turned to a statuesque woman of forty-five or fifty. "Please follow me," she said.

The woman escorted them down the hall to Thomas Morgan's office—three offices the size of Carolyn's could have fit inside.

Meg again seemed taken by the surroundings, while Nick made sure to ignore them. "Good to see you again, Mr. Morgan," Nick announced in his best bank examiner's voice, then gestured toward Meg. "This is my associate, Meg Taylor."

"Ms. Taylor." Morgan shook both their hands, then indicated the man standing to his right. "And of course, Mr. Ford, you and Harmond are already acquainted."

Harmond Rhodes, Smith Pettit's general counsel. He introduced himself to Meg.

"Harmond would like to sit in on our discussion, if you have no objection," Morgan said.

"That would be fine." In truth, Nick would have much preferred to talk to Morgan without benefit of legal counsel, but the request was more than reasonable.

The four of them fit easily around an antique oval table.

Rhodes folded his hands in front of him, cleared his throat, and said, "You expressed a great deal of urgency when you called this morning."

Nick nodded. "Some things had come to my attention, and I felt dealing with them quickly and efficiently might be in both our interests."

"Certainly a quick and judicious disposition of this entire matter has always been Smith Pettit's priority."

Pat answer, but Nick gave Rhodes high marks for eloquence. There would be no give aways today, not on Rhodes's part, but then Nick didn't intend to direct all his questions at Rhodes. "Perhaps we can get right to the matter at hand, then," he said.

"Certainly."

"We'd like to ask Mr. Morgan about Smith Pettit's contract with Tremont Engineering." Rhodes and Morgan shared a quick glance at the mention of Tremont. A nervous glance? Nick couldn't be sure.

"If you could be more specific?"

"The billing records we have show three payments to Tremont totaling $4,787,000, is that correct?"

Rhodes looked at Morgan, and Morgan glanced upward, as if doing some quick mental calculations in his head. After a few seconds Morgan said, "I don't have the exact figures in front of me, but it sounds like you're in the right neighborhood."

That Morgan even knew the name Tremont Engineering off the top of his head, let alone the approximate payments under its subcontract with Smith Pettit, piqued Nick's interest. Perhaps Morgan was simply a hands-on CEO with a good memory for detail. Then again, perhaps Morgan had paid special attention to putting the details of the Tremont subcontract to memory. If the latter was the case, Nick had to wonder why.

"And what services did Tremont provide in return for those payments?" Nick asked.

"Tremont was to provide the design work for the dam's turbines. Their specifications, the turbine beds, the—"

Nick interrupted, having focused on one key word. "*Was* to provide the design work for the turbines? Didn't they?"

Morgan looked at Rhodes; a short whispered conference followed. "We never received any designs, no," Morgan said.

"Nothing?" Nick said.

"No."

During the exchange Meg busily flipped through the Tremont subcontract. Having found what she searched for, she said, "According to your contract with Tremont, the designs were to have been delivered to you over four months ago."

"As of today we have received nothing from Tremont," Morgan repeated.

"And yet you've paid them almost five million dollars?" Nick asked, adopting a suitably astonished tone.

"That is correct."

"Do you *expect* to see anything from Tremont in the future?"

Again, Morgan and Rhodes paired off in a private whispered conference. "Frankly," Morgan said after a moment, "at this point we're pessimistic."

"Then I assume you have taken steps to enforce the contract."

"What do you mean?" Rhodes asked.

"Have you demanded Tremont perform its obligations and produce the designs? Have you written them letters? Filed a lawsuit?"

Rhodes tapped a pen on a legal pad; he didn't look at Morgan before answering. "Representatives of Smith Pettit engaged Andrew McKenzie, the president of Tremont, in a series of discussions. The net results were . . . let's say less than encouraging."

Interesting that *both* the CEO and the general counsel should know so many specifics concerning Tremont. "You have informed the Chinese of Tremont's lack of progress?" Nick asked.

Rhodes nodded.

"And their reaction?"

Rhodes looked at Morgan, who shrugged slightly while answering. "They seemed . . . unconcerned."

"Unless I'm missing something, without turbine designs you don't have turbines, and without turbines you don't have a hydroelectric dam. How could they be unconcerned?"

Morgan's head vibrated quickly left and right. "The construction of the hydroelectric dams is not in jeopardy, Mr. Ford. In fact, the turbines have already been manufactured."

"How? Without designs?"

"Smith Pettit completed all phases of design work called for by Tremont."

"*You* completed them?"

"We stand behind the work of our subcontractors," Morgan said proudly. "In this case we had little choice but to assume their responsibilities."

"So, in essence," Nick said incredulously, "Tremont was paid almost five million dollars for nothing."

"That is the way it turned out, yes."

"And was that the way it was intended?" Nick countered.

Once more the two engaged in a private exchange. Then Rhodes said, "Certainly not from our point. When Tremont didn't perform, we, as you just heard, were forced to assume the obligation. That's money out of our pocket."

"Five million out of your pocket?"

"That," Rhodes said hesitantly, "would be hard to estimate."

Nick signaled to Meg, who held up two stapled documents for Morgan and Rhodes to see. Meg said, "I have here two separate construction bids for hydro-electric dams, both submitted by Smith Pettit within the last two years. Each bid breaks out costs for design, including for turbines."

Nick looked at Morgan. "Do you know how much Smith Pettit bid in these two cases, Mr. Morgan? For the design of the turbines?"

Morgan's eyes dropped. "Not offhand."

Meg made a show of opening and reading from each document in turn. "In the first case, $2,821,000, in the second . . . $2,758,000 . . . That's a pretty large disparity: two point seven, two point eight million versus five million dollars. A factor of almost two."

Sweat appeared on Morgan's lip.

"Can you explain the disparity, Mr. Morgan?" Nick asked.

Rhodes laid his hand on Morgan's forearm. "Tom, don't answer that."

"Do you have any reason to believe the money you paid to Tremont went into engineering design?" Nick asked, pressing the offensive.

"We have no evidence to conclude otherwise, Mr. Ford," Rhodes replied.

Nick then interlaced his fingers and studied the two men. Neither would match his stare. "I'll be frank with you, Mr. Morgan, Mr. Rhodes. I think this whole thing stinks. I think the subcontract with Tremont was grossly overpriced, and I think you had no reasonable expectation Tremont was going to perform its obligations."

Nick paused for effect and got it.

"I'll give you my theory," he continued. "This looks suspiciously like a kickback scheme. Simple enough to work out. An arrangement between you and Tremont. They inflate their charges, pass on a bill to you. The five million becomes a line item in the bill you present to the Chinese: design work, Tremont Engineering. The Chinese pay—the tab, subsidized by U.S. dollars, doesn't look quite so high to them. Then Tremont kicks back enough cash to you to cover your engineering costs and provide a tidy profit. That's illegal, but hey, so what? Everybody gets rich, everybody stays happy."

"That *never* happened," Morgan insisted.

Rhodes set a hand on Morgan's arm, quieting him. "Tom," he said, "let me handle this." Heatedly, he turned on Nick. "We've tried to be accommodating, Mr. Ford. You asked for a meeting, and we made ourselves available. We thought you had something urgent to discuss. Instead you rehash a bunch of unfounded allegations that lack even the—"

"Rehash?" Nick interrupted, holding up a hand.

"Yes, rehash. And unless you have something else you'd like to discuss, I think this meeting is over."

*Rehash a bunch of unfounded allegations?* Nick looked at Meg, then back at Rhodes. "Mr. Rhodes, I don't remember anyone raising this subject matter with you previously."

"Then you might want to improve your lines of communications with your staff, because I discussed all this with Mr. Johnson over two weeks ago."

*Mr. Johnson. Scott.* Nick inhaled audibly. "Scott Johnson?"

Rhodes nodded.

"He asked you these same questions two weeks ago?"

Rhodes nodded again, smugly. "And our answers haven't changed. I suggest you check with him."

Nick bit his lip, lost suddenly in thought.

Meg cleared her throat. She said, "Scott . . . Mr. Johnson . . . is dead. He was murdered while investigating this case."

Rhodes's eyebrows jumped; his voice broke. "I'm sorry . . . very sorry. I had no idea. Forgive me. But certainly you don't think, aren't suggesting, his death had anything to do with his investigation."

"Actually," Meg said, "we think it might."

The answer shocked Rhodes to silence and raised Nick from his stupor. He stabbed a finger in Rhodes's direction. "You say you've had this discussion in the past . . . say Scott Johnson raised, I'm raising, unfounded allegations. Okay, then you explain why you paid Tremont Engineering almost five million dollars for work they never accomplished, because I don't see an explanation."

Morgan and Rhodes sat mutely.

Nick frowned. "You're hiding something. I know it. And if I need to personally review every receipt, every account entry, to find what, then that's what I'll do. But let me warn you, if I find you've held something back we won't just be talking a civil action. I'll do my best to see each of you in a federal penitentiary."

"Mr. Ford, I protest," Rhodes said indignantly. "That was uncalled for."

Nick slapped a hand on the conference table. "You heard Ms. Taylor. My best friend was investigating this case, and now he's dead. I'll do what I have to to find out why. Feel free to take that as a threat—if I

need to be blunt to get my answers, then I'll be blunt."
Nick stood and began to pack his briefcase. It took a
moment before Meg realized she should do the same.

"Mr. Ford . . ." Rhodes said anxiously after a short
conference with Morgan.

Nick snapped his briefcase closed. "Yes?"

"Please, take a seat."

Uncertain whether to leave or stay, Nick appraised
the two men. Finally, he sat down.

"Can I be candid?" Rhodes asked, arms wide in a
sign of surrender.

"It would be a welcome change."

"Off the record?"

"If you mean can Ms. Taylor stop taking notes, sure.
She'll set down her pen. But understand that I don't
keep confidences—anything you tell me, it's fair game
to use."

Rhodes nodded reluctantly, then sighed, as if unsure
where to start. "All right. I want you to try and understand what we're faced with when we negotiate a contract of this sort. The Chinese government approaches
us, indicates it would like to offer us a contract, a
huge contract. We're interested, of course, and start
negotiations; then a few conditions pop up. To the
Chinese, perquisites of one sort or another are
commonplace."

"You don't mean perquisites, you mean pay*offs*."

Rhodes smiled frostily. "Characterize them any way
you like, but remember, you're applying American
sensibilities to a very different culture with traditions
dating back thousands of years. A culture we are suddenly thrown into. It's sink or swim. In China it is
the normal course, even polite, to extend . . . considerations."

"And in this case what were the *considerations*?"

Rhodes ran a hand through his hair before answering. "The Chinese placed certain conditions on us.
One being that we subcontract out some of the work."

"To companies of your choosing?"

Rhodes looked again at Morgan, who said cautiously, "Of course, we always reserve the right to subcontract out any of the work, at our discretion, but here the Chinese were thinking a bit more specifically. They asked that we subcontract out the turbine design work to Tremont."

Nick chewed lightly on his tongue as he considered the information. "Did you suggest to the Chinese that there might be better subcontractors to choose from?"

"We did. As far as we were able to discern, Tremont Engineering had little expertise in the field of hydroelectric-project construction, but . . . well, the Chinese were quite insistent, and when someone offers you an almost two-billion-dollar contract, and there are only a few strings, you accept the strings."

"Whether the subcontractor was capable of performing the work or not?"

Morgan aimed a pen at Nick as a teacher might a ruler. "There's nothing illegal or unethical in what we did, Mr. Ford. Anything Tremont couldn't handle, we'd assume responsibility for, out of our own pockets. That's what we planned, and that's what we did. If someone got rich off the subcontracts, it wasn't us."

Nick let the comment pass and moved on. "How did you determine the payment to Tremont?"

"They submitted an estimate."

"Did you negotiate it?"

"No," Morgan mumbled to the floor. "The Chinese made it clear we should accept the bid as received."

Nick tapped the end of a pencil on the table. He glanced at Meg, his head cocked, making it clear to all that Morgan's answers did not sit well with him. Finally Nick asked, "You had no prior relationship with Tremont?"

"No," Rhodes answered earnestly.

"With Andrew McKenzie or with any of Tremont's other officers or directors?"

"No."

"Received no finder's fees, refunds, or other payments for subcontracting work to them?"

"Absolutely not," Rhodes declared, clearly offended by the implication. "Mr. Ford, we've freely admitted to some instances of overbilling. As to other allegations you have made against us, well, we both have our point of view, but this business with Tremont, we've been candid with you, told you everything we know."

"Then why, Mr. Morgan, Mr. Rhodes"—Nick looked from one to the other—"why do you think the Chinese insisted you hire Tremont? Why hire a company with no experience, at a premium price?"

Morgan developed a sudden interest in his watch band, leaving Rhodes to deal with the question. "To tell you the truth," Rhodes confessed, "I never cared to ask. But I'll give you the same advice I gave Mr. Johnson."

"What was that?"

"I told him to pose the question to the president of Tremont, Andrew McKenzie."

An hour later Morgan's secretary escorted Nick and Meg to the elevator. When the door had shut, Meg turned to Nick. "We're following in Scott's footsteps, aren't we Nick? Pursuing the same path."

Nick nodded. "Where's Tremont headquartered again?"

Meg shifted some papers and read from her notes. "Birmingham, Alabama."

"Didn't Scott say, when he called you, that he was on some sort of tour of Southern cities?"

"Uh-huh."

Nick rubbed his brow as he thought. Rhodes had told Scott to pose his questions to the president of Tremont, Andrew McKenzie. Had Scott taken the advice?

"Meg," Nick said, "I'm going to need you tonight. I want you to get on the computer and learn all you can about McKenzie and Tremont Engineering. I'll give you a list of data bases to search. Clear tomorrow too. I think we'll be taking another flight."

"Birmingham?" Meg asked.

"Yeah."

"You think Scott went there, to check out Andrew McKenzie?"

"All I know is Scott learned something, and we have to find out what. So far we've just been sniffing around the edges. Maybe this McKenzie has answers, maybe he doesn't, but I think it's worth a flight to find out, don't you?"

# 23

Andrew McKenzie took the turn into the parking space at twenty-five miles an hour. The BMW's tires screeched but held, something his old Pontiac would never have done. He slammed on the brakes, stopped inches short of the curb. Shit, this was one awesome machine. Nine months old, and he still hadn't gotten over it.

He turned off the engine, reached for the door, then thought better of it and sank back into the bucket seat. He was wasted after a dozen, maybe more, drinks down at Stillwaters. He'd made a stab at some hot number at the bar. He couldn't remember her name, but she was damn cute. Poured into those tight jeans, with motherfucking kick-ass tits.

A few less beers and maybe—no, definitely—he would have made it with her. Maybe she'd be back tomorrow; if not, maybe one of her friends would be— they were all fuckable. At that age almost all of them were.

He turned up the volume on the car stereo, already at three-quarters of it max. The car, his clothes, his skin, reverberated with the low basses of heavy metal. Kick-ass tits and kick-ass music, he thought as he reached under the seat for the half pint of scotch he kept there. High, he planned to balance on the plateau all night long if possible. Hell, he didn't have anything scheduled tomorrow—he could get as fucked up as he wanted. The idea appealed to him.

Maybe he could call someone? Sarah? No, that bitch wouldn't give him the time of day. Ginnie? Maybe. If her boyfriend wasn't there, she'd come over. Man, it'd be good to get some from Ginnie. He felt as horny as hell.

The half pint was almost empty, just some wash in the bottom. McKenzie swore to himself. He kept more inside, but that meant he'd have to move. He turned off the car stereo and opened the door. He rose unsteadily.

Fuck, that's when it really hit you, when you stood. He steadied himself against the hood of the car. A dozen deep breaths did nothing to clear his mind. Maybe Ginnie would have to wait—suddenly bed didn't sound like such a bad idea.

McKenzie made his way up the walkway. He fumbled with his keys, dropped them, recovered them, and finally found the keyhole. Once in the elevator he pushed the button for the eighth floor before slumping against the wall. Now that he had the car, the next thing on his list was a new pad. When he'd moved in, it hadn't seemed so bad, but that was two years ago, and things had changed dramatically since then. He could now afford much, much better.

Christ, maybe he should move into the Birmingham hills—something near the country club. He'd buy the kind of place he belonged in, the kind of place he deserved.

McKenzie swung open the door to his apartment; his hand went for the light switch. A look at the place confirmed his thinking. "*A fucking dump,*" he yelled to no one.

He remembered the remains of a steak in the refrigerator. He could go for that. Why, he wondered, did drinking, drugs, sex—all the good things in life—make you hungry?

He walked into the kitchen and flipped on the light. Two Asian men in dark suits sat at the kitchen table, one stout, a bit fleshy, the other not much taller but powerful with heavy brows and features.

McKenzie, startled, stumbled back against the wall. "Jesus . . ." he started.

"McKenzie," said Li calmly. "My name is Li. I am a business partner of Deputy Ambassador Jiang's."

The even voice took the edge off McKenzie's surprise, and he fought to regain his composure. With the realization neither man had yet to make an aggressive move, he found his confidence and voice. "What the hell are you doing in my house?"

Li's answer came matter-of-factly. "You were told someone would come, if they needed to . . . if you didn't hold up your end of the bargain."

McKenzie suddenly wished he was not so fucked up. His mind was working too slowly to give him a feel for the situation, and his body could not be counted on if things got physical. Trying to sound sober, in control, he said, "I deal directly with the deputy ambassador, not a couple of his lackeys. Now get out."

Li shook his head decisively. "Deputy Ambassador Jiang has been . . . reassigned. You will deal with *me* or I shall instruct my associate"—Li gestured to his side, at Pu-Yi—"to deal with *you.*"

McKenzie backed down, averted his eyes to the floor—what choice did he have? "You scared the shit out of me, you know. I've only dealt with Jiang, no one else." He looked up at the wall clock, his voice moving to anger. "It's one-thirty in the fucking morning. Say what you came to say and get out."

Li sat silently, motionless; his eyes continued to bore into McKenzie's. Then he said, "Nice car."

McKenzie didn't answer; his mind whirred.

Li repeated his comment, breaking McKenzie's train of thought. "*Real* nice car."

Liquor dulled the apprehension McKenzie felt. They needed him, gotta remember that. Nothing to be worried about. *"God damn right it is."*

"And expensive," Li added after a pause.

"I can afford it."

"Of course you can . . . but I am under the impression you and the deputy ambassador agreed to certain restrictions on your lifestyle."

A lecture? At one-thirty in the morning? McKenzie was not in the mood. "Shit, so it's a nice car? What, you want me to drive around in a fucking ghetto cruiser the rest of my life?"

Li's smile held no warmth. "Cars like that attract attention."

McKenzie ignored the comment and moved for the liquor bottles under the sink. Why the hell did he have to put up with this shit? His life was his life. What the hell did they care; they had gotten their share, hadn't they? If he wanted to ride things out in style, so what?

McKenzie poured himself some scotch and took a stiff drink before continuing. "I don't give a damn if you've got a problem with my car."

Pu-Yi stood. His right hand wrapped into a fist; the muscles of his forearm bunched.

"What other things have you bought?" Li asked.

"You want an itemized list?" McKenzie said, not quite as confident this time. "Look around you, see the palace I'm living in? Like a king . . . I'm living like a fucking king, right?"

"You've had too much to drink."

"No shit." McKenzie lifted his glass and took another healthy gulp. "Now, what are you doing here?"

"I am under the impression you were told to wait to buy anything until the subcontract was awarded, then use restraint. And you were supposed to keep up appearances at work, put in eight-hour days, hire additional staff. You agreed to this. A contract . . . a matter of honor."

"So I lied, sue me. In the meantime, get to the reason for your visit or get out. I don't like people breaking into my house in the middle of the night."

"Our business association is now over. You were warned."

Pu-Yi took a step forward, his eyes flashing violence, and alarm bells screamed in McKenzie's mind. "Hey . . . just wait a minute."

Pu-Yi pulled a handgun from his pocket and pointed it at McKenzie's chest.

"The rules were clear," Li said.

McKenzie's eyes went wide. He had a gun in his bedroom night table—too far away. Fuck it, this wasn't turning out the way he envisioned at all. He choked out his words. "You're screwing with my mind, right?"

"No."

"The car? Man, it's just a car, *that's all it is*. No one's gonna notice."

"People have *already* noticed. They'll come, they'll ask questions. You have attracted attention, Mr. McKenzie. We can't have that."

McKenzie backed up, his mind racing, searching for a line of retreat. "Okay, okay. So maybe I did screw up a bit. I admit that. I'll sell the car. Play things straight, any way you want."

Li paused for a moment, then stood and placed a hand on Pu-Yi's arm. The arm lowered, the gun went with it.

"One more chance, McKenzie," Li said. "I am not the deputy ambassador . . . *I* expect *complete* cooperation. Will I have it?"

"Yes."

"Good, because I think you know what will happen if I don't." Li circled McKenzie. "Do you know a man named Scott Johnson?"

McKenzie shook his head. "No."

"Are you sure? Young, thin, black hair, works for the General Accounting Office in Washington."

Li now stood behind McKenzie, but McKenzie kept his eyes forward, focused on the powerfully built man with the gun. "I'm sure," he said nervously.

"Funny, because I have it on good authority that Johnson was here, in Birmingham, investigating you. And I also have reason to believe he didn't leave empty-handed. In fact, I'm quite sure he didn't leave empty-handed because a few days later he was some place he shouldn't have been. Now, what I'm curious to know from you, Mr. McKenzie, is what did Johnson learn and how."

*What the hell was the man talking about?* "I have no idea."

"C'mon, Mr. McKenzie. Did you get drunk, maybe say something at a bar you shouldn't have? Or do you keep records . . . secret records of our operation that Johnson could have somehow gotten his hands on? Or maybe you just decided to talk to save your own skin?"

McKenzie kept his eyes from rising to the acoustic ceiling tile almost directly above Li. *Was it possible, could this Johnson have somehow broken into the apartment, found what was hidden there?* "None of those things happened. Believe me, I've played things by the book."

"Don't insult me, McKenzie." Li smashed his free hand on the table for emphasis. "You broke your word once, and after knowing you for all of five minutes, I am convinced you are capable of doing it again. Please cooperate or"—Li shrugged and gestured again to Pu-Yi—"I'm sure my associate would be most happy to resort to alternative methods of persuasion."

McKenzie backed against the wall. "Man, you don't need to do that. Really. If I had anything to tell you, I would."

Pu-Yi started toward McKenzie; hate shone from his eyes.

"You have your goon touch me, and I'll go to the police," McKenzie wailed. "I'll take you down; I'll take the operation down."

Li shook his head slowly. "That would be a very bad mistake. Pu-Yi, tell our friend what happened to the last man who threatened to run to the police."

Pu-Yi smiled, flashed a set of uneven teeth. "I removed his feet . . . with a hacksaw," he said.

"Needless to say," Li added with a sarcastic grin, "the man didn't run far. I think it would be better if you cooperated with us."

McKenzie's eyes darted.

"Mr. McKenzie, my patience is wearing thin. Let me make something clear to you. You tell me what I want to know, and when I walk out of this apartment, you're alive. You don't, and . . . I think you know what happens. You have ten seconds, I'll count them out. When I reach ten, you're out of options. One, two, three . . ."

"I swear to God, I've never met a Scott Johnson."

"Four, five . . ."

"I didn't talk to anyone. No one."

Pu-Yi raised the handgun, aimed the barrel at McKenzie's chest.

"Six, seven, eight . . ."

"You've got to believe me."

"Nine, t—"

"All right." McKenzie raised a hand. "It's the only thing I can think of, but maybe . . . You were right. I did keep some records hidden here. As insurance . . . that's all. In case you guys didn't live up to your side of the bargain. But I've given them to no one. This Johnson would have had to break in here, and—"

"Where are they?" Li demanded.

"I . . . just need a stepladder," McKenzie said hurriedly. "In the closet."

McKenzie removed the stepladder and set it up in the kitchen. From the top step, he pushed on one of the ceiling tiles, moving it up and to the side. His hands went through the opening and brought down a square metal box. He set it on the table.

Pu-Yi opened it and pulled a computer disk from the box. He handed it to Li.

"This is the only copy?" Li asked, inspecting the disk.

"Yes."

"You're not lying again, are you?"

"No, I swear to God, that's it."

"And you've told no one else about our little operation? You've never met Scott Johnson or told anyone about this computer disk?"

"I swear."

Li bobbed his head once. "I believe you. Johnson must have broken in." Li pointed at the ceiling, to the tile McKenzie had pushed aside. "You made his job easy . . . see how one side of the tile is stained a shade darker? You might have worn gloves, Mr. McKenzie."

Li shrugged. "And now it's time I kept my promise. I walk out of this apartment with you still alive." Li tucked the computer disk into his suit pocket, then turned to Pu-Yi. "Stay with our friend, Pu-Yi. Keep him company."

Li walked toward the door.

"Hey, wait a minute," McKenzie yelled, taking a step forward, only to have the barrel of Pu-Yi's gun rammed in his chest. "I gave you what you wanted. I told the truth."

Li opened the door. "Good-bye, Mr. McKenzie."

Pu-Yi chuckled as Li closed the door. "You're a stupid son of a bitch, McKenzie. You know that?"

McKenzie's stomach tightened. No, he wasn't that stupid, but what choice had he had? And what choice did he have now? He sprang forward in desperation, one hand aimed for Pu-Yi's throat, the other for the gun in Pu-Yi's hand.

To Pu-Yi, McKenzie's charge came absurdly slow, like a lumbering cow. He sidestepped it easily and hooked one thick arm around McKenzie's neck. The other still held the gun. He pressed its barrel against McKenzie's temple.

McKenzie stopped struggling immediately.

"What were you going to do?" Pu-Yi hissed in his ear. "Fight me?" He jammed the gun barrel hard against McKenzie's skull. "Fight me now, asshole."

Pu-Yi felt McKenzie's body shudder, heard a weak whimper, and realized McKenzie had started to cry.

Like a woman. Weak. Without courage.

A feeling took Pu-Yi then—the rage—and he tightened his hold, the muscles of his biceps bulging and his forearm digging farther into McKenzie's throat, shutting off the sobs. His other hand, the one that held the gun, he placed on the back of McKenzie's head, and used it to drive McKenzie's head forward.

Not even a gasp escaped McKenzie as his windpipe collapsed. For a moment he grabbed his throat, attempted to loosen the iron-like band that choked the life from him. Then he clawed wildly at Pu-Yi, reaching up and behind him.

Pu-Yi felt nails rake the right side of his face; he jerked back harder.

McKenzie tried to push backward with his legs to no effect—Pu-Yi had braced himself, and outweighed McKenzie by at least twenty pounds.

Eyes bulging, McKenzie's struggles grew first more frantic, then they slowed. A couple of dozen seconds later they stopped entirely. His body hung limply from Pu-Yi's arm, feet dragging on the floor.

Surprisingly light, was Pu-Yi's first thought, now that the struggle was over. He kept his arm muscles taut and counted to a hundred, then let McKenzie's body sink to the floor.

He remembered his own face then, and his hand went to it. He swore as the fingers came away tipped in red. Stupid, to have allowed himself to be marked. He pulled a handkerchief from his pocket and wiped the fresh rivulets of blood from his face.

From a pocket Pu-Yi removed a jackknife. Opening the smallest blade, he carefully scraped clean the underside of the fingernails of McKenzie's right hand, the one that had scratched his face, then buffed them quickly with the handkerchief. Finished, he examined McKenzie's face. Blue; bloodshot eyes popping from sockets.

"You're not a pretty boy anymore," Pu-Yi whispered, then hoisted McKenzie back to his feet and began to drag him toward the balcony.

## 24

From behind the counter the police sergeant looked from the ID to Nick and Meg, back to the ID again, then scratched his jaw determinedly. "The General Accounting Office?"

Nick nodded, accustomed to the reaction—more puzzlement than respect. "That's right," he confirmed.

The sergeant's confused look remained. "You two from the state house?"

"No. Washington. GAO's a federal agency."

"Huh . . . didn't know that. And what is it you want with the sheriff?"

"Information, I hope," Nick answered patiently. "On an investigation I'm working on." That threw the sergeant, as Nick thought it might. Even people who had heard of the GAO rarely knew they conducted investigations.

"You guys just like regular police? Someone doctors their books, they call you—that sort of thing?" the sergeant asked, still looking at Nick's card.

There was no use in explaining or taking offense. "Something like that." Nick smiled, lips pressed together.

The sergeant nodded, clearly unimpressed, and scratched his chestnut hair, coifed a bit too carefully. "Maybe I can help you?"

"Thank you, Sergeant, but if the sheriff's available, I'd like to talk to him."

"All right, Mr. Ford, Miss Taylor," the sergeant said after a pause. "Why don't you just take a seat right over there and I'll go tell the sheriff you're here?" He pointed across the counter at a folding chair against the wall, then disappeared into the back offices with Nick's card.

Nick offered the chair to Meg; she refused it. They both remained standing, Nick surveying his surroundings. Wood paneling, tile floor. Plaques, safety fliers, and wanted posters on the walls. The station appeared workmanlike and very clean. Nick figured the force must be small—probably a couple dozen cops at most—to match the small town. Cobbs Fork, thirty minutes from downtown Birmingham. A main street lined with old men—chawing, watching, judging.

The station had no air conditioning; two fans circulated hot air. Nick loosened his tie, finding it oppressively hot and humid, hard to take a full breath. He rolled up his sleeves, trying unsuccessfully to cool himself.

The sergeant reappeared after a lengthy absence and crooked his finger in Nick's direction. He led Nick into a cramped office which bore no resemblance to the orderly and clean public area. An imposing bald man, tall with a well-lined face and dark stains around his armpits, sat behind a steel desk. The man rose and stuck out his hand. "Sheriff Connors," he announced.

Nick took the sheriff's hand and returned the strong, firm grip.

The sheriff gave Nick a quick appraising glance. Nick had seen the look before; he knew what the man thought: a goddamn bean counter from Washington. Not that it wasn't true, Nick supposed—he fit the bill. He felt about as out of place here as he imagined the sheriff would in D.C.

Nick cast his eyes down, then swore at himself for breaking the sheriff's stare. Bad enough men like this intimidated him at times, did he have to let them know it? It wasn't a matter of fear, certainly not envy, just discomfort. Men like the sheriff didn't follow the niceties: the easy patter of polite conversations, the conventions of dress and decorum. It bothered Nick that his position, his looks and dress, created a look of derision in the sheriff's eyes, a gulf Nick must work hard to bridge.

The sheriff said, "The sergeant says you two are

with the . . . General Accounting Office, I believe he said."

"That's right," Nick said, Meg echoing him.

"Investigators?"

"Right. Office of Special Investigations."

Sheriff Connors nodded. "Forgive me for saying so, but you two look more like the pencil-pusher type."

Meg, her jaw set, said, "Nowadays we use calculators and computers."

The sheriff laughed. "And what brings the General Accounting Office's Office of Special Investigations to our little town?"

Nick took an immediate dislike to the large man. "I came down to question somebody: Andrew McKenzie."

Sheriff Connors rubbed his temple. "Name doesn't ring a bell."

"I just left his apartment building, found out he took a bad fall last night. He's dead. I think your men were called to the scene."

Sheriff Connors looked at the sergeant. "Would that be the . . . what was it, Earl? The Eastbrook apartments?"

The sergeant nodded. "Must be."

"That's it," Nick verified.

Sheriff Connors eased his bulk back into the chair. "Yeah, sure, one of our men answered the call last night." He reached for a pack of cigarettes lying on his desk, knocked one out for himself, then held the pack for Nick, who shook his head. "Bad timing," the sheriff continued. "Why'd you want to talk to this McKenny?"

"McKen*zie*," Nick corrected. "His name surfaced in one of our investigations."

"What exactly is it you were looking into?"

"Billing irregularities in a federal contract."

The sheriff immediately lost all interest. "Billing irregularities, huh?"

"We wanted to talk to McKenzie about it. A matter of routine."

Sheriff Connors kicked his boots onto the desk. "Looks like your routine came a day too late."

The sergeant made a halfhearted attempt to suppress a laugh.

Nick rolled with the comment. "Can you tell me what happened?"

"I read the report this morning, but . . . hold on a second." Sheriff Connors picked up his phone. "Tom, is Arnie around? . . . Good. Could you send him in here?" The sheriff placed the receiver back on its cradle. "Arnie . . . Officer Gordon . . . was on the scene. You can hear it from the horse's mouth."

A young, lanky cop with a sunken chest and acne scars across his cheekbones ambled in a moment later. The sheriff pointed at Nick. "Arnie, this here is Mr. Nick Ford, and this is Miss Meg Taylor. They came all the way from Washington, D.C., to talk to us about that accident victim you covered last night. Andrew McKenzie."

The young cop, eyes wide, stuttered a "Uh-huh."

"Can you fill them in?"

"Sure can," Arnie replied eagerly and turned toward Nick. "Not much to tell really. What do you want to know?"

"The circumstances of death."

Arnie screwed up his eyes, as if recounting last night's events was a Herculean effort. "Got a call about two in the morning. One of the apartment owners discovered the body, on the parking lot. Victim had landed on concrete, head first. Eight floors below his balcony. A real mess." Arnie delivered the last sentence with a schoolboy's zeal.

Sheriff Connors cut in. "Mr. Ford came down here to question Mr. McKenzie about some billing irregularities. I'm thinking he has a notion McKenzie's death wasn't accidental."

Arnie shook his head. "If you're thinking it wasn't an accident, Mr. Ford, I think you're on the wrong track."

Sheriff Connors tapped his ash into the tray, then took a puff and aimed the smoke in Nick's direction.

"Why?" Nick asked.

"McKenzie's apartment wasn't disturbed. No money taken from his pockets, no sign of a struggle. We searched his place, didn't find anything to make us suspicious. We *did* find an overturned stepladder on the balcony and a busted lightbulb in the balcony's fixture. Seems pretty clear what happened: while replacing the lightbulb he lost his balance."

Nick nodded. "Sounds reasonable." Easy enough, of course, to push someone off a balcony, then bust a lightbulb and overturn a ladder, but he saw no reason to argue the possibility. "Coroner confirm the fall killed him?"

"Sure did. Told us something else too: McKenzie's blood-alcohol level was .21."

"The man wasn't feeling any pain," Sheriff Connors contributed. "A minor blessing, I suppose."

"We have witnesses who saw him leave a bar shortly after one in the morning," Arnie said. "From what they said, he was in no condition to step up on a ladder."

"Makes you wonder," Meg said, "why he got it into his head to change a busted lightbulb after all those drinks."

Sheriff Connors answered. "You find out why drunks insist on driving eighty when they can't handle fifteen, miss, and you'll have your answer."

Caution might well be an early casualty of drinking, but that didn't explain away the convenient timing of McKenzie's death, not to Nick's satisfaction. He directed another question at Arnie. "You dust for prints?"

"On the doorknobs, the stepladder. I didn't see any reason to dust the rest of the apartment after we got the coroner's preliminary report."

"Neighbors see or hear anything?"

"No."

"You have a file on McKenzie?"

"No. Never been in trouble as far as we know. Heads a small engineering firm in Birmingham. Inherited ownership from his father, I understand. A bit of a playboy. That's about all we know about him."

"Unless you have something else to tell us, that is," Sheriff Connors interrupted, a hint of a smile curling his lips.

Nick shook his head, and after a pause he said, "I'd like to see McKenzie's apartment, if that's possible."

Sheriff Connors looked hard at Nick for a moment, then shrugged. "Why not? We're always happy to help out our federal brethren. Arnie, why don't you run Mr. Ford and Miss Taylor over to the apartment? . . . Anything else we can do for you, Mr. Ford?"

There *was* something else, and Nick was about to blurt it out, ready to use his federal clout in the battle sure to follow, when he thought of Scott.

Nick forced himself to smile, then let the words come out as they would have from Scott, who had used a hundred similar lines in Nick's presence in the past. "Just one thing. . . . Name of a good restaurant for lunch. Something simple—nothing that doesn't have a napkin dispenser on the table. Barbecue, chicken fried steak. I don't get down South nearly as much as I should."

For the first time the sheriff's face softened. He and each of his three officers offered a favorite. Nick followed up quickly on the newfound goodwill. "And, Sheriff," he said, "could you call the coroner, tell him I'll be flying in another medical examiner to confirm his preliminary opinion?"

The goodwill dissipated instantly. "The coroner's report seems to fit the facts, Mr. Ford. Drunk, McKenzie fell off the balcony. The fall killed him. Why do you need another examination?" The sheriff's other question—who the hell are you to come into *my* town and tell *me* how to do *my* job?—went unstated but clearly conveyed.

Nick again thought of Scott. "It's paperwork and

bureaucracy, Sheriff. The D.C. way of doing things. Do I think another examination is necessary? No. Will my boss get on my case if I don't get one? Hell, yes. I'd appreciate it if you smoothed things over with the coroner, let him know it's a matter of routine, that's all."

Reluctantly, the sheriff nodded. Scott would have been proud.

# 25

Nick and Meg stood when Dr. Samuels, a tall, dignified man who compared favorably to the idealized television persona of a doctor, leaned into the waiting room. "Mr. Ford . . . Ms. Taylor," he announced, then disappeared.

Dr. Samuels had an excellent reputation as a forensic pathologist, perhaps due in no small part to extensive practice—a dubious benefit of being one of the medical examiners for Washington, D.C., the off-and-on murder capital of America. Nick was lucky to have gotten him to fly down on such short notice. An unusually slow day in D.C., evidently.

Nick and Meg followed Dr. Samuels through the door marked CORONER'S OFFICE, EXAMINING ROOM, in black block letters.

McKenzie lay naked on a large waist-high stainless steel table. A Y-shaped incision marked his body from just under each of the armpits to the bottom of the sternum, then down in a straight line to the pubic bone. The incision bulged open slightly, irregular masses visible underneath. Nick tried to keep his eyes from the area above McKenzie's shoulders, but his eyes were drawn there in spite of himself. McKenzie's features were identifiable, barely, but not especially pleasant to look at.

A scale hung over one end of the table—to weigh organs stripped from the cadavers; a large sink with a heavy-duty spray attachment was built into the table's other end. An antiseptic smell, exceptionally strong, pervaded the room, masking more unwelcome scents, Nick guessed.

It was the first autopsy room Nick had ever visited. So far, surprisingly, he had managed to remain analyti-

cal about the experience. Dr. Samuels's attitude
helped: professional, unemotional, almost as if showing Nick and Meg under the hood of his car.

Nick looked at Meg. Her face had gone white, but
her breathing seemed controlled. "You okay?" he
asked.

She nodded shortly, and Nick turned to the coroner.
"Have you finished your examination, Doctor?"

"Yes," Dr. Samuels confirmed, and he briefly summarized what that entailed in clinical detail.

"And what did you find?"

"Of course, I'll have to wait to see the results of
the lab and toxicology tests. . . ."

"Of course."

The doctor shrugged. "Frankly, at this point I see
no sound basis for challenging the coroner's preliminary report. Death caused by a fall."

"Could he have been pushed?" Meg asked.

Dr. Samuels paused. "Certainly possible, just no evidence to suggest he was."

"How about thrown off the balcony?" Nick suggested. "Killed first, then thrown?"

Dr. Samuels reached two hands under McKenzie's
right thigh and raised it for Nick's and Meg's inspection. "See the blotching?"

Nick would have been content with the oral explanation. He glanced quickly, then nodded.

"Liver mortis," Dr. Samuels explained. "The pooling of blood in a dead body. When blood stops circulating on death, the red blood cells settle with gravity
over time, giving the skin underneath the body a red-
dish, mottled color. By examining the resultant pattern
of skin discoloration, it's possible to determine the
position of the body after death. In this case the discoloration on the corpse is consistent with the position
the police found the body."

Dr. Samuels lowered McKenzie's thigh and picked
up a medical chart. "Algor mortis—the temperature
of death—tells much the same story. A live body, as
you know, maintains a constant temperature of ap-

proximately 98.6 degrees Fahrenheit. After death the body temperature falls about a degree an hour, depending on conditions. The coroner tested body temperature through the anal cavity. 96.1 degrees. Factor in the loss of blood, the ambient temperature, the result: I'd say the victim died within two hours of the time the coroner arrived at the scene, a half hour or so before the police were called."

Nick kept himself from shuddering. A very cold science. "So in your opinion, Doctor, McKenzie *was* alive when he fell from the balcony."

Dr. Samuels shook his head. "I didn't say that. What I can say is that if he was killed and thrown over the balcony, the two events were closely linked in time. Mr. McKenzie wasn't, for instance, killed across town, transported to his apartment in a car's trunk, then thrown off the balcony. We would see a different pattern of blotching—evidence of the body's prior position—and a lower body temperature."

Dr. Samuels crooked his finger, and Nick and Meg followed him to the head of the examining table. Dr. Samuels pointed at the corpse. "As you can see, the back and right side of the victim's head, his right shoulder and spinal column, are crushed. Damages consistent with a fall from eight stories. Falling victims often land on their backs or sides; the position of the body wasn't suspicious in that respect. I could find no other evidence of violence to the body. However, the fall would likely have obscured prior injury to the neck and cranial region."

Meg said, "So if McKenzie was . . . say hit on the head, then thrown off the balcony . . ."

The doctor finished Meg's thought. "I wouldn't be able to distinguish the separate traumas."

Interesting, but as Nick thought it over, not overly helpful. He stroked his chin. "Doctor, couldn't everything you've told us be said about *every* accidental falling victim? If I've understood you correctly, you've found no actual evidence of wrongdoing."

"That's correct, Mr. Ford. Although there are three

things—not exactly what I'd call hard evidence—that I noticed. Things one would classify as peculiar."

Nick and Meg exchanged quick glances. "And they are?" Nick asked.

"From my examination of the body and the photographs of the scene, the blood loss surprised me. Less than I would have expected."

"One of the cops said the scene was a mess," Meg said.

"I can imagine in the eyes of a police officer it would appear to be. What I'm referring to is bleeding from the resultant trauma. In the case of a falling victim, a body that strikes the ground alive bleeds more than one that strikes the ground already dead. A live body, the blood's still under pressure; a dead body, the heart's stopped pumping. No pressure, less bleeding."

"I don't understand. Now you seem to be saying McKenzie *was* dead before he struck the ground."

"Not at all. Again, Mr. Ford, I'm only talking possibilities. The amount of blood loss was less than I would have expected, but not unreasonably so. The deceased may have been alive when he fell; he may have been dead. I couldn't say with any certainty."

Nick kept his eyes from going to the ceiling. "Just possibilities."

"Exactly. Another thing . . . I inspected the victim's clothing. On his trousers I found a large urine stain."

"Not uncommon for a person's bladder to empty on death, is it, Doctor?"

"No, not unusual at all. What's unusual about this stain, however, is its shape. A wide streak down the length of his pants."

"What's unusual about that?"

"Gravity, Mr. Ford. The police found the victim lying on his back eight floors below his balcony, right? If he had expelled his bladder on death, and death occurred on the ground below his apartment, why wasn't the stain pooled around his crotch and the seat of his pants? Instead it ran down the *length* of the victim's pants."

Meg caught the doctor's reasoning. "As if the victim died in an upright position. Perhaps as he was lifted over a balcony?"

"That's conjecture, Ms. Taylor. But, yes, that would be consistent with what I found. Then again, I cannot prove that urine stain wasn't from a day ago, a week ago."

"You said you noticed three curious things," Nick prompted.

"Yes. The victim's . . . well, perhaps it's better if I showed you." Dr. Samuels moved around the examining table to McKenzie's left side. "I checked the victim's fingernails. I was looking for skin samples, blood samples, preserved under the deceased's nails—evidence of a struggle."

Nick's eyebrows arched. "You found something?"

"See for yourself." Dr. Samuels lifted McKenzie's lifeless left hand by the wrist.

Nick noticed a trace substance under McKenzie's nails. "Is it skin?"

"No. Dirt. Nothing unusual." Dr. Samuels set down McKenzie's left hand and walked around the examining table. Nick and Meg followed, confused. The doctor lifted McKenzie's right hand this time. "Now take a look at the right hand."

"I don't see anything."

"Correct. That's what gave me pause. Look under his nails again."

Nick did. They were clean.

After a moment Dr. Samuels said, "Clean. *Perfectly* clean."

Nick saw where the doctor was going. "You're saying the nails on his right hand have been cleaned."

"It appears so. Either the deceased cleaned the nails of his right hand, and *only* his right hand, shortly before he died, or someone else did after the fact. The latter possibility raises intriguing questions."

Nick's mind weighed possibilities. "Let me see if

I've got this, Doctor. McKenzie is attacked. He struggles, perhaps scratches his assailant with his right hand. Then he's killed. The assailant destroys the incriminating evidence by cleaning the blood and tissue from under McKenzie's fingernails, then throws McKenzie off the balcony."

Dr. Samuels shrugged. "That, Mr. Ford, is a string of conclusions I myself have not put forward. I have just made observations. I will tell you this, though: nothing I have observed would be *inconsistent* with the scenario you suggest. But let me be clear, we have allowed ourselves to make suppositions. Suppositions aren't enough for me to challenge a finding of accidental death."

"I wouldn't ask you to challenge the finding, Doctor," Nick said. "In fact, I understand your position completely. Do me a favor, though. The urine stain, the fingernails, make notes, take a few pictures, if you could, and send them to us. For our files."

Nick took the two sodas from the stewardess and handed one to Meg, who sat next to him in the window seat. Meg's hand trembled, spilling 7-Up on her skirt.

"You okay?" Nick asked.

"Fine," Meg said, though Nick noticed her hand continued to shake.

"That was my first autopsy too," Nick said. "Not very pleasant, was it?"

Meg shook her head. "No, but . . ." She gulped. "The autopsy isn't what's bothering me, Nick."

"Then what is? Because something sure has you spooked."

Meg took a deep breath. "I guess I've just let my imagination get the better of me."

"Meaning?"

Meg shrugged, embarrassed. "I'm nervous. Worried. Scott was investigating this case, now he's dead. We go to interview McKenzie, now he's dead too."

Nick gave voice to his own thoughts: "You think,

somehow, someone's been keeping a step ahead of us all along?"

"I'm not sure, but if they are . . . Nick, two people are dead, both probably murdered. Are we next?"

Nick hadn't considered the possibility. He was a government accountant; people didn't murder government accountants. At least that's what he had always believed before Scott's death. He shook his head forcefully, as much to convince himself as to convince Meg. "No, Meg. Really, we don't have anything to worry about."

Meg nodded. "Like I said, I let my imagination run away with me. You're right . . . I know that. It's just . . ." Her voice trailed off.

"Of course I'm right," Nick said, sounding more confident than he felt. Scott dead, McKenzie dead. *Could* they be in danger?

On the way home from the airport, Nick shared a cab with Meg. The cab dropped her off first, and he manufactured an excuse to escort her up to her apartment. He walked through each room before leaving.

# 26

J. T. Frasier settled into his desk chair like an old man, everything he did slowed in tempo. His head sank onto a clenched fist; he bit his forefinger between the first and second knuckle. He tried to think, but his normally orderly mind wouldn't cooperate—random thoughts, mainly fears, flashed through his consciousness.

Finally, Frasier reached for his phone, though he did not pick up the receiver immediately. He stared at it a moment instead; then his eyes traveled upward, settling on a black-and-white photo of him and his father. They stood on the deck of the *Intrepid,* the small sailboat his father once kept in Pensacola. Of all the photos adorning his office walls—and there were many: photos of him shaking hands with CEOs, governors, senators—it was his favorite.

The boat had been little better than scrap when his father bought it. They refurbished her together, replacing the rigging, patching the sails, sanding and refinishing every inch of her hull and teak deck. His father passed away five years ago, and though Frasier rarely sailed her anymore, he still kept the boat in perfect condition.

He lowered his eyes again, ashamed.

*Everything had been laid out for him. It would have been such a damn easy ride.*

Retirement was only ten years away; he could have looked forward to a generous consulting contract requiring little more than dinner with the board of directors once a month or so. His stock options alone were worth over fourteen million dollars. Why the hell had he risked everything? And for what? An indiscretion, a sick obsession.

Maybe people would have understood if he had come forward in the beginning. Asked forgiveness, sought help. But not now—now things had gone too far. He had no alternative but to play ball.

Why had he been convinced that he could get away with anything? And why had he ever thought he could deal with John Li?

It was so easy to deceive one's self.

Frasier picked up the receiver. Li preferred face-to-face meetings, but in this case who cared what the son of a bitch preferred? Things had gone terribly wrong, again.

He dialed Li's personal line; a pleasant, female voice answered with "John Li's office, may I help you?"

"May I speak to him?"

"I'm sorry, sir, but Mr. Li's in a meeting right now. May I take a message?"

"This is very important, could you please get him out of the meeting? I know he'll want to talk to me."

"I'm sorry, sir. If you'd just leave your number, I'm sure—"

The small amount of patience Frasier started the call with deserted him. "*I'm sure* I have no interest in leaving my number. I want to talk to Mr. Li immediately."

"Sir, I—"

"What's your name?" Frasier demanded.

"Excuse me?"

"I *said,* what is your name?"

"Susan."

"Okay, Susan, I'm going to tell you what you're going to do. You're going to march into whatever meeting Mr. Li is attending and tell him he has an urgent call. It's an emergency. Got it?"

"Your name is?"

"Tell Mr. Li we played a hole of golf recently. *One* hole. He'll know who I am."

"I really don't think—" the woman began.

Frasier drained the last bit of fight from her. "Do it. Don't argue, just *do it.*"

"Just a moment, sir."

Less than two minutes went by before the secretary's now chastened voice again came over the line. "Please hold for Mr. Li."

Li's voice came next over the line, relaxed but somewhat impatient. "Mr. Frasier, I didn't expect to hear from you."

"I didn't expect to call."

"I believe you are aware our normal protocol requires—"

"The hell with normal protocol." From the first Frasier hadn't liked Li, hadn't liked the way he talked, the heavy jowls and small eyes that seemed too self-satisfied. Now his feelings had moved beyond dislike.

"I was told you had an emergency," Li said.

"You bet your ass I do."

"Then we should meet. I could make some time later to—"

"No more golf courses," Frasier interrupted. "We'll do this now. My line's secure."

"Very well. What is it?"

Frasier ran his free hand through his hair; he willed his voice not to break. "*What is it?* God dammit, let's not play this game again."

"I'm afraid I have no idea what you are talking about."

"Over the last couple of days I passed you information. Credit reports and a memo from Ford's desk, a report on Ford's visit to Smith Pettit. The information incriminated McKenzie. Do you remember that?"

"Yes."

"Today I got another report—McKenzie's dead."

Li said nothing, and Frasier continued. "He *fell* from his eighth-floor apartment."

"Accidents do happen," Li said matter-of-factly.

"You had him killed, didn't you?"

"Would it surprise you to know Mr. McKenzie had a complete set of financials for his company—a true

set—stored on a computer disk in his apartment? I
don't need to tell you the damage such evidence could
have caused us. I believe Scott Johnson may have gotten a look at that disk; I wanted to make sure he was
the last."

"*A true set of financials?* Dammit, Li, if Johnson
made copies . . ."

"Relax, Mr. Frasier. We searched Johnson's car;
you had his office searched. If Johnson had made copies, they would have surfaced by now. I did what I
had to do. I'm afraid Mr. McKenzie could no longer
be trusted."

"McKenzie was one of your men. You picked him,
God dammit. I didn't."

"No, in fact I did not pick McKenzie, but you, *you*
passed on the information that Ford was about to interview him. *You* did that. Now you tell me, *what the
hell did you think would happen?*"

Frasier's mouth went dry; he said nothing, and after
a moment Li continued. "I'm waiting for an answer.
What did you think would happen? You wanted the
problem solved; that's why you came to me. Well, I
took care of it, like *you* wanted."

Frasier's breathing echoed in the phone as his mind
raced. He had only passed on information, that's all.
*That's all,* he repeated to himself. He closed his eyes,
fighting to compose himself. Couldn't he just go back
in time, to before Li, to before the insanity?

"This has got to stop," he said.

Li let Frasier's sentence settle before answering, his
voice soft. "You should not lose sleep over this Mc-
Kenzie. Trust me, he wasn't worth it."

Frasier reached for a paper clip, began straightening
it with his left hand—a nervous habit; dozens were
scattered across his desk. What choice did he have but
to move forward? Li owned a part of Frasier's soul,
and Frasier knew it. Certainly, there was no going
back.

"You fucked up," Frasier said sternly.

"I did what necessity required, and because of that we all sleep easier."

Frasier clenched his teeth. "Sleep easier? You're not following me, Li. I said you *fucked up,* and I meant it. You didn't solve a goddamn thing by killing this man. Do you understand what I'm saying: you didn't make things better; you didn't solve the problem. You made things *worse.*"

The other line went silent. Finally Li said, "Explain."

"Ford called in a forensic specialist to examine McKenzie. He must have found something, because Ford's now convinced McKenzie's death wasn't an accident."

"What did he find?" Li asked, for the first time sounding anxious.

"I don't know, not yet."

The other line went momentarily silent again. "It's a bluff. He didn't find anything."

"I don't give a damn if it's a bluff or not. One way or the other it means the case will draw more attention. Do you understand now?"

"Unfortunate."

Frasier tired of hearing that word. "Unfortunate," like an earthquake or tornado or an act of God. "I hold you, your people, responsible."

"The business we are engaged in entails risks. That can't be avoided. Would you have preferred Ford had reached McKenzie? Had convinced him to talk? Had gotten hold of McKenzie's disk? If you want to guarantee there will be no further unfortunate incidents, stop the investigation. Stop the hearings. Stop Ford."

"We've discussed this before—"

"We're discussing it again."

"He's an high-ranking employee of a federal agency, for God's sake."

"He's an insignificant insect who continues to irritate. No more arguments—you *will* take more aggressive action to stop Ford."

"And how do you suggest I do that?"

"I believe in insurance, Mr. Frasier. Contingency plans. I put a few things into motion months ago in case Mr. Ford became overly bothersome. I think he has. . . . The next hearing is Thursday?"

"Yes."

"Expect a package in the mail tomorrow. You'll find it interesting, I believe. Use your connections, see that the contents are delivered to the appropriate parties *before* Thursday. There should be enough inside to haul in Ford's chain. If not . . . well, I'll be compelled to consider more drastic and final alternatives."

Frasier let the now straightened paper clip fall from his hand as the sentence lingered. "What do you mean by that?"

"I think I've made myself clear. Too much chain to play with and a dog can end up choking itself. Ford will be silenced, one way or the other."

Frasier's mouth went dry. It took a second before he could respond. "You can't," he said.

"Oh, but I assure you I can. In fact, it would be extremely simple. A hit and run, an apparent mugging, a faked suicide . . . any number of ways. You must understand, Mr. Frasier, one man's overzealous curiosity is threatening us. Very plainly, we can't have that. You either use your connections and my package to deal with the matter, or . . ." Li let the sentence hang. "I suggest you don't disappoint me."

Frasier let the phone slip from his ear. Should he disconnect the line and try to run away? How far would he get if he did? From every corner people pulled his strings, like a marionette. He felt himself sinking deeper into madness, but had no idea how to extricate himself.

He heard Li call his name, at first quietly, then louder.

Frasier slowly raised the phone. He closed his eyes. "All right," he whispered. "I'll look for your package. And I'll do what I can."

"No," Li corrected him, "you will do what you *must*."

# 27

Nick checked his watch. The hearing would begin any minute. The senators had already arrived, most had taken their seats; they simply waited on the call to order from Chairman Callahan.

Meg plopped a stack of documents on the witness table, then took the seat to Nick's right. "Nervous?" he asked her.

Meg shook her head.

"Good, because I thought I'd let you handle the opening statement."

Meg's eyes went round. "I . . ."

Nick laughed softly. "A joke, Meg." Their relationship had warmed a bit over the last few days—fine with Nick, now that the ground rules had been set.

"Funny." She smiled unevenly, then nudged Nick and pointed at the balcony. "Looks like your Q Rating's fallen."

Nick looked at the balcony, at the one C-Span camera there. "Q Rating?"

"Yeah, Hollywood uses the term to score name recognition," Meg explained. "Star quality. Didn't you say CNN *and* C-Span televised the last hearing? Looks like CNN crossed you off the list."

Nick nodded. It didn't surprise him. CNN had covered the first session with the expectation of fireworks; instead they got a civil—in television language read low ratings—hearing. Civility was back-page news, and evidently they decided not to waste their equipment on another boring afternoon session. C-Span, on the other hand, thrived on the mundane.

CNN's absence didn't bother Nick; the print media was still quite adequately represented, and he would gladly sacrifice the dubious benefits of television expo-

sure for another hearing as well mannered as the last.
An unlikely prospect, according to Carolyn.

Smith Pettit had called Nick yesterday afternoon
with a final settlement offer—fifty million dollars. Nick
had almost dropped the phone. *Fifty million,* when he
had documented overbillings of less than thirty million? Carolyn had counseled him to accept the offer—
in her words, "The settlement makes the public
whole . . . more than whole. Your job's over; let the
FBI handle the investigation into Scott's death, Mc-
Kenzie's death—that's their job." *She was right. He
knew she was right, but—* He rejected the offer, even
after Carolyn had turned harsh, the teacher questioning the reasoning of the student. Intuition told
Nick he had something bigger than billing irregularities by the tail, and the only way he'd ever find out
what was to keep digging. Carolyn's last words were of
warning: "You don't agree to this deal, I understand
Whitford's ready to play hardball." When Carolyn
"understood" something, it was pretty much a
guarantee.

Hardball, from Whitford, an unpleasant prospect.

Nick nudged Meg, who was still focused on the C-
Span camera. "Forget about Q Ratings," he said,
pointing at Senator Callahan, who now held a gavel
in his hands. "We're about to start."

Callahan gave a brief opening statement. Nick's was
briefer still. Thirty seconds at most, then he prepared
to jump to the meat of his testimony. "There have
been significant developments since the last hearing,"
Nick announced. "I would like to start by summarizing
certain findings that are of crucial—"

A senator cleared his throat loudly, interrupting
Nick. Eyes flipped in the sound's direction, toward
Senator Charles Whitford III, who stared a long moment at Nick before speaking, his voice resonating in
the now still chamber. "Mr. Chairman, I believe the
last hearing ended during the questioning phase. If the
committee has no objection, I would like to make a

few additional inquiries of our esteemed witness before he continues with his statement."

Chairman Callahan looked left, then right, and, encountering no dissent, nodded. "You may proceed."

Senator Whitford kept his eyes locked on Nick, adding a disarming smile. "Mr. Ford, over the last month or so I've listened to hours and hours of figures, estimates, and projections from your office—if nothing else the absolute volume of statistics has been stunning. My colleagues and I are always heartened to find the taxpayers' money being so diligently spent by bureaucrats such as yourself." Senator Whitford spat out "bureaucrats" like a curse. "Congratulations to you and your team; you must be very pleased with yourselves."

The senator paused, but Nick said nothing, unwilling to acknowledge the insincerely offered praise. He had a sudden vision of Whitford as an ancient consul of Rome, about to turn his thumb down.

Senator Whitford eventually resumed. "Mr. Ford, your title is what?"

"Senior Auditor, Special Investigations Division."

"And how long have you held your current position?"

"Senior auditor? Seven years."

Senator Whitford puckered his lips and wagged a finger in Nick's direction. "That's not quite accurate, is it?"

"Excuse me?"

"I believe that until a few days ago you were acting assistant comptroller of the Government Division, isn't that correct?" Senator Whitford demanded.

"Unofficially, but I had reserved the option to—"

"*Yes* or *no,* Mr. Ford," the senator interrupted, frowning.

"Unofficially . . . yes. I was."

"I see. You were an assistant comptroller, but are no longer. As to the reason, it is my understanding that . . . how should I say it . . . you did not see eye to eye with your superiors. Is that correct?"

"The choice to give up the assistant comptroller position was my own, Senator."

"I'm sure it was." The senator shrugged sarcastically. "Just as I'm sure your *demotion* from assistant comptroller to senior auditor had nothing whatsoever to do with your professional fitness."

A cheap twisting of words that Nick started to object to, but Senator Whitford spoke over him: "I wonder, Mr. Ford, if you might have made a rush to judgment about Smith Pettit an older and wiser head might not have made?"

"It is not my place to *judge* anyone, Senator," Nick countered.

"Certainly your presence here is not quite so innocuous as you would have us believe. You have made recommendations to the committee, correct?"

Nick took a deep breath. Take your time, he reminded himself. "Yes, sir, based on the evidence we collected."

"We've heard your *evidence,* reams of it, but now we're trying to grasp something more amorphous: the truth. . . . Who is your direct boss in the Special Investigations Division?"

"Dennis Lindsay."

"And his boss?"

"Carolyn Reed."

"Carolyn Reed, the comptroller general of the GAO?"

"Yes, sir."

"You respect their judgment?"

"Yes, sir," Nick answered, deciding it would not further his cause to answer no with regard to Dennis.

"And have you ever had occasion to discuss the audit of the Yünnan Project with them?"

"It's come up a few times," Nick conceded.

"I'm sure it has. Mr. Ford, has Ms. Reed or Mr. Lindsay ever suggested you seemed overly caught up in this audit and might consider recusing yourself from it?"

Whitford's sources were good, Nick gave him that. "I don't remember exactly—"

"I can call them as witnesses, Mr. Ford," Senator Whitford interrupted, "if you need your memory refreshed."

"If I may finish my thought, Senator. I don't remember their exact words, but yes, they did at one point suggest something to that effect."

Senator Whitford nodded slowly. "I see. So two older, wiser heads, people with valuable extra years of experience, offer their advice and you ignored it, is that correct?" The senator punctuated the sentence by slapping the bench in front of him.

"Senator, as I said, I value Ms. Reed's opinion, I value Mr. Lindsay's opinion, but *I* am in charge of the audit, and in that capacity *I* must make decisions *I* am comfortable with."

Senator Whitford pursed his lips while undertaking another series of slow nods. Six times his head rocked forward. "You've got the keys to daddy's car, son, but with privilege comes responsibility."

Nick swallowed a comment and forced a half smile instead. It was no time to be baited, not now, when Whitford clearly sought his head. "I can assure you, I take my responsibilities very seriously, Senator."

Another series of damn nods. "I'm sure you do, Mr. Ford. I'm sure you do." The senator pointed a finger at Nick. "Now, let's get to the facts in this case. For those of us who aren't as well versed in financial statements as yourself, can we simplify things? According to you, in plain English, there were cost overruns in the Yünnan Project contract?"

"Significant cost overruns, sir, and incurred by Smith Pettit, in my estimation, with the intent—"

The senator lifted his hand; his voice took on a harsh edge. "Let's never mind your view of their intent for a moment. Let me put it this way, but for the cost overruns we wouldn't be meeting here today, isn't that correct?"

"I suppose so . . . yes."

"I agree. Now, Mr. Ford, can you explain what a cost-plus contract is?"

Nick nodded. "Certainly. Let's say Company A contracts with Company B to perform some task. Under a cost-plus contract, Company A reimburses Company B for all of its costs *plus* an additional amount equal to some percentage of those costs. The 'plus' is essentially Company B's profit margin. A cost-plus contract eliminates a fixed-dollar bid's inherent risk. It insures a reasonable profit to the contractor, but keeps either side from reaping a windfall."

"A very concise explanation," Senator Whitford said. "I thank you. You are the author of an article entitled 'Cost-Plus Contracting, Uses and Abuses,' are you not?"

It took a moment for Nick to remember the article in question, then he said, "Co-author."

"Co-author." The senator nodded his head seriously. "I've had the chance, yesterday, to peruse the article." He drew out peruse, like peru-u-u-s-s-se. "I came across an interesting passage at one point." Senator Whitford held up a piece of paper. "May I read it to you?"

"Of course."

The senator made a show of removing his reading glasses from his suit breast pocket. He put them on, balancing them near the end of his nose. "I quote," he read, " 'Cost overruns are a common and predictable byproduct of cost-plus contracting.' " Senator Whitford raised his head, looked at Nick from above his glasses. "Do you remember writing that, sir?"

"If it's in the article, I assume I did."

"I can assure you, you did. Now, the Yünnan Project contract is a cost-plus contract, isn't that right?"

Nick nodded.

"For the record, sir."

"That's correct."

"Therefore, at the time the contract was signed, according to your own writings, the government should have expected there would be cost overruns."

"The article was making reference to historical evidence."

"And I've lived long enough to learn history can teach us a thing or two about the present." Scattered laughs followed the aside; Nick realized Whitford had the audience in his pocket. "By your own account, Mr. Ford, the government could have predicted cost overruns, yet when there are cost overruns, you wave your hands in indignation and talk of imposing Draconian penalties against Smith Pettit."

"Sir, the D.C. police may be able to predict there will be X number of murders a week in this city. That doesn't mean they don't do everything they can to investigate those murders and bring the murderers to justice."

Senator Whitford pounced immediately. "Sir, are you now comparing the executives of Smith Pettit to *murderers*?"

It was becoming clear to Nick he was way out of his league; Whitford was twisting everything he said. He took a moment to collect himself—there were ten rounds to a fight and he had to keep his feet. "Of course not. . . . I am simply presenting evidence as I have been called upon by the committee to do. I make no recommendation of whether legal action should be taken against any of the parties involved."

"But you do, sir. By using terms such as 'gross negligence' and 'fraud,' you have pervaded these proceedings with an aura of illegality, implied that some very good people should go to jail."

"I'm not saying anyone should go to jail."

"How very charitable, Mr. Ford. How very charitable. Then you are prepared to withdraw your charges against Smith Pettit?"

"The *GAO's* charges," Nick corrected.

Senator Whitford pounded the bench sharply. "Do you recommend they be withdrawn or not?"

"I do not," Nick stated firmly.

"Then, Mr. Ford, I sincerely hope *you* are withdrawn, because I have reason to believe you are not

only incompetent to hold the job of assistant comptroller, you are incompetent to hold any position
within the GAO."

Senator Raine's turn to thump the bench. *"Mr.
Chairman!"* she shouted, coming to Nick's defense,
but she did not even slow Senator Whitford down.

"Mr. Ford," Senator Whitford continued, "do you
mean to sit there and tell me you have not singled
out Smith Pettit for persecution?"

*"Absolutely not,"* Nick fired back.

"I see. I am holding in my hand a report prepared
by your office, dated yesterday, entitled 'Status report,
documented billing irregularities, Yünnan Project.'"
Senator Whitford lifted the report for all to see. "You
are familiar with it?"

"I am."

"In fact, your office delivered copies to the members of this subcommittee earlier this morning in antic-
ipation of the hearing."

Nick glanced at Meg; she nodded. "That's correct,"
Nick confirmed.

"You have a copy in front of you?"

Meg slid him a copy.

"I do."

"Could you turn to page three?"

Nick did.

"I draw your attention to item seven, entertainment
and travel expense. Could you read the figure
printed there?"

Nick felt off balance. Was this a feint, or was the
senator on to something? "Nine hundred and seventy-
six thousand dollars."

"Which represents what?"

"Entertainment expenses we have documented as
inappropriate."

"Now I go to Appendix F. These are the itemized
entries that underlie the nine hundred and seventy-six
thousand dollars, correct?"

"Correct."

The senator pulled off his reading glasses, scratched

his cheek with one of the stems. "In my over forty years in the Senate, I've relied on figures provided by the GAO countless times, never once doubted their accuracy . . . until today. This morning I felt compelled to do something which for me was unprecedented—I had my staff verify the figures. Add each of the couple of thousand entries. Check it and recheck it. . . . They found something rather peculiar, Mr. Ford. Your figures don't add up."

Nick looked down at the status report, as if the error Whitford had alluded to might jump out of the page at him. "There must be some mistake," he muttered.

"I assure you there is, but it was not made on our part."

Nick guessed just the opposite. Senate staff members? With calculators? A recipe for disaster. "Excuse me, Senator, but an error is highly unlikely. All entries are entered into a spread sheet . . . they're automatically tallied by computer."

"Shortly before the commencement of today's hearing, one of the big five accounting firms was kind enough to double-check my staff's calculations. I repeat, the error is not on our part."

Nick's confidence flagged. "I'll recheck the tally, Senator. If there has been a mistake, I'll issue an amended report along with my apologies."

"You might want to check a number of tallies while you're at it, Mr. Ford," Senator Whitford said stiffly, "because this wasn't the only problem my staff identified. They located over a half dozen instances which call into question the GAO's skill in arithmetic."

Nick turned to Meg—production of the status report had been her responsibility. She appeared flustered as she scanned the numbers. "That's very hard to believe," Nick stammered.

"I agree. Almost as hard to believe as the pattern they identified. If the mistakes were random, one would expect some tallies to be low, some high. Odd thing was, all of the incorrect tallies identified by my staff were high. All *over*stated improper billings. Do you have an explanation for that, Mr. Ford?"

Nick shook his head.

"Could it be that your have *purposefully* overstated figures, Mr. Ford?"

Nick turned to Chairman Callahan. "I object, strenuously, to the senator assailing my motives."

Senator Whitford leaned into his microphone. "Either your motives or your competence. I can't help assailing one or the other. Need I repeat the question a second time, Mr. Ford?"

"That comment was out of line," Senator Raine objected.

Chairman Callahan ignored the objection. "Mr. Ford, if you will answer the question, we can move on."

"I did *not* purposefully overstate any figures," Nick emphasized each word with a pointed finger.

Senator Whitford seemed to mull the answer over for a moment before proceeding. "You originally made the decision to audit the Yünnan Project?"

"Yes . . . after evidence of billing irregularities was brought to my attention."

"And after you pointed out these billing irregularities to Smith Pettit, they arranged a meeting with you, correct?"

"Yes."

"They admitted to some inadvertent errors, and offered a reasonable settlement, did they not?"

Nick shook his head. "They offered a settlement, but no, it was not reasonable."

"In *your* opinion."

"And that of my staff."

A quick exchange; Nick hadn't faltered. Senator Whitford paused, hands in the position of prayer, elbows on the bench, index fingers supporting his forehead. After a moment he lifted his head. "Subsequently, Smith Pettit raised their settlement offer a number of times, as I understand it, to avoid

the expense and bad publicity that would accompany
an audit and hearing. Is that correct?"

"They raised their settlement offer, that is correct.
I have my own views as to their motivation."

"As I do of yours, Mr. Ford, but let's stick to facts
for the moment. Plenty of time to get to your
motivations. . . . You rejected each offer?"

*My motivations?* Nick took a moment to clear his
mind and concentrate on the question. "Each offer
was inadequate," he said finally.

"Their offer of twenty million dollars was
inadequate?"

"Yes."

"Their offer of twenty-five million dollars was
inadequate?"

"Yes."

"And their offer of *thirty* million dollars, you considered that inadequate as well?" Senator Whitford
asked incredulously.

"I have already presented to this committee evidence—"

"*Yes or no,* Mr. Ford?"

"Yes."

"Smith Pettit's last offer, I believe, was *fifty million
dollars.*" Whitford paused, letting the subcommittee
ponder the figure, then asked, "That's a rather large
sum, wouldn't you say?"

"We have already documented almost thirty million
dollars of improper billing, and—"

Senator Whitford interrupted. "Yes, yes, we've
heard *your* calculations. My turn now. You rejected
the offer, correct?"

"Things have come to my attention, Senator. Revelations of a nature which—"

"Mr. Ford," Senator Whitford thundered. "Answer
the question. You rejected the offer, *correct*?"

"Yes."

"Once again against the advice of Carolyn Reed,
the comptroller general of the GAO . . . is that also
correct?"

"Yes."

"I see. . . . Do you know what the profits of Smith Pettit were last year, Mr. Ford?"

A misleading question. Last year Smith Pettit acquired a French construction company; that had adversely affected profits. The year before, and before that stretching back a decade and more, the picture looked quite a bit rosier. "Somewhere in the neighborhood of eighty million, but last year—"

"Eighty million?" Senator Whitford broke in.

"But that doesn't show the whole—" Nick tried again.

"Mr. Chairman, could you please instruct the witness to answer the question without delving into the irrelevancies he seems to have such a fondness for?"

Chairman Callahan took orders well. "Mr. Ford," he scolded, "please listen to the question and answer succinctly; you'll have the chance to make additional statements later in the hearings."

Nick nodded, unchastened, and Senator Whitford continued.

"Eighty million dollars. And you want Smith Pettit to forfeit what? More than fifty million, evidently. That leaves a profit of, at a maximum, thirty million dollars. Now, thirty million dollars profit probably sounds like a lot of money to most of us, but then again everything is relative. What is or is not a lot of profit depends on the capitalization of Smith Pettit. Do you know what the value of Smith Pettit is, Mr. Ford, the whole company?"

Nick had a rough idea. "Approximately a billion dollars," he guessed.

"At last," Senator Whitford said with mock relief, "a figure you and I can agree on. A billion dollars, a very large concern. Let's lop off a few zeros and turn that into something we can all relate to. A billion-dollar company making a thirty-million-dollar profit would be the same as a, oh, a thousand-dollar company making a thirty-dollar profit. That's something even I can understand." Again, muffled laughs from the audience. "I've got a financial planner, a very good one—someday, believe it or not, I'm going to have to retire." The laughs came stronger this time. "If I invested a thousand dollars in an enterprise which only returned thirty dollars a year, *a three percent return,* what advice do you think my financial planner would give me?"

Nick's jaw muscles tensed. "I wouldn't have any idea."

"I would. He would tell me in no uncertain terms to sell. My God, Treasuries are paying almost seven percent; even U.S. savings bonds are paying four and one half. Don't you think, Mr. Ford, pursuing an award against Smith Pettit which would erase their razor-thin profit margin and push them into the red could drive tens of thousands of Smith Pettit shareholders to reach the same conclusion my financial planner would reach? Could drive them to sell their shares?"

Nick shrugged. "I wouldn't know."

Senator Whitford raised his eyes. "Come now, you're an educated man with an understanding of economics. If the profits go down dramatically, what is the likely result?"

"Some might sell, yes."

"And the share price of Smith Pettit stock? Wouldn't it fall?"

"I suppose there would be downward pressure on the stock, yes."

"In fact, Smith Pettit stock has already fallen significantly, hasn't it?"

"I believe so."

"You believe so?" Senator Whitford snapped. "How about fifteen percent so far this year? What I'm wondering is, was that more or less than you hoped for?"

Nick straightened in his chair, tilted his head slightly. "Excuse me?"

"I said, was that more or less than you hoped for?"

Nick said nothing, confused, and Senator Raine

broke into the discussion. "Mr. Chairman," she said, "I'm having trouble establishing the relevance of the senator's line of questioning."

Senator Whitford feigned bewilderment. "Then let me make myself clear. What have we learned so far today? Mr. Ford has doggedly and irrationally pursued Smith Pettit during this audit. He ignored counsel to withdraw from the audit from both his direct superior and the head of the GAO. He ignored his own writings, wherein he recognizes cost overruns as inherent byproducts of cost-plus contracts. He presents figures to this committee which are universally flawed in a manner prejudicial to Smith Pettit. In direct contravention of his superiors' wishes he rejects all offers of settlement by Smith Pettit, and as a result Smith Pettit's stock price falls precipitously."

"What are you implying, Senator?" Senator Raine asked.

"Not implying, Senator. *Charging.* I *charge* that Mr. Ford rejected *every* attempt by Smith Pettit to reach a reasonable and palatable settlement because he did not *want* a settlement. I *charge* that what he wanted was this hearing . . . a chance to plaster Smith Pettit's name across the headlines, not for the sake of the taxpayers but for his own selfish reasons, reasons that may have included pecuniary gain."

Hands covered microphones as commotion broke out among the senators behind the bench. Camera shutters clicked in rapid succession.

Nick attempted to slow his heart. *Evidence? Of pecuniary gain?* He fought to control his voice without success. "*Senator Whitford,* as a member of the Senate, in this chamber you are immune from the laws of slander and can *suggest* anything you please . . . but if you *ever* repeat those lies outside this chamber, rest assured I will direct my lawyer to institute legal proceedings."

Chairman Callahan pounded his gavel, his face red. "*Mr. Ford,* I will not have you threatening a member of this committee."

Nick had exploded, strategically a blunder, but he couldn't back down now. Besides, he didn't feel in the mood to give quarter, not on this point. "And *I* will not have lies spread unchallenged."

Senator Whitford waved the chairman off. "Mr. Ford, within these chambers our forefathers had the foresight to grant immunity to legislators specifically so we could speak the truth without fear of reprisal. That is what I have always done, and what I will always do. You, sir, *shall not* bully me into doing otherwise."

Senator Raine added her voice to the mix. "Mr. Chairman, I *object*. For the senator to make such an inference, protected by immunity or not, seems to be of the grossest type of negligence. I ask that he produce evidence of his charges or withdraw them."

"If it pleases the members of the committee," Senator Whitford said, "I will be more than glad to do so. Since our last hearing certain abuses . . . alleged abuses . . . of power have come to my attention. They called into question Mr. Ford's findings . . . and his integrity. I've investigated those allegations and am prepared to share my findings."

More shutters clicked in what was now an otherwise silent hearing room. All eyes, including Meg's, bounced between Senator Whitford and Nick, waiting on the senator's next words. They came after a long, pregnant pause.

"Mr. Ford, how much do you make?" Whitford asked.

Thrown off balance, Nick shook his head, as if he didn't understand the question.

"At your job," Senator Whitford explained. "Your salary. How much do you make?"

"Eighty-one thousand dollars a year."

"A very good salary, I think most people would agree. Then again, what does a partner at one of the big accounting firms make?"

"I wouldn't know."

"C'mon, Mr. Ford," Senator Whitford coaxed. "Three hundred thousand, four hundred thousand?"

Nick shrugged. "Some do, I imagine."

"More than some, Mr. Ford, I can assure you. And I can assure you of something else, many of them aren't nearly as smart as you are. That must upset you at times."

"No, sir, it does not."

The senator bobbed his head. "So you say. . . . Are you familiar with a man named Chen Tao-tzi, Mr. Ford?"

*Chen Tao-tzi?* Where had he heard that name? Lowered eyebrows formed a deep cleft above Nick's nose.

"Mr. Ford?"

"The name sounds familiar."

"Familiar? But you simply can't place it, is that correct? Perhaps I can assist your memory. Chen Tao-tzi resides in Hong Kong. I have here a log of Chen Tao-tzi's telephone calls during the last few months. A total of four calls were placed to your number, Mr. Ford. Each call lasted on the average three and one half minutes."

*Chen Tao-tzi. Hong Kong. The informant who'd called periodically.* "Yes, I remember now."

"Suddenly it's all coming back to you, is that right?" Senator Whitford asked sarcastically.

"You jogged my memory, correct."

"Well, now that your memory is *jogged*, perhaps you can tell us in what context you know Chen Tao-tzi."

*What did Chen Tao-tzi have to do with this hearing?* Nick racked his mind for answers but came up empty. Whitford obviously had an ax suspended, ready to fall, but where? When? "He called my office for the first time about two months ago," Nick answered hesitantly, "said he had information on the Yünnan Project audit."

"Information?"

"Yes. Evidence of billing improprieties."

"So?" Senator Whitford said, as if expecting Nick to continue.

"I'm sorry?"

"Chen Tao-tzi called you *four* times. He must have been a wealth of information. Can you tell me what bits of important evidence he has passed on to you?"

Nick paused, trying to guess where Senator Whitford was headed.

"Mr. Ford?" the senator prompted.

"Well, he didn't . . . That is to say, as it turns out . . ."

Nick paused again, and Senator Whitford exploded. "*Mr. Ford,* will you stop hemming and hawing and answer my question? Anyone with the brains of a six-year-old can understand it. The reporter, I'm sure, will be happy to read it back to you as often as you need to hear it."

Senator Raine, obviously having reached her boiling point, cut in heatedly. "The witness has every right to answer in his own way."

Senator Whitford fired back with venom. "The *witness* has an *obligation* to answer. And I will sit here with the committee all day if necessary to get it. *Mr. Ford?*"

Nick had learned his lesson—hesitation created the impression he had something to hide. This time he answered immediately, confidently. "He passed on no information of value."

Senator Whitford leaned forward, his face displaying surprise. "Did I hear you correctly, Mr. Ford? Did you say *none*? You accepted four calls from Chen Tao-tzi and received nothing, no information, in return?"

"That's correct. He promised information but did not deliver."

"So you chatted about your home life, is that it?"

Nick did not dignify the question with an answer, and Senator Whitford moved on: "May I suggest you did in fact have conversations, but the information flowed in the opposite direction—from you to him."

"I don't know what you're talking about."

The senator refitted his glasses and opened a red folder. He lifted a thin stack of papers in the air. "I hold in my hand copies of brokerage confirmations. Trades executed by Chen Tao-tzi through a Hong Kong broker. It seems Mr. Chen sold shares of a particular company short four times in the last two months. Do you know what a short sale is, Mr. Ford?"

Nick bit the bottom of his lip before answering. Wherever this was going, it didn't sound good. "It's in essence a bet that the price of a stock will go down."

"Correct. And what stock do you think was sold short by Mr. Chen?"

Nick shook his head. "I have no idea."

"Would it surprise you to know it was Smith Pettit?"

*Dammit.* Nick's heart jumped; his body tensed. "Yes."

"Four short sales, each within one half hour of speaking to you. How do you explain that, Mr. Ford?"

Nick couldn't keep emotion from his voice. "I can't," he said, rattled.

"Do you have any overseas bank accounts, Mr. Ford?" Senator Whitford asked, buffeting Nick with shotgunned questions.

"No."

"None?"

"No."

"No money in a Caribbean bank?"

"No."

"Then either the record-keeping department of the Royal Bahamian BanCorp is in desperate need of an overhaul, or you've had another memory lapse, because I hold in my hand an account statement in the name of Nicholas Ford of Washington D.C., U.S.A., in the amount of $107,000."

Four photographers had taken up kneeling positions to the front of the bench behind which the senators sat. Nick found himself staring into their camera lenses as the shutters fired nonstop. He said nothing, his mind running in circles.

"Mr. Chairman," Senator Whitford continued after a moment, "I suggest that a fraud has been perpe-

trated upon this committee by Mr. Ford. I suggest that
he contrived to drive down the price of Smith Pettit's
stock, and conspired with Mr. Chen Tao-tzi to profit
as a result by selling Smith's Pettit stock short. I move
that these proceedings be suspended until such time
as Mr. Ford has retained legal counsel, at which time
I will move to drop the investigation against Smith
Pettit and refer Mr. Ford's case to the Justice Department for prosecution."

With a look at Senator Raine, Chairman Callahan
said, "These are serious charges you have raised
against a man with a solid, impeccable record. I hope,
Senator, you are confident of your sources."

"I am. And as I have a number of other questions
I would like to ask Mr. Ford when the hearings resume, I ask a subpoena be prepared to insure his
attendance."

With little of her prior enthusiasm, Senator Raine
objected. "Mr. Chairman, I must confess to being startled by some of the evidence the senator from Alabama has produced, yet I must continue to decry his
theatrics. There is absolutely no reason to subpoena
Mr. Ford. To infer that he might not appear at the
next hearing of his own volition is an unjustified slap
at his long and honorable record as a civil servant."

Senator Whitford tipped his head. "Mr. Chairman,
I believe I have presented sufficient evidence to call
into question Mr. Ford's *honorable* record. However,
I defer to the senator from Maine. If Senator Raine
stands prepared to guarantee Mr. Ford's presence,
then I shall, with some amount of trepidation, I confess, withdraw my request."

"Very well," Chairman Callahan said. "Mr. Ford"—
Nick finally raised his eyes; his mouth hung half
open—"Senator Whitford gave you a good piece of
advice. Find a lawyer, a good one. We'll reconvene in
two weeks."

Nick heard the bang of the gavel, felt Meg's hand
grip his forearm. Then the crowd of reporters closed
around him.

# 28

The receptionist's look—consoling and sympathetic—told Nick everything. Eight-thirty in the morning and the talk had already begun. Probably had been going on nonstop from the night before.

Down the hall Nick could see Judy's head buried in the *Washington Post*. He had seen the articles, knew what she was reading. No time like the present to break the ice. A few yards from her he called out, loud enough for others to hear. "So, Judy, what did you think?"

Startled, she raised her head and hurriedly ditched the paper behind her desk. "Nick, I'm so sorry about . . ."

She couldn't get the words out; Nick helped her. "Thank you, Judy. Really."

"What they're implying, it's terrible. How can they print those lies?"

The question, said with absolute trust, void of suspicion, warmed Nick. He forced a confident smile. "Forget the print media. I'm thinking my future lies in television, what about you?"

After a moment of indecision Judy laughed, a relief for both of them.

"Did you watch?" he asked.

Judy nodded, then growled under her breath, face pulled tight. "That guy was a real bastard."

"Senator Whitford?" Nick asked, as if the name had not been on his lips all morning.

"Yeah." She balled her fists. "I wanted to punch him out."

"Go for the chin—rumor is he's got a glass jaw."

They laughed again, and the tension level retreated further. A few more quips and Nick headed into his office. "Any messages?" he asked, calling back over his shoulder.

"On your desk. Pretty good-sized pile."

Nick didn't plan on returning them anytime soon. "I don't want to be disturbed, okay? If anybody asks, say I'm in a meeting."

He shut the door, and as it closed, so did his charade. He swallowed hard, took a deep breath; his shoulders slumped. He'd get through this somehow.

The pile of messages on his desk was as deep as Judy had indicated. He flipped through them quickly, recognizing most of the names. A couple were friends, calling, he guessed, to offer their support. A couple of reporters' names jumped from the stack—poison; he had learned that much from his eleven years. Their come-on was always the same. "Hey," they'd say, "here's your chance to set the record straight, to get out your side of the story." It always sounded good; the only problem came when you opened the paper a few days later to find the smiling, friendly, just-between-you-and-me reporter had somehow managed to bury a shiv between your shoulder blades. He threw the reporters' messages in the wastebasket without further deliberation.

Nick's eyes drifted up from the messages, unfocused. His heart beat urgently; he rubbed his forehead absently. So much for controlling his emotions and putting yesterday behind him.

Nick had been given copies of the four brokerage slips. They were real. Chen Tao-tzi had sold Smith Pettit stock short four times, just as Senator Whitford had indicated. *Had Nick played the dupe? Had Chen Tao-tzi called Nick under the pretense of informer to take the pulse of the Yünnan Project audit and trade on the results?*

The bank account in the Bahamas, how did that fit into all this? Nick had been shown the account papers. There was no signature on file, but the money was there, and under his name. *Who had deposited it and why?*

Chairman Callahan was right about one thing—he would need a very good lawyer.

And what of the ongoing investigation and the revelations he never got the chance to voice during the hearing? What of Scott?

Nick couldn't think of that now, couldn't deal with it any more than he could yesterday's hearing. He dialed Carolyn's number and learned she was out of the office, then threw himself into a position paper prepared by the Accounting and Information Management Division—a proposal on new accounting standards. Anything to take his mind off the hearing and give him a chance to regain his bearings. Dry and complicated, the paper fit the bill. He pulled a red pen from his desk and began reading, marking comments in the margin as he proceeded. Every few paragraphs his eyes drifted upward and he found himself staring at the wall.

"Nick . . ."

At the whisper, Nick looked up to see Judy, standing half in and half out of his office. Nick rarely if ever had to repeat orders. He had told Judy he didn't want to be disturbed and had meant it.

Judy seemed to read his mind. "Sorry, but Carolyn's secretary just called with a message. Carolyn would like you to meet her at the Dirksen Senate Dining Room for lunch. Twelve sharp."

Another lunch with Carolyn—Nick would have been honored given different circumstances. He nodded in resignation and put down his pen. As hard as he tried, his mind refused to refocus on work.

Nick recognized a few people. Here and there a senator, a cabinet officer, an agency head. The faceless, however, filled the bulk of the dining room: clerks, interns, and staff. Tourists took the remaining seats, easily recognizable by their shorts and I LOVE D.C. handbags.

He had eaten here—the Dirksen Senate Dining Room—before, but not for a number of years. When

he started with the GAO he came regularly for the
cheap, all-you-can-eat lunch buffets, both pluses given
his limited resources at the time. The reason he frequented the restaurant so often, however, had less to
do with the plentiful, inexpensive food than it did the
clientele. For a while he kept a checklist: three weeks
and he had spotted two-thirds of the U.S. Senate. It
had amazed him. Not just that he, Nick Ford, ate in
the company of senators, but that tourists from Ames,
Iowa, did also. All shared the same buffet line, the
same food, the same tables. Of course, after eleven
years the novelty of seeing senators had worn off, but
Nick's pride in a country whose leaders ate side by
side with tourists stood undiminished.

Today, however, Nick wished he was anywhere else
but here. He felt on display. Of all places, why had
Carolyn forced him to come here?

He ordered a glass of iced tea from the waitress, an
older woman who joked easily with him. If she knew
who Nick was, knew the difficulties he was in, she
didn't let on. She had probably worked there for decades, he guessed. Seen senators come and go, Republicans and Democrats, and outlasted all but a handful.

He checked his watch: 12:12. Unusual for Carolyn
to be late.

Nick resumed his sweep of the room. Another thing
he liked about the dining hall, the decor had not
changed. Same red leather chairs, simple white table-
cloths with fresh flowers, and marble colonnades. It
pleased him somehow that current fashions had not
penetrated here.

His eyes swept left, back across the room, and met
those of Carolyn. He found her sporting a forced
smile.

Nick stood as she approached.

"Sorry I'm late," Carolyn said on drawing near.
"Got tied up. Have you been waiting long?"

"Just got here," Nick lied.

Carolyn pointed at the buffet. "Want to jump in
line?"

Nick nodded and let Carolyn lead the way.

The mussels were a specialty, steamed and ladled with butter. The soup was too: navy bean. Nick settled for the two, forgoing the multiple types of vegetables and carved leg of lamb. Carolyn, he noticed on starting back for the table, had settled for even less: the navy bean soup and a roll.

Again at the table, Nick mixed the soup with his spoon absently. "Carolyn," he said finally, "about the hearing—"

Carolyn shook his head. "Not now, Nick. When we're done eating, why don't you escort me to the Capitol? We'll talk about the hearing on the way."

The condemned prisoner eating his last meal—the parallel was too close to miss. Whatever appetite Nick had—little to begin with—deserted him. He continued to play with his soup as Carolyn talked of old times, times, Nick guessed, unlikely to be repeated.

They paid the bill, Carolyn's treat, then started for the basement level. An underground rail line ran between the lower level of the Senate Office Building and the underbelly of the Capitol. Few people utilized the subway; it existed primarily for the convenience of senators.

As they waited for the next set of cars, alone on the clean and well-kept subway platform, Carolyn commented, her voice consoling, "Whitford can be a son of a bitch, can't he?"

An understatement in Nick's estimation. "You don't have to convince me. The whole thing was like a bad dream—the man gutted me in front of a national TV audience and made it look effortless."

Carolyn tugged at her earlobe. "I know. I watched. He's good at it. Been doing it since before you were born."

"Jesus, I'll give him that. The foul-up with the spreadsheets didn't help. All in all, I played the part of the lamb being led to the slaughter well, don't you think?" Nick tried to smile.

Carolyn patted him on the arm. "It's the oldest defense tactic there is: put the witness on trial."

"And that's how we arrive at the truth?"

Carolyn shook her head. "Hearings before the age of TV were bad; with TV they're terrible. There's a new theory on how you win these things—you throw a bomb at the other side. Joe six-pack doesn't understand facts and figures, but he sure as hell knows when someone's made to squirm. That's the way the game is played. Politics, you've heard the word before. And the rules are . . . flexible . . . malleable . . . breakable. Take your pick or select all three."

Nick heard a soft rumble. A line of subway cars soon appeared from a bend down the tracks. The individual cars were small, maybe seven feet square, and sat four. "I'm starting to wonder if there are any rules at all anymore. Whitford ambushed me. The brokerage confirmations, the bank account statements . . . I can't explain those right now, but they're phony, or there's been a mistake, something. I'll get to the bottom of it, Carolyn, but how do I regain my reputation? How do I do that?"

Nick took a step away from the tracks as the cars neared. Research assistant, that had been his first position with the GAO—it didn't sound half bad to him now. The subway cars pulled to a stop. Nick and Carolyn entered the last car, sat on opposing bench seats. The subway door shut a second later, locking them in privacy.

"Nick," Carolyn asked as the subway pulled from the station, "what you just said now, about the confirmations and account statements, I believe you but . . . I've got to ask this, okay? Are you sure you're telling me everything?"

Nick let his head fall back against the glass panel topping his bench seat. "C'mon, Carolyn."

She looked down. "Sorry, but it's part of my job to ask. Phony or not, the evidence Whitford raised is pretty hard to ignore. People are going to want answers."

*Too bad he didn't have any.* "I'm clean, Carolyn. I have nothing to hide."

"You have dirty laundry, you air it now, understand? Now I can help you, later I can't."

"I've always been up-front with you, Carolyn. Always."

Carolyn seemed distracted by the answer; she nodded, face blank. "Okay," she said after a pause. "I believe you, but that doesn't solve our problem."

Nick's eyebrows arched. "Problem?"

Carolyn's eyes stayed down. She paused, then stumbled through an explanation. "Nick, my job, it's not always as unsullied as I wish it was. Politics plays a role. So does public perception."

Nick read between the lines. "What are you saying?"

She refused to meet his stare. "I'm saying I think you have to focus on yourself right now. You can't let work get in the way. There's some explanation for everything that came out at the hearing, and we'll find it, but in the meantime, I think, considering the allegations . . ." Carolyn let the sentence dangle.

"Are you suggesting I step down?"

"No. No. At least not permanently . . . but I am suggesting, for your own good, you think about a leave of absence."

Nick would be lying to himself if he said he hadn't seen this coming, but so early, and from Carolyn? Nick shut his eyes and let his head fall forward. The rhythmic sound of wheels on tracks spurred his thoughts.

Carolyn pleaded with him to understand. "Dammit, Nick, put yourself in my shoes. You've been accused of manipulating an investigation for personal gain. Evidence has been produced supporting the allegations. What would you like me to do? Huh? . . . I want you to sit out the next few weeks, until things quiet down. Do it of your own volition. When this all blows over, your position will be waiting for you."

Carolyn paused, giving Nick a chance to comment.

When he let the opportunity pass, she continued. "I know it's not fair. Personally I think it sucks, but it's reality. I've got to do this thing by the book. Allegations have been raised. There is significant evidence as to their veracity. That means either you take my suggestion or . . ." Her voice trailed off.

"Or you'll make it an order?"

Carolyn nodded once, eyes closed. "One way or the other you're going to be relieved from all work, including Smith Pettit. I'd rather the decision came from you."

"Who would take over my work load, take over Smith Pettit?"

"Forget work, Nick. Worry about yourself, understand? Excuse me, but you're in deep, deep shit."

Nick slumped in his seat, deflated. "What the hell happened, Carolyn?" he asked after a few seconds. "What in God's name happened?"

"I'm sorry, Nick. You don't know how sorry I am."

"I'm sorry too." Nick straightened, composed himself. "I'll have my request for a leave of absence on your desk within the hour."

The train began to slow as it approached the station under the Capitol.

"Nick, I told you, I have to do this by the book. I'm going to ask you to go straight home . . . not to return to the office."

*As if he were a criminal? As if he couldn't be trusted?* "That's standing by me?" Nick asked sarcastically.

Shame-faced, Carolyn explained: "You know procedure. I should have had security escort you from your office this morning. I didn't want to do that to you; I hoped to save you the embarrassment. So I asked you out to lunch instead. And as to sticking by you, half the Senate just saw me eating lunch with you. I'm in your corner, and if they didn't know that before, they know it now."

That explained why Carolyn had picked the Senate

Dining Room for lunch—he felt foolish for doubting her. The train pulled to a stop, and Nick stood.

As the door to the car opened, Carolyn said, "I think it's for the best, Nick. I really do." She left the car, faced him from the platform. "You getting out?"

Nick shook his head. "I'll take it back to the Senate Office Building. Catch a cab home from there."

Carolyn smiled thinly. "You can get through this. Just take care of yourself, okay?"

A bell sounded, a signal the train's doors would soon be closing. Voice flat, Nick said, "It seems, Carolyn, someone's already taken care of me."

The car door shut, separating Nick and Carolyn; then the train rumbled slowly from the Capitol station.

## 29

Nick sat on his couch, hunched forward, two hands cupping a tumbler as if it contained a precious fluid he could not trust to the grip of one. Periodically, between sips, he took his eyes from the floor to the ceiling and back again. It was seven p.m. He had arrived home at three-thirty, mixed his first gin and tonic at four, dropped on the couch, and had not moved since except to refill his glass—he'd forgotten how many times.

Reason told Nick he could ill afford such self-destructive behavior, but somehow reason seemed irrelevant. Grief, anger and impotence—the feelings needed to be masked, and alcohol did the job quite well.

He tilted the glass, straining the drink between his teeth.

*The stares, the whispers.* In the rest rooms, the halls, the cafeteria, from secretaries to division heads, Nick imagined the topics were the same: did he do it? Would you have guessed? Even those who had offered a supportive word had entertained uncertainty behind their eyes.

He let his forehead sink to the lip of the tumbler.

On the coffee table in front of him lay a folded copy of the *Washington Post*. Nick's eyes swept the page-eight column, covering the hearing and accusations. Thank God they hadn't included a photo—as it was, he had felt on display coming home, imagining every person he passed had read the article and somehow recognized him.

The sharks would circle soon; blood already stained the water.

Nick looked down and noticed his gin and tonic had disappeared again. He rose to fix himself another.

Three ice cubes, a little tonic, the balance gin; he had dispensed with the lime slices a few drinks ago. He then returned to the couch.

As long as he believed in himself, it didn't matter who condemned him—isn't that what he had always assumed? Now he understood the crushing weight of accusations, of suspicion. And their cost. Who was left to uncover what happened to Scott now?

The doorbell rang, breaking Nick's thoughts; he swung his head in the direction of the front door.

The sound drew instant sweat from his palms as the possibilities flashed through his mind: newspaper reporters, television cameras. How quickly he had fallen to the level of a cornered animal cowering in shadows.

The bell rang again, but Nick remained frozen, glass poised halfway to lips. The silence lingered this time. Had whoever rung the doorbell given up? Were they headed for the elevator this very second?

Nick set his drink on the coffee table and hurried, almost frantically, to the peephole in the door and looked out.

*Meg.*

She stood on the other side of the door, her image distorted by the fish-eye lens, the forefinger of one hand poised near the bell.

Nick saw her pause, then turn and start slowly for the elevator. He delayed only a moment longer before pulling the door open. She spun, mouth agape on seeing him, clearly uncertain of what to say or do.

He greeted her, his face a mask concealing all emotion.

Seeing her there, three feet distant, eyes turned to the floor, Nick realized how little he had left. Family gone, Scott gone, and his job—the sense of himself he had grasped fiercely and built a life upon—now gone as well. And Meg? It was too late to pull her to him; he had already pushed her away.

And yet she stood at the entrance to his apartment. *Why?*

Nick moved from the doorway. "Come in."

Meg entered uneasily, shuffling to the center of the living room. After Nick pushed the door shut, she said hesitantly, "I stopped by your office earlier . . . you were already gone."

He nodded. "A leave of absence. Carolyn thought it might be in my best interests. The GAO will make an announcement tomorrow." How easy to say, so much harder to accept.

"I . . . I'm sorry."

"Me too." He forced a smile. "Can I get you a drink?" He gestured toward the coffee table, to the drink he had set there. "I've already helped myself," he said, as if that wasn't obvious from his slurred speech.

Meg shook her head. "No, I just came to . . . After yesterday, I wanted to apologize."

"For what?"

"The spreadsheets," she said.

He had his answer—guilt had brought her to his door. Or was that only part of it?

"They were my responsibility," Meg continued. "And Senator Whitford was right; the tallies were off. All in one direction, just as he said. I don't—don't know how it happened."

Nick sank to the couch. He took a long drink, then said, "I'm not sitting at home with a drink in my hand because of inaccuracies in a spreadsheet. You heard the charges, the evidence."

Meg began to pace the room. "But I . . . Whitford, the committee, they attacked you over those spread-sheets, and it wasn't your fault. You placed me in charge of producing them. *I was in charge.*"

"Meg . . ." He intended to tell her what was done was done, to forget about it, but realized suddenly she needed to accept responsibility. He let her. "Okay, something got screwed up and you were in charge . . . welcome to the GAO. Now, what are you going to do about it?"

"I don't know . . ."

"If I was still your acting boss, I'd tell you 'I don't know' doesn't cut it."

Meg's fist pounded an imaginary lectern. "I spent most of last night at the office trying to figure out what could have happened; I still don't have an explanation. It just doesn't make any sense. The numbers shouldn't have been off."

"Go through the old drafts," Nick suggested calmly, "retrace your steps, check the backup copies on your computer, on your secretary's computer. You'll find the answer. I have faith in you."

She raised her eyes quizzically, as if startled to hear him say so. Did she blush then, or was he imagining things? "I'll try," she said.

"Good." Nick lifted his drink, downed it in three large gulps. "Now, if you'll excuse me, time for another fill-up." He moved to the kitchen counter.

"Are you all right, Nick?"

"I'm absolutely great. Why do you ask?"

He turned to find her biting her lip. "Sorry," he said. "I didn't mean to . . . I'm doing okay." He held up his glass. "Sure you don't want one . . . only you can keep me from drinking alone. I've got wine, if you'd like."

Meg nodded. "All right."

"Chardonnay?"

"Fine."

He poured the drinks, handed Meg hers, and indicated a chair. "Just throw the laundry on the carpet. . . . I'll get to it sooner or later."

She folded the two shirts that lay on the chair and set them in a neat pile on a side table, then spent the next few moments staring at her drink in silence. Nick finally spoke: "I didn't do it, Meg. In case you're wondering. None of it."

"You didn't have to tell me that."

"No, but I guess I wanted to." Nick poked the ice cubes floating in his drink. "There must be talk. At the office. And I . . . I just wanted you to know."

Meg set her wineglass on the table and leaned

toward him. "Nick, the charges, now that you've brought them up. The bank in the Bahamas, the account in your name. That didn't just happen; it wasn't just a clerical mistake. Someone opened that account to discredit you. I have to believe that."

Nick held his head in his hand. "Possible."

"More than possible. Remember the other day I asked you if we might be in some danger . . . with what happened to Scott, to McKenzie. What if I was right? What if someone wanted you off the Yünnan Project audit just like they wanted Scott off? Well, now they've gotten their wish, haven't they? It wasn't murder, but every bit as effective—someone neutralized you before you could place what you'd learned into evidence before the Senate committee."

Nick had discounted Meg's fears before; no longer. He paused, considering her words. "Let's say you're right," he said finally. "What can I do about it? I've got a lawyer—a good lawyer. Beyond that, I have to trust the authorities. The truth *will* come out . . . I believe that."

"Dennis *is* the authority in this case, Nick. You can't leave it to him. You've got to do . . . something . . . I don't know what. But if you sit in your apartment and don't try—"

"What the hell do you want me to do?" Nick exploded, and then, on seeing Meg's face fall, lowered his voice. "Hey, I apologize. Really. I know you were trying to help, it's just . . . I guess I have a long history of running from my problems; maybe that's the way I like it. . . . Don't worry, everything's going to work out."

Meg shook her head almost imperceptibly. "I hope so." She took a drink of wine, then ran the tip of her index finger back and forth along its rim. "Nick, I know we've had our . . . some friction," she said quietly, "but if I can help, in any way, any way whatsoever, let me know, okay?"

*Friction?* That's how she interpreted his cold shoulder? Nick's heart flipped. "My turn to apologize, okay? If I've been a bit cold since Scott . . . since he died, well . . . it's not your fault. It has nothing to do with you. It's me. It's the way I am. It's . . ." He felt water build in his eyes and wiped them uselessly. He looked away, embarrassed.

"Nick?" Meg whispered softly.

He stood and walked to the window. With his back to her, he drew his sleeve across his face. "Sorry, I don't usually do that kind of thing. Too much to drink, I guess." His head spun—the gin, Scott, Whitford, Meg, so many things. He shut his eyes and let his forehead rest against the glass of the window; it felt cool, comforting.

A hand touched his shoulder lightly. Meg had followed him to the window.

A single tear started down his face, and this time he didn't stop it. He kept his eyes shut, swallowed hard, and opened his mouth. The words came slowly.

"You started to ask me once why I missed Scott's funeral."

"I heard you had car trouble."

"That's what I told people, but the truth is I . . . I just couldn't."

"I think I understand," Meg whispered.

Nick shook his head. "No. No, you don't." He took a deep breath, forcing himself onward. "When I was eight," he said, barely audible, "my parents jumped in the car to go to the grocery store."

He saw himself on the pier again, his mom telling him to put down the fishing pole and come along. "They wanted me to come with them, but I wouldn't. I told them I wanted to fish; I told them I was old enough to stay home alone. They left without me."

Nick paused, collecting himself. "They said they'd only be gone a few minutes. A half hour went by, then an hour. Then a squad car pulled into the driveway." Meg's hand tightened on his shoulder.

Nick heard the sheriff's words again: matter-of-fact, as if to say, "This is life, kid, get used to it." "A tourist ran a stop sign," Nick continued. "Broadsided them. They died instantly, the sheriff said."

Meg stroked his shoulder. "I'm so sorry, Nick." Her voice trembled with emotion.

Nick nodded. It took a moment before he could go on. "I stayed at a neighbor's for the night; the next day my aunt arrived. I didn't have any brothers, sisters, grandparents, just her. She lived out East—I hardly knew her."

More pictures came to him. His aunt standing in the doorway. She had checked his tie, his suit coat, his shoes. "We'll leave for the funeral in a half hour," she had said. "I'll call you." And she had. From the bottom of the stairs. "It's time to say good-bye," she had called.

Good-bye? To his parents? He was eight, and was being asked to say good-bye to the two people who had been his whole life?

"The funeral was that weekend," Nick went on. "I was to drive with my aunt . . . to be pitied and plucked at by people I hardly knew. But when my aunt came to my room to get me, I was gone. I had hid. Maybe I couldn't stand the thought of seeing my parents go into the ground. Maybe not seeing it made it less final. Maybe I was just scared. Or maybe I felt guilty. If I had gone with them to the store, hadn't argued . . . Who knows? . . . No one knew where I was. My aunt, understandably, became frantic. She called the police, neighbors. They didn't find me until that night, after the funeral."

His aunt's face filled his mind now; she had pulled back the sheet in the far corner of his parents' closet and found him. Curled in a ball. Wrapped in the smells of his mother and father.

Nick rubbed the heels of his hands deep into his eye sockets. "It all came back to me before Scott's funeral," he said, "as if it had happened all over. Down to the guilt: if I had taken Scott's call, if he had had a chance to fill me in on his investigation . . . And so I hid. Like an eight-year-old. Like a child."

"It wasn't your fault," Meg whispered.

Nick lifted his head from the window, turned toward Meg. Her face was streaked; her hand covered her mouth.

"If I acted strange, it was just that everyone I've ever been close to . . ." Nick's voice faded to nothing.

"I'm so, so sorry, Nick," Meg said. "So sorry."

Nick nodded, all at once embarrassed at his tears, his show of emotion. He pulled himself upright, took a deep breath, and escaped to the security of his drink. He finished it quickly and started to the counter for another.

*Why was he wallowing in things almost three decades old? His problem wasn't in the past; it had to do with allegations made only the day before. Why wasn't he dealing with the present?* Maybe, he realized, because the present had just blown up in his face. The wall behind which he had shielded himself had crumbled, and the memories had come crashing forward.

Nick returned to the couch, and Meg sat beside him. "Would you tell me about your parents, Nick?" she asked.

He leaned back, closed his eyes, and did, beginning with the physical descriptions ingrained in his mind by the photo he carried in his pocket. Then the memories started, each one calling to mind another, and then another. Their games of charades; the long walks; the bonfires; the canoe that flipped, sending them all into the water.

Nick laughed. For the first time he could remember, he thought of his parents and laughed. His father's face, so stern when the canoe went over. Then came his mother's smirk, the break in his father's glare, and soon all of them were howling.

"Every snowfall, if it was good packing, my dad and I would make a snowman. Mom would come out with a scarf and something for its eyes and nose. We'd ambush her. Pelt her, softly, with a couple of snowballs. She'd laugh and fire back. . . . Funny, how much I liked winters then. My hands would get so cold I had to run them under warm water to regain their feeling, but I never minded somehow. A dumb thing to think of, I suppose. . . . I remember once . . ."

Sometime before eleven Nick finished one story and never started another. He drifted off to sleep, carried by a dozen stiff drinks. The next morning, late, he woke to find himself alone, covered with the quilt off his bed. On the coffee table, he discovered a short note: "I let myself out. Meg."

# 30

"Beautiful," Senator Whitford said, a whiskey and water in hand, eyes tracing the snow-capped mountain peaks in front of him. He stood on a balcony of rough-hewn white pine, connected to an eight-thousand-square-foot lodge of the same construction. "You know I hate to disparage the South in any manner, but this surely puts my place in the Smokies to shame."

J. T. Frasier nodded as he swished the ice and scotch in his glass, then took a gulp. He set one hand on the balcony's railing. "I fell in love with Aspen out of high school. Spent one winter here before college, skiing during the day, waiting tables at night. I almost stayed and joined the ranks of the ski bums . . . but Dad wouldn't have it. It was back to good old Virginia. I swore I'd come back someday."

"I'd say you have done so in style, sir."

Frasier took another drink. "My daughter says I'm just one more capitalist carving up the landscape, trying to get close to what he loves and ruining it by squeezing too tight."

"She ever use this place?"

Frasier smiled. "All the time."

Senator Whitford nodded, as if sharing a private joke. "You get assigned the guilt; she takes victimhood *and* the hot tub, huh? Well, I wouldn't worry too much. I'd say Aspen's a long way from being ruined." Senator Whitford stared again at the mountains, then turned the discussion back to business. "We've set the date for the next hearing, two weeks from Thursday. All parties will agree to the settlement—that'll put the investigation to bed. For good."

Frasier set down his now empty drink and nervously

rubbed his hands together. "I hope to God you're right."

"You know what we did to Ford. He's out of the picture for good, and without him the GAO will sign off, guaranteed. No other agencies are investigating. We've got nothing but clear sailing ahead."

"You're sure Smith Pettit's on board?"

Senator Whitford nodded. "They were caught skimming from the public trough, and they know it. The settlement's going to cost them a few dollars, but things have been made clear to them: they'll more than make up the loss in future government business. Their board of directors will rubber-stamp the settlement agreement, don't worry."

Frasier looked down at his drink, then slowly nodded. "I just want it to be over. I want everything to go back the way it was. . . . I want to be able to sleep again at night."

Senator Whitford clapped a hand over Frasier's shoulder. "J.T., I've never lost a night of sleep in my life. You just get your mind right, and everything's going to work out. The GAO will pack up its calculators and go home, wait and see. It *is* over."

Frasier, tight-lipped, nodded again. "Want another drink?"

Senator Whitford shook his head. "Seventy-eight years of living takes one holy toll on a bladder. Believe me, it is *not* something to look forward to. If I don't want to start wearing goddamn diapers, I make sure to quit at two."

Frasier shrugged indifferently. He filled his glass from a bottle of scotch set on the bar built into the back corner of the balcony. "I haven't drunk so much since college."

"Well, just watch yourself. It is not the time to do something stupid. Joshua blew his trumpet, and our walls *did not* come tumbling down. Now, join me in a toast to that." Senator Whitford raised what little remained of his drink.

J. T. Frasier smirked. A good portion of his new

glass of scotch disappeared with the toast. He returned to the balcony's railing, again taking in the vista. "Can I tell you a secret?"

Senator Whitford joined him by the railing. "I'd be honored."

"This is a beautiful house, with one of the best views in the valley. I got exactly what I wished for years ago, but if you want to know the truth, I had a hell of a lot more fun out here when I was waiting tables, living with three other guys in a one-bedroom apartment."

Senator Whitford nodded. "Anytime you want to sign over the deed, you let me know."

Frasier took another drink of scotch without comment.

# 31

Pedestrians coursed below. All with someplace to go, all with some purpose. Nick watched them for a few moments, then lowered and latched the window, shutting out all evidence of activity.

He turned back to the television, to a mind-numbing daytime talk show designed, like its many brethren, to make its viewers feel better about themselves by parading an endless stream of troubled souls across the screen. A symptom of modern culture, Nick supposed, to establish one's own worth not by deeds or actions, but by pointing fingers at others, as fingers were now being pointed at him.

Nick's eleven years of accomplishments with the GAO had earned him scant public recognition, just a quiet respect from peers—all he had ever desired. But a hint of scandal and suddenly scores of reporters clamored for an interview. Overnight he had become newsworthy. No longer a person but a story, to be shaped and molded to fit the appetite of the audience.

His lawyer had been unequivocal in his advice: say nothing, keep out of sight, let the media circus wear itself out. Then you'll be able to fight this thing on the basis of facts, not sentiment. And so, for nearly a week now, as the half dozen reporters camped out on his doorstep shrank to three, then one, then finally none, Nick had secreted himself in his apartment—a self-imposed incarceration.

To Nick's side, the phone rang.

He barely stirred at the sound, just a slight twist of the neck; he had weaned himself from answering after a half dozen earlier bothersome exchanges. His answering machine now screened the calls. He returned only a small fraction, to his lawyer, of course, his secretary, Judy, a few friends, and the single call from Carolyn.

Carolyn had inquired after him politely, even warmly, but had made things clear. "I can't tell you anything," she had said. "Not about the investigation, not who's running it, nothing. I'm sorry, but I'm in a difficult position here. You have to understand that."

Meg had called as well. It had been late, after nine, and her voice had reverberated through his apartment. "Hi," she had started, sounding uncertain. "This is Meg. . . . Just wanted to see how you were doing. . . . I don't know if you're around, but I wondered . . . do you want to meet somewhere maybe? Catch a coffee or something. . . . Tonight or some other time. Just call. I . . . Give me a call, huh?"

He hadn't. Not by design, not because he didn't want to—he did, more than he wished to admit—not for reasons he could fully understand. Hours had passed as he looked at the phone, and with their passing, calling Meg became that much harder, made it all the more certain he wouldn't. Then it was the next day, and then the day after.

He was lying to himself if he thought time could make Meg's call go away. It wouldn't. The call was a reality, and so was Meg—both weighed on his mind now more than ever—but what did he have to offer her now?

The phone rang a third time and pulled Nick from his thoughts.

On the fourth ring his answering machine clicked on. "This is Nick Ford," the machine dutifully reported. "I can't come to the phone right now, but if you'll leave a message, I'll get back to you as soon as I can."

A voice came over the machine's speaker: "Nick, it's Harry, at the *Sentinel*."

Harry Sanders. A junior editor at the *Washington Sentinel*. Nick and Scott had dealt with Harry frequently in the past, and never had a reason to regret doing so. A good source, Harry was not only professional, he knew when not to be.

"Give me a call," Harry continued. "I want to give you a heads-up on something. I'll be at the office until six toni—"

*A heads up?* Nick made an instant decision: he'd take a chance that Harry's offer of a heads-up was more than a simple come-on. He grabbed for the phone. "Harry."

Harry did not seem shocked to hear Nick's voice. "Screening your calls, Nick?" he commented.

"Surprised?"

"Given the circumstances, no, I guess not."

"You said something about a heads-up," Nick pressed, short-circuiting the inevitable expression of sympathy.

"Right. This Sunday's edition. National section, front page. Three columns, starting above the fold."

"On me?" Nick asked, already knowing the answer.

"Afraid so. It's part one of a series on bureaucratic corruption." Harry's voice drifted away.

Nick exhaled loudly. "How bad is it going to be?"

"Bad. I've seen a draft. Story goes out of its way to crucify you . . . does a fairly good job of it too."

Nick swore to himself. "Anything I can do?"

"Not really, unless . . .." The phone line went silent.

"I'm listening," Nick urged.

"Nick, there's got to be more to your story. I know you're leery of the press, but . . . Look, if you want a chance to tell your side, explain the bank account, put a different spin on things, there might still be time for a rewrite. I can promise you even-handed treatment."

Nick trusted Harry to keep his word, but that didn't change the facts: there was no story to tell. It was all some sort of terrible screw-up—that's all—and Nick told Harry as much.

"If that's the way you want to leave things," Harry responded, clearly skeptical. "I just thought . . . Hey, we let it go at that, then. I've done my duty, now how are you doing? Hanging in there?"

"Never better," Nick responded sarcastically before softening his voice. "Thanks for calling, Harry. Letting me know what's coming. Really."

"No problem. You take care."

"I'll try. Bye, Harry."

"Oh, Nick?"

Nick returned the phone's receiver to his ear. "Yeah?"

"Almost forgot. I wanted to ask you about that murder a few months ago. The Chinese woman. Anything ever come of that?"

*Murder?* Nick had no idea what Harry was referring to.

"You know, the woman found in the dumpster," Harry added.

"Doesn't ring a bell, Harry."

"Your boss . . . what's his name?"

"Dennis Lindsay?"

"Right, Lindsay. Hasn't he called you about it?"

At the mention of Dennis, Nick sank to the couch, instantly suspicious. "No. No he hasn't. Why should he?"

"Hold on a moment, let's see if I can find it." Nick heard a shuffling of papers, then Harry's voice returned. "Yeah, here it is. I called Lindsay, faxed him a copy on . . . Monday, I think. It's an article from our paper dated . . . let's see, about three months ago. I'll read it to you." Harry cleared his throat and began. 'Last night sanitation workers discovered the body of Suyuan Chunnu, nineteen, in a trash dumpster in an alley off Woodruff Avenue. The deceased had been severely beaten, her hands mutilated. Cause of death has not yet been determined by the coroner. The police are investigating.' "

Harry paused. "Lindsay didn't call you on this?"

*Mutilated hands?* "No," Nick confirmed a second time.

"Thought he would have by now. I didn't call you

directly because . . . Well, I knew you had a lot on your mind."

"The article said the woman's hands were mutilated?"

"Right. Our report on Scott's death used almost identical language. The cops asked us to avoid specifics. You know how they worry about copycats, weeding out false confessions. Anyway, one of our copy editors remembered the article about the woman in the dumpster and commented on the similarity. So I dug the article out. Thought you guys might be interested."

"I am," Nick said, then added quickly, "You know any of the details?"

"You mean her hands? Yeah, I know the details. Both of the woman's forefingers were shot off, Nick. Right above the first knuckle."

*Shot off, right above the first knuckle, just like Scott's.* Nick's stomach tightened.

"I passed the information on to Lindsay," Harry went on. "Thought he might want to look into it . . . see if it was more than a coincidence. I figured he'd talk to you about it. Maybe Scott had met this woman before, maybe . . . I don't know, I just thought it was worth checking."

*Two index fingers shot off.*

"Nick?"

"Yeah, I'm here." He closed his eyes for a moment. "Do you know any other details? Where the woman lived, worked, leads, things like that?" He reached for a pencil as Harry answered.

"All I know is what's in the file in front of me. Hold on a second while I . . . Yeah, here are the pleasant facts. The woman had been beaten. There was evidence of sexual activity, vaginal and anal. A fair amount of trauma, not your *Joy of Sex* kind of stuff. Death was from strangulation. Coroner's not sure what caliber of gun was used to blow off her fingers, but did determine she was alive when it happened. The woman, Suyuan Chunnu"—Harry spelled the name—"was born in China. As near as anyone can tell, she entered the country eight months ago, illegally. No family here."

Nick jotted notes on the margin of an old newspaper. "You have a home address?" Nick asked.

The line went silent; Nick heard more shuffling of paper. "No, just work. Evidently some sort of sweatshop. You know how it goes, Nick. An illegal comes to the country, gets roped into one of these shops, and that's it . . . they're little better than an indentured servant. And if they complain to the authorities they risk deportation, so most keep their mouth shut. It's pretty grim for most of them."

"What's the address?"

Harry read it off. "Of course, it might be shut down by now. Then again, I don't know if cracking down on sweatshops is high on the cops' priority list these days, not with this city's problems."

Nick wrote the address, then asked, "Anything else?"

"Nope. Now you know as much as I do." Harry's voice turned tentative: "Nick, if you do . . . at some later date . . . decide to give your side of the story . . ."

Nick understood Harry's drift immediately. "If I talk to anybody, I talk to you first. Okay? But let me repeat, I don't have anything to tell. That's the truth."

"Sure, Nick. Sure."

Nick shook his head. "Bye, Harry. And thanks again."

Nick dropped the receiver to its base, then paced the room.

*Fingers shot off, just like Scott's. The murdered woman, Suyuan Chunnu, Chinese. Could this all have something to do with the Yünnan Project audit, as Meg theorized?*

Nick recalled Harry's surprise: "Lindsay hasn't called you yet?" Next, Meg's words came to him. Her admonition: "Dennis is the authority in this case, Nick. You can't leave it to him. You've got to do . . . something . . . I don't know what."

Perhaps Meg was right. But if he couldn't leave things to Dennis, couldn't leave things to the GAO, then who could he turn to?

He looked at the coffee table, at the scribbled notes of Harry's call and the address written there, underlined twice, of the sweatshop where Suyuan Chunnu had once worked.

Who could he count on? He resigned himself to the only answer and started for the kitchen and the D.C. street map kept in one of its drawers.

## 32

The street on which Suyuan Chunnu once worked stretched from affluence to despair. Nick followed it the entire range, as neat homes and cafés gave way to rundown apartments and pawnshops. Along with the deteriorating neighborhood the mix of races shifted, from white to Hispanic, black, and Asian.

Counting down the addresses as he drove, Nick found the number he was looking for above the door of what appeared to be an abandoned storehouse. A half block farther, at the first available parking spot, he pulled to the side of the street.

Nick couldn't help but notice that his car stood out from its neighbors, as he himself did on the walk back to the storehouse. Strange and somewhat unnerving to feel suddenly in the minority, to attract stares and wonder what thoughts hid behind them.

Nick peered through the storehouse's dirty windows. He saw old and rusting bits of machinery—fly wheels and fan motors and tangles of insulated electrical wire—but no activity and no lights. Perhaps Harry had been wrong, perhaps the D.C. cops had found time to close this particular sweatshop.

The entrance stood at the storehouse's far corner; Nick tried the door, expecting to find it locked—it wasn't. He hesitated momentarily, then stepped into a hallway; the door creaked closed behind him. From above, somewhere along the flight of stairs before him, came a buzz of activity. Voices, footsteps, machinery, all muted and mixed.

Nick followed the narrow passage upward, taking the stairs worn bare to wood one at a time, cautiously, as latent fears made themselves known. *What was he doing here? Alone? In this neighborhood, in this build-*

*ing? No one knew he had come; no one would know
where to look if he disappeared.*

Nick forced himself on; he'd come too far to turn
around.

One flight and the noise grew louder, more distinct.
Many voices, sharp exchanges. Another flight and
Nick came to a small landing. The voices, the sounds,
came from an opening on its far side marked by an
oscillating fan circulating humid and stuffy air.

Nick hesitated at the side of the fan, seeking clues
to the occupants beyond. Their voices were now dis-
tinguishable, as was the language they spoke—
Chinese.

Nick stepped forward past the fan and into the
opening, his senses instantly immersed in noise and
commotion. He looked upon a large, high-ceilinged
room, its windows painted over in off white. Rows of
fluorescent lights along the ceiling, most burned out
and blackened, lent the room at most a marginal
illumination.

A grid of tables covered the sagging floor, each with
sewing machine and operator. Nick did a quick count.
Three dozen figures, all Asian, bent over the humming
machines: men, women, old, young.

Most of the workers wore dark pants and white
shirts, but here and there a splash of color—red, yellow—appeared on the women. Otherwise no discern-
ible distinction existed between the sexes. A real
equal-opportunity position.

The workers chattered among themselves, but their
eyes rarely left their work. Paid on production, Nick
guessed, they concentrated on the job. No one took
notice as he entered the room.

The workers moved quickly, effortlessly, stitching
together precut swatches of denim, then adding pockets, zippers, and belt loops. Minutes, and a new folded
pair of jeans lay on a stack of the same while another
swatch of denim began to take shape. The work went
quickly; still it amazed Nick more of the assembly
wasn't mechanized. Maybe this particular shop was

too small to afford the equipment, or maybe the illegal workers were just too cheap not to take full advantage of.

A few feet from him an older man—he looked mid-sixties, but Nick guessed this type of labor might add a premature stoop and a dozen phantom years—sorted designer labels from a box set on the floor. All counterfeit, Nick assumed, but that would be of little concern to the legions of discounters and street vendors more interested in labels than authenticity.

Nick squatted, balanced on the heels of his shoes, next to the old man. "Excuse me," he said loudly, speaking over the clamor.

Immediately a silence rippled outward; heads turned at his voice. The old man, however, offered Nick only an expressionless glance before continuing his work.

Nick asked if there was someone in charge, someone he could talk to. The man pointed at the entrance. Nick followed the man's line of sight but saw nobody. "Perhaps I can ask you a few questions."

The old man paused in his work, then rose and left for the landing. Unsure whether the man intended to bring help or just escape an annoyance, Nick remained. He reached into the box, selected a leather label—Polo by Ralph Lauren—then left his heels, drawing himself to his full height.

The room had quieted, sewing machines and conversations. Nick scanned left, then right, everywhere met by stares. The old man, he noticed on looking back toward the landing, had disappeared.

Nick spent a moment twirling the leather patch between the forefinger and thumb of his right hand self-consciously. Another few seconds and he decided a more aggressive course of action was called for. He pulled his wallet from his pocket, held it above his head, the GAO identification card hanging free, and announced loudly: "I'm with the General Accounting Office . . . Special Investigations. A woman worked here a few months ago—Suyuan Chunnu. Does anyone remember her?"

No hand shot up, no voice broke the silence. *Had they understood the question?*

Nick stepped into the center of the room and tried again. "Suyuan Chunnu. She was nineteen. I'd like to speak with anyone who remembers her. Anything you tell me will be kept absolutely confidential."

He rotated in place, seeking eye contact with every worker as he repeated Suyuan's name for the third and fourth time. Most regarded him dumbly, but one girl—a bit on the plain side with ungainly hair and thick, dark-rimmed glasses—avoided his eyes. Nick lowered his hand, the one holding the ID and started toward her. A voice to his rear caused him to spin.

"What you want here, mister?"

The speaker was Chinese, short, balding, already red in the face. He struggled with the zipper on his pants as he walked purposefully in Nick's direction. Pulled from the bathroom by the old man, Nick guessed.

If their height disparity—Nick stood a good five inches taller—intimidated the balding man, he didn't show it. A few paces from Nick, he repeated angrily, "What you want here?"

"Who are you?" Nick asked.

"Supervisor. What you want?"

Nick flashed his ID. "A woman worked here. Suyuan Chunnu."

The supervisor's eyebrows bumped up a fraction. "Many women work here."

"I'm only concerned with one—Suyuan Chunnu. She was murdered, about three months ago. You remember her?" he asked.

The man considered for a moment, then shook his head. "No. You go now."

"I know she worked here. I need to ask you some questions. About her. About her death."

Two more men suddenly appeared at the landing. They took up positions on each side of Nick. "You go now," the supervisor yelled again.

"I'm not looking to cause any trouble, I just want to—"

The supervisor reached out and bumped Nick on the upper arm. "You go now, mister."

Nick stood his ground, arms crossed. "When my questions about Suyuan Chunnu are answered, I'll leave," he said coolly, feeling anything but.

The supervisor unloosed a stream of piercing Chinese, and the faces of the two men to Nick's sides turned cold.

Nick peered back over his shoulder, seeking unsuccessfully for the girl in the thick glasses. Only when the two men began to advance did Nick retreat. He sidestepped the supervisor, who proceeded to launch another salvo of what Nick assumed to be obscenities.

Instinct told Nick that to flee in fear would be a mistake, might trigger an assault. Instead, his back to the three men, he descended the stairs slowly, deliberately, as if leaving of his own accord. The supervisor continued to yell but didn't follow.

Not until he stepped out on the street, into the welcoming sunlight, did his heartbeat slow. *Jesus Christ, what the hell had he been thinking?*

Nick took a series of long, deep breaths, then started unsteadily for his car. His hands trembled as he unlocked the driver's door. He'd handled the threat of violence better than he would have imagined, but now, after the threat had passed— He sat in the bucket seat, let his head fall back on the rest, and worked on controlling his breathing.

Nick looked at the storehouse. If he wanted answers out of the supervisor, he'd have to involve the GAO. Of course, then he'd have to admit undertaking an unauthorized investigation—his lawyer would love him for that.

What choice did he have?

Nick thought suddenly of the girl in the thick glasses. She knew Suyuan Chunnu, he'd bet on it. Questioned alone . . .

He checked his watch. Quarter past three. He had

nowhere to go, nothing to do. For a minute he deliberated, and then, mind made up, locked his door and settled back into the seat. He'd wait, at least until dark.

Shortly after five-thirty workers began to file from the storehouse's front door: groups of two and three, and then, finally, the girl in the thick glasses.

She left in the company of an older woman, but after exchanging a few words the two split in different directions. Alone and walking quickly, as if in a hurry to distance herself from the storehouse, the girl passed Nick on the opposite side of the street. At the first intersection she turned right and soon disappeared from view.

Nick started his car, merged into the now heavy rush-hour traffic, and followed. By the time he had negotiated two lanes of traffic and rounded the first corner, the girl had melded into the sidewalk traffic. He cruised slowly in the right lane, searching the passing profiles. After a block he spotted her and pulled to the side of the street some fifty yards farther on at the first empty parking spot. He exited the car and waited.

The girl did not notice Nick at first. When she did, her eyes jumped swiftly from recognition to panic. Nick held up his hands, palms out. "Miss," he said, "if I could just talk to you for a few moments . . ."

The girl glanced over her shoulder nervously.

"Just a few questions," Nick continued, "about Suyuan Chunnu."

"I cannot help you," she said in accented but otherwise perfect English, then sped past him.

Nick matched her pace. "Did you know Suyuan?"

The girl kept her eyes focused forward and charged ahead, but after twenty or thirty yards, when it became apparent that ignoring Nick was not going to make him go away, she stopped abruptly and turned on him. "If someone sees me talking to you . . ."

"Please," Nick pleaded. "It's important."

Her eyes darted back down the street; when they returned to Nick, they showed indecision.

"Please," Nick repeated. "I need your help."

He could almost read the girl's deliberations as she lowered her head and drew her upper lip into her mouth. Finally she said under her breath, "There is a small park, a playground, on Whittier Street and Fourth. Do you know it?"

Nick shook his head. "But I can find it."

"Be there in an hour," she said, then hurried off down the street. Nick made no attempt to follow.


Nick checked his watch: 6:55. Either the girl was running late, or wasn't coming. He scanned the park again: a few mothers with infants, children playing near the swings. No way he could have missed her.

Maybe he should have been less trusting.

He left the bench he'd been sitting on and began a slow lap around the park. Head down, hands folded behind his back, he considered his next move. Instead of alternatives, however, he foresaw only dead ends. He kicked a pebble, watched it hop across the sidewalk and disappear into sparse brown grass.

A voice caused him to raise his head. The girl from the sweatshop stood before him, dressed in jeans and T-shirt. Much prettier somehow than he remembered—more stylish. She'd removed the thick glasses, pulled back her hair, and for the first time Nick took note of the delicate features and clear eyes he so admired in the Chinese, especially among their youth. Girl her age, Nick thought, should be in college, picking among suitors. A few more years in a sweatshop and there might not be many to pick from.

"You came," he said, conceding surprise.

"I was not going to, but . . ." She looked away, clearly ill at ease.

"I'm glad you did. My name's Nick. Nick Ford." Nick paused, hoping the girl might reciprocate. She did not disappoint.

"I am Jing-mei," she said after a moment's hesitation.

Nick pointed down the sidewalk. "Would you like to walk, Jing-mei?"

She shrugged and fell in step beside him.

"You knew Suyuan Chunnu?" Nick asked after a few seconds of silence.

Jing-mei cast her eyes to the sidewalk. "Why do you wish to know about Suyuan?"

"You know she was murdered?"

Jing-mei nodded solemnly.

"It's possible whoever murdered Suyuan murdered a friend of mine."

She turned her head, appraised him, then continued on in silence. Finally, she acknowledged, "We came across together."

"Came across?"

"From China," Jing-mei explained, "on a freighter."

*A freighter? Not a passenger ship.* "How long ago was that?"

"Eight months."

Eyebrows raised, Nick said, "You speak excellent English after only eight months."

Jing-mei's eyes flared, showed their first sign of life. "I have studied English since I was a small child. Because I work in . . . in that place . . . you assume I am uneducated."

Nick regretted his choice of words. He assured Jing-mei that he had meant no insult, but she seemed unwilling to easily forgive. "Many of the people I work with have been to universities," she said. "One is a doctor, one an engineer. Does that surprise you?"

A doctor sewing together blue jeans in a sweatshop? Yeah, that surprised him, and he admitted as much. Jing-mei seemed to appreciate the truthful response. "Intelligence and individual ability are valued in America, therefore the intelligent and able come. They understand there will be sacrifices, but also understand the rewards of freedom—for them and their children."

"Is that why you came?" Nick asked.

Jing-mei nodded. "Yes. To fulfill my dreams . . . And my father's."

Nick sensed Jing-mei wished to elaborate and allowed her time to do so. They walked on without speaking, Nick focused on the skyline: peaked roofs of row houses etched against a steadily darkening sky. He liked this girl, he decided.

Eventually, Jing-mei said, "You know of the Cultural Revolution?"

Nick nodded.

"My father was a junior professor in Beijing when Mao called for the purge of 'counterrevolutionaries.' The counterrevolutionaries Mao had in mind were the educated: professionals, intellectuals. That was in 1966. The Red Guard—children, really, many of my father's students among them—closed the university where he taught. They sent him first to a reeducation camp, then to the countryside where his talents as a poet were put to use cleaning pigsties. He was lucky, I guess. They shot many of his fellow teachers.

"Years later, he married. I was born to him late in life. By that time the excesses of the revolution had been halted, but not corrected—the universities had never reopened to him. He farmed ten acres, made a modest living, enough to keep us fed and under shelter. My education he undertook himself. He taught me English, philosophy, mathematics. You must be prepared, my child, he used to say, for the day when the people shed their oppressors." Her hand stole quickly to the corner of her eye, dabbed, and returned.

Nick studied the girl's face, transformed by passion, jaw forward, teeth clenched. Society had crippled her childhood; fate had crippled his own. Which was preferable? At least she had a government to hate, he decided. He had nothing so definitive.

"Evidently, my father grew tired of waiting for the people," Jing-mei went on. "On my last birthday, my eighteenth, he presented me with a great gift—passage to America. I don't know how he raised the money . . . he would not tell me."

"And you are working, making jeans, to repay him?" Nick asked.

She nodded. "Fifteen thousand dollars. For my parents, for most rural Chinese, an incredible sum, a fortune. But I will repay them—fifteen thousand and many times more—in thanks and to send a message."

"A message?"

"In my village, out of sixty or so children, only eighteen were girls. Everyone knew why, but few talked of it." Her voice faltered, and she needed a few seconds before she could continue. "China has a one-child policy, and girls are not prized. A girl is assumed to be a liability, cannot be counted on to support her parents in their old age as a boy can. And so in the countryside many newborn girls are delivered in secret, and die in secret."

Nick bowed his head. "I'm sorry."

"I am too, Mr. Ford. And so I will prove them wrong."

They had circled the park and now passed the swings for a second time. The peals of laughter from the children—girls and boys—underlined Jing-mei's account. Nick directed the discussion back to his investigation. "You say you arrived by freighter," he said. "I'm assuming you were smuggled into the U.S. illegally."

Jing-mei paused, obviously anxious at the question. "Suyuan was a good friend. I want to help, but . . . I cannot, will not, go back there."

"You're not going back," Nick assured her. "Immigration laws don't concern me right now. I'm here to find out who killed Suyuan . . . that's all."

Jing-mei ran her tongue over her lips, then nodded. "It was as you say. I was smuggled into the country. So was Suyuan."

"The freighter you arrived on, do you remember where it docked? What port?"

She shook her head. "No."

"Near D.C.? New York?"

"We spent two weeks locked in the ship's hold. At port, we were loaded in the back of trucks without windows and driven here. I don't know where we docked; I wasn't supposed to."

"What about the name of the ship?"

"That I know. The *Shansi*. It was stamped on a life preserver in the hold." Jing-mei spelled the name, and Nick made a mental note of it.

"And how did you and Suyuan find jobs?"

"The job was part of the contract."

Nick didn't understand, and Jing-mei explained: "The price for entry to America was twenty-five thousand dollars; my father could raise only fifteen. The remaining ten thousand dollars I must work off."

"At the place I visited today?"

Jing-mei shrugged. "That place, another place . . . wherever I am sent. Three years, then I'll have my freedom."

"Three years to work off ten thousand dollars?" Nick snorted. "That's only three thousand and some a year."

"There are quicker ways to work off the money," the girl mumbled. "Luckily I am considered too plain."

It took a few seconds before Nick grasped the girl's meaning. All at once her transformation made sense. The thick glasses, the unstylish haircut—more artifice than nature. "And Suyuan?"

"Suyuan was beautiful."

"She became a prostitute?"

Jing-mei shook her head. "She was asked, but she refused."

"And that's why she was killed?" Nick guessed.

"She refused, now she's dead. The message was clear. We are little more than chattel, Mr. Ford; your laws do not apply to us or shield us."

Nick felt suddenly protective of Jing-mei. "Who was responsible? The supervisor I met?"

Jing-mei tossed her head dismissively. "He is nothing."

"Then who?"

"I don't know," Jing-mei replied, rubbing her hands together nervously. "I don't think I want to know." She looked to her watch then and said, "It's getting late, I must go now."

"A few more questions . . ."

"No. I must go."

Nick pulled a business card from his wallet and gave it to her; she hurriedly stuffed it in her jeans pocket. "And if I need to get in touch with you?" Nick asked.

"Don't," Jing-mei said. "I have told you everything—for Suyuan—that is all I can do." With that she veered from him. "I must go." Half running, half walking, she crossed the street.

Nick almost shouted after her, an offer of help, money, anything she might need, but he didn't, and in less than a minute he lost sight of her. The opportunity had passed.

# 33

Nick heard the fax machine engage and started immediately for his study, where it rested beside the computer. Thin thermal fax paper curled from the machine's top. He straightened it to read the heading on the first page: "Federal Maritime Commission," it said—the fax Nick had been expecting.

The machine idled after spitting out three pages, and Nick ripped the sheets free. The cover page was short, just a quick note from a Federal Maritime Commission member for whom Nick had done a few favors in the past: "Hope this is what you're looking for. Glad to have been of service . . . Wayne." Nick's eyes tracked downward and found exactly what he had been looking for, a copy of the manifest from the *Shansi,* the freighter Jing-mei said she'd been smuggled to America on.

Two columns marked the manifest, the first a list of the *Shansi's* ports of call. Nick ran his finger down the column, searching for any within the United States. He found only three, all at the same place: a shipyard in Norfolk, Virginia. Sliding his finger to the right, he checked the corresponding dates of entry. The first two dates meant nothing to him, the third a great deal. *July 21.*

The date jumped out at him, snapping his spine straight.

The *Shansi* had docked at Norfolk on July 21, the *same day* Scott had been murdered.

Nick sank to a chair. The *same day.* Too much of a coincidence to ignore. His mind connected dots: Suyuan Chunnu and Scott, their hands similarly mutilated; Suyuan and the *Shansi,* the freighter she'd been smug-

gled to America on; and now, completing the circle,
Scott and the *Shansi.*

Nick pulled a road atlas from a shelf above his computer. He knew roughly Norfolk's location, but felt a
need to pinpoint it. He turned to the state map of
Virginia and did. Norfolk lay some one hundred and
eighty miles south and east of D.C., at the base of the
Chesapeake, along the Atlantic coast.

*Along the coast.* Again Nick's mind clicked. Scott
had told Meg his investigations were leading him to
the coast. To Norfolk? Nick wondered. And Carolyn
had said the police believed Scott's body had been
moved. From Norfolk?

Nick folded the fax, marked the Virginia state map
with it, and stuck the road atlas under his arm. Then
he scooped up his car keys and made for the apartment's underground parking structure. He did not
waste time to deliberate the drive south; he just
started. What he expected to discover in Norfolk he
couldn't say. Maybe after seeing the shipyard—the
workers, the ships at dock, the freight—something
would come to him, a hint of what Scott had uncovered. Maybe he'd walk through the gate, talk to a
foreman or a secretary on some pretext, and chance
upon a discovery. Or maybe—more likely—he'd learn
nothing at all. Maybe, in truth, he just needed to see
for himself the place where Scott might have died.

As traffic thinned out of D.C. and interstate turned
to state highway to two-lane rural route, Nick reaped
an unseen benefit of the drive—he began to relax.

As a rule he preferred the clean lines and order of
a city. On those rare occasions when he wanted to
enjoy the country he did so his way: from behind large
picture windows at bed and breakfasts, beach houses,
and resorts, not through a windshield. But just being
out of D.C., away from phones and headlines, was a
release. Taking secondary roads added three-quarters
of an hour to his drive, but he didn't mind. Since the
last Senate hearing he'd barely been able to think, and

enjoyed the luxury of letting his mind wander, as it did now.

The passing countryside—fields of peanuts, tobacco, and cotton bounded by scrub pine and interrupted by the occasional barn or one-story house invariably in need of paint—raced by in hypnotic measure, recalling distant memories. A dark green pickup truck with white-wall tires, jeans rolled above the ankle, roadside vegetable stands.

Nick stopped at a gas station to purchase a more detailed Virginia map, and an old, stooped man in neat overalls cleaned his windshield. *Cleaned his windshield.* My God, when had he last seen a gas station attendant clean anybody's windshield? For that matter, when had he last seen an attendant?

Small towns gave way to urban sprawl as Nick approached, then crossed, the James River into Norfolk. Whatever charms graced the city—few along the path he drove—disappeared entirely as he neared the port area. Even the air smacked faintly of oil.

He stopped by the side of the street and checked his map. He had only to turn right at the next T in the road, pass the U.S. naval base, then start counting down the miles.

He drove on.

Another five minutes and Nick again pulled to the side of the road. To his left, a couple of hundred yards below the rise on which he had parked, stood a square, nondescript warehouse circled by a tall cyclone fence. Fixed to that fence was a weather-beaten sign. Kiajong Shipping, it read.

Tired of sitting, Nick shifted uneasily in the car seat. Two hours and he'd seen nothing. No ship, no workers. The docks and parking lot stood empty, as did the pad on his lap in which he had planned to record observations.

So much for learning anything. Nick checked his watch—it was late, nearing seven.

*Now what, Nick? Now that you've gone off on your wild-goose chase to no end, what next?*

Nick finished his coffee and watched the sun close on the horizon, wondering if Scott had done the same from this spot a few short weeks ago.

*Was it only weeks? It seemed so much longer.*

Nick started his car; he wouldn't drive home, not tonight. He'd take a room in Norfolk and return to the shipyard early the next day. Scott had learned something here, Nick felt certain—perhaps he'd discover what in the morning.

Retracing his drive, Nick sighted the familiar sign of a national hotel chain just past the port area. He checked in. A vending machine in the lobby provided dinner: two granola bars and an apple juice.

Nick retreated to his room, hung his shirt in the closet, and carefully folded his pants over the back of the room's one chair. In the bathroom he followed routine diligently—brushed and flossed his teeth, took a shower, clipped his nails. Anything to prolong activity.

Finished, he sat on the edge of the bathtub, head cupped in hands. Loneliness and sorrow caught him then, for no reason and for so many reasons. He drew air sharply through his nose, teeth clenched tightly.

*He'd be cleared, would get his job back. He'd find the persons responsible for Scott's death. Things would assume their old order; everything would be okay.*

Even as Nick told himself these things, he knew the root cause of his depression lay deeper than the accusations he faced, deeper even than the desire to avenge Scott. It had to do with purpose and meaning. And it had to do with Meg.

Nick made for the other room and the television remote on the table between the twin double beds. He pushed the power button and filled the otherwise darkened room with a bluish glare. Flipping through the channels, he came to a financial network and turned up the volume. Three analysts debated fiscal policy. Nick obliged himself to critique their opinions, sometimes nodding in agreement, other times running

counterarguments through his head. He forced himself
to logic, and if the depression didn't lift as a result, at
least he managed to choke off its worst effects. A
restless sleep eventually found him.

Nick was showered, dressed, and at the front desk
by sunrise. The counter hosted a slot for room keys,
and Nick dropped his through.

At the noise a woman appeared from a back office.
"Thought I heard something out here. You checking
out?"

Nick nodded, and the woman moved to a computer
behind the counter. "Room number, please."

Nick's mind went blank. "Ah . . . Sorry, I can't remember. I just dropped the key through the slot and—"

"Your name, sir?"

"Ford. Nick Ford."

The woman punched in his name. "Here we are,
Room 272." She smiled. "No additional charges, Mr.
Ford. You're all set. Have a nice day."

Nick froze as the woman started for the back office.
Of course she'd be able to pull up the name of a guest
on the computer. Stupid of him not to think of it, but
then he had always left the legwork to others. If Scott
had stayed here, stayed in Norfolk—

"Excuse me," he called, and the woman turned.
Nick reached for his wallet and removed his GAO
identification card. "I'm trying to trace a man's movements. I wonder if you could check your computer and
tell me if he stayed here within the last few months?"

The woman scrutinized Nick's identification, then
shrugged. "Sure," she said, and returned to her computer. "What's the name?"

"Scott Johnson."

The woman typed in Scott's name, then frowned.
"A Thomas Johnson, a Michael Johnson, a Lois Johnson, but no Scott. Sorry. Can I help you with anything else?"

"Maybe." Nick pulled the Norfolk map from his
luggage and spread it out on the reception desk. "How
well do you know your competition?" he asked.

# 34

Shirtsleeves rolled up, frustrated and hot, Nick reentered his car. He reached for the Norfolk map, picked up a pen, and X'ed out the last motel.

He swore silently.

The desk receptionist had been incredibly accurate. With the aid of the yellow pages she had marked sixteen hotels and motels on his map within a five-mile radius of the port, and all turned out to be no more than a block from where she'd indicated. Not that it had done him any good; closing on five hours and he'd learned nothing. He'd worked his way inward, toward the port, crossing off hotels as he went. No one had turned up a guest record of a Scott Johnson.

Compounding his bad luck, twice that morning he had swung by Kiajong Shipping, each time finding the same thing he had found the night before—no activity. The place looked empty.

Nick had three choices now: he could broaden his search of hotels beyond the five-mile radius he had arbitrarily set, he could hang out indefinitely in Norfolk waiting for activity at the shipyard, or he could head home. He leaned toward the last option. If Scott *had* spent the night in Norfolk, by no means a certainty, he would likely have taken a room near the port—a five-mile radius seemed reasonable. As for hanging out in Norfolk, Nick decided his time might be better spent hitting up connections in the FBI and the Commerce Department for a rundown on Kiajong Shipping.

Nick checked the map for bearings. East two blocks to the port road, then north a mile to the highway which would take him back across the James River. He swung out of the hotel's parking lot and a few blocks later into a gas station's. His fuel gauge showed less than an eighth of a tank.

He filled up, bought a soda for the ride home, and asked to use the men's room. The attendant, his biceps marked by barbed-wire tattoos, handed him a key chained to a bulky metal plate.

The men's room met Nick's expectations only because he had had none. The floor had not seen a broom or mop in recent memory; the sink was rust-stained from a constant drip; two dispensers of condoms substituted for a mirror. Nick searched for a relatively clean place to set his soda can, and settled for pinning it under his arm. A row of curled and yellowed business cards was tacked to the wall above the urinal—services that might pique dockworkers' and seamen's interests: nine-hundred phone lines, escort services, and rooming houses.

The last pair of cards caught his eye. *Rooming houses.* Both advertised their vicinity to the port.

The desk clerk had marked neither on Nick's map that morning; not surprising given their rather unique form of advertising. Nick could guess what the rooms were like, just the type of seamy place that might appeal to Scott while playing detective.

Nick zipped his pants and ripped the two cards from the wall. Worth checking out, he decided.

Nick's visit to the first rooming house, as seamy as he imagined, served only to increase his frustration, and he entered the second, the closest to Kiajong Shipping, with lowered expectations. Behind the beaten and peeling counter, a pale bearded man with pronounced hollows under his eyes and a cigarette dangling from his lip greeted him with indifference.

"Hi," Nick said as he approached the desk.

The clerk nodded absently as he extracted the cigarette from his mouth. "Room?"

"No."

The clerk tucked a thumb behind a large silver belt buckle and glowered. "What can I do for you, then?"

"I'm trying to track the movements of a man."

"Good luck." The clerk answered perfunctorily, leaving the "fuck you" unspoken. The cigarette went back into his mouth for a quick puff.

"I think he might have stayed here a couple of weeks ago."

"Was that supposed to be a question, mister?"

Nick nodded. "Yeah, I suppose it was. I was hoping you could check your guest list."

The clerk took a long drag, burning almost a half inch of cigarette to ash as he studied Nick. "Can't do that."

"Why not?"

"My policy is I don't open up my guest registry to every shithole who walks through the door, that's why." The clerk leaned forward over the counter aggressively. "Any other questions?"

Nick pulled out his identification, held it up for the clerk to see. "I'm not just any shithole; I'm a federal shithole. With the General Accounting Office, Office of Special Investigations."

The clerk gave Nick's ID only a passing glance, but it had its effect. The man adopted a less threatening posture, and when he spoke again sounded a bit less sure of himself. "Well, I'm sure your mama must be real proud, but unless there's a warrant in there too, I can't help you."

This wasn't Nick's type of game, but he'd had practice of late and he pressed his advantage. "I'm trying to keep this simple, okay? Save yourself some major headaches and cooperate. I give you the man's name, you check your records. The man didn't stay here, I leave, that simple. His name was Scott Johnson and—"

"Scott Johnson?" the clerk interrupted.

"Yes."

The clerk shook his head, a flat, self-satisfied smile on his face. "So I'm not the first one the fucker stiffed, huh?"

"Excuse me?"

"You're investigating him, right?" The clerk dropped the stub of his cigarette into an empty soda can. "Good. Son of a bitch seemed like a nice enough guy, but those are the ones you have to look out for, aren't they? Do me a favor, mister, nail his ass for me."

Glad to be suddenly on the clerk's good side, but uncertain why, Nick shook his head as if to clear it. "I'm sorry, I'm not following you."

"Scott Johnson. The asshole stiffed me. Checked in, stayed two nights, never came back."

"Mr. . . . ?"

"Schneider."

"You remember him, Mr. Schneider? Scott Johnson?"

"I think I just said I did, didn't I? Dark hair, lanky. A little younger than you. Took me for eight-eighty bucks, or at least tried to. I tend to remember people like that."

*Scott had come to Norfolk! Had investigated Kiajong Shipping!* Nick felt a rush of excitement. "You have an imprint of his credit card?"

Schneider pointed at a sign on the counter that said, NO CREDIT CARDS. "I took it up the ass long enough. You have any idea what Visa, Mastercard were charging me? Three and a half, four percent off the top. I deal only in cash."

More likely the credit card companies didn't deal with Mr. Schneider, Nick guessed. "Then what did you mean by he *tried* to take you for eighty-eight bucks?"

"Someone skips out on me, I don't rely on credit cards or anybody's good nature. And I don't listen to excuses. I lock their things up, tight. Padlock them in my storage room. Amazing how many assholes suddenly discover a few extra bucks in their wallets when that happens."

*Padlock them in a storage room.* "You have some of Mr. Johnson's property?"

"Sure as hell do. Worth a bit more than eighty-eight

bucks too, I'm betting. Not many clothes, but one of those fold up computers—it can't be cheap."

*Scott's laptop.* Nick forced his voice toward calm. "Mr. Schneider, I'd be very interested in taking a look at Scott Johnson's things."

Schneider shrugged. "You pay his bill, and you can take them the hell away with you for all I care."

Nick reached for his wallet, began counting out money. "That was eighty-eight dollars?"

Schneider's eyes betrayed greed as they locked on Nick's fold of bills. "Plus interest."

Nick pulled out another twenty.

"Hell, mister, I could've sold his damn computer for a hell of a lot more than a hundred and eight dollars."

Nick added his last four twenties to the pile, then showed his empty wallet to the clerk.

Satisfied, Schneider scratched his fingers in the air. "The money," he said.

Nick held the stack just beyond Schneider's reach. "After you give me his things."

Schneider nodded eagerly. "You got yourself a deal." With that he disappeared into the back room.

# 35

Nick stared at the computer screen, a pencil locked sidewise in his mouth, his face illuminated dimly. He sat in his GAO office, lights off, door closed; no one had seen him enter other than the night security guard, and Nick intended to keep it that way.

"Tremont Engineering," the screen said, and below that "Password" followed by six spaces. He looked at the scratch pad to his side. Across the top: ANDREW F. MCKENZIE, and below, various anagrams and abbreviations. He removed the pencil from his teeth and scribbled another—ANDYFM—then typed the letters into the computer. He pressed Enter, the screen went momentarily black, then, as had happened at least three dozen times before, "Invalid User ID" flashed on the screen.

Nick threw his pencil across his office. "Dammit," he swore silently to no one.

He turned to the window, looked at the darkening horizon beyond, and saw his own reflection there, a disembodied, frowning face glowing faintly. He closed his eyes and rubbed his temples, frustrated at his lack of progress.

To his side lay a manual, a software user's guide. He tapped a finger against its spine, then with a groan opened it to page one and began to read anew, recommitting himself to making sense of the instructions.

Fifteen pages later, he felt lost and started over, this time underlining sentences in the manual as he went.

A door creaked open behind him, and with it a wedge of light from the hallway swung across his office wall and engulfed him. He swiveled on his chair.

Meg stood there, as surprised to see him as he was her.

"*Meg.*"

"*Nick* . . . Sorry . . ." she stuttered. "I didn't think you would . . . Didn't think anybody would be here." She looked down, red in the face. "I was going to check something. On your computer. I'll . . . Sorry." She looked at him uncertainly.

"Come in." He waved to her, his throat suddenly dry.

She stepped forward hesitantly as he cleared the screen he had been viewing and popped a floppy disk from the computer. "Want to shut the door?" he asked.

Meg did, enveloping herself in near darkness. She reached out and found the light switch.

Unsure of what to say or how to give voice to all he felt, Nick jumped to the obvious question: "How have you been doing?"

"Good." Meg shuffled her feet. "Yourself?"

"Okay. You're here late, for a Sunday. I expected the place to be empty."

Meg smiled flatly. "I sort of thought the same thing." She said it as a question—strictly speaking, Nick shouldn't be in the office and Meg knew it.

"Yeah, well . . ." Nick fidgeted with a tape dispenser instead of finishing the thought. Finally he said, "Meg . . . the message you left me . . . I meant to get back to you."

She looked away. "You've had a lot on your mind. You don't have to explain."

"Actually, I think maybe I do." Nick's right foot began to vibrate, and he pressed it hard to the floor. "Though I'm not sure if I can. I've . . . It meant a lot to me, you coming over the other night. It helped."

Meg raised her eyes to his, still uncertain. "I'm glad."

"I've spent a lifetime facing problems on my own, Meg. Out of necessity. Maybe that's not a very good habit, but it's a habit that dies hard." Nick felt the heat rise in his face and cleared his throat. "You said you wanted to check something?"

Meg nodded. "I'm still trying to run down the cause of the spreadsheet errors."

"This late? On a weekend?"

"My schedule's full up; all I've got is after hours."

Nick indicated a chair, and Meg sat. Now that they'd turned to work, her words seemed to flow easier: "Since you've left, I've tried about everything I could think of. Reviewed old drafts, ran a diagnostic on my computer, but keep coming back to square one: what happened, shouldn't have happened. The spreadsheet tallies automatically—there's no human element involved. And it's not as if the spreadsheet program's new to the market; if it had bugs, people would have discovered them by now. Right?"

Nick bobbed his head. "I would have thought so."

"Me too. So, well . . . I'm just about out of ideas."

"You run a virus scan?" Nick asked.

"A couple of them. Best the GAO has."

"And?"

"Didn't find a thing. So tonight I started sorting through my computer's allocation units, comparing disk space against— Well, it's complicated, but I uncovered a hidden file."

Nick raised his eyebrows. "The cause of the problem?"

"Not exactly, but . . . The file was camouflaged, Nick. Attached to the start-up program. As if someone didn't want it found. It occurred to me that—" Meg paused. "You're going to think I'm crazy."

"Go ahead," he encouraged her.

"Well," she began tentatively, "once we talked about the possibility that somehow someone was keeping a step ahead of our investigation . . . do you remember that?"

Nick nodded. "I remember."

"I'm not saying we were right, but if we were, I might know how they managed it. Let's say someone got access to our computers, hacked into them and planted a file . . . the file I found tonight."

Nick lifted his eyebrows in disbelief. "Why would anybody want to do that?"

"The file I found, it's some sort of user log. It creates a record, a list, of every keystoke, every command, typed into its host computer. Someone with access to the file could learn everything that's been done on that computer. On my computer." Meg evidently read Nick's face because she raised her hands defensively. "Okay, the file *might* simply be a relic from a prior user, *might* serve any number of purposes, but I got a brand-new computer when I joined the GAO, Nick. Where'd this file come from? And like I said, the way the file was hidden . . . it got me to thinking."

Nick shook his head. "C'mon, Meg, no one just hacks into a GAO computer. We've got pretty damn good fire walls here."

"So does the Pentagon and it's been hacked into before." Meg shrugged. "Anyway, it's the only explanation I've come up with for what happened to the spreadsheet."

"So someone hacked into the system and planted the user log on your computer. While they were at it they manually corrupted the spreadsheet. Is that it?"

Meg nodded. "Far-fetched or not, that's the theory. I came to your office to test it. If someone *was* trying to monitor our investigation . . . well, I'm guessing my computer wouldn't have been the only one they paid a visit to."

"You want to check whether I have the same hidden file on my hard drive," Nick guessed.

Meg nodded.

Nick rose and offered his chair to Meg. "Be my guest."

"Thanks." She brushed past him and assumed control of the computer. Her hands, until then folded stiffly before her, came alive over the keyboard. Nick tried to follow her actions and the changing screens, but soon became hopelessly lost.

Three or four minutes passed, then Meg stopped

suddenly and rapped her knuckles against Nick's desk. "Got it," she said triumphantly.

Nick peered over her shoulder, surprised and suddenly anxious. "What?"

"The user log. Same place on your computer, attached to the start-up program."

Nick saw a column of words, letters, and symbols stretching the height of the screen. *Had* someone hacked into his computer after all? "What am I looking at?" he asked.

Meg gestured at the computer monitor. "A record of the commands typed on your computer in inverse chronological order. See, on the top here. That's the last command you input. You closed a screen." Her finger traced down the column. "Before that you had typed Enter, and before that a series of letters: A-N-D-Y-F-M." She looked at Nick inquisitively.

Nick ignored her confusion. "You really think someone has been monitoring our investigation through our computers? Through this hidden file?"

Meg took a deep breath. "I'm not sure. But I checked some other computers on my floor—they don't have the same file. I find that odd, don't you?" Without waiting for Nick to answer, Meg pointed again at the computer monitor. "Nick, the letters you were inputting: M-C-K-E-N-Z. A-F-M-C-K-E. E-I-Z-N-E-K; are they variations on Andrew McKenzie's name . . . the owner of Tremont Engineering?"

"I . . ." Nick paused. "I don't know if I want to get you involved in this."

Meg's frown indicated her disapproval. "If it involves McKenzie, I *want* to be involved. Unless, of course, you think I wouldn't be up to it."

"No. No." Nick shook his head to emphasize the point. "In fact, I could use your help. It's just . . . I'm in pretty deep trouble, Meg. You're better off steering clear."

"I'm not worried. Tell me how I can help." Meg looked up at him, eyes unflinching, and held the stare until he nodded slowly.

"Okay," Nick said. "Those strings of letters, they're my rather inept attempts at breaking a password."

Meg cocked her head and Nick explained. He described his activities of the last few days: the sweat shop, his conversation with Jing-mei, the manifest of the *Shansi* and the resulting trip to Norfolk, Kiajong Shipping, and the rooming house. "I've gone through everything stored on Scott's laptop . . . found nothing of interest. Then I noticed a disk in the floppy drive." He held up the disk he had set next to the computer. "I tried to open it—that's when I hit the roadblock. I got a screen, 'Tremont Engineering' across the top, room for a six-character password below."

Meg said nothing, her eyes wide in rapt attention.

Nick lifted an inch-thick software guide, flashing its cover toward Meg. "I came here for this." He didn't need to expound, Meg would recognize it—software designed to defeat encryption systems and passwords, this particular one the intellectual product of the GAO. "But I can't make heads or tails of it, to be honest." He shrugged. "So I gave up and started punching in guesses. The string of letters you saw, those were variations on McKenzie's name. I tried variations of Tremont Engineering before that. Haven't gotten anywhere."

"I'm trained in that software," Meg said.

He nodded. "I thought you might be."

She held out her hand and he handed her the disk. She inserted it into the floppy disk drive, then rubbed her hands together. "Okay," she said, "let's see if we can crack it."

"Wait a second, Meg . . ."

She raised her eyebrows. "What is it?"

"The user log, can you disable it?"

Meg grinned sheepishly. "Better if someone doesn't have a record of what we're doing right now, huh? . . . Yeah, I can disable it."

Soon Nick was forgotten; the computer held Meg's full attention. He sat behind her, his eyes tracing the gentle curves of her shoulders, idling on her neck.

"I've disabled the user log," Meg announced after five minutes. Success in breaking the password did not come as easily. Another half hour passed and with it Meg's confidence. "Arrgh," she screamed finally, running both hands through her hair.

Nick leaned toward the computer, one hand on the desk, the other on the back of Meg's chair. "No luck?"

"I'm not getting anywhere. Whatever lock-out's installed on this disk, it's real, real good."

"Scott must have got in. How did he manage it?"

Meg shook her head. "I don't know. Maybe he's just a better guesser than you are. If I knew a little more about McKenzie—his birthday, his mom's maiden name, the names of his childhood pets—I'd make a few guesses myself."

"What do you suggest we do?"

Meg shrugged. "The computer lab can crack this. I'm sure of it. I know my way around the basic theories, but they're the experts. If nothing else, they'll have the GAO's mainframe run through the entire universe of possibilities. With a six-character password that could take a while, maybe even a few days, but they'll get it done."

"Days?"

"I don't know what else to suggest, Nick."

Nick looked to the ceiling. "There has to be another answer. If we can figure out how Scott did—" Nick stopped mid-sentence. His face went momentarily blank.

"What is it?" Meg asked.

Nick bit the knuckle of his thumb. "I'm just wondering if . . ." Nick's briefcase leaned against the wall; he grabbed it and popped its snaps, revealing a laptop. He handed it to Meg.

"Scott's?" Meg guessed.

"Yeah. I told you I reviewed its files. What I should have said was I reviewed all the files listed in the directory."

Meg caught his drift. Excitedly, she opened the laptop and started the machine. "The user log?"

Nick nodded. "Let's say you're right: someone *was* monitoring your computer, my computer. Why not Scott's as well? And if the user log is on Scott's computer—"

Meg interrupted, finishing his thought. "It's going to list all the commands Scott inputted. So if he typed the correct password at some point, we'll have a record of it."

Nick nodded again, smiling now. "That's what I was thinking."

Less than a minute elapsed before Meg announced success. "It's here, Nick. The user log. Same place, attached to the start-up program." She pressed a key and displayed the file.

Nick's chest tightened as the screen filled. It produced a strange feeling in him, accessing this last record of Scott's life.

Meg used a pencil to point at the screen. "Okay, going backward. He's powered down his machine. Before that he's scrolling. Probably on some data base. Yeah, see. He's on Internet, using a search engine. Looking for a name: 'J. T. Frasier.'" Meg turned to Nick. "J. T. Frasier. I've never heard of him, have you?"

Nick shook his head, and Meg continued to scroll down. "How about a John Li?" she asked.

"No," Nick confirmed again, making a mental note of both names.

"Well, Scott seemed to want to learn as much as he could about them. He used a number of search engines, Yahoo, Alta Vista, Webcrawler."

Nick said, "Let's focus on the password for now. We'll go back through the commands one by one later on and see how Frasier and Li might fit into this."

Meg scrolled down the page. "Okay, we'll be looking for a series of letters or numbers, no more than six characters long. The floppy disk goes in his A drive, so he'd have had to access his A drive before inputting the password. So look for either the characters or the A-drive command, and—"

"Meg?"

"Huh?"

"Scroll back a bit."

She did.

"There. *Stop*." Nick pointed at the screen, to six capital letters. Y-U-N-N-A-N. They looked at each other. "I should have thought of that," Nick said. "Give it a try."

Meg swiveled from Scott's laptop to Nick's computer. After Password, she punched in six letters: Y-U-N-N-A-N. This time the familiar window, "Invalid User ID." did not flash on the screen. Instead the screen blinked, and a file directory appeared.

They were in.

# 36

Li reached for his phone, annoyed at being disturbed at such a late hour. "What is it?"

The apologetic voice was that of his special assistant. "Sorry to disturb you, Mr. Li. Mr. J. T. Frasier's on the line. He says it's urgent."

"Have him hold," Li said after a moment's pause.

Li hung up the phone and turned back to the brief biography on his desk, skimmed it for a second time. A photo was attached: the chief executive officer of a regional telecommunications firm. A tan, aristocratic man, smug in Li's estimation.

Li's eyes traveled from the photo to the four women standing silently in front of him. Each had much to commend herself—all were young, twenty to twenty-seven, all were beautiful by standards anywhere in the world, and all had excellent references. Li's index finger flanked his nose as he compared and contrasted attributes. He hesitated, then, the decision made, he lowered his finger deliberately twice, pointing out two of the girls to the madame standing by their side.

His choices were opposite extremes. The first girl had blond hair and an athletic build; she looked ripe and eager, with somewhat vacant eyes. The second, the oldest in the group, appeared demure, intelligent, with a certain vulnerability. Both displayed enough class not to be obvious.

The madame smiled, no doubt pleased to be collecting double the fee she expected.

A married man with no record of frequenting prostitutes, Li had no reason to believe either of the two ladies would catch more than the chief executive officer's eye, but as a good host—Li was throwing a party the following night for a small group of Chinese and

American businessmen—he prepared for every possible contingency. Li underlined "moderate to heavy drinker, martinis," on the biography. Enough drinks and even a happily married man's head might be turned by an extraordinary figure.

The chief executive officer's file would go into a wall safe; with luck explicit videos would follow. The women's hotel rooms would feature concealed cameras; the women were experts on positioning their lovemaking for best effect. Li had no immediate plans to use any resulting videos, but the chief executive headed a powerful company, and having hooks in such a person could prove useful. He had collected many such videos over the years, a hidden pile of assets he had withdrawn from only occasionally, but always to good effect.

J. T. Frasier's was there. Li laughed to himself for misjudging the man so badly. Three times he had hired women at least as attractive as these to seduce Frasier, and each time they had failed miserably. A devoted husband, Li had concluded sadly, but chance intervened to prove otherwise. Li had simply been dangling the wrong bait.

He had realized his error a few years back at a party he threw which J. T. Frasier attended. Another of the invitees, a homosexual, had a predilection for young, athletic men; Li had accommodated his tastes by procuring a well-proportioned twenty-year-old for the evening. During the course of the party Li had noticed Frasier's eyes tracking the young man at odd moments. Idle curiosity, Li had wondered, or something more?

Intrigued by the possibilities, Li had pulled the young man aside and amended his orders. Aided by alcohol, the seduction had been accomplished with relative ease. The evening ended with the young man and J. T. Frasier spending a few hours in a hotel room together. Frasier had eagerly submitted to a host of indignities, the young man in Li's employ making good use of the toys and restraints at his disposal. All filmed, most explicitly.

A few days later Frasier had received a copy of the video at his office—special delivery. Li had waited a few days before making contact. How quickly the captain of industry had been reduced to panic. Li had negotiated with a desperate man, and knew things would go as planned.

Fear of ridicule: a powerful man's Achilles' heel.

Li closed the chief executive's file and put him out of mind. There had been dozens like him in the past; there would be dozens more in the future. He looked back at the women. Normally, he would have sampled the talents of the two he selected, but this evening he felt tired, and the waiting call from J. T. Frasier annoyed him. He waved his hand at the madame and she quickly shuttled the women from the room.

Li picked a hand-rolled Corona cigar from a wooden box on his desk. He sliced a neat V in its end, then held a lighter to the tip. He drew the rich smoke into his mouth and let its flavor swirl within, like a fine wine, before exhaling. Only then did he again pick up his phone and press the flashing button on his telephone.

"Mr. Frasier," Li said, "I understand you have something urgent to discuss."

"You kept me waiting for . . . for almost ten minutes," Frasier sputtered.

"And you, Mr. Frasier," Li replied stiffly, "have again chosen to ignore protocol by calling me directly."

"It's an emergency, dammit. We have a problem."

Such a desperate, pleading tone—Li was not used to allying himself with so weak a man. "Correct me if I'm wrong, but I believe you made yourself very clear the last time we spoke: you didn't like the way I solved your problems."

"It's different this time," Frasier explained sheepishly. "There's no other choice. It's Ford; he has a copy of McKenzie's disk . . . Tremont Engineering's financials."

Li stopped rolling the cigar between thumb and forefinger and swore to himself. He now understood Frasier's panic. "How did he get it?" he asked pointedly.

"All I know is he loaded the disk onto his office computer about an hour ago. I don't know where he got it or how he got it."

"Is he alone?"

"I don't know that either, but on a weekend, at this hour, the GAO building should be nearly empty. He hasn't called anyone—the phone line's been clear."

"What has he learned?"

"He's begun to shift through Tremont's financials but . . . I have no idea if he's guessed their significance."

Li set the cigar on the ashtray, pressed his hands together in a praying position, and hung his head in thought. There was enough on that disk to take them all down. What Ford had guessed or hadn't guessed was irrelevant now. He had seen the contents of the disk—that alone sealed his fate. Li intended to say just that when he stopped himself. Better perhaps if he took the opportunity to remind Frasier of his station.

"What," Li asked, "would you have me do?"

"I . . ." Frasier started, then added hurriedly, "He can't be allowed to talk."

"And how would you advise we stop him?"

Frasier paused, then whispered hoarsely, "There's only one way. You know that."

"Are you suggesting what I think, Mr. Frasier?" Silence greeted his question, and Li tried again. "Mr. Frasier?"

"God help me, just do it."

Li picked up the cigar, puffed, and blew the resulting plume of smoke toward the ceiling. "You are at home?"

"Yes."

"Stay by your phone. I'll need updates on Ford's

activities, and perhaps the assistance of those who work with you. And, Mr. Frasier?"

Frasier grunted.

"Remember," Li continued, "what I do, I do at your request. I will, at some time, ask for payment, and that payment will be of my choosing. Is that clear?"

"Just get it done, Li," Frasier said, and with that the line went dead.

Li spent the next ten minutes considering alternatives as, putter in hand, he tapped golf balls at an overturned cup lying on the office carpet.

Wipe your mind of emotion and focus on the objective, he schooled himself. See the ball fall in the hole. Head down, elbows locked, pendulum swing, Li mentally ran down the checklist. Ball after ball rammed home.

It was, as he had learned, all a matter of the setup, then the all-important follow-through.

# 37

"We've got to tell the FBI . . . somebody," Meg said, her face animated. She sat directly to Nick's side behind his office desk.

Nick checked his watch; it was just after four a.m. They'd worked nonstop since nine the night before, but the time had passed quickly, almost unnoticed—both rode a high. Seven hours and the pieces of the puzzle had fallen almost into place. "I'm going to try once more."

He pressed redial. Four rings and an answering machine clicked on. Nick listened to the now familiar recording: "This is Carolyn Reed. Please leave a message at the tone, and I'll get back to you as soon as I'm able." He hung up—he'd left two messages already; a third would serve no purpose.

"She must be out of town," he muttered.

"So what do we do now?" Meg asked.

"I'm not sure," he said, then rose from his chair and stood by the window. He looked out on the dark street below, devoid of all activity. His mind swam with facts, dates, figures. They painted an incredible picture, one he first doubted, then debated, and now accepted.

"Either we wait until business hours and try Carolyn again, or we go straight to the Justice Department. Let's think about it for a while."

Nick continued to stare at the street until he caught Meg's reflection in the window. Beautiful, his first thought. All night long he'd been conscious of her—her smell, her smile, and, the few times they accidentally brushed against each other, her touch.

"How are you doing?" he asked.

She looked up at him, unaware he could see her. "I don't feel tired, if that's what you mean."

"Good—it'll probably be a long day." *And by the end of it would he be vindicated?* "Thanks, Meg, for your help. Without you . . . I'd probably still be sitting in my apartment feeling sorry for myself."

Nick saw Meg smile, then quickly brush her eyes with a hand. Did she care that deeply for him? Did she care as much as he cared for—

Nick stopped in thought as a new reflection appeared above Meg's, standing in the doorway, smiling blackly.

*Dennis.*

Nick spun to face him, his mouth dropping open.

Dennis spoke first, ignoring Meg: "I'm surprised to see you here, Ford. Leave of *absence* usually means just that."

Nick didn't allow Dennis the satisfaction of an excuse; instead he countered, "At four a.m. on a Monday morning, I'm sort of surprised to see you as well."

Dennis shrugged. "You're not the only one with too much work and too little time. Once in a while an early start can't be avoided, though I might want to make it a habit—this morning has already paid an interesting dividend." He walked behind the desk, turned his head to view the computer screen. "What are you two working on?"

Nick looked at Meg. Neither had even considered calling Dennis with their discoveries, but Dennis was now here, and how could they say nothing? To a superior? Dennis would know about everything soon enough; there was no reason to keep him in the dark, not any longer.

Nick and Meg exchanged a quick nod, then Nick turned to Dennis. "I think you better look at this. I've tried Carolyn at home for the last couple of hours, but so far I haven't been able to get her."

Dennis examined the computer screen. "What is it?"

"The financials of Tremont Engineering," Meg said.

"Tremont Engineering? From the Yünnan Project audit? We've already examined their financials."

Nick shook his head. "No. We examined a duplicate set of books. A phony set." Nick pointed at the computer screen. "Now we've got the real thing."

Dennis drummed his fingers on Nick's desk. "Where'd you get them?"

Nick started at the beginning. "I got a call from Harry Sanders. From the *Washington Sentinel*."

"Sanders?" Dennis appeared puzzled for a moment, then nodded thoughtfully. "Right, Sanders. He called me a while ago, something about a tip?"

"A murder with an m.o. similar to Scott's," Nick said.

Dennis snapped his finger. "That was it. Sounded sort of far-fetched, as I recall."

*And you sat on the lead, didn't you, Dennis?* "Well, it wasn't, not as it turned out." As he had to Meg the night before, Nick recounted his activities of the last few days: the sweatshop, Jing-mei, the manifest of the *Shansi* and the resulting trip to Norfolk, Kiajong Shipping, and the rooming house. "I found a disk with Scott's things." Nick pointed at his computer. "That's what was on it."

Nick expected a rise out of Dennis, a lecture about conducting an unauthorized investigation. Instead Dennis seemed oddly unnerved by Nick's news. He wiped the back of his hand across his upper lip. "What have you found?"

"From what we can tell, Tremont Engineering wasn't an ongoing concern. It was a front, a conduit for laundering money for a smuggling operation." Nick paused, letting the bomb shell settle. Dennis's reaction—reserved—was a bit of a disappointment.

"Here," Nick said, "let me show you." He grabbed the mouse and scrolled up the computer screen. Suddenly he stopped and pointed. "Look at this credit, here. On April 3, a three hundred and fifty thousand dollar deposit. Received from Smith Pettit under the subcontract. Okay, if we jump a moment"—Nick opened another file on the disk—"to accounts payable, we see a corresponding series of debits. The same day the money's received, almost all of the money, over ninety percent of it, goes out in wire transfers."

"To pay expenses, I'd assume," Dennis said.

Nick shook his head emphatically. "I don't think so. Three hundred and fifty thousand dollars in expenses? Not payroll but *expenses*? And all paid out on the same day?"

"It's possible. Do you know where the money went?"

Nick played with the computer screen, then pointed. "It's all right here. Fed wire numbers, ABA numbers for the banks."

"You know whose accounts they are?"

"One of them," Nick said.

Dennis's eyes went round. "Whose?"

"Mine."

Dennis drew back, obviously confused, and Nick explained. "Remember the hearing? Whitford's accusations? Allegedly I've been tipping off a Hong Kong businessman, Chen Tao-tzi, telling him to short Smith Pettit stock. Chen supposedly sent a portion of the profits to me. Whitford produced bank records showing the deposits."

Dennis nodded.

Nick shuffled through a pile of papers and held up a bank statement. "Here's a copy of Whitford's evidence. An account in my name down in the Bahamas, with four deposits over the last few months. Take the first, a deposit of $26,000 on June 27." Nick pointed again to the computer screen. "Now look back at Tremont's financials. On *June 27* Tremont wired out *$26,000*. I can trace *each* of the four deposits back to Tremont . . . dates and amounts are identical."

Meg said, "Nick was set up. For months money flowing from Tremont has been used to establish the bogus deposits in his name. An insurance policy, I suppose. Ready to be cashed in if he ever got too close to the truth."

Nick expected Dennis to appear incredulous; instead he seemed shaken by the revelations. "Set up by who?" Dennis asked.

"Meg and I have a few hunches." He told Dennis of finding the hidden file, the user log, on Scott's computer, and Meg's thoughts as to how it got there. "Thanks to the log, we know what Scott was doing before he was murdered. Primarily, researching two people, a J. T. Frasier and a John Li. You ever heard of them?"

Dennis shook his head. "No."

"We did our own research. Wasn't hard to learn something about J. T. Frasier. He's head of A-tek. You've heard of it, I'm sure. Hi-tech company, microprocessors, software. Does a lot of government contracting, especially with the Pentagon. Guts of smart bombs, guidance systems, that sort of thing."

Dennis nodded sourly. "I'm familiar with the company."

"John Li's a different story. We didn't come up with too much on him, just a few quick mentions, but a friend of mine in the State Department was a bit more helpful, once he forgave me for getting him up at one in the morning."

Nick grabbed a fax off his desk. "John Li is a Chinese citizen of mixed Caucasian-Asian blood. He founded a trading company in Hong Kong twenty years ago; it's become very successful. Through numerous subsidiaries Li owns controlling interests in over two dozen companies, most of them involved in shipping . . . the import-export business. One of those companies caught my eye . . . Kiajong Shipping."

Dennis stared at Nick blankly, so Nick explained. "Kiajong Shipping is where the *Shansi* docked," Nick reminded him. "The ship Jing-mei came to America on." Nick again read from the fax. "Now, this is where it gets interesting. Li has brokered numerous deals between American and Chinese businessmen. Word is he has high-placed connections in Polytech, the arms conglomerate controlled by the People's Liberation Army."

"So Scott researched a couple of people, what of it?" Dennis asked sharply.

"Meg and I have a theory. We can't prove it, not yet, but . . . It adds up, Dennis."

"I'm listening."

"Okay, we know Chinese immigrants have been smuggled into this country through Norfolk at the shipyards of Kiajong Shipping. And John Li owns Kiajong Shipping. Therefore I'm guessing John Li's involved in the smuggling. In fact, I'm guessing he's behind it. Now if Li's expertise is moving things in and out of the country, why assume his product is limited to Chinese immigrants? If Li smuggles people, he'll smuggle anything, and I'm guessing he does."

"I'm still missing the significance of all this."

Meg broke in. "Think about it, Dennis. Scott told me he was going to light off fireworks, had uncovered something incredible. Okay, we know he was researching Li and Frasier. Li we're pretty sure is a smuggler, and Frasier, he runs a company which manufactures cutting-edge arms components. Now, what do you think the connection is?"

Dennis shook his head dumbly, leaving Nick to explain. "We think Li smuggles illegal Chinese immigrants into the country, and we think he smuggles hi-tech arms components out. We think he gets those components from J. T. Frasier . . . from A-tek . . . and sells them to China."

Dennis found a seat and sank onto it. "That's quite a leap."

Meg shook her head. "We don't think so. Li has ties to the upper echelon of Polytech and the PLA, remember? This whole thing makes sense."

"Back up a minute." Dennis turned to Nick. "You started off talking about Tremont Engineering's financials. I don't get the connection. How do the financials, the Yünnan Project, fit into all this?"

"Look," Nick said, "if I'm right, the government of China, the PLA, somebody, has to pay off Frasier and Li, right? That's a problem. Wire transfers from China can be a bit incriminating. So they need to launder the money. Send it through a conduit, an ostensibly legitimate business, so it comes out clean. That's what I think they did. Smith Pettit told us they were as good as *ordered* by China to offer a subcontract to Tremont. And what was Tremont? Nothing. A dummy corporation run by a puppet—McKenzie. Now, why would the Chinese *insist* Smith Pettit subcontract out a sizable chunk of work to an incompetent design firm?"

"I wouldn't know."

"Don't you see, Tremont's the conduit. As the Yünnan Project goes forward, the Chinese make payments to Smith Pettit. Smith Pettit in turn sends money, clean money, to Tremont. And what does Tremont do with it? Most it wire-transfers to Li and Frasier—the payoff—and McKenzie keeps a share for his troubles. A made-to-order money-laundering scheme."

"Now the kicker, Dennis," Meg added. "The Yünnan Project, all payments to Tremont under its subcontract, are funded ninety percent by the Chinese and *ten* percent by *U.S.* taxpayers. Think of it. The taxpayers of this country are *subsidizing* the smuggling of U.S. arms to the tune of ten percent."

Dennis frowned. "If you're right," he said skeptically.

"Simple enough to prove," Nick said, "all we have to do is trace the wire transfers from Tremont. They may jump around the country a bit, but eventually some are going to end up in the pocket of Frasier and some, maybe through the accounts of Kiajong Shipping, in the pocket of Li. I'm sure of it. A few subpoenas, and we'll uncover everyone involved. That's why we've been trying Carolyn. We want to move on this, fast. We've been debating whether it's time to bypass Carolyn and call the FBI directly or—"

"No," Dennis interrupted, shaking his head vehemently. "Carolyn's going to want to be in on the

ground floor of this." He tapped an index finger
against his temple. "I know she was at a conference
in Virginia. . . . Look, let me go to my office, I've got
some phone numbers there." Dennis stood. "Give me
some time to track her down. Don't talk to anyone . . .
*anyone* . . . until I get back."

Nick nodded. "Sure," he said as Dennis scuttled
from the office.

Meg waited maybe fifteen seconds before whispering, "Did you see that, he turned white. You're about
to be a hero; I think that's got him sick."

Nick smiled. "If I know Dennis, he'll get over it.
By the time he reaches Carolyn, he'll probably be
claiming half the credit, but who cares anymore? I feel
pretty good right now and nothing's gonna ruin that."

Fifteen minutes later the phone rang; Nick grabbed
it anxiously. "Dennis?"

"Yeah."

"Did you find her?"

"I tried. No luck. But I did the next best thing."

"What's that?" Nick asked.

"I've got Senator Whitford holding on the other
line."

*"Whitford?"*

On the mention of Whitford's name, Meg moved to
Nick's side, a questioning look on her face.

"Yeah," Dennis answered. "I woke him up. I
thought about what you said, and you were right—we
can't just sit on this information. Whitford was the
logical person to contact. He's up to speed on the
investigation, he's the power on the Energy and Commerce committee, and he chairs the Armed Services
committee."

"Geez, Dennis. Whitford? Why didn't you talk to
me first?"

Dennis's voice turned cold. "One, I didn't think it
would be a problem, and two, I'm your boss, remember? I don't have to consult you."

Meg clutched Nick's shoulder and mouthed,

"What's happening?" Nick held up a finger and spoke again into the receiver: "Well, you should have consulted me, because I'm not going to tell him anything."

"I've already given the senator an outline of your investigation, Nick. Consider it an order if that makes it easier for you. As soon as we find Carolyn, she'll be included in the loop."

Nick considered his position for a moment and realized he had little room to maneuver. "All right," he agreed reluctantly. "Put him on."

Another second and the familiar drawl sounded over the line. "Mr. Ford, I hear you have a story to tell me. . . ."

# 38

At the appointed time and the appointed place, Li's gray sedan pulled to the side of the street. From the shadows of a brownstone's stoop Pu-Yi appeared; Li thrust open the back door of the sedan and Pu-Yi entered. The car then continued its course, winding through the streets headed nowhere.

Pu-Yi bowed his head in deference.

Li barely glanced in Pu-Yi's direction. "You are clear on your orders?" he demanded.

Pu-Yi nodded. "Yes, sir."

"Repeat them for me."

Pu-Yi did, satisfactorily.

"It must be made to look like a mugging," Li said. "Remove his wallet, his watch, take her purse and jewelry."

Pu-Yi nodded.

"There can be no mistakes this time."

"I understand, sir."

"Be sure that you do," Li said sternly. He passed on a few final instructions, then, their business concluded, signaled the driver to return to the pickup site. There, Pu-Yi exited the car. It drove off immediately; there were no good-byes.

The car drove only a few miles before Li again signaled the driver to stop.

He had arrived a half hour before sunrise. The night sky was clear, the humidity had finally broken, and he looked forward to the walk along the reflecting pool stretching from the Washington Monument to the Lincoln Memorial, both lighted, each glowing white and pure.

So different from what lay a mile in any direction: a crumbling D.C. infrastructure encapsulating poverty.

·

A lesson there: governments didn't take care of you, ideologies didn't take care of you, you had to take care of yourself, even in America.

Li came here sometimes, at night, early in the morning, to think. The place had an order and clarity, a Grecian balance, that inspired the same in his thoughts. Such a clean, tranquil atmosphere, unlike Tiananmen Square with its mishmash of monuments and obtrusive cadre of PLA soldiers and less obvious undercover police.

That the buildings lacked the emotional character of some Chinese architecture—were in fact almost dull—was not lost on him, however. They in some way reflected much of America: technically impressive, but comfortable, overfed, and somehow mundane.

The walk was therapeutic, to cleanse his mind of the events that would soon unfold. He had, of course, ordered killings before, and no doubt would again—killing, in itself, never bothered him. The morality that equated killing with evil, mercy with good, had been propagated by the masses to protect themselves from the powerful. Li ascribed to his own set of rules. On reaching the Lincoln Memorial, he ascended the steps and read the inscription above Lincoln's statue he had read many times before: "In this temple, as in the hearts of the people for whom he saved the union, the memory of Abraham Lincoln is enshrined forever."

To the south of Tiananmen Square stood a strikingly similar memorial, Chairman Mao's Mausoleum. Inside, seated much like Lincoln, was a massive white statue of Mao, a mural of the mountains and rivers of China behind him.

Every country had its heroes. Flaws were glossed over, be they Mao's or Lincoln's. Unfortunately or fortunately, however—Li had no opinion on the matter—America had become like a pretty teenage girl who dwelt on every mark of acne, every extra half inch of fat, until she convinced herself she was ugly. The Vietnam memorial to his left was symptomatic: where the other memorials within his sight praised

America's successes, that memorial dwelt upon failure; where other memorials gleamed white, its dark polished surface threw reflections but had no light of its own. When America built its next statue on the Capitol mall, and the next after that, they would be to her supposed victims, Li predicted, and a country that no longer glorified the noble was doomed to ignobility.

What an interesting time to live, to have witnessed the fall of one great empire, the USSR, and to watch the erosion of another, the USA. A fertile field for the oldest empire in the world to rise once again to world prominence.

Not that Li believed in the Chinese communist system, far from it; he had given up believing in any system at all. Now he believed only in himself, a lesson he had learned years ago in Beijing.

Through most of his youth Li had been an outcast due to his mixed blood, a gift from a father he had never met. A minor British official appointed to Great Britain's Beijing consulate, his father saw Li's mother, just eighteen at the time, as infinitely attractive but wholly unsuited for marriage. His appointment in Beijing over, he left Li's mother with child and John Li with a greater problem, for the Chinese prized nothing more than a pure blood line.

But in 1972, when John Li turned seventeen, he developed a close friendship with a boy one year his senior, Wei Ziyang. Unlike the other boys and girls who ignored Li, or worse, Wei sought out Li's company, seemed to enjoy it. In the universities of China a growing underground of intellectuals discussed concepts of freedom of the press and freedom of expression. Wei was a member of their circles—people who cared more for Li's ideas than his background. Li attended just two meetings with Wei's friends before his mother found out. She attacked him viciously with a bamboo rod.

"You don't understand," his mother explained to him later, after regaining her composure. "I know what you think of me. You think I embrace what has been drilled into my head by the party: communism is the savior of the peasants and the working class, and all those who oppose the party are enemies of the people. I never have. *Never*."

Li was too shocked to say anything—his mother had been a member of the party as long as he could remember.

"No," his mother continued. "I'll tell you what I have faith in: myself. I trust no one to look after me, no one to provide for me. Every government, every organization, every person, will use you, and enslave you, if you let them. History is a river. It *will* follow its course. If you swim against the current, you go nowhere. You eventually drown. Let history go where it must—you keep alive."

His mother forbade him to see Wei again, and to ensure he obeyed her orders, she shipped Li off to live with relatives in Guangzhou. There he learned the value of his mother's advice—he relied on himself, and within a few years established a flourishing business smuggling Western consumer goods across the border from Hong Kong. Soon no one commented on his rounded eyes or size, at least not to his face.

Fourteen years later came the *xuécháo,* the Chinese student uprising, known in the West as the Tiananmen Square massacre. Led by a dedicated group of students, nearly a million protesters crammed Tiananmen Square and its surrounds. Workers, even policemen, aided the students; the ideal of democracy seemed almost within their grasp. But then, unexpectedly, the more than quarter million troops deployed around Beijing attacked. Heavy tanks and armored vehicles made short work of the barricades hastily erected by the protesters, crushing anyone who got in their way. Troops with automatic weapons strafed the crowds on the street. Several thousand casualties, maybe more.

Li learned later that his old friend, Wei Ziyang, had helped organize the students. After crushing the protests, the Chinese committed Wei to a mental institution; he died there two years later from "complications."

If not for his mother's stern hand and good advice, Li might have shared his friend's fate. He took the lesson to heart. He would willingly espouse communism as long as communists ran China. When the communists fell, so would his avocation. Communism, capitalism, democracy, he could live comfortably with any, for all were merely labels, and therefore meaningless; only his life held value.

Li looked at the horizon. The stars had all but disappeared, and the black and purple hues of night were rapidly giving way to the dark oranges of early morning. He started down the steps of the memorial, back to the edge of the reflecting pool.

As the sun made its first appearance, he began.

Standing erect, his chest slightly concave, feet shoulder distance apart, Li sank smoothly into his knees. His weight balanced over fixed feet, a stable base, he moved from the waist, right, then left in an endless circle, his hands and arms maintaining continuity.

Each movement flowed rhythmically, slowly, deliberately, adding a sudden grace to his bulky body.

He let his hands rise, floating at an impossibly slow pace, till they were shoulder height, palms down, then brought them to his body and let them sink while he exhaled, and repeated the process.

In China, Hong Kong, all over the Far East, at sunrise young and old could be found in parks or public squares doing just as he, practicing—"playing" was the preferred term—*taijiquan,* t'ai chi ch'uan. The discipline, as always, brought harmony to his mind—the yin and the yang, the active and passive, in balance.

His body moved as if in slow-motion dance, arms flowing wide into the White Crane Spreads Wings posture. His *taijiquan* master prescribed ninety-one exercise forms; this morning Li intended to concentrate on the low forms, the strenuous postures.

He planned to finish with the most strenuous position of them all: Tiger, Poised for Attack.

# 39

Nick punched in Dennis's extension and received an anxious "Hello" from the other end. "It's me," Nick said. "You ready to head to Whitford's?"

Nick's earlier discussion with Senator Whitford had been brief and to the point. Nick had given the senator a thumbnail sketch of the investigation, after which Whitford had asked the three of them, Nick, Meg, and Dennis, to meet him at his congressional office by five-thirty a.m.

It was now five-fifteen.

"What time is it?" Dennis asked. "Quarter after five? Dammit, I'm not ready. I have to finish up a memo for my secretary to type and—I need a few more minutes. You're still taking Meg's car, right?"

"Yes," Nick said.

"Okay, you better take off without me."

"We can wait," Nick offered.

"No, don't keep the senator waiting. I'll be maybe fifteen, twenty minutes behind you . . . maybe less."

Nick tried to sound disappointed. "You're sure?"

"Yes. Start right in with the senator. I won't be long." With that the line went dead.

Nick shoved a few last papers in a briefcase; then he and Meg started for the elevator. Once outside, they made for Meg's car, parked a block and a half from the GAO building.

Their shoes echoed off the deserted sidewalk, and Nick was reminded of their walk home from the charity event. How uncomfortable he felt then, and how very comfortable now.

"Explanations of the user log, breaking the password, all the computer stuff, I'll look for you to handle," Nick said.

Meg nodded confidently, her face lit warmly by the orange hues of sunrise.

"That leaves me with the financials, the wire transfers, Scott's research on Frasier and Li, and—" Nick stopped in mid-stride; he pounded the fist of one hand into the palm of the other.

"What is it?" Meg asked.

Nick shook his head, upset with himself. "The fax. From my friend at the State Department. The background check on John Li. I left it in my office."

"Want to go back?" Meg suggested.

Nick looked at his watch. "No. I don't want to be late."

Meg turned and pointed at a bank of phones they'd just passed. "Give Dennis a call. He can bring it over with him.

"Good idea." Nick set down the briefcase and searched his pocket for change. He produced a couple of quarters.

Meg pointed fifty yards up the street to a black Honda. "I'll meet you at the car." She picked up Nick's briefcase and headed toward the car as he walked back to the phones.

For the last thirty minutes Pu-Yi had watched the newer-model black Honda, knowing Ford and the woman would come. Finally, through the dim morning light, he saw two people exit the GAO building and begin to walk in his direction. Pu-Yi stepped back into the shadow of a doorway and watched the approaching figures. It was almost a block before he made a positive identification. Immediately he left the doorway and started in their direction carrying a folded newspaper, feigning interest in the front page.

The plan was simple: confront the two as they entered the car. Shoot Ford immediately, leave the woman and her car in the inner city for the police to find: a carjacking and a violent rape, both victims deceased. Tabloid fodder.

Li had vetoed the use of a silencer. Only professionals used silencers, and as Li had made very clear, the shooting must not look suspicious.

Pu-Yi peered above the newspaper. Down the block Ford and the woman had stopped, seemed to be engaged in conversation. Then they separated, the woman continuing on, Ford turning back to stop at a bank of pay phones.

*Now what?* Ford, as the primary target, should be disposed of first; the woman was of secondary importance. But Pu-Yi had seen Ford hand the woman his briefcase. If it held the copy of McKenzie's disk, and the woman drove off with it—

The choice was clear: the woman must be dealt with first.

Pu-Yi considered his weaponry. The snub-nosed .38 in the right pocket of his windbreaker would effectively remove the woman, but the gun blast would alert Ford. The knife in his left pocket, on the other hand, had its advantages—the woman would die quietly in his arms. One problem: Pu-Yi was not so sure he wanted the woman to die, at least not so quickly. Not when he had so many uses for her.

Better, perhaps, to keep the woman alive and use her to draw Ford in.

Yes, Pu-Yi decided, keeping the woman alive, for a time, had multiple advantages.

Nick, lifted the pay phone's receiver and deposited the quarters in the coin slot. He casually scanned the sidewalk as he waited for a dial tone. To his left, a woman scuttled away from him clutching a grocery bag. To his right, past Meg, a man in a blue windbreaker approached reading a newspaper. Otherwise the sidewalk was empty. The street was almost as deserted, just a few passing cars.

At the dial tone Nick punched in Dennis's number with a shaking hand.

*A few minutes now and he'd be in Whitford's office. Then the story would come out and the nightmare would end. His reputation, his sense of self, restored.*

As Dennis's line rang, Nick's eyes found Meg and followed her as she neared her car. He smiled thinking of her. His eyes then tracked to the side, to the man in the windbreaker a half dozen yards beyond Meg. Asian, Nick now realized. He could just make out the man's features in the morning light: a broad face, what looked like a long scratch on his right cheek.

A "hello" came over the phone breathlessly, and Nick turned his attention back to the phone.

"Dennis, it's Nick." He saw the face of the Asian man again in his mind. A scratch along the cheek. *A scratch?* Why was that important?

The line went silent for moment, then Dennis squeaked, "Nick?"

"Yeah," Nick answered. "I forgot something in my office, the fax from the State Department on John Li. Could you bring it along with you?" *Why was the scratch important?*

"Where are you calling from?" Dennis asked.

"The street. From a pay phone." *A scratch.*

"Sure, Nick. I can bring it."

"Good, it's right by my—" Nick started. A long scratch, as if someone's fingernails had raked the man. *As if someone's fingernails had raked the man.*

Nick's stomach dropped as he suddenly remembered: the autopsy outside Birmingham. McKenzie, the owner of Tremont Engineering. The medical examiner had noted the fingernails of one of McKenzie's hands had been cleaned. Nick had followed the examiner's inference: McKenzie had scratched someone before he'd died, and that someone had not wanted to leave skin traces under McKenzie's nails.

Nick jerked his head urgently in Meg's direction, letting the receiver fall to swing by its cord.

Pu-Yi closed on the woman's back, admiring her shape as he did so. Fit, athletic, but one could never tell. Sometimes the unfit were the ones that fought fiercely to cling to life while the fit succumbed surprisingly quickly. He found himself hoping that that would not be the case.

The woman opened the door of the Honda and placed the briefcase in the backseat. A few steps and Pu-Yi would be to her. One slap hard to the face should do it. The woman would scream in terror, and Ford would come running to her aid—it was his nature. Pu-Yi would be waiting, knife in hand.

Pu-Yi grabbed the woman's shoulder, spun her around easily. Their eyes locked momentarily, hers showing a hint of fear, then annoyance. "What are y—" she started, when his blow took her across the face and knocked her against the car. First lesson, he thought, speak only when spoken to. He reached out to pull her to him.

Nick crashed into the Asian man in stride, sending him sprawling to the sidewalk and knocking the gun from his hand. Nick's first concern was Meg—she seemed dazed, unable to protect herself. He pushed her into the rear seat of the Honda, flipped the lock, and shut the door. He turned in time to receive a straight-legged kick to the shoulder.

The Asian man leapt for the car door, swearing on finding it locked, and incidentally granting Nick the second he needed to recover his feet. The man turned back on Nick, and Nick retreated.

*Run. Draw the man away from Meg. Outdistance him.*

Nick sidestepped a large metal trash basket, using it as a temporary barrier, and when the man continued to advance, he pushed the basket over at the man and began to run. He cut across the street, dodging easily through the sparse traffic. A blast of horns sounded behind him, indicating, he hoped, his follower's passage had not been so trouble-free.

After a dozen frantic strides Nick risked a glance over his shoulder. His heart stalled—the man was there, running behind him, and in his hand something glinted. A knife. The man now held a *knife*.

Nick flew around the first corner he came to, then risked another glance to his rear. The man had closed the distance between them.

At the end of the block Nick realized he was slowing. His breathing had turned ragged, his legs heavy. A few more seconds and the man would be on him. He saw no alternative but to turn and face the attack. What would he do then? Untrained fists against a knife?

The obvious answer flashed through his mind: what would he do then? *He would die.*

Nick spotted a wooden chair propped by someone's stoop. He veered, steps ahead of his attacker, and reached the chair, swung it outward as shield and weapon.

The man in the windbreaker stopped short of Nick. Saying nothing, his face cold, he began to circle Nick slowly, the knife tracing small figure eights in the air.

Nick's gut tightened. He yelled out, calling for help, as the man lunged forward. Nick blocked with the chair, rapping the man on the wrist with one of its legs, but the knife did not clatter to the ground as Nick hoped.

Nick yelled again, his voice cracking with fear. A window above him opened, and then another, but no voices came from the shadows within. It was a mistake to look to the windows. The man lunged again, and this time grabbed the chair and wrested if from Nick's grasp.

The man stooped and swung out a leg, catching Nick at the back of the knees. One second Nick was standing, the next his head cracked concrete. He looked up, saw the man, saw the knife, saw both about to descend on him, the images swimming as he fought unconsciousness.

Meg spun the wheel and gunned the engine, thinking not of her own safety, but only that she must stop what was about to happen. The car flew over the curb, catapulting her against the roof of the car and knocking her momentarily into blackness. She didn't see Pu-Yi turn, his face pure panic, nor did she feel the grille of the car take him at the hips, knocking him beneath the undercarriage. She did feel the chain-link fence that came next and managed to slam the brakes to the floor, slowing the car slightly before it skidded sideways into the brick wall of an office building.

Nick heard the car clear the curb at the same time Pu-Yi did. He rolled to the side, escaping Pu-Yi's fate by a yard.

Still dizzy, Nick started after the car, but stopped momentarily when Pu-Yi's body appeared from underneath it. He prepared to leap on the man and wrestle the gun from him; a look at the twisted joints and the crushed chest smeared crimson told him it wouldn't be necessary.

The car had stalled, the driver's side up against a brick wall. Nick ran to the passenger's door and ripped it open. Slumped forward, Meg's head rested against the steering wheel. "Meg," he yelled, panicked.

She opened her eyes; her hand went to her forehead. "I'm okay," she said weakly, a bead of blood laying a path to her eyebrow. He pulled Meg's body away from the steering wheel. The rivulet of blood from her forehead had now wound its way past her eyes and continued on toward her chin. "Can you move?" he asked.

She nodded, but winced when she tried. "It hurts," she groaned through clenched teeth.

"All right, let's see if we can slide you out." He put his hands under her body, lifted and pulled simultaneously. She slid easily. So light. He picked her up in his arms.

Her head rested on his shoulder; her hands gripped his shirt fiercely.

Nick laid Meg on a small patch of grass; he knelt beside her, making a quick examination. Her eyes looked clear. He traced the bleeding to a one-inch scrape on her forehead that didn't appear serious, but might mask a concussion.

"Stay here," he whispered, then made his way back to Pu-Yi's body. He had not noticed Pu-Yi's face at first, and now averted his eyes. The car's undercarriage had skinned his forehead and one cheek to bone. The knife lay a few feet from Pu-Yi's outstretched hand; Nick left it there, his first diagnosis correct: the man was dead and a threat no longer.

A crowd had yet to gather, but a half dozen pedestrians crept forward, steadily gathering their courage. "Get help," Nick yelled to deaf ears, and it took two additional attempts before a man sped off presumably to do just that.

Returning to Meg's side, Nick lay beside her, propping himself on one elbow. He set a hand gently on her neck. "How are you?"

"I'll be okay," she said with great effort, raising a trembling hand to her head. "My face . . ."

"Still regal," Nick said. They shared the memory with a smile, but after a few seconds Meg's fell flat. Another moment and her face went completely slack.

"Meg?" Nick's eyes bulged in horror when she didn't answer. He squeezed her hand, but her fingers remained limp and unresponsive.

"Meg?" he tried again, yelling this time. He brushed back the rivulet of blood from her forehead, as if that might in some way help to heal her. It didn't; Meg's eyes remained closed.

In the distance he heard the wail of sirens, more than one. He cradled Meg's head in his arms and rocked, repeating her name again and again.

# 40

Senator Whitford spotted the limo and strode resolutely to its side.

J. T. Frasier's driver stood by the passenger door. He acknowledged the senator with a quick nod of the head as he held open the limo's back door. Senator Whitford climbed into the bench seat across from Frasier.

Frasier appeared shaken—his shoulders drooped, his eyes darted. The only greeting he offered was an unpleasant glare, even after the driver pushed the door shut from the outside, locking the two in privacy.

Senator Whitford tipped his head. "J. T."

Frasier gritted his teeth and started in immediately. "Dammit, this can't be happening. You've got to shut him up."

Senator Whitford shook his head. "It's too late for that now. Too many people know Ford's story; too many have copies of the disk. Once they audit your inventory records . . . There's no way to shut this thing up, not anymore."

Frasier twisted his wedding ring nervously around his finger.

"We've got a real problem, J. T.," the senator said.

"You think I'm some sort of dumbass?" Frasier spat. "You don't have to tell *me* there's a goddamn problem." He pounded his fist on his thigh. "We've got to stop him."

"Li tried and failed. Blame him, not me. What would you have me do at this point? Walk into the police station and drag him out? With reporters all the hell over the place? With the Justice Department and the FBI involved? I repeat, we've lost the opportunity to control the situation. We have to prepare for the worst."

Frasier half covered his mouth, eyes dilated. "They won't believe him."

"They won't have to believe him—they'll have facts. Ford has the disk, the financial records. Li's reportedly skipped the country, but that's where the good news ends."

Frasier fell back into his seat, his fear now palpable. "You've got to do something."

Extreme pressure, high stakes, and Frasier looked ready to fold—not what Whitford had hoped. He said calmly, "I've been in town for all of two hours. In that time I've talked to the attorney general, the head of the FBI, and the D.C. police commissioner, and now I'm here talking to you. I'm doing what I can, but frankly, at this point that's not much more than monitoring the situation."

Senator Whitford paused, his hands folded in front of him. "Remember, J. T., *you* made the deal with the devil. *You* violated a score of export laws and got caught. All *we* ever did was offer you a possible way out. We thought if you worked with us we could protect you, but circumstances now make that impossible. I want you to consider something, J. T. I regret this, I really do, but I think if we were to offer you up to investigators we could—"

"*Offer me up?* Did you say *offer me up?* Fuck that. You hear me, *fuck that.* This isn't coming out. None of it. I played along with you guys. You said if I did, everything would be okay. I'm holding you to that. You *understand?* I did what you asked, and now you had better stand by me."

Senator Whitford's voice turned cold. "I will stand by you, to the extent I'm able. The more . . . embarrassing . . . aspects of your transgressions, those never need see the light of day. And I give you my word, I'll do everything in my power to make sure you're given a light sentence, that you serve it in a minimum-security prison. But you *are* going to have to take a fall if we are to salvage the situation . . . do you understand? There *will be* indictments, but we can limit the damage to our operation. You made your own bed, J. T. We kept you out of it for a long time, but now you've got to go quietly. Accept that."

"Indictments. God dammit, you promised me. You *promised me*. I did everything I could for you, and now you talk to me about goddamn indictments?"

Senator Whitford's eyes grew hard. "I want to make this clear: you've got one last card to play. It may not be a winner, but if you follow our story, our script, you just might cut your losses considerably."

Fraiser's face reddened. "The hell if I'm going to be indicted. No one's going to throw J. T. Frasier to the wolves. Nobody. You hear me? You make this go away, or I tell everything I know. *Everything!*"

"That can't happen," the senator said forcefully. "You know that."

"Well, it's *gonna* happen. I'm not playing some sort of goddamn scapegoat."

"Calm down, J. T. Telling everything is *not* an option."

"*Then you fucking fix things.* I go down, and you and a lot of others are going with me. I don't care how much damage I cause. Do you read me?"

Whitford looked at Frasier, then, finally, nodded once.

"Good." Frasier smiled for the first time. "My Gulfstream's at Dulles. I'm going there now. In a few hours I should be back in Raleigh. If I'm going to have to face questions, I'll do it from there, where I've got some influence. Not that I expect I'll have to use it, because by the time I touch down you'll have figured out a plan to extricate me from any involvement, right?"

Senator Whitford said nothing, and Frasier pointed a finger at his chest. "Dammit, I don't care how you have to do it, but I don't want my name dragged through the mud. You just make sure I never have to show up on the stand . . . that I never have to testify . . . because you know what happens if I do. Have I made myself clear?"

Again Senator Whitford nodded. *You*, he said to himself, *have made yourself absolutely clear.*

# 41

Slumped forward on a teak bench, head balanced in one hand, John Li stared vacantly at the cabin cruiser's wake, a straight line stretching as far as he could see and beyond. His eyes periodically sank, then snapped open, his mind dulled by the constant drone of the boat's diesel engine, his body's reserves sapped by a long and active night.

He checked his watch. Twelve-thirty p.m. The sun glared. Another hot day in a series of hot days. Even the wind blew hot. Li rose reluctantly and stretched, his back and knees protesting the effort. Sweat glued the polo shirt he wore to his chest and back.

A search of the drawers and cabinets of the boat's small cabin produced a tube of sunscreen. Returning to the deck, he squeezed a generous puddle on his palm. Sleep, in a soft bed with clean sheets, dominated Li's thoughts as he rubbed the lotion over the exposed pale skin of his scalp, face, and arms.

Yes, Pu-Yi had failed him badly. Yes, his operations in America were for all intents and purposes over—a great loss—but Li chose to focus on the positive. He had escaped arrest, if only by a few hours, and between his accounts in Singapore and Switzerland he had over twenty million dollars tucked away, more than enough to live comfortably. And he still had allies in high places. After all, hadn't General Soong come to his aid? Arranged for him to be ferried off the coast and picked up by a Chinese freighter?

Li reached for the pair of binoculars that rested on the bench, raised them to his eyes and scanned the horizon. Empty. A seamless transition from blue water to blue sky. He checked his watch again: 12:36. It wouldn't be long now.

He heard the engine of the boat rev down and realized it had been slipped into neutral. The boat slowly coasted to a stop. Li glanced to the two men, both Chinese, who stood squarely at the helm on the upper deck, hard-eyed and unconcerned by the sun. General Soong's men.

"Why are we stopping?" Li yelled.

One of the men, muscular, wearing no shirt, scanned the horizon, his hand shielding his eyes. "There," he said in coarse Cantonese, pointing off the stern. "The freighter." He nodded to the other man on the upper deck, who cut the engines. They both descended a short ladder to the rear deck.

Li scanned the horizon in turn, his hand shielding his eyes. "I don't see anything."

The man moved behind Li, pointed over Li's shoulder. "There."

Li strained his eyes. "I can't see any—" he started.

The blackjack was already out of the muscular man's pocket and cupped in his hand. He struck from behind, swiftly and with an efficiency of motion. One short, vicious swing.

Li's mind exploded in light. A flash, an instant of comprehension that things had gone terribly wrong, then blackness.

The two men worked quickly, without speaking. A canvas tarp secured with ropes covered a corner of the deck. One of the men untied the ropes; the other folded back the tarp, revealing a fifty-gallon metal drum lying on its side, three life preservers wedged underneath to keep it from rolling. Together they righted the drum. Quarter-sized holes, two dozen or so, were cut in its top. Its other end was similarly perforated—cut with a blow torch shortly before they left dock.

They lifted Li and dropped him in. Ignobly, head first.

The men made a last check of the horizon. Still clear, the only movement a half dozen seagulls riding lazy two-foot swells off the stern, hoping for fish scraps.

The muscular man tilted the drum, enough so each man could get a hand under it. Together they lifted, resting much of the drum's weight against the boat's side. A concerted push and it went over into the water—landed with a splat that sent the seagulls into the air.

The drum floated high for a long moment, until one side dipped as water gushed through the holes in its end. The drum upended, then filled quickly. Steadily, smoothly, in less than ten seconds the ocean took it.

A stream of bubbles rising from the deep blue marked its decent; soon those too disappeared.

One hour back to dock. As his partner started the boat toward shore, the muscular man entered the boat's cabin and exited with a warm Coke, wishing it were tea instead.

The man didn't hate this part of the job, didn't love it either. It just was. The way a farmer felt, he supposed, about slaughtering his livestock: an essential chore best tackled dispassionately. Not evil, not wrong, just necessary.

He had known Li only a couple of hours. His initial reaction was of a shrewd, intelligent man. But then, that was the problem, wasn't it? Li knew too much. A potential embarrassment neither General Soong nor China could afford, or so he had been told.

The man twisted off the bottle cap and arched it over the side. A seagull swooped, investigating.

Five thousand feet of water this far out. Tremendous pressure at the ocean floor, almost a mile down. The man remembered stories told him as a boy, one in particular, of a deep-sea diver whose safety line tore. The diver fell into an undersea rift and had to be buried in his dive helmet, the water pressure having caused his body to implode. Quite probably a childhood myth, but the man wondered, nonetheless, what the weight of a mile's worth of water would do to Li's body.

He turned his eyes, and mind, from the water. He drained the Coke, then stretched out on a bench. Sleep came easily.

# 42

Captain Jeffrey Harkins stripped off his headset and threw it angrily at the cockpit controls. The old man would be pissed. Normally easy enough to get along with—almost pleasant—when Frasier got a bug up his ass he could be a pain, and today he had a *huge* bug up his ass. He just couldn't get back to Raleigh fast enough. And who would be blamed for the delay? Jeffrey fucking Harkins, that's who.

A commercial pilot wouldn't have to put up with this shit. They had the union behind them if anyone tried to get in their face. He had the credentials to work anywhere; why he ever thought flying a corporate jet would be hot shit he'd never understand.

Harkins swallowed his pride. For now at least Frasier still signed the paychecks. Time to kiss some butt. He found Frasier working diligently on a drink in one of the six goat-leather seats mounted in the passenger compartment. Startled, Frasier looked up as Harkins approached.

"We ready to take off?" Frasier asked anxiously.

"Not quite, sir," Harkins responded, bending over Frasier's seat. He hated calling Frasier sir. On the commercial airlines the pilots were the ones called sir, the way it should be. "I just got a call from the tower. We're being asked to hold."

Frasier turned white. "Why?"

"Tower got a call from Bethesda. Seems some kid spilled his motorcycle early this morning. The doctors salvaged his liver; they need it shipped to Benson ASAP. Someone's on the critical list down there . . . needs a transplant."

Frasier at first seemed relieved, then annoyed. "What does that have to do with us?"

"Benson's less than forty miles from Raleigh, sir. The tower checked all commercial and private flights . . . we'd get it down there quickest."

"They want us to take the kid's liver?"

"Yes, sir."

"Dammit." Frasier hit the flight tray with his fist, splashing some of his drink on his pants. He looked up at Harkins, incensed. "No. Absolutely not. We don't have time for that."

Jesus Christ, Harkins thought, a life was at stake. He had never considered himself a great humanitarian, but he wouldn't think twice about bending his schedule a bit for something like this. "Yes, sir, I told them that."

"Then what the hell are we doing here? The law doesn't require us to wait, does it?" Frasier asked.

"No, sir." Harkins shook his head. "Problem is the tower. They determine our flight priority, and if we refuse this request, I think they'd . . . excuse me, sir . . . fuck us. I wouldn't plan on getting our flight clearance anytime soon."

"Hell." Frasier took a number of deep breaths, then asked impatiently, "When is it coming?"

"The liver? Tower said it shouldn't be any more than ten minutes."

"Does that mean we lose our takeoff priority?"

"No, sir. That's the good part. If it gets here on time, we'll probably be ahead of the game. Tower'll assign us call-name 'lifeguard.' That means once the package is on board, we have priority all the way— takeoff to landing clearance in Raleigh."

Frasier turned his head to the window, then back to Harkins. He wet his lips. "Okay. We wait the ten minutes. But if it's not here by then, I don't care what the tower says. You call them and tell them that. You tell them we have an emergency of our own to deal with."

"Yes, sir."

Harkins started back for the cockpit, mimicking Frasier to himself: *You call them and tell them that. You tell them we have an emergency of our own to deal with.* The hell with that. The tower wouldn't give him the time of day with that type of whining. No, he'd have to wait it out and hope the goddamn thing got here on time.

Maybe passengers were the problem—they gave you nothing but shit. Flying for Federal Express, UPS, maybe that was where it was at. Damn right. Maybe the time had come to send around his résumé. The market was tight right now, but he understood you had a pretty good chance if you were willing to take a foreign assignment. Fed Ex flew out of the Philippines; that wouldn't suck—the girls there were supposed to be something.

Harkins monitored his watch. At ten minutes on the dot he spotted a black car approaching across the tarmac. He jumped out of the hatch and waited. The car came to a stop, and a man exited carrying a small cooler sealed with a few wraps of duct tape. An Igloo brand cooler, Harkins noticed. Seemed as strange as shit to be carrying around a human liver in something usually reserved for beer.

The man from the car handed Harkins the cooler. All right, Hawkins thought, breaking a smile: his name would be washed from the shit list, and someone in Benson would get a brand spanking new liver. Not a bad day, all and all. And with priority clearance they'd probably even end up shaving time from the flight— that should make the old man's pecker stand up.

After exchanging a few words, Harkins jumped back into the jet, broke the good news to Frasier, and started down the preflight checklist.

# 43

Nick walked to the doctor's side, fighting the urge to break into a run.

"She woke about two hours ago," the doctor said, then referred to the medical chart he held in his hand. "Blood pressure, vital signs, all good. Her EEG appears normal. We've asked her simple questions—she's answered coherently. Her memory doesn't seem to be affected. We're hopeful there's no brain damage."

Anything but that, Nick prayed.

"She's exhausted, Mr. Ford, and in great pain. Normally we wouldn't allow her visitors—she's not out of danger yet—but she was insistent and . . . Please, keep it short and try not to excite her."

Nick stopped at the threshold to the hospital room, as if to stall off a reality he didn't care to face. Inside the room—the focus of the tangle of tubes, IV's and electronic monitors, all white and chrome with digital readouts and LCD graphs—lay Meg, appearing very small.

"We operated yesterday," the doctor whispered. "Three broken ribs where she slammed into the steering wheel." The doctor pointed at a spot on his own chest. "Her left kidney was severely lacerated—we had to remove it. Some internal bleeding . . . nothing serious. I mentioned the head injury already."

Nick ordered his foot to move forward, but it didn't obey. Swirling in the back of his mind, nearing consciousness, were images from the past. His parents. Scott.

After a moment of silence the doctor said, "You may go in if you want, Mr. Ford."

Nick shut his eyes, forced his hands to fists to keep

them from trembling. His aunt's voice: *It's time to say good-bye, Nick. Time to say good-bye.*

"Nick?" The sound reached beyond his closed eyes, into his convoluted thoughts, and pulled him back to the present. He opened his eyes.

"Is that you, Nick?" Meg asked from her bed, her voice weak and raspy.

Nick moved quickly to Meg's bedside, ghosts of the past instantly supplanted. Her face, that portion not covered by bandages or obscured by the respirator, looked pale and waxy.

"You had me so worried. I thought . . . How are you doing?" Nick reached down and wrapped his hand around Meg's. It felt cold—too cold for something living. He squeezed lightly, and her eyes opened wider.

"I'm fine. Just fine." Her smile seemed to come at great effort, and it disappeared on her next words. "I talked to the police. Briefly. They told me what happened. The man I hit . . ."

"You saved my life, Meg."

For the first time showing strength, she clutched his hand. "I saw you run," she said, "and I didn't know what was happening, then he chased you. I got in the front seat, started the car, followed, and when I saw he had a knife . . ."

Nick set his hand on her shoulder. "You didn't have a choice."

"I . . . I didn't want to kill anybody."

"Let's worry about you, huh?"

"Who was he? Why did he attack us?"

Nick glanced at the doctor still standing behind him. "When you get better we'll discuss it, okay?"

"Please, Nick. I have to know."

Nick glanced again at the doctor, then pulled a chair to Meg's bedside and sat down. "The evidence we gathered . . . we were right. About almost everything. The FBI has reached the same conclusions we did: John Li was smuggling hi-tech goods out of the U.S.

with the aid of Frasier. Li and Frasier found out we were on to them; they wanted us silenced."

"How, Nick? How did they find out we were on them?"

Nick shook his head, irritated with himself. "Stupidity, Meg. I didn't think. The user logs you uncovered . . ."

"Yeah."

"The logs *were* planted, just as you guessed, and that's not all. Our computer modems had been replaced. Li and Frasier had access to our computers anytime they wanted. They could either download the user log and review the record of our keystrokes, or they could monitor us in real time. We disabled the user log, Meg, but it never occurred to me they would have bugged my modem as well. That's how they learned we'd accessed Tremont's financials. Of course, they didn't know what we had learned, what we had guessed, or even who we had told, so they sent someone to assess the situation."

"Sent someone?"

Nick nodded, then explained: "The wire transfers from Tremont . . . remember there were four sets. One went to the account in my name in the Bahamas. The FBI traced the other three. One went to Li through Kiajong Shipping, one to Frasier, as we guessed. The last set of wire transfers . . ."

"Yes?" Meg prompted.

"The wires jumped around a bit, but they ended up in Dennis's hands."

*"Dennis?"* The monitors above Meg reflected her shock—their easy rhythms spiked, then turned erratic. She struggled to a more upright position.

Nick nodded, tight-lipped. "Which explains what he was doing in the offices at four in the morning. We told him what we'd uncovered; we told him everything. And remember, you commented he turned white at the news. It had nothing to do with his dislike for me, Meg. It had to do with saving his own skin. When he left my office, supposedly to find Carolyn's

number, he must have contacted someone . . . maybe
Li . . . and reported what we'd found."

"I . . . I can't believe that."

"He sent us out on the street, Meg. He stayed inside
on some excuse, but sent us out to an ambush. And
now Dennis can't be found. He's disappeared. It all
adds up. Li or Frasier must have got to him months
ago, paid him to deflect the GAO's investigation. He
tried so hard to make me give up the Yünnan audit,
to take charge of it himself, to hinder my investigation.
Now I know why. But to set us up for murder . . ."
Nick's voice faded away in anger.

Meg's eyes lowered as if in deep thought. Finally
she said, "Li and Frasier, they're in custody?"

Nick shook his head. "The FBI thinks Li's left the
country. His apartment, his offices, both were cleaned
out. They raided Kiajong Shipping; all they found was
a couple of laser target designators—part of a missile-
guidance system—packed in a drum of bearing oil.
Frasier's dead. His corporate jet went down yesterday,
a few hours after we were attacked, on its way out of
D.C. Frasier was on it. The FBI's going on the as-
sumption Li silenced him . . . had an explosive placed
on Frasier's jet."

He looked at her gaunt face, the bloodless skin.
"Hey, enough. We can talk more later."

Meg ignored his words. "What about you now?
The accusations?"

"All dropped. Carolyn's reappointed me to assistant
comptroller. I even got an apology from Senator Whitford." Nick straightened, puffed out his chest, and
looked down his nose, trying his best to look and
sound like the senator. " 'Your country owes you a
great apology, Mr. Ford, and an undying debt of grati-
tude. I will do all in my power to see that the full force
of law is brought to bear against the truly guilty.' "

At great effort, Meg laughed. Nick joined her but
stopped abruptly on feeling the doctor's hand on his
shoulder. "I think," Nick said, "the doctor is telling
me you need your rest."

Meg looked over Nick's shoulder at the doctor. "Just a moment more."

The doctor nodded and retreated to the doorway.

"They took one of my kidneys."

"I'm sorry, Meg. They had no choice."

"I know . . . severe internal lacerations. A miracle the broken ribs didn't end up puncturing a lung, that's what they told me."

"The ribs will mend, and the kidney, you've got another one." Nick grinned, fighting back tears. "Hey, your office is only a few doors down from the bathroom anyway."

Meg started to chuckle again; then a wave of pain stole her face. "Oh, that hurts."

"I don't want you to hurt."

"It's really not so bad if I don't move. They have me on drugs . . . some really good ones."

"Lucky you . . . Hey, before I go, I've got a message for you."

"Hmm?"

"An order to get better . . . it's from the President."

"Of the United States?"

Nick nodded. "Someone from his staff will be calling you soon. To invite you to a reception the President's hosting Saturday night. We're not exactly the guests of honor—there'll be over two hundred guests—but we're on the A list. With the President's approval rating what it is, he can use all the heroes around him he can get." Nick laughed at Meg's shocked expression. "Don't look so surprised. We *are* heroes . . . at least you are. Front-page news."

"I don't feel like a hero."

"There are at least ten reporters downstairs who would tell you otherwise."

Meg looked down at her body, then up and to the right, following the length of IV tube running from her arm. "A reception *this* Saturday night? Five days from now?" she repeated.

Nick nodded. "I told them we might not be able to make it."

"What do you mean *we*?"

"I told them we're a package."

Meg's face turned stern. "Go."

"We'll see."

"Not we'll see . . . go. Really, I insist. I want a full report, what the President says to you, what the First Lady wears, what's served for dinner."

"Meg . . ."

She continued to look at him sternly.

"Okay," he said, admitting defeat. "I'll go."

"Good. And a word of advice, that old tux you own . . . replace it. One of these times you're going to sit down and . . . Well, I don't think that's quite the splash you wish to make at the White House."

Nick smiled. "I'll buy a new one, promise."

Meg nodded, satisfied. Her eyes sank closed. "I'm so tired."

"You should sleep now."

"Would you stay, Nick? Just for a moment."

"Sure," he whispered, his chin shaking slightly.

"I'll just close my eyes for a second . . . just a second." Her eyes closed, and in a few moments her breathing relaxed. Nick flipped his eyes to the heart monitor; it showed a steady, even blip.

The doctor crept to Nick's side. "Mr. Ford, it's time to go."

Nick nodded reluctantly and followed the doctor from the room.

# 44

Nick used his bath towel to wipe the mirror clean of steam, then covered his face with shaving cream. He shaved, relathered, then shaved again. It was a big day; he wanted to look his best.

He had laid out his tux before showering, and dressing went quickly, all except the cuff links. It took him a few minutes to master the necessary one-handed stab.

Nick turned, judging his image in profile. The pants fell neatly, breaking just above the shoe, his jacket didn't pull and displayed no trace of polyester sheen, the shirtsleeves showed a half inch below the jacket sleeves, and the bow tie was small and classic. Most important, he'd jumped that hard-to-define line—he wore the suit, not vice versa. The six hundred dollars he laid out for the new tux had been well spent; Meg had been right about that.

He had seen her that morning, sat with her for over an hour before the doctor shooed him away. Thinking of Meg, he smiled. She still seemed small and lost among the tubes and monitors, but she didn't tire as easily and the color had almost returned to her face. The improvements were easy to see; she would get well quickly now.

He had again mentioned skipping the White House diner—he wasn't the hero, Meg was—but she wouldn't hear of it. She had insisted, and he could refuse her nothing.

He'd been to the White House once before, a few weeks after he took the job with the GAO. He had joined a tourist group. An almost too wholesome-looking youth had led them on a brief tour. "This," Nick remembered the young man saying as they entered a large oval room, its carpet a shade of royal blue, "is the Blue Room. James Monroe ordered many of the furnishings. The Blue Room serves as the main reception area for guests of the President. . . ."

Nick Ford, guest of the President. He liked the sound of that, and gave his ego rein.

Nick stuck out an arm, practicing. "Mr. President."

He'd been briefed on protocol by the chief of staff's office earlier in the day. ". . . Dinner will be served in the State Dining Room—an usher will show you to your seat. We ask that you remain standing until the President and First Lady have entered the room and taken their appointed place at the head of the table. There will then be a brief introductory remark by the President, followed by. . . ."

Was it all designed to make you a bit nervous? Make you feel like a peasant about to rub elbows with royalty? If it was, it had worked. He became suddenly aware of the moisture on his palms and rubbed them together self-consciously. Everything would be fine. He'd accept the President's praise in Meg's name and pass it on to her.

Almost three hours yet before he was due at the White House. Ridiculous to be ready three hours early. Then again, how often did one attend a White House reception?

He again admired his reflection. The ringing of the phone kept him from adjusting his bow tie for the dozenth time. He lifted the receiver from the bedside table. "Hello?"

"Mr. Ford?"

The voice sounded familiar: female, with a Chinese accent. Before Nick had a chance to place it, the voice came again. "This is Jing-mei. I am the girl from the—"

"I know who you are, Jing-mei," Nick interrupted with warmth and surprise. The girl from the sweatshop. He remembered that he'd given her his card. "How are you?"

"I . . . I have a problem. I think you might be able to help me."

"Anything. Anything in my power." He meant that. Already, on his own initiative, he'd contacted Immigration and discussed her circumstances on a no-names basis. The discussion had been mildly encouraging, and he had set up a face-to-face meeting the following week. "What is it?"

"Could you come? Meet me now?"

Nick checked his watch. "I'd like to meet with you, Jing-mei. In fact, I've been thinking lately . . . about your situation. I'd like to tell you about it. Unfortunately, tonight I have a previous engagement. Tomorrow my schedule's wide open. You name the place, the time, and I'll be there."

"I have to see you, today," Jing-mei persisted. "It won't take long."

Nick debated for a moment. "Maybe if you came here, to my apartment?"

"I'm sorry, but I can't do that. I am staying with . . . a friend . . . I feel safer here."

At once alarmed, Nick asked, "Are you in danger? Should I call the police?"

"No, *don't* call the police. Everything will be all right if I can talk to you. I helped you, now I'm asking you to do the same."

That logic was hard to defeat. "All right," Nick said. "I've got . . . maybe an hour and a half to spare." Time enough, if he rushed, to see Jing-mei, return, straighten up, and get to the Capitol.

"An hour and a half will be plenty. Thank you, Mr. Ford."

"I owe you the thanks, Jing-mei. Tell me where you are and I'll leave right now."

The address Jing-mei gave Nick led him to an apartment house in a middle-class neighborhood on D.C.'s north side. The lobby door was locked. Nick pushed the button next to apartment 503—the apartment number Jing-mei had given him—on the building directory. A voice, too distorted to positively identify, came from the speaker a few seconds later: "Hello."

"It's Nick Ford," he said.

In response a buzzer sounded, and Nick gained entry to the lobby. He took the elevator to the fifth floor and knocked on the door to apartment 503. Jing-mei opened it.

Nick tipped his head. "Jing-mei." She greeted him with an odd expression, a reaction, he assumed, to his formal attire. He tugged lightly on his tux lapel. "It's for a dinner tonight. I'd already dressed by the time you called."

She nodded, though her expression remained fixed. "Thank you for coming," she said as she waved him in.

Nick entered, and Jing-mei closed the door behind him. "I said I owe you the thanks," Nick said, "and I meant it. If it hadn't have been for you, I—" He stopped abruptly; his head snapped to the rear of the apartment, to the man who appeared suddenly from the back room.

*Dennis.*

Eyes hollowed out and bloodshot. Clothes rumpled.

On seeing Nick, a wry smile sprung to Dennis's lips. "Nice threads," he said.

Nick backed toward the door. He didn't see a gun, but his hair bristled just the same. A trap. A setup, and he'd walked right into it.

After a moment of silence, Dennis dead-panned: "What's the matter, have you forgotten me already? Out of sight, out of mind, is that it?"

"Dennis . . ." Nick mumbled.

"Ding, ding, ding. We have a winner."

Nick glanced toward Jing-mei. She seemed dumb-founded by Nick's reaction. "Don't blame her," Dennis said, reading Nick's mind. "She thinks we're buddies."

"Why would she think that?"

Dennis raised his hands and smiled. "I can be fairly

convincing when I want to be." He walked to the center of the room.

"You do not work together?" Jing-mei asked innocently.

"We did," Nick answered, eyes glued to Dennis. "Not anymore." He circled Dennis cautiously, inspecting his surroundings. Nicely appointed but not lavish. A railroad apartment, Nick guessed. He could see a kitchen beyond the room he stood in, and beyond that what looked to be a bedroom, both empty.

"How did you find her, Dennis?" Nick asked.

Dennis shrugged. "Wasn't hard. You told me quite a bit about her, remember? The place she worked, the address. I looked her up . . . waited for her to leave work, just like you did. Then suggested she call you. I could have called myself, but I have a feeling you wouldn't have agreed to meet me."

"You're right about that." Nick started for a cordless phone which lay on a coffee table. "I'm calling the police."

Dennis beat him to the phone and placed his hand over it. "Wait. Hear me out, Ford. I brought you here for a reason."

"I don't give a damn about your reason, not with Meg in the hospital." Nick wrested the phone from Dennis's grasp and pushed the On button.

"Then listen for Jing-mei's sake."

*Jing-mei's sake?* Was that supposed to be a threat?

Dennis raised a hand, palm forward, as if taking an oath. "She's in trouble, Ford. Serious trouble. I can't help her, but you might be able to."

Nick looked at Jing-mei, her head lowered, biting her bottom lip. Reluctantly, he turned the phone off. "What kind of trouble?"

"She broke a code. At your urging. She *talked*."

Nick shook his head. "Everything Jing-mei told me is under seal. Nobody should know . . ." He jerked his head back to Dennis. "Unless you leaked the information?"

Dennis rubbed his face nervously, eyes darting. "It

doesn't matter anymore *how* the information leaked, just that it did. To help you, Jing-mei crossed some ruthless people. When the news gets to them, and it will soon, they're going to make an example of her."

"You son of a bitch." Nick took an aggressive step forward but stopped as Dennis retreated to the far wall. Nick turned to Jing-mei. "I'm sorry. I never meant to put you in danger. You'll be protected. I promise you that."

"In case you've forgotten," Dennis said, "she's here illegally. You go to the police and she'll be deported. Her welcoming committee in China would be as vicious as any here."

Nick placed a hand lightly on Jing-mei's shoulder. "We're going to file a petition for political asylum with Immigration. I've already done some of the groundwork. You're not going back to China . . . no way."

Jing-mei raised her eyes to Nick. "I trust you, Mr. Ford."

Dennis began to clap. "Bravo." He pointed at Nick. "You see, Jing-mei, what did I tell you? A command performance. The man's a boy scout." Suddenly, Dennis turned serious. "That's why I called you here, Ford. That's why I want you on my side."

"I have no interest in being on your side." Nick emphasized the point by sticking a finger in Dennis's face.

"Without me Jing-mei would have been dead by the end of the week. I think I deserve something for that good deed. Besides, you owe me. You fucked me over pretty good."

"I did what?" Nick felt heat rise in his face. "*I* didn't put Meg in the hospital. *I* didn't betray the GAO's trust, betray my country. *You* did those things."

Dennis laughed shortly before his face went blank. "You don't understand a damn thing, do you?"

"I understand loyalty. I understand justice."

Dennis grimaced and shook his head. "No, you understand regulations and accounting standards . . . that's all."

"Turn yourself in, Dennis, or I will."

Dennis smiled frostily. "Turn myself in? That's not the kind of justice I'm interested in. I'd be dead within twenty-four hours."

Nick tilted his head. *Dead? Within twenty-four hours?* "What are you talking about?"

Dennis sought out the nearest chair. He stared for a moment out the window before answering, his tone subdued. "I'm an embarrassment, Ford. You've made me one. An embarrassment to people who don't like embarrassments. But I'm alive, and with or without your help, I'm going to stay that way. If I'm lucky, maybe I can even make my way out of the country. Hell, who knows, I might even live to see my seventieth birthday, but I'm not going to put any money on it. That's how I'm fucked, Ford. You did that. Funny, though, now you're the only one I can trust. The only one I can turn to."

"I don't . . ." Nick cleared his throat. "I don't understand."

"Because you're a boy scout, just like I said. You always have been. A goddamn boy scout."

"If you mean I know the difference between right and wrong—"

"Right and wrong?" Dennis shouted. "Is that the only thing you get off on? The terms mean *nothing*— labels invented by powerful men to pen in the sheep. They had you pegged from the start. You *never* would have understood."

Nick went silent as he considered Dennis's words. "Who are 'they'?" he asked finally. "The Chinese?"

Dennis ran his free hand through his hair, then chuckled sarcastically. "The Chinese. The goddamn Chinese were puppets from the start. Marionettes on a string."

"You worked for them," Nick said, his finger this time aimed at Dennis's chest.

"I *never* worked for the Chinese."

"I saw the financials, remember, Dennis. Li bought you."

Dennis shook his head slowly. "I never met the man, never had any dealings with him."

*Was Dennis crazy? Did he actually think Nick would believe his lies?* Nick looked at Jing-mei, but if anything she seemed more confused than he.

"And the money wired to your account?" Nick asked.

"Window dressing. Part of the game. I didn't keep a penny."

Dennis had lied to him so many times, and yet— Something about his demeanor gave Nick pause. *Should I hear him out,* Nick wondered, *or go immediately to the police?*

Dennis said, "Your curiosity's aroused, isn't it, Ford? I can see it in your face. I've planted the seeds of suspicion, and that mind of yours is whirring—that's what I need. You see, Ford, you *are* my only hope. As it is, I know only enough to be dangerous. Only enough to be silenced. I don't know the why. And until I do I'm expendable. You're going to help me get what I need. For once I'll be the one to benefit from your talent for digging out the truth."

Nick's eyes narrowed. "Why would I help you?"

"Because I know you, Ford—it's in your nature to follow up loose ends. I'll give you names, dates, everything I know. You can do the rest."

Nick paced the apartment, hands on hips. Both Jing-mei and Dennis tracked his progress, saying nothing. "All right," Nick said eventually. "Let's say I'm willing to give you the benefit of the doubt. Let's assume you really do have a story to tell. Fine, we got to the police, *then* I help you."

Dennis shook his head. "So I can end up a statistic like J. T. Frasier? . . . Maybe I haven't been clear— the police *can't* protect me, Ford, not from the people I'm involved with. I go to the authorities, I enter police custody, and I'll end up dead. Maybe they'll say I tried to escape, grabbed a gun, or jumped from a window, who knows, but the outcome will not be in question. No, *you* have to help me. We uncover the whole truth; then we blow the lid on it and no one will be able to touch us."

*"They" again.* Who was Dennis referring to, and were they, not Li, responsible for Frasier's death? Nick caught himself, realized his curiosity *was* aroused. Just as Dennis had predicted, the investigator in Nick had stirred. "You say you weren't working for the Chinese, then who?"

"Powerful people." Dennis shook his head again, in resignation this time. "You're not going to believe me."

"Try me," Nick snapped.

"I told you your problem . . . you're a boy scout. I have my own problem: I'm the good soldier. I followed orders." Dennis reached into his jacket. Nick flinched, bringing a smile from Dennis. "Easy, Nick. I don't have a gun." He removed a thin fold of papers and held them out.

Nick grabbed the papers and gave them a perfunctory examination. Each was covered with columns of dates and what looked like telephone numbers. "What are they?" Nick asked.

"Proof. Of what I'm about to tell you."

Nick looked again at the papers.

"Those," Dennis continued, "are the phone records for my office at the GAO, both incoming and outgoing calls over the last week. An original, unaltered log. Look at the phone numbers closely. Something should jump out at you."

Nothing did. After a half minute, Nick said, "If there's something here, I don't—"

A loud rap sounded on the door, interrupting Nick. A moment later a voice came from the hallway: "Electrician."

Dennis put his finger to his mouth.

The knocking came again. "We've got an electrical circuit out. We think we've traced the overload to your apartment."

Dennis stole to the door and looked through the peephole. On the other side stood a man carrying a toolbox and dressed in blue work clothes with ZIMMER ELECTRIC embroidered above the right breast pocket.

The knocking repeated a third time. "Hello . . ."

While Dennis retreated from the doorway, index finger still crossed over mouth, Nick sought out the nearest lamp. He turned its switch—nothing happened.

More knocking.

Nick went next to the window; it overlooked the street. He waved Dennis over and pointed out a van below, ZIMMER ELECTRIC printed on its side. He whispered, "The electricity's out, and there's a van below . . . what's the problem?"

Dennis's face had gone white. He swallowed once and whispered in return, "Everything." He closed his eyes, clearly panicked. "The setup's too sophisticated for the men after Jing-mei . . . that means they're after us." He gritted his teeth. "Dammit, someone must have followed you here from your apartment . . . has probably heard everything we've said."

*Followed him?* Nick skewed his eyes. "You're crazy, Dennis. Paranoid. How could anyone hear what we've said?"

Dennis scanned the apartment desperately, answering Nick almost as an afterthought. "A parabolic dish from the street, passively through the phone lines, any number of ways."

"All right," the voice from the hallway announced, "the superintendent gave me a passkey. In case anybody's there, I'm coming in."

"Jing-mei," Dennis said urgently under his breath, pointing at the door, "try to get rid of him."

Jing-mei nodded uncertainly, then called out, "Just a moment." She approached the door. "We don't have any problems here," she said.

An insistent voice came from the hallway: "We've got a whole circuit out downstairs, and all the wiring loops up through your apartment. I gotta check it out, ma'am."

Dennis whispered to Jing-mei, "Stall him," then ran toward the rear of the apartment. Nick tucked the papers Dennis had given him into his coat pocket, then followed.

As Jing-mei argued with the electrician, Dennis pulled a butcher knife from a cutlery block in the kitchen and ran into the back bedroom. His head flipped side to side, and Nick mirrored the movement. The bedroom was small: a bed, a chair, a dresser, one window, a bathroom off to the left.

Dennis ran to the window, slid it up, and peered outside. He froze for a moment, then drew back from the window and leaned against the wall, his chest rising and falling in shallow heaves, perspiration showing on his upper lip and forehead. Nick looked out the window for himself. There was no fire escape, nothing between him and the pavement five floors below. He might possibly survive the jump, but almost certainly would break his legs in the process.

Dennis swore under his breath, then said, "At least they're going to take you down with me, Ford. That's the only thing that gives me any comfort. We're in the same boat to hell."

As the incessant banging on the apartment's front door continued, fear finally took Nick, tightening his rib cage and squeezing his stomach.

The man made an instant decision. His ruse had failed, and direct action was now called for. He set his toolbox on the ground and opened it, lid toward the door's peephole, obscuring the contents within. His hand went into the box; when it came out it held a 9mm automatic equipped with a silencer.

He fired three shots to the immediate right of the doorknob, splintering the jamb. A hard kick and the door banged open. Two hands on the gun, the man swung the barrel toward the only movement within

the apartment: the young Chinese girl, standing stupefied like a deer caught in headlights.

The scream building in Jing-mei's throat never got
a chance to exit. The man pulled the trigger twice;
both bullets took Jing-mei in the throat, rocking her
head forward and her body to the ground. Her limbs
shook violently for a few seconds as thousands of
nerves fired in unison; then the life went out of her.

First mark accounted for.

The man closed the apartment door, then moved
forward, gun sweeping in front of him in a short arc—
eleven o'clock, one o'clock, eleven o'clock, one
o'clock. He had memorized the floorplan to the apartment before stepping inside. A one-bedroom railroad
apartment: a living room, a kitchen, and a bedroom
with connecting bath. No one could get past him. He
would clear each room, one after the other.

The room he stood in, the living room, had one
closet. He pumped two bullets into it, waist high, to
the left, then the right. He opened the door and
jumped back. Empty, just a vacuum cleaner and
clutter.

The kitchen came next. He hesitated, listening. All
was silent, and he continued forward.

Nick heard the front door burst open. From where
he stood, he could not see the gunman raise his
weapon and fire, but did see the aftermath. His first
thought on seeing the spray of blood and flesh issue
from the back of Jing-mei's neck was to rush forward
in aid. But his body overruled his mind, held his feet
in place until reason returned. Jing-mei was beyond
help.

Two more *pops* sounded, and Nick and Dennis ran
for cover. Nick to the bathroom, Dennis to one side of
the bedroom door. Dennis clutched the butcher knife
fiercely, his knuckles white.

*Paranoid.* Nick had called Dennis paranoid. And
now— Jing-mei lay dead, and they were next.

Nick's mind shifted through possibilities and just as

quickly discarded them. Run? Run where? Jump? Five stories? Attack? With what?

Suddenly the wall to the opposite side of the doorway from Dennis exploded. One moment it was intact, the next moment two holes the size of fists appeared, a hollow cone of plaster and wallpaper jutting from each.

Nick realized, a fraction of a second late, what would come next. Before he could shout a warning, two blossoms of red appeared on Dennis's front, one on his chest, the other just above his groin.

Dennis managed just one step, then his eyes rolled up and he fell. He landed facedown and lay motionless. The two blossoms of blood on his front were mirrored on his back, where the bullets had entered. As Nick's eyes locked on spreading red, another bullet ripped into Dennis's skull.

Reflexively, Nick stepped back from the bathroom door. He forced his mind to again consider alternatives—there were none.

He shut the bathroom door and fixed its lock. How long would the door hold the man? And then? What would it feel like, a bullet tearing into his body?

There was a small window over the bathtub, and Nick jumped inside the tub and pounded it open. Given the alternative, a jump of five stories seemed far less daunting than a few moments earlier, but the window was small, impossibly small. He'd never fit through it.

Nick's knees went weak. There was no way out. The man would finish him with a bullet in the brain, just as he'd finished Dennis. The end of everything.

With satisfaction the man saw the body fall to the floor. Only amateurs felt safe from a 9mm bullet behind a wall of wafer-thin plaster. Dead amateurs.

He noted the hair, the body type. Lindsay. He pumped an insurance bullet into the downed man's brain. That left Ford, now a cornered, and therefore dangerous, animal. He proceeded cautiously.

His gun's clip held fourteen rounds; he'd used twelve, leaving two. Perhaps enough to finish his assignment, but there was no reason to take chances. He popped the clip and within a second inserted a full replacement. Fourteen rounds, one target.

The man jumped into the room, instantly taking in its configuration. A double bed, a chair, and the door to the bathroom. He fired one shot, a dull pop, through the chair's upholstery, and two more through the mattress of the bed. All three were met with silence.

That left the bathroom. He raised his gun and aimed for the center of its door.

*"Phhtt."* A bullet slapped the wall inches from Nick's head. Bits of tile stung his left cheek. Another bullet struck almost instantly, this one waist high, two feet to his right. Instinctively Nick fell flat against the bottom of the tub. A hail of bullets followed.

Nick covered his head with his hands as tile fragments rained from above. A few bullets hit the iron tub, their ricocheting ringing loudly in his ears. Then the noise stopped.

Nick's mind spun; he had only seconds now. The man would come through the door. If Nick did nothing, he would die. He had to move. Had to search the bathroom for some sort of weapon. Had to find something, anything, that might give him a fighting chance at life.

All was silent beyond the bullet-ridden door. Still the man popped the gun's clip and inserted a third. Ford was dead or playing dead. Either way the time had come to end things.

"Ford," the man urged, "come out."

Silence.

Cruelty wasn't a character trait of the man, not by nature, but there were realities to face, one being that at the end of the day he had to look his wife and child in the eye. And so he did not think of Ford as a human being, did not think of Ford's friends or dreams or fears. He thought only of his own job, nothing more.

He sent three bullets into the jamb, just to the side of the knob, then kicked in the bathroom door.

Startled, Nick reared back as the door jamb exploded suddenly. He had left the tub and now stood just to the side of the door, his back against a pedestal sink. He knew what would come next, and a fraction of a second later it did—the door burst open from the strength of his attacker's kick.

Nick had to act immediately, in that instant before his attacker fully regained his balance.

Arm cocked, Nick forced himself to movement, leaning into the open doorway, eyes locking on those of the other man. Nick held a can found under the sink, and as the man's gun rose toward Nick's chest, Nick slung the arm holding the can forward. Blue crystals sprayed from the open can, streaming toward the man, fanning out like lead pellets from a shotgun.

The crystals slapped the man across the face, dropping him instantly to his knees.

The man screamed in agony as the drain cleaner burned out his eyes.

Nick surprised himself—he showed no mercy. He rushed forward and kicked the man hard in the temple; the man crumpled to his side and after two equally vicious kicks remained still.

Nick retreated to the wall to his rear and slumped against it, riding down to a sitting position, trying to catch his breath. He held his head in his hands, the reality of all that had happened in the last few minutes striking home. Dennis lay dead, the carpet underneath his head a growing stain of red; in the other room Jing-mei lay dead; before him his attacker lay blinded, perhaps dead as well.

A voice came to Nick then: *Run. Here, in this apartment, you are in danger.* He heeded the voice and scrambled on all fours to the gun of the downed man.

The weapon's weight surprised him; its lethal potential struck home.

Nick ran for the front door, the gun held poised for use. He paused over Jing-mei for just a moment. Too long. Her staring eyes seared their way into his memory.

Less than a minute later Nick was out of the building and on the street, the gun and the hand holding it tucked from view within the tux coat.

He ran blindly until his lungs gave out.

# 45

A vast rectangular hall with a hundred-feet-high barrel-vaulted ceiling bisected the center of Union Station, the hub of D.C. train and subway travel, yet Nick felt claustrophobic. It was the crowd: a scurrying throng of late-afternoon commuters.

He had jumped the Metro, uncertain of where to go, what to do, knowing only that his car might be watched and he had to put as much distance between himself and the apartment as he could. He had gotten off at Union Station—the idea of being surrounded by people appealed to him, gave him a sense of security, but his feelings had changed dramatically. Dressed in formal wear, he hardly melded into the background.

As he walked the length of the hall, his eyes swung from face to face to face; each appeared briefly out of the jostling mob in front of him, then folded into his wake. He realized what any cop could have told him: a crowd gave an advantage to the hunter, not the hunted.

*The hunted?*

According to Dennis, that's what he was, and how could he doubt Dennis any longer?

Jing-mei's image came to him then: at her neck a red scarf of blood, and above an unblemished face with eyes mercifully closed. Dennis's image now, his face far from unblemished, marred by a gaping exit wound. And Nick would have been next. He could hear the gunman calling: "Ford, come out." *Ford.* The man had known his name—he hadn't come just for Jing-mei and Dennis, but for Nick as well.

What had Dennis said? "At least they're going to take you down with me, Ford. That's the only thing that gives me any comfort. We're in the same boat to hell."

Nick spotted a police officer stationed by the ticket booths and retreated into the flow of pedestrians.

A part of his brain screamed at the idiocy. *Two people were dead, one disabled—you have to go to the police.* Another part of his brain ran an endless loop of Dennis's warnings: "The police *can't* protect me, Ford, not from the people I'm involved with. I go to the authorities, I enter police custody, and I'll end up dead."

Would Nick suffer the same fate if he called the police?

What had Dennis said about himself, that he was "an embarrassment to people who didn't like embarrassments?" Would the "powerful people" who had removed Frasier, who had hunted Dennis, assume Nick had learned all from Dennis? Was Nick himself now the embarrassment, the next in line for removal?

Nick berated himself for conjuring conspiracies, but immediately Jing-mei's and Dennis's images returned. Two people *were* dead. He wasn't conjuring that.

Nick crossed the hall to a rest room. He sat in a stall, door closed, trying unsuccessfully to organize his thoughts. From his coat pocket he pulled the phone records Dennis had given him.

The sheets were marked with four columns: the first the date, the second time of day, the third outgoing phone numbers, the fourth incoming phone numbers. He flipped through the pages, finding it hard to concentrate, waiting for something to "jump out at him"—Dennis's words. Nothing did. All he saw was a swirl of meaningless numbers, mostly local with a smattering of area codes around the country. *This was Dennis's proof?*

Nick did a quick approximation: there were five pages and maybe sixty phone entries a page. That meant he would have to run a check on three hundred phone numbers.

Nick slammed his hand on the side of the stall.

*You can't just do nothing. All your life you've ig-
nored crises in the hope they'd go away. They never
did, and this one won't either. No more hiding in clos-
ets. Time to face things head-on.*

Nick took a deep breath, gathered himself, and left
the rest room. He walked by the police officer toward
an exit. He wouldn't go to the police, not after what
had happened, not after Dennis's warnings. Instead he
would go to the one person he could trust. Someone
with as much power as any who might be after him.

# 46

No name marked the driveway, just an address and a black metal gate—shut—but Nick recognized it just the same. Over the years he had been, if not a regular visitor, at least an occasional one. The house was invisible from the road. In the soft light of dusk he saw only a long, woods-flanked drive that disappeared in a gentle bend.

"That's it," Nick told the cab driver, and pointed through the right window.

Ten yards beyond the gate, the cab slowed and moved toward the shoulder, prepared to execute a Y-turn. As its headlights flashed across the side of the road, Nick caught a glint of reflected light through the windshield.

Nick's heart stalled. "Drive on," he said urgently, sinking low in the backseat.

"Excuse me?"

*"Drive on."*

The cab did, and a short distance up the road Nick spied the rear quarter of a car tucked into the woods.

*A stakeout? Was someone a step ahead of him? Had they figured he might come here to contact Carolyn?*

Nick had the cab driver turn right at the first corner and pull to the side of the road. He exited the cab with an excuse of wanting to surprise somebody, and stood in place as the cab drove off, prepared to turn his face aside if anyone passed. Not surprisingly, no one did. The neighborhood, a sleepy upper-income D.C. enclave with cul-de-sacs and ten-acre lots, saw little traffic.

Once the cab had disappeared, Nick took his bearings and set off. There was one property separating him from Carolyn's; he planned to cross it and make his way directly to Carolyn's door, skirting the front gate.

His pace turned rapid.

Cloaked by trees, he passed through Carolyn's neighbor's property without incident, then ran into a brick wall, literally. It was maybe a foot higher than his reach, and seemed to circle Carolyn's entire property. He walked its length for a bit, then glanced quickly in both directions—all clear.

Nick moved to the base of the wall and jumped. Both hands gripped brick, and for a moment he hung in stasis like some great side of beef in a cold room, unable to pull himself up, unwilling to release his grip. Then his feet came to his arms' aid, dug into the brick, lending him the additional strength to struggle to the top of the wall.

And then he was over.

He landed badly, falling to all fours, then backed against the wall, his breathing heavy, and waited. Three minutes went by; he heard nothing. Again doubts took him—what was he doing here; what if Carolyn was out; why hadn't he called the police? He drove doubt away the only way he knew how: action. He stood and began to move forward through Carolyn's heavily wooded lot.

A few dozen yards and Nick came to Carolyn's drive. He moved down it, toward her house, sticking to its edge, concealed among trees and underbrush. Thirty seconds and he spotted a sliver of red brick. Soon the breadth of a stately colonial opened up to him.

Carolyn lived alone, no dogs, no domestic help. He'd ring her doorbell, and if home, she'd let him in. She'd know what to do; she *always* did.

A sound. To his rear. The gate squeaking open.

Nick sprinted for cover behind the trunk of a massive oak tree to his right. For a moment he heard nothing more, then the hum of an automobile engine. He risked a quick glance, and spotted a black Lincoln approaching; he pulled his head back sharply.

The auto slowed—he could hear its engine wind down—and stopped. Directly to his side. Its door opened.

*Who was it? Had he been seen?*

Nick inhaled, willing his body to contract. Desperately, he scanned the woods, marking escape routes.

A solid thud then—the car door being shut—and soon the engine drone faded down the driveway.

Nick held still for twenty long seconds, then hearing nothing, chanced another glance. The Lincoln had pulled to a stop by Carolyn's front door. A man exited, holding a cane. The cap the man wore did not obscure the white locks that curled at the collar of his shirt.

Nick recognized him immediately: Senator Whitford.

Senator Whitford started up the walk toward Carolyn's home. The door opened while he was still ten paces distant, and Carolyn appeared at the threshold. No greeting passed between them, not that Nick could make out, as Whitford stepped past Carolyn and disappeared inside.

Nick's forehead sank to his hand. He had hoped to find Carolyn alone. Now he would either have to tell his story to Whitford as well, or wait until Whitford left and—

A sharp crack sounded to Nick's rear.

He froze; his heart beat loudly in his ears. Through the beats he recognized another sound: a rustle of dead leaves, and another, and another. Careful footsteps somewhere to his rear. Nick turned, twisting his neck and body, not daring to move his feet and advertise his presence as someone else had advertised theirs.

Through the tangle of underbrush and low-hanging leaves cut by dark branches, an object took shape. A man, moving slowly in the woods, maybe thirty yards away. Nick could make out no more in the faint light.

The man picked his way back toward the front gate. Nick's mind worked quickly: Whitford must have left the man off. Why? Simply a Secret Service agent to guard the senator, or something more?

The man soon disappeared, subsumed by the foliage, and still Nick waited, two minutes, five minutes, before risking his first step.

He moved agonizingly slow then, each footstep carefully planned, avoiding branches, avoiding leaves. Once a twig snapped under his weight, and he again froze, forcing himself to count to a hundred before daring to look back in the direction of the hidden man. He heard and saw nothing, and started forward once more.

A stretch of lawn surrounded Carolyn's house; Nick knelt at its edge, steeling himself. Thirty yards of open green and he'd be at the front door. And if Whitford was there, so what? Everything would be okay once he had a chance to talk to Carolyn.

Nick sprinted noiselessly to the front door, his hand to his chest, holding the handgun in place in the tux's breast pocket. No one yelled or followed. Adrenaline coursed his body; he took a dozen long breaths to calm himself, then rang the doorbell.

## 47

Carolyn's eyes snapped wide on seeing Nick; she stepped back, startled. *"Nick,"* she said.

He brushed past her through the open door, and she pushed it shut behind him, stupefied. "What are you doing here? The gate . . . how did you get in?"

Nick ignored her question. "I've got something important to tell you." He scanned the sitting room. "Where's the senator?"

Carolyn pointed toward her study.

"Good, I can tell you both."

Carolyn tilted her head, confusion stamped on her face, and started for the study. Nick followed.

The senator, attired in a summer suit, olive this time, over a light blue-striped shirt, sat in an armchair to the side of a large cherry desk. On seeing Nick, his mouth dropped and the color drained from his face.

"Mr. Ford," he said feebly, then looked at Carolyn for explanation. She shook her head, indicating she had received none herself.

The senator started to rise, and Nick held up a hand. "Please . . . sit. You too, Carolyn. Something's happened. I'll need your help—both of you. . . . Dennis contacted me."

"Dennis?" Carolyn exclaimed.

Nick nodded and explained quickly, starting with Jing-mei's call and finishing with Dennis's allegations. "Dennis said he never worked for the Chinese, that they were nothing but, in his words, marionettes on a string. He said he worked for powerful people. . . . I wouldn't believe who, he said."

After a pause Whitford scoffed. "Well, it seems Mr. Lindsay has nothing if not a vivid imagination. You've been had, Mr. Ford."

"Had?" Nick looked at Whitford. "I thought so too at first. Then a man kicked in the front door of the apartment. He killed Jing-mei . . . and Dennis."

Carolyn's head snapped in Whitford's direction.

"He tried to kill me too," Nick added.

"Someone tried to kill *you*, Nick?" Carolyn swallowed hard. "Today, before you came here?"

Nick nodded.

Carolyn's hand went to her temple. "Who, Nick? Do you have any idea?"

Nick shook his head. "A man knocked on the door, pretended to be an electrician. Dennis guessed somehow that it was a ploy. He said the man was coming for him, and for me. Then the man broke down the door." Nick pulled the gun from his breast pocket, cradled in his hands. Senator Whitford and Carolyn raised their eyebrows on seeing it.

"He carried this," Nick said, raising the gun. "There's a silencer attached." In his mind, Nick saw the bullets take Jing-mei at the neck. "I was lucky to get away. He had me pinned in a bathroom, and . . . I might have killed him. I'm not sure. I ran. There was nothing I could do for Dennis or Jing-mei."

Carolyn glared in Whitford's direction as Nick continued: "I haven't called the police. According to Dennis, they would get to me, even in police protection . . . if I went to the police I'd end up dead. After what happened, I gave Dennis the benefit of the doubt and came here instead."

Carolyn clutched her chest. "Charles . . ."

Senator Whitford waved Carolyn off dismissively. "Now, just hold on a moment," he said. "Lindsay never identified this 'they' he kept talking about, right?"

"Like I told you, only generically: powerful people, I wasn't going to believe who. He never got a chance to tell me more." Nick reached again into his breast pocket and pulled out the papers Dennis had given him. "Dennis did give me this; said it was proof."

"What is it?" Carolyn asked.

Nick handed her the papers. "A log of incoming and outgoing phone calls from Dennis's office. An unaltered log, Dennis called it. He said something would jump out at me, but"—Nick shrugged—"nothing has so far."

Senator Whitford frowned and stuck out his hand for the papers. Carolyn passed them to him. Whitford flipped the pages quickly and with a "Hrrumph" threw them on the desk. "Mr. Ford," he said, "thank God you're okay. And given what you just went through, I can understand your being a bit confused—"

Nick started to object, but Whitford spoke over him. "However," he added sternly, "I think you must bear in mind Dennis Lindsay was a *fugitive*. Whatever he may have told you should, I think, be taken with a great deal of salt. I hold little stock in shadowy references to 'powerful people,' not when the whereabouts of John Li, a criminal of flesh and blood, is unknown. Why didn't Lindsay want you to go to the police? I would think the answer was obvious—because the police would have arrested him, that's why. As to his other motives in bringing you to the apartment, I don't pretend to say, but I put them down to the actions of a desperate man."

The senator's calm self-assurance was contagious. What had a moment ago seemed so certain to Nick seemed much less so now. He looked at Carolyn and saw his doubt reflected there.

"According to you, Mr. Ford," Senator Whitford said, "two people, maybe three, are dead. I think it's high time we did something about that." The senator reached into his suit coat, removed a thin black book. "I'm calling the Justice Department."

"The senator might be right, Nick," Carolyn said tentatively.

"Of course I am," Whitford agreed, the color finally returning to his face.

Nick felt suddenly foolish. Perhaps the senator *was* right . . . to have believed Dennis, the man who had lied all along, who had been in on everything from the start, who had set him up, set Meg up, on their way to the senator's, and who—

Nick stopped in thought. On the way to the senator's.

His mouth went dry. *On the way to the senator's.*

An adrenaline rush pushed Nick's senses on edge. He reached for the sheaf of papers Whitford had set on the desk—Dennis's proof—and set the handgun down in its place. Nick turned to the last page, to the log of calls on the morning he and Meg had been attacked. It jumped out at him then, just as Dennis had predicted it would.

Nick's hand began to tremble as he continued to stare at the page. Stupid of him not to have seen it before. He had repeatedly searched for a phone number he might recognize, but it was not what was *on* the page that should have jumped out at him, but what *wasn't.*

Senator Whitford had stood, picked up the phone, and was about to dial.

"Senator, could you please put down the phone?" Nick said softly, as if lost in thought.

"Excuse me?" the senator said.

Nick's voice turned forceful. "I said, could you please put down the phone."

Perplexed, the senator said, "Mr. Ford, it is imperative the authorities become involved. I don't see any other course."

*Powerful people, Dennis had said. You won't believe it, Dennis had said.* Nick stared momentarily at the gun on the desk, then reached for it, suddenly very conscious of its weight, its deadly purpose. He raised it slowly with a shaking hand and pointed it at the senator. "I'm afraid I'll have to insist."

As Whitford lowered the phone, Carolyn's eyes went wide. "Nick? Have you gone mad?"

*Had* he gone mad? Maybe. He directed the barrel of the gun to the two chairs flanking the cherry desk and fought unsuccessfully to keep his voice from cracking. "Please, sit. Both of you."

"Mr. Ford," the senator said indignantly, drawing himself to his full height. "I don't know what in the hell is going on here, but I insist on an explanation. Immediately."

Nick's heart thumped loudly, confusing his thoughts. What had he done? To draw a weapon on a United States senator? Like a dog who sensed fear, an emboldened Whitford started toward him. One step, two steps, an arm's length away. Reaching out now for the gun.

Nick saw Meg's face in his mind, and anger flared suddenly within him, bringing with it resolve. He raised the gun to Whitford's eye level. "I said *sit*," he repeated in a commanding voice that surprised even him.

Whitford paused; his face reflected first surprise, then indecision. Nick could guess the senator's thoughts: *Would this man pull the trigger? A moment ago I would have said no, but now—*

Finally Whitford snorted, turned, and sat as directed. Carolyn followed suit, and Nick felt a surge of relief. He'd won the first battle. What now?

"What in God's name are you doing, Nick?" Carolyn asked again.

"Looking for answers," Nick answered, his voice even. He took control of the center of the room, assessing Whitford as he did so. The senator was cool, very cool; either that or Nick had it all wrong.

"You wave a gun in my face, in the senator's face, and that's your explanation? What's this all about?" Carolyn demanded.

In reply, Nick flipped the phone log onto Carolyn's lap. "Take a look. Last page. Early morning, around five. There's a series of calls from and to Dennis's office. See them?"

Carolyn nodded. "What do they mean?"

Nick stared at Whitford, watched his face again go white. "I think the senator knows. Let's see if I'm right." Nick backed to the phone, the gun all the while trained on the senator's chest. He picked up the receiver. "Read the number off to me, Carolyn."

"Nick—"

*"Read it off to me, Carolyn,"* he repeated. This time she did, and Nick dialed the number. Three rings and a formal voice answered. Nick's mind worked quickly to assimilate the information and develop a strategy. He identified himself as Senator Whitford's personal assistant and feigned confusion about an outstanding bill, then poised the question that meant everything to him. His heart stalled before the answer came. If he was wrong—

He wasn't.

Nick had the man on the other line first repeat himself, then elaborate. Finally, Nick offered his thanks and slowly let the receiver fall to its base. Until that moment Whitford's betrayal had seemed certain but somehow unreal. No longer. The reality struck Nick hard.

"I demand to know just what you think you're doing, Mr. Ford," Senator Whitford yelled.

Eyebrows low, almost in a squint, Carolyn repeated Nick's name several times, seeking answers as well.

After a pause Nick said, "The number you read off, Carolyn, connected me to the Sussex Hotel in Manhattan." By the way Whitford's eyes darted, Nick guessed the senator knew what was coming.

Confused, Carolyn cocked her head but remained mute. Senator Whitford rushed to fill the silence. "Mr. Ford, I don't know what it is you're trying to prove here, and frankly, right now I don't care. What I do know is that if you don't set that gun down *immediately,* you will be facing serious charges."

"I don't think so, Senator. You see, I finally understand Dennis's proof. In the early morning of August 9—slightly before Meg and I were attacked—there were a total of three calls to and from Dennis's office. All involving the number I just called. The Sussex Hotel in Manhattan. Problem is, Senator, I talked to you that morning. Dennis patched me through, remember?"

Senator Whitford's face went blank.

"Remember?" Nick asked again. "Dennis called you, then connected us. *You* asked Meg and I to meet you at your Senate office in one hour. *One hour,* Senator. One hour for you to get dressed and get to your office." Nick turned to Carolyn. "That's what finally jumped out at me, Carolyn. Three calls that morning, all from or to a two-one-two area code—Manhattan, but no *local* call. That's what I finally noticed . . . something was missing. The call Dennis *made to the senator's.* You do live in the city, don't you, Senator Whitford? A local call."

Whitford said nothing; his eyes radiated hate.

"Charles . . . ?" Carolyn said, anxiously.

"The Sussex Hotel," Nick went on, "just confirmed that Senator Whitford spent Sunday night, August 8, at their hotel."

"That's a lie," the senator said.

Nick shook his head. "The hotel manager pulled up your bill, Senator. You signed out, *personally,* on Monday morning. What I find hard to understand, then, is how you planned to meet me in your office that morning, Senator. How were you going to make it from Manhattan to D.C. in only *one* hour?"

Whitford opened his mouth, but no words came.

"Of course, you never intended to go to your office, did you, Senator? The manager said you signed out at eight forty-five, three hours *after* we were to meet. No, all you cared about was getting us out on the street. Out on the street where Li's man could silence us before we had a chance to talk. You did your part, Dennis, your lackey, played his . . . You *lied,* Senator, but since Meg and I were the only ones who could have caught you in that lie, you weren't concerned— you didn't expect us to be around to complain. A powerful man, Dennis said. I just never imagined how powerful."

Carolyn's eyes narrowed, and skipped again to Whitford. He avoided her stare.

Whitford banged the end of his cane down on the floor. "I've had just about enough of this, young man," he barked. "I am a United States senator, and if you don't put that gun down now, you'll be seeing nothing but the inside of a jail until you're as old as I am." He started to rise.

Nick held the gun at the senator's chest and fought to keep his voice from breaking. "Senator, don't test me."

Whitford's face turned cold. "And don't threaten me, son. I'm too old to scare."

"This gun is silenced—I've heard it fired today, at me. It barely makes a noise, like a champagne cork, that's all. I *will* do it—I don't see that I have any choice. The police aren't an option—Dennis said I go to them, I end up dead, and more than ever I have reason to believe what he said."

Whitford fell back into his chair as Nick canvassed the room. Only two entrances, the double door he had come through and a door to a screened-in porch looking out over the backyard. He moved to the double doors, listened at them for a moment, then asked, "Is there anybody else in the house?"

Carolyn shook her head.

Nick locked the double doors, then started around the room, shutting drapes as he went. "Dennis, his involvement surprised me, but somehow I can deal with it, but you, Senator . . ."

"Charles?" Carolyn said, eyes wide, a note of disbelief in her voice.

Whitford continued to glare at Nick, still refusing to meet Carolyn's eyes.

"The man who murdered Dennis and Jing-mei, you sent him, Senator, didn't you?" Nick pressed.

"I have no idea what you're talking about."

"Carolyn, I think the senator came here for a reason . . . as a precaution in case I tried to contact you. If you don't believe me, walk to your front gate.

There's a man there, hidden in the woods. He arrived with the senator. I think that man's waiting for me, and I don't think he has a warm welcome in mind."

"Charles," Carolyn asked again, and when he didn't answer, the breath went out of her body. *"Charles?"* she repeated after a few moments, now red in the face. Her pupils dilated, the familiar wrinkles around her eyes stretched taut. "You son of a bitch," she exclaimed suddenly. "You goddamn *son of a bitch*."

Carolyn dropped her head into her hands and spoke tonelessly. "Nick, I can't take this anymore. I can't sleep . . . can't eat . . . can't . . . I have to tell you something."

"Carolyn—" Whitford started, but Carolyn flared at him. "Not anymore. You targeted Nick, you bastard. Things are going to end, and they're going to end now." She closed her eyes. "What happened? God, what happened? It was all so clear in the beginning. No one was supposed to . . ." Her voice faded.

Nick reached out his hand, the one not holding a gun, and laid it on her forearm. "What was so clear?"

"She has nothing to say," Whitford said desperately. "Nor do I. I am ordering you, as a United States sen—"

Carolyn interrupted, in the strong voice Nick had heard so many times before. "Tell him, Charles. This ends *now*. No more deaths. Tell Nick *everything* . . . or I will."

"Carolyn, there's no reason to—"

*"Tell him,* Charles."

For a moment Whitford's face darkened. He looked from Nick to Carolyn and back, opened his mouth to speak twice, then finally settled back into his seat. His face muscles relaxed; his jaw unbunched.

"Very well. Perhaps Mr. Ford does deserve some answers. Carolyn, why don't you offer the young man a drink, or if you'd prefer—" Whitford produced a lighter, set it on the desk to his side, then lifted a cigar from the inside pocket of his jacket.

Nick shook his head. "No, thank you."

Whitford shrugged and let the cigar drop back into the pocket. "You should enjoy the pleasures of life while you can, young man. My doctor limits me to a cigar a week—please don't be offended if I don't take this occasion to avail myself of it. I prefer the porch at my home, on the swing."

"And I'd prefer you to get to the point, Senator."

"Getting to the point, a trait I admire but don't often emulate. A fault of mine—I blame it on my Southern roots. We like to spread a little honey before eating our bread."

"I just saw two people killed, Senator. I don't want rhetoric, I want an explanation."

"All right, then, let's get to it." Whitford locked onto Nick's eyes and held his gaze for a half dozen long seconds. "Mr. Ford, I've been a senator since 1956—one hell of a long time. I've held office during the cold war, the civil rights movement, Vietnam, Watergate, and Desert Storm. In that time I've taken stands on thousands of issues, some popular, some not, but every six years like clockwork Alabama voters send me back to the Senate. Why? Because they know I'll fight for God, the United States, and Alabama, in that order. I always have, and always will. And I think, sir, I've earned the benefit of the doubt on that score."

Nick deadpanned, "All you've earned, Senator, is time enough to tell your story."

"Threats don't become you, Mr. Ford." Whitford shrugged. "But then again, how can I blame you? I suppose much of the unpleasantness might have been avoided if we had had this talk sooner. I take partial responsibility for that. Your file, Mr. Ford, indicates you are a man who plays things by the book. A man who follows the letter of the law. Admirable qualities both, but unfortunately it has been my experience that sometimes exigencies arise that the law doesn't contemplate. Would you have seen that? Would you have been flexible? Your psychological profile said no. And so we kept you in the dark, and now . . . Now it seems we must tell you everything anyway, and . . ."

Whitford paused. "Things happened, unfortunate things . . . but we never intended it that way. *Never.*" Nick could feel himself being appraised. "What I'm about to tell you, at Carolyn's urging, involves U.S. national security. I'd like you to agree not to dis-close—"

"I won't agree to a damn thing, Senator."

Whitford nodded glumly. He looked out the window for a moment, then at Carolyn, who stared at him icily as she repeated: "Tell him *everything,* Charles."

"It seems," Whitford said, turning back toward Nick, "I'm forced to rely on your patriotism. A rather archaic notion, don't you think?"

Nick said nothing, looking instead at Carolyn, who turned her stare to the floor.

"I've known, the government's known," Whitford continued finally, "all about John Li's operation for over two years."

# 48

Nick looked at the senator, incredulous. His mouth dropped. "You *what*?"

Senator Whitford nodded. "Over two years," he repeated.

*Over two years!* Nick struggled to make sense of Whitford's words. "Carolyn, is that true?" he asked finally.

She nodded slowly, looking past him.

"You knew about Li's operation for two years, knew he was smuggling arms from the country? Then why didn't you shut him down?"

"The sixty-four-thousand-dollar question." Whitford picked up a pencil from his desk and spun it in his fingers. "I'm not a hawk, Mr. Ford. Never have been. I've seen war, watched young men die horrible deaths. Believe me, I never want to see that happen again. But I also understand the causes of war. Rule number one: weakness invites aggression. Unfortunately, the majority of Americans no longer agree with me. The USSR dissolved; we triumphed spectacularly in the Gulf War. The public *feels* safe, and so we're downsizing our military. Do you realize the U.S. presently has only the eighth largest army in the world? The *eighth*."

Whitford beat his cane on the ground for emphasis. "No matter what the public may *feel,* the world is *not* a safe place. We *must* remain strong, *must* take precautions. Facts remain facts, and the fact that's most concerned me over the last few years is that China, the most populous country in the world, a country which, at her core, remains a dictatorship dominated by hard-line communists, a country with a horrendous human rights record, is expanding and upgrading its military as fast as possible."

Whitford locked on Nick's eyes, as if willing him to understand the import of his speech. Nick returned his stare coldly, and Whitford went on.

"We won the cold war with the USSR for one over-riding reason: the strength of our economy. The USSR simply could not afford to compete in an era of hi-tech, expensive weapons systems. She was never an economic power, only a military one. China is a wholly different animal.

"Go into a K-mart sometime, Mr. Ford. Grab a power saw off the shelf, or an electric drill, or a pair of pliers, any pair. Odds are 'Made in China' will be stamped on its side. Look at garden equipment, calculators, Barbie dolls, lamps, tennis shoes, even artificial Christmas trees, for God's sake. China *is*—present tense—an economic power, and it's only the beginning. Now she has reclaimed Hong Kong, an economic power in its own right, and her appetite is whetted. Think of Japan—a country of a hundred and fifty million or so people, but with a GNP rivaling our own. Now imagine a China, with a population well over one point two *billion,* every bit as technically advanced as Japan. It will happen . . . a decade from now, maybe two or three, but it will happen. What will we be faced with then, Mr. Ford?"

Nick glanced at the door, imagining a knock would sound any minute—the man from the woods, checking on his charge. Was Whitford stalling for just such an opportunity to yell out? "I think you had Dennis killed, Senator," Nick said impatiently. "I think you tried to have me killed. And you tell me about China? What are you getting at?"

"I'm painting a picture, sir. A dangerous one. And if you have patience, I'll answer all your questions shortly." The senator leaned in toward Nick and lowered his voice, like a favorite uncle passing on the wisdom of a lifetime. "Where will China employ its new military might, Mr. Ford? Any guesses? How about Korea? China has encouraged North Korea's saber rattling toward South Korea for years. Tensions in the demilitarized zone between the two are at historic highs. Or the Spratly Island chain, the choke point of Japan's oil-supply lifeline? China, Vietnam, and the Philippines all claim the chain, but China has recently escalated tensions by seizing certain key islands. Or the most likely spot—Taiwan—which China claims as a possession and threatens to retake by force? China has massed troops and battleships across the Taiwan Straight, has conducted ballistic-missile and artillery tests off Taiwan's coast. How long before she makes good on her threats and invades?

"Who will intercede, Mr. Ford? Russia? A decade ago maybe; today, no. Russia has neither the capability nor the desire to confront China. Europe? The European powers have not been able to effectively project power overseas since the Second World War. Japan? Don't count on it, not with her almost nonexistent military and absolute dependence on China's raw materials. I'll tell you who will intercede, who will come to the aid of her allies just as she has time and time again: we will. The United States of America.

"What will be the cost, Mr. Ford? How many lives will we lose? And do you doubt that China will consider posturing with nuclear weapons? Count on it, that's the Pentagon's position. They believe the communist regime stands ready to sacrifice millions to reach its goal; people are, after all, one of its most abundant and cheapest commodities. If you still doubt China's resolve, recall her involvement in the Vietnam War, in the Korean War. Remember what befell the people of Tibet, and never forget the butchery of Tiananmen Square."

Nick's right hand had begun to shake; he shifted the gun to his left and waved it at Whitford. "Enough, Senator. I don't need a history lesson; I don't need a briefing on China. I need answers. Get to the point."

"The point, sir? That is the point. Like so many Americans, you're ignorant. You sit in comfortable houses with washing machines and microwave ovens and movies of the week, and don't want to think about the possibility of war. Someday you may have no choice.

"I chair the Senate Armed Services committee; I *know* the facts. China has two point nine million men in her army. Is the U.S. a superior military force today? Yes, but Pentagon projections say that could change by 2010. China is on a purchasing binge: billions of dollars worth of Russian military equipment: submarines, jets, rockets, ballistic-missile technology. She now has at her disposal six dozen Sukhoi Su-27 long-range Russian fighters, two Russian kilo-class submarines, over a dozen intercontinental missiles that target the continental U.S., many more which target Taiwan. That's only the beginning. She has orders for more of each with Russia and the Ukraine, and she continues to work with Israel on the F-10, a new fighter to be manufactured in China incorporating F-16 technology. She's developed her own anti-ship missiles based on the French Exocet which could keep the U.S. Navy at bay. She's developing the supersonic, swing-wing Hong-7 tactical bomber, and has obtained in-flight refueling technology from Iran. She's tried to buy an aircraft carrier, and may be trying to build one.

"What do you notice about these items, Mr. Ford? Submarines, bombers, intercontinental missiles, aircraft carriers? China is procuring *offensive* weapons meant for *projecting* power, not defending her soil."

Nick remained stone-faced. "And if I accept all you've said? So what? You've made no attempt to explain why I was attacked, why Meg was attacked, why Dennis, Jing-mei, and Scott are dead. Then you tell me China must be contained, say she's a military threat, and yet you do *nothing* to prevent her from smuggling hi-tech arms. Your own words damn you, Senator."

"My own words *vindicate* me, young man. You just don't understand . . . not yet."

"Then make me understand, Senator. I'm running out of patience."

Senator Whitford nodded. "Shortly before the British handed back Hong Kong, on the highway running north from Hong Kong through the New Territories to Guangzhou, a truck ran off the road. The driver died in the accident. When the local police examined the truck's cargo—wooden crates supposedly full of machine tools—they found a complex piece of electronic gear they couldn't identify. They alerted British intelligence; British intelligence called in the National Security Agency, the NSA. Turned out to be an artillery-control system for a MLRS rocket launcher—an A-tek product."

Nick placed the name instantly. *A-tek.* J. T. Frasier had headed up A-tek. He still didn't know where Whitford was headed, but for the first time he became absorbed in the story.

Whitford continued. "The NSA traced the cargo to the port of Hong Kong, then to Kiajong Shipping of Norfolk. That led them to John Li. The NSA investigated very quietly, searching for the leak. How had the control system found its way into John Li's hands? Their investigations pointed to A-tek's CEO, J. T. Frasier. Once they had accumulated sufficient evidence against him, the NSA confronted Frasier. Accused him of a host of crimes, including treason. I understand that after a rather lengthy interrogation Mr. Frasier broke down, and the story came out. It seems Mr. Frasier had certain . . . predilections . . . he kept from his wife and business associates. Mr. Li, however, managed to procure a video featuring Mr. Frasier engaged in these activities. A very explicit video, I understand. Mr. Frasier, another man, and a number of sexual toys.

"Li approached Mr. Frasier with a business arrangement: the tape in exchange for an A-tek computer chip. Li made it as easy as possible for Frasier—the chip was an obsolete design of no value. Blackmail, to which Mr. Frasier succumbed. A mistake. As you might expect, Li soon made other demands, threatening to expose Mr. Frasier as a sexual deviant *and* a traitor if he didn't cooperate."

Whitford shrugged. "Mr. Li sank the hooks deeper and deeper; in the end he owned Mr. Frasier's soul."

Carolyn's head rose slowly. "Nick," she started before her voice broke. She swallowed and tried again. "You know how much military hardware is smuggled from this country, to China, to the Middle East, everywhere. We've done studies, we've made recommendations, but we've never been able to stop it . . . not even slow it down. And that doesn't even take into consideration the voluntary transfer of technology to hostile governments. The money involved, it's enormous. Our own corporations sell us out. For God's sake, our own government is not above suspicion. You *know* that."

"So we give up? Give Li a pass?"

"No, Mr. Ford," Whitford said, resuming control of the conversation, "but instead of hitting our heads against a wall, why not try a different tack? Why not use Li's operation to suit *our* purposes for once? What happens to moles we uncover within our borders? Sometimes we arrest them, but often it's in our interest to turn them, to convince them to work for us. Double agents. Such an opportunity was offered Mr. Frasier, the alternative being exposure and jail. He accepted, and became a U.S. intelligence *asset*. An asset *you* threatened."

Carolyn said hesitantly, "No one counted on Smith Pettit inflating billings, no one counted on a GAO investigation, and no one counted on you being put in charge of it. The NSA studied your background, your record, and everything they learned heightened their concern. You're too good at your job, Nick. Worse, you're incorruptible. They feared your audit of the Yünnan Project might lead you to Tremont Engineering, the money-laundering scheme, and eventually to Frasier and the smuggling ring. They feared you might blow Li's operation wide open, and the NSA's plans along with it, and couldn't take that risk."

Nick shut his eyes, just for a second. Everything he knew fell into place: Carolyn's urging to settle the Smith Pettit audit, his promotion. His promotion? Assistant comptroller at thirty-five—a trick, a ploy, an illusion. *My God, what a self-important fool he'd been.* "So you stopped me."

Carolyn looked down and nodded shortly.

"She did her duty, Mr. Ford," Whitford cut in. "Only her duty. And at my prompting, I may add. She promoted you out of our hair, then loaded you with so much work you had no time for your old casework."

By her own admission, Carolyn had stopped him. Had *betrayed* him. Had she also set up Scott, set up McKenzie? Set up Meg and him? Nick fought the answer with his heart even as his mind accepted.

Carolyn continued to stare at the floor as Whitford continued. "Dennis Lindsay took over the Yünnan Project audit. Him we could control. We told him only enough to carry out orders . . . he asked no questions. Unfortunately, for everyone concerned, you didn't leave well enough alone. You put yourself back in the picture."

"And at the hearings it was your turn to stop me, Senator?"

Whitford shrugged. " 'Extremism in the defense of liberty is not extremism.' Barry Goldwater said something to that effect, I believe. You should have agreed to a settlement, Mr. Ford. Things would have been so much easier."

"Li was kept apprised of the progress of my investigation?" Nick guessed.

"It was imperative Li remain a step in front of you," Whitford said. "You can understand that now, can't you? As you know, your computer and phone were bugged—we did that. Anything else Dennis Lindsay or Carolyn learned of your activities, they passed on to me, and I passed on to J. T. Frasier. J. T. Frasier then relayed the information to Li. Li, of course, knew nothing of our involvement, the government's involvement. He simply believed Frasier had Lindsay in his pocket. The wire transfers to Lindsay just completed the picture in Li's eyes."

Nick felt sick. "Why?" He looked at Carolyn. "Why did you do it?" She didn't answer, and Nick raised his voice. "*Dammit, why?* You've known Scott for years, since he started work. And Meg . . . Why, Carolyn?"

Finally, Whitford said, "Because she's a patriot, Mr. Ford. Because she loves her country." He turned to Carolyn. "Would you like to explain the technical aspects, Carolyn?"

Nick looked at her expectantly. "Carolyn?"

Her right hand, balled into a tight fist, covered half her mouth. She spoke quietly, her voice enfeebled. "Computer viruses, you know what they are, Nick."

*Computer viruses?* Nick paused, thrown off guard. "Of course."

Carolyn explained anyway, speaking in a detached manner, like an automaton reading off a list of specifications. "Computer viruses spread by contact: they're either loaded onto a computer from an infected floppy disk or CD-ROM, downloaded via telephone modem from an on-line service, or imported from another computer or peripheral. The first viruses infected computers instantly and visibly. Pretty innocuous and easy to eradicate. Next, hackers devised dormant viruses—viruses designed to spread widely before revealing themselves . . . almost like the HIV virus in humans."

*Why was Carolyn briefing him on viruses?* Nick fought to make the connection.

"We have 'stealth' strains now," Carolyn went on. "Viruses which employ cloaking systems to mask their identity. They're aided by encryption systems, and polymorphic encryption systems which shift form after each infection. Camouflaged, they're invisible to the electronic scrutiny of all but the most advanced antivirus programs."

Nick had a hunch and played it out. "During the

hearings our data files and spreadsheets—the inflated numbers—you were responsible? A virus?"

Whitford answered. "I apologize for that, Mr. Ford. We needed to discredit your testimony."

"What do viruses have to do with any of this?"

Carolyn took a moment to collect her thoughts. "In today's world, if you have important data on your computer, the best thing you can do is keep it quarantined—no contact, no infection. The virus designers know this, and entice users to break quarantine by posting attractive programs on bulletin boards. Pandora's boxes, Trojan horses. They look attractive, but you download one, open it up, and boom. You blow up. It's a lesson the government took to heart."

"Mr. Ford"—Whitford hunched forward, his two hands resting on the tip of his cane— "we've offered China a Pandora's box."

*A Pandora's box?* "I don't understand," Nick said.

"A fact from the Gulf War—you can look it up in the papers; it leaked before we could classify it. Several weeks before Desert Storm, U.S. intelligence officers learned of a plan to smuggle a computer printer from Amman, Jordan, to a Baghdad military installation. The Iraqis intended to tie the printer into the computer network which coordinated its air-defense batteries. The U.S. intelligence officers got access to the printer, replaced one of its microchips with a specially altered replica—a computer virus embedded in its electronic circuits."

Whitford sat back and grinned. "The printer infected the computer; the computer infected Iraq's entire air-defense system. *Boom!*" Whitford threw his hands apart. "The virus wreaked havoc. Every time an Iraqi technician opened a file on his computer, the screen went blank. It didn't win the war for us, but it damn well helped, and it opened up the government's eyes to the possibilities."

Nick's eyes opened as well. Incredible. He let the gun sink. "The software, the chips, the weapon components Frasier made available to Li . . . ?"

Whitford now literally beamed. "We dictated to Frasier exactly what he would pass to Li; we infected every item beforehand."

"Nick," Carolyn said, "no way are the Chinese going to break these encryption codes. They're decades ahead of anything ever imagined in the private sector. Some of the best minds in the country have confirmed that to my satisfaction. And the chips? The viruses are burned into their microcircuits."

What had Dennis said: the Chinese were mere puppets . . . marionettes on a string? Nick stared at Whitford and Carolyn, awestruck, as Whitford went on.

"The Pentagon's examined some of the software the Chinese currently use in their T-72 tanks and MIGs—crap. Obsolete years ago. The Chinese'll grab this stuff, plug it in, and test it. It'll perform incredibly, just as it was designed to do. So what'll the Chinese do? They'll copy it; they'll employ it in every one of their tanks, their planes, their subs, their radar installations, their ships, thinking they've upgraded their army. But each peripheral we let them steal—range finders, helmet sensors—each piece of software they smuggle has the same embedded virus. And once our little virus gets its claws into their machinery, it ain't ever letting go, son."

"But haven't you given up our technological edge?" Nick asked, still struggling to come to grips with what he'd heard.

"Have we given away *some* technological secrets? Sure, ones we concluded the Chinese would buy or steal or develop soon enough anyway. But look at what we've gained, a chance to infect the Red Army. And the poetic justice of it all—the Chinese will have done it to *themselves*."

Nick let the gun drop all the way to his side. "Exactly what will this virus do?"

Whitford said, "Until we activate it, nothing. Every component will function as designed. But every piece J. T. Frasier leaked to Li is designed to link to equipment with 'ears.' Link to fighters, tanks, subs, and personnel carriers. All pieces of equipment which have the capability to *receive* radio, laser, or infrared signals. We can actually *communicate* with our virus, Mr. Ford. Give it instructions by specially coded message."

Carolyn nodded. "It's all true, Nick."

"Let me give you an example," Whitford said, animated. "Say China decides to invade Taiwan. A squadron of Chinese Su-27's leads the advance attack and meets one of our squadrons; they engage each other. Suddenly one of our fighters transmits a specially coded message over military radio frequencies. Think of each of the Su-27's as one computer network; the infected software or chip, our software, our chip, is tied into that network. It 'hears' the transmission; the virus activates. Suddenly all hell breaks loose. The virus shuts down the Su-27's navigational systems, its fire-control systems, its communication capabilities. Dogfight over. We win without a goddamn shot being fired."

Nick's eyes blurred. Was it really possible? He answered his own question: if young college hackers could successfully insert viruses into the computer systems of Fortune 500 companies, what couldn't the government do with all its resources?

Whitford's voice turned somber. "I pray constructive engagement is effective, Mr. Ford. We all do. We pray China buys into American culture—from Disney to democracy—but if that doesn't happen, we better be prepared for the alternative. That's what this was all about. Our military is being gutted—we *need* an insurance policy. A safety valve. One I hope to God we never have to test."

"How do I now you haven't made up everything you've told me?" Nick asked.

"You have the word of a senior senator and the comptroller general of the GAO."

"Congress approved the plan?"

Whitford shook his head. "It's a 'black' program . . . no congressional or White House oversight. *Very few* people know, for obvious reasons. If the secret gets out, the operation's worthless."

"What's your authority, then? For this kind of covert action you'd have to get the approval of—"

"*Dammit,* Ford," Whitford yelled, cutting Nick off. "Haven't you heard what I said: China launches a nuclear missile, we might be able to disarm it. China invades Taiwan or South Korea, we might be able to shut a good slice of their army down. Forget the damn approvals for a moment. We may have won a war China doesn't even know it fought . . . a bloodless victory."

*Scott, Jing-mei, Dennis?* "Not bloodless, Senator. There have been a few casualties."

Whitford slammed his cane against the floor. "Carolyn thinks the world of you. Frankly, I'm having a little trouble understanding why. I don't give—"

Carolyn put her hand out, silencing Whitford, then said, "What happened to Scott, we had nothing to do with it. We had no idea he was investigating on his own—*you know that.* He stumbled onto Li's operation, and . . . Li's men caught him, Nick. At Kiajong Shipping yard. We didn't know anything about it. They just . . ." Carolyn's voice faded away.

"Mutilated his hands, then killed him," Nick said, finishing Carolyn's sentence. "And the subcontractor in Birmingham . . . McKenzie?"

Carolyn rubbed her forehead. "Things spiraled out of control. Li was informed of your leads . . . that you were going to question McKenzie. The intent was to give Li a chance to cover his tracks, that's all."

"I'd say he covered them pretty good, wouldn't you?"

"McKenzie was a *traitor* to the United States of America," Whitford trumpeted. "He was killed—I'm sorry about that—but what would you have us do: flush the operation down the drain in *his* memory?"

Nick clenched his teeth. "Instead you left Li free to attack me, to attack Meg."

"You've got to believe me, Nick," Carolyn said, "I knew nothing about that."

Nick turned on Whitford. "And you, Senator?"

"You had the disk, enough evidence to expose Li's entire operation. Yes, I set you up, but not for murder. Li's man was to rob you of the disk, that's all. I swear it." Whitford shook his head. "You were removed from your post, dammit. If you had stopped your investigations, nothing would have happened to you or to Miss Taylor. We had the situation under control."

"Tell that to Meg." Nick raised the gun again; his hand shook. It would be so simple to pull the trigger. An accessory to all that had happened to Scott, Meg, dead in the time it took a nerve impulse to go from his brain to his finger.

Whitford took a deep breath. When he continued, he spoke emotionally. "You have my heartfelt apologies. I know what you probably think of me, but you're wrong. If I could take the young girl's place, I would. Without hesitation. But I can't. And now we must all deal with realities. The merit of the operation remains. Our safety valve, the Pandora's box, still exists. Still protects you and me. Protects every child who hopes to grow up someday and realize the fruits of this great nation. How will revealing all that has happened do anything but hurt those prospects?"

"People *died*."

Whitford set his jaw. "Don't give me that sanctimonious bullshit. Open your eyes. The game's rough, welcome to the real world. We wear white gloves only to hide the bruises on our knuckles. Let me repeat, *no one* was supposed to be killed. It was an accident . . . out of our control. Yes, people died. They have in the past, and will in the future. Are we supposed to fall on our swords? If we are, at what price, Mr. Ford?"

"And so the killing goes on. Dennis, Jing-mei."

"I don't know who attacked you today. Maybe it was Li's men, maybe not. But I promise you this: If it was a rogue element in the government, whoever was responsible will be found and punished. There are limits, Mr. Ford."

*Were there?* Nick wondered. "And the man inside Carolyn's gate?"

"A Secret Service agent . . . nothing more. Here to keep watch for Dennis . . . as I said, I had no idea he was dead."

Blood roared in Nick's ears. He imagined Whitford as a snake, hypnotizing and confusing the issues. "We're a government of laws. We can't . . . The public has to know."

"Ford," Whitford yelled, "my God, think of what you're saying. Think of the strategic edge we've gained. We've wheeled thousands of miniature Trojan horses inside China's gates, and we can open the trapdoors anytime we like."

*The promise of a bloodless war—did anyone have a right to forfeit that?* Emotion fought logic in Nick's mind. He shut his eyes. Was this about Whitford or Carolyn, or about the thousands, maybe hundreds of thousands of lives that Whitford said might hang in the balance? "Sorry, I can't ignore the last month," Nick said finally, eyes hard in resolve. "Too much has happened."

Whitford stroked his chin, then nodded slowly. "All right," he said weakly. "Maybe too much *has* happened. Maybe Carolyn and I must face the consequences of our actions. So be it. But, Mr. Ford, don't ruin all we've worked for. Don't let the end of our careers stand for nothing. Work with us."

"How?"

"By keeping it out of the papers. By maintaining the integrity of the operation. I promise you, Mr. Ford, that I will testify before a closed session of the Senate. I'll write a confession, cooperate in any way you'd like."

Carolyn eagerly seized on the idea. "Whatever you want, Nick," she echoed.

A closed session of the Senate? The truth revealed. Other, better minds could weigh the operation and

consider the alternatives. It made sense to Nick. The
Senate could investigate and determine whether to lay
bare the operation. Either way, it would not be on
Nick's head alone to decide.

Whitford pointed his cane at Nick's gun. "I think
you can set that down now," he said. "We're all on
the same side."

Nick's mind continued to whirl. How could he, one
man, play jury? Maybe Whitford was telling the truth.
Maybe Nick could lay grave injustices at the senator's
feet, at Carolyn's feet, but perhaps murder was not
among them. And if he shunned vigilante justice, that
meant he had to go to the authorities—why not the
Senate?

Nick lowered the gun to the desk, his right hand
still wrapped about its grip.

Whitford heaved a sigh. "Strange, Mr. Ford, but the
idea of confessing, letting the Senate take action . . .
no matter what that may mean to me personally . . .
somehow it's liberating." He turned his legs to the
side, rubbed them vigorously with the palms of his
hands. "Excuse me while I stretch my legs . . . have
to do it every half hour or so, another of my doctor's
orders. Only thing that keeps the blood flowing." He
groaned as he rose, placing most of his weight on the
cane. "I hate using a cane, but it keeps me out of a
wheelchair. Maybe it's just vanity . . . Roosevelt ran
the country from a wheelchair, did a fairly good job
of it too."

Nick concentrated on their next move. He asked,
"How would we set up a closed session of the
Senate?"

Carolyn answered. "We can get on the phone right
now, Nick. You name the senators; we tell them
everything."

Whitford, to Nick's left now, nodded. "Two senators, three senators, a half dozen. Whoever you feel
most comfortable with."

Nick started cataloging senators in his mind. Senator
Raine for sure. And Senator McCaskey. Maybe Senator—

From the extreme left of his peripheral vision, Nick caught a blur of motion, the only warning. A blow from Whitford's cane—hard, biting—struck Nick across the wrists, breaking his hold on the gun.

Nick looked up at Whitford, now standing over him, face contorted in violence. His effort to raise an arm in defense came an instant late, and the second stroke cracked the back of his skull.

Nick fought to gain his feet, but the cane came down again, then again, on his shoulders, then the back of his neck.

Nick fell off the chair, rolled to the ground. He thought he heard a voice, Carolyn's voice, yelling something, and then he was on all fours. He saw Whitford's shoes, just for a moment, polished black and shiny. Then the cane cracked down once more, and Nick's head exploded in a flash of light.

# 49

"My God, Charles, did you kill him?" Words—Carolyn's words—filtered through to Nick's consciousness. He rolled his eyes but couldn't open them. He didn't seem to have power over his body, not yet.

Two fingers pressed against Nick's neck, and then came Carolyn's voice, choked with emotion. "There's still a pulse. Thank God."

Feeling crept back to Nick's body. To his head first. The pain almost caused him to black out again.

*"Why?"* he heard Carolyn ask, her voice close. "For Christ's sake, why?"

Nick worked to open his eyes; still they wouldn't obey. The sharp pain, centered at the back of his head, grew stronger. Piercing.

"You heard him, Carolyn," Whitford said, coldly. "We tried to explain . . . *we tried*. He wouldn't listen."

Nick managed to open his eyes then, just for a moment, and in that instant caught Carolyn, stooping at his side, hovering over him. And Whitford, the cane still clutched tightly in his fist. Then their images began to go fuzzy, to lose their focus, and the room began a slow spin. Nick shut his eyes again and fought to retain consciousness.

"What about the closed session of the Senate? We could have—" Nick heard Carolyn say desperately, only to have Whitford interrupt.

"When have you ever, *ever* known the Senate to keep a secret, Carolyn? Open session, closed session, it wouldn't have made any difference. We *tried* to explain."

"We could have tried harder."

*"He wouldn't listen . . .* I'm sorry, Carolyn. God, I'm sorry, but he didn't leave me any choice."

"I've got to call a doctor." Nick heard steps—Carolyn moving toward the phone.

*"No,"* Whitford shouted.

"What do you mean, no?"

Nick opened his eyes again. The pain was still there but was duller now, bearable. *Have to get to my feet, protect myself.*

"Everything we've worked for will be lost. Too much is at stake, Carolyn. You know that. We both know that." There was a short pause. "I'm going to get someone in here," Whitford said.

"Who?"

Whitford didn't answer.

"The man at the gate?"

Another pause, longer this time.

"Charles . . . Charles, look at me. You brought the man at the gate along in case Nick showed, didn't you?"

"Stay here." Whitford started for the double doors.

"You lied, didn't you? You knew about the attack on Dennis and Nick today . . . *Charles*?"

Whitford turned; his voice flared. "What do you think, Carolyn? God damn right I knew about it. And if Li's man had done the job right the first time, like he was supposed to, this all would have been over a long time ago. Ford doesn't understand necessities, and I don't have time to make him understand. He threatens everything—the national security interests of this country. By now the scene of the shooting's been sanitized. There's nothing to link us to it."

Carolyn's mouth dropped open; it was a moment before she could speak. "What happened to you?"

"What happened to *me*?" Whitford barked. "Nothing happened to me. What I want to know is, what happened to *you*? Alternatives, remember? Put them on the scale: one man's life against tens of thousands . . . maybe millions. How naive are you? This isn't a game, and Ford won't be the first to die for his country. How's this: Li had nothing to do with Frasier's death and it sure wasn't an accident. Satisfied? That's reality, Carolyn, now deal with it." He started again toward the doors.

*"Charles."*

Nick coughed involuntarily. A series that racked his body.

Whitford spun, faced Nick. "He's waking up. Hand me the gun."

Carolyn picked the gun off the desk and cradled it to her breast. "No."

Nick pulled a hand in toward his body, tried to push himself to hands and knees. He groaned at the feeble and failed attempt.

"The gun, Carolyn," Whitford insisted again, taking a step in her direction.

*"No."*

Whitford turned the cane in his hand, gripping its end. "Very well." He raised the cane over Nick, the heavy silver handle poised like a club head.

"Don't do it, Charles."

Whitford looked to her, saw the barrel of the gun was now pointed in his direction, its tip vibrating in time with her trembling hand. He paused, gauging her as he had earlier gauged Nick. "This is hard for you, I know," he said softly. "But it has to be done. With time you'll see that."

Nick again tried to raise himself, and once more he failed. *Have to move. Have to roll. Do something.* He looked up, into Whitford's eyes—hate shone down on him as the cane began its descent.

The cane dropped in a smooth arc. Gathering speed. Nick tensed his body, eyes wide.

A muffled splat then, and with it the cane's trajectory jumped right. Its velocity slowed. Nick continued to stare upward, saw surprise, then fear flood Whitford's eyes as he bent double, forearms clamped against his right side, holding in a growing patch of red.

The senator staggered for a moment, mouthed something in Carolyn's direction, then crumpled in on himself and fell to the ground. He landed facing Nick, only a few feet distant. And as gravity took Whitford's slack skin, molding a distorted death mask, Nick for the first time noticed Whitford's neck: thin, with flaps of flesh pooling above his shirt collar. And Whitford's hands, marred by pea-sized liver spots.

No longer a powerful man, no longer a man to fear.

Nick fought his way to his elbow and finally a sitting position. A rush of blood, and his head again swam. He closed his eyes, held the back of his head, and hung on to consciousness desperately. A few seconds later he turned to Carolyn, sitting at the chair behind the cherry desk staring off into space, the gun still in her hands.

Only then did Nick fully realize what had happened. "Carolyn . . ." he said, and ran out of words.

"He would have killed you," she replied, looking through Nick, speaking to no one.

"We should call someone . . . a doctor."

Carolyn regarded Whitford for a moment, then shook her head. "He's dead."

Meeting Whitford's glazed eyes, open but unseeing, Nick realized she was right.

Tears started down Carolyn's face. "What happened?" Her voice came remote and broken. "What in God's name happened?"

"I'd like to call the police now, Carolyn," Nick said gently.

Her eyes jumped up and flared. *"No,"* she insisted fiercely.

"Carolyn . . . it's over now."

She trained the gun in his direction. "No, it's not over."

Nick dipped his head once, signaling agreement, and the gun barrel drifted downward. They sat, he staring at her, she staring blankly at Whitford. Finally, she said, "In the beginning everything seemed so clear. The things that happened . . . I swear to God, Nick, I didn't know. After McKenzie fell from his balcony, I harbored some doubts, but kept them locked away. I don't think I wanted to face them. And what I . . .

we . . . were trying to do . . . it was so important. What happened to Scott, the attack on Meg, on you . . . You were all off the case, *dammit. You should have been off the case.* No one had any reason to touch you, that's what I thought."

Nick shut his eyes.

"Forgive me, Nick." Carolyn's voice dropped to almost a whisper. "I'm so sorry. So very sorry." She paused, then continued. "I wasn't in on things in the beginning. When you initiated the audit of the Yünnan Project, I knew nothing. They didn't think they needed me then, didn't think you'd delve into the subcontracts, thought Senator Whitford could control the scope of the audit from the bench. They were wrong. They came to me then. Told me everything you've heard today and asked my help.

"Nick, Burt Knowles *was* planning to retire. I would have strongly considered you for his position anyway . . . believe that. You know how I respect your abilities, it's just that . . . Their motivation, their purpose, was sound—Whitford was right about that. Don't you see? All I did was promote you—that was supposed to be the end of my involvement. If I knew how the lies would trap me, involve me . . . knew what was going to happen to Scott, to Meg, to you, do you think I ever would have agreed?"

Carolyn shook her head violently. "Was I wrong? Wrong to help a cause that started out just? Decisions aren't black and white, Nick, they're shades of gray. Good *and* bad, right *and* wrong, inseparable sometimes. And all you can do is balance the two and choose the alternative you *think* will do the most good. If you were in my position, maybe you'd understand. Senators, cabinet members, come to me and say national security requires bending the law just a bit. At first you tell them no, but over time you see there *are* times the law *doesn't* serve justice. Do you understand what I'm saying? Men and women of courage serve their country, not a rule book."

"With all that's happened, I find it hard to call Senator Whitford a man of courage."

Carolyn raised her head. "Senator Whitford was a good man. A solid man, who loved his country. He just believed in what he was doing so desperately that he"—she looked at Whitford's fallen body—"he lost his compass. A number of people lost their compass."

"Who, Carolyn? Give me names."

She shook her head. "You think exposing them would help? I don't. Sometimes revealing a wrong causes more harm than good. Yes, Nixon was a flawed character; yes, he covered up Watergate, but did exposing his role help this country or did it cripple us? First we lost our sense of America's place in the world; then Nixon lost support for the bombing raids of North Vietnam. Soon we lost Vietnam; then came Cambodia and the Khmer Rouge. One million Cambodians killed, how many Vietnamese boat people, all because of high-minded people who insisted we expose our dirty laundry. Was it really worth it? Things went on in the Kennedy administration every bit as criminal as Watergate. If they'd been disclosed, would JFK have had the moral authority to face down the Russians during the Cuban missile crisis? It's not a game out there, Nick. The world plays for keeps, not gold stars. I believe in what I did. Called upon to serve my country, I served. I have no regrets about my decision, just the way . . . the way everything's turned out."

"People have to take responsibility. . . ."

"I can't *avoid* it. Do you think I've slept through a night in the last month? Do you think my stomach didn't sour every time I spoke with you? My hands are dirty. So dirty I can't ever get them clean. . . . All I can try to do is help."

Carolyn picked up the phone, pinned it between her shoulder and ear, then punched in a number.

"What are you doing?" Nick said.

"I'm going to try to give you something more tangible than apologies." After a couple of seconds, she spoke into the phone. "This is Carolyn Reed." A long pause, perhaps a full minute, followed.

Nick looked at Carolyn questioningly. Her face gave him no clue as to what would come next.

When Carolyn spoke again, her voice was gruff. "I just learned someone targeted Nick Ford today." After another pause, Carolyn continued; Nick monitored her side of the conversation. "Senator Whitford confirmed the fact. . . . I'm not calling to argue what you knew or didn't know. . . . What do I want? I want the order rescinded, immediately. . . . No, I don't believe you. . . . Immediately. You have no choice . . . I'll tell you why, because a few hours ago I put together four packets of information, everything I know about the project. Names, dates, events. I've mailed them, using various carriers, various drop points to confidants. With each I included a letter with simple instructions. If Nick Ford should disappear or die, in an accident or otherwise, the information in those packets is to be released to the newspapers. . . . Otherwise they remain buried, of course. . . . Believe me, I have thought this out. . . . Why? Because Ford's an innocent man. . . . No, he's not a threat. I've convinced him that the men who came after him were sent by John Li. A hit against Dennis Lindsay that he got in the middle of. It would make sense if you do what you can to support that fiction. . . . Talking to me won't do any good. . . . You're right, you don't have much choice. Rescind the order. . . . Good. . . . The senator's with me right now. . . . Unfortunately, he can't; he's indisposed. . . . Where am I? I'm in hell, Director. I've been there for quite some time."

Carolyn hung up the phone and looked at Nick. "Your get out of jail free card," she whispered after a moment.

Nick had followed enough of the conversation to understand what had transpired. "The packets of information?" he asked.

"A lie—I've put together nothing, mailed nothing—but they don't know that. I do know names, Nick.

Dates and events. They can't risk all I know making its way to the press. . . . You're safe now—they don't dare touch you—but I won't give you the tools to destroy what we did."

"And if I go to the newspapers or the police anyway?"

"Would anybody believe you? Without hard evidence, I'd bet not. And you'll have canceled your insurance policy. Think of what's happened, and you tell me: how long before you'd have an accident or disappear? Your decision, Nick. Alternatives, just like I had. Just like the senator had. . . . I'm going to have a glass of port. Would you like to join me?"

"I don't feel like a drink."

She shrugged. "Well I do. I don't have much time left."

*Not much time left?* Something in the tone of Carolyn's voice gave Nick pause.

"It's one of the bottles Harry put up years ago."

Harry, her husband who had died of cancer a few years back.

"Opened it last night," Carolyn continued. "The second bottle I tried—the first had turned. I thought for a moment they'd all gone bad, like Harry and I." She poured herself a glass, a generous portion, then reseated herself. She didn't drink immediately, just spun the stem of the glass slowly between her forefinger and thumb.

"The 'iron lady,' that's what they've always called me. You've probably called me that, just never to my face. Tough, determined. Men said I had balls. And I never minded. That's the image I cultivated, because that's who I thought I was. Want to know something?"

"What?"

"I'm weak, Nick. A coward. Just like Harry."

"I've never thought of you, or Harry, as cowards, Carolyn," he said softly.

She laughed. "A few days ago I might have half agreed with you, but not about Harry. I just never let you, never let *anyone,* see what he had become in those last few years. I kept up the charade, telling everyone Harry this, Harry that; then I'd dress him up once a month or so for a grand appearance . . . for all of a half hour. Any more and people would have known. . . . In the end he was like a baby. He soiled his pants two, three times a day, and he'd cry because he couldn't do anything about it . . . this strong man who used to lift me in his arms as if I weighed no more than a bag of groceries. You know, he got so thin I could almost wrap my hand around his calf. Around his *calf,* Nick."

"I'm sorry," he whispered. "I didn't know."

"I didn't want *anybody* to know. I lived with the man for three years like that—an invalid who couldn't give love, didn't even *try* to provide companionship, just demanded—three years while the love slowly drained from me, day after day. In the end all I could see was a selfish old man. God forgive me, but I couldn't recall the love anymore. I just couldn't."

Nick looked to the pool of blood growing around the senator.

"Do you want to know how much of a coward Harry was, Nick?" Carolyn went on. "After he died, I found something locked in one of his drawers that made me hate him. A loaded handgun. I never knew he had a handgun, but it was there. A stack of notes too. Fourteen. Drafts of a letter from him to me, the first dated two years before he died, the last one month before. Suicide notes, Nick. Harry planned to commit suicide. For *two years* he planned to commit suicide."

"I can't judge him for that, Carolyn."

"*I have* judged him, and you've got it all wrong. Harry wasn't a coward because he contemplated suicide, Harry was a coward because he planned suicide for two years and *never pulled the trigger*. . . . There, I've said it. God forgive me if he can. If Harry had been strong, he would have pulled the trigger and saved our love. Instead he became a pitiable shell of a man who cried himself to sleep in self-pity, and I couldn't, *couldn't,* remember him as anything else."

"I can't find it in myself to blame him," Nick said, "or you, for that matter."

"But *I* did blame Harry, Nick. I cursed him more times than you would believe. You know what, though, I've stopped. A few days ago, for the first time I remembered the old Harry. I forgave him, and I actually missed him. Maybe it's empathy. . . . I pulled out Harry's gun a few days ago. The same one he never could bring himself to use. I found the bullets, loaded it, but— I couldn't even aim it at myself. Perhaps I had too high of an opinion of myself to destroy this body in such a . . . personal . . . manner. I came to the conclusion I'm every bit as weak as he. Every bit as weak."

"Then put the gun down."

"No. Things have changed in the last half hour. There's no going back now. As you said, people have to take responsibility. I think I can do that now. Remembering Harry, the way he was once . . . knowing he'll be waiting for me . . . that helps."

She shook her head as if to clear it, then looked at Nick, her eyes pleading. "One thing, Nick. I don't have any right to ask, but . . . Forgive me. It'll help, somehow. It'll make it easier."

Nick looked down.

"Please, Nick."

Nick nodded. "I forgive you."

"Thank you." Carolyn bowed her head in acceptance. When she raised it again, her eyes had brightened. "Suddenly, I feel so alive. For the first time in years." She took a deep breath. "The air tastes fresh and smells so wonderful. My skin's tingling. I've heard impending death can do that . . . heighten the senses. A benefit I wasn't expecting . . . helps make it worth it, these last few minutes, as if I'm experiencing life anew."

*Impending death.* Nick looked at the gun in Carolyn's hand. "Carolyn," he whispered, "give me the gun."

She ignored him. "I've lived in this house most of my adult life. I'll end it here too." She got to her feet and moved to the window facing the east and pulled the drapes open. "It's such a beautiful night, Nick; I don't want to miss a moment. The air . . . so clear. Look at the stars, the moon. So long since I even bothered to look. Don't make the same mistake. It's right out your window, every evening. But today . . . it's something special today. The most beautiful view I've ever seen."

"Carolyn, give me the gun," Nick tried again.

"No. The decisions I made, funny, but I still think they're the right ones. Problem is, I can't live with the aftermath. Leave now, Nick. Out the back."

"I won't."

"They'll be coming soon. They'll trace the call and send someone to deal with me. It would be better if they didn't find you here."

"It would be better if they didn't find either of us here."

"What they'll find of me will do them no good, but it will serve a purpose. Once I'm gone, they'll accept my story . . . they'll have no choice . . . and you'll be safe. No one will dare touch you, Nick . . . my word on that. Now go."

Nick shook his head.

Carolyn looked at him quizzically, then reached for the cigar lighter Whitford had set on the desk. She stood, then backed slowly to the window. She snapped the lighter open, flicked it once; a half-inch flame sprang from its top.

"I'm afraid," Carolyn said, "I'm not going to give you any choice." She held lighter and flame to the drapes.

"Carolyn," Nick yelled, jumping to his feet.

Carolyn held the gun steady. "Don't, Nick. It's the only way."

The drapes caught; Carolyn continued: "They'll find

me, find the senator, and cover things up. 'Freak Fire Takes Life of Senator and Comptroller General,' will be the headline and, as far as the public will ever know, the truth. As long as you stick to your story, you'll have nothing to fear."

The flames licked upward slowly for a moment or two, then, as if enjoying the taste, began to consume material hungrily. Smoke pooled near the ceiling.

"Come with me, Carolyn," Nick pleaded, cautiously advancing. One step, two steps.

She shook her head and said calmly, "No."

Within seconds inch-long flames grew to foot-long flames. Seconds more and the entire length of drape turned to a pillar of fiery red. Flames fanned across the ceiling, cutting through smoke now a half foot thick.

"Stop," Carolyn ordered, gun still steady in her hands, and Nick obeyed. "This fire's for me, and for the senator. Our hell, not yours. Go. Now."

Nick stood for another few seconds as the blaze spread, first warming, then beginning to sear his cheeks, his hands, every piece of exposed skin. The black smoke curled around him, finally forcing him to his knees in a fit of coughs.

From there, through the thickening haze, he looked at Carolyn and saw only her silhouette, like some stone statue set against a backdrop of yellows and reds. Only this statue started to move, to spread its arms wide as if welcoming the flames about to engulf it.

The heat unbearable, the smoke almost to the floor, Nick's instinct for survival took over. He covered his mouth with a hand and bolted for the back door. One bounce off the door jamb and he was on the porch, and from there stumbled out to the backyard.

Hands on knees, Nick greedily sucked in air. Rasping. Only when his lungs had partially cleared did he again think of Carolyn. A glance at the house told him he could do nothing for her. Smoke poured out onto the porch, flames followed, pushing through the doors, pressing flat against the windows.

Nick's scalp tightened. Head bowed, he whispered, "Carolyn"—a silently offered prayer he could spare only a second for. The smoke, the fire, would bring the man lying in wait at the front gate.

Nick ran across Carolyn's back lawn without looking back. He made the woods, then scaled Carolyn's back wall. He had covered five blocks before he heard the first fire engine.

# 50

"Again?"

Nick turned his face from the window and met the eyes of the cab driver in the rearview mirror. He nodded. "Yeah."

They had already rounded the Ellipse, the large circular plot of land to the south of the White House grounds, five times. Or was it six? Nick had lost count.

He turned back to his right, to the window. The stolid architecture of the Commerce Building passed from view, giving way to the south face of the White House, the floodlights about its base lending it a virginal white glow. Inside, the President's reception would be well underway. Nick could still gain admittance, seek the President's ear, or the ear of one of his chief advisers and tell them—

Tell them what? Nick asked himself.

Seeking the truth at all costs had so far led only to death and suffering. Could he expect any less from a full airing of Carolyn's and Whitford's crimes? The ability to shut down an army, the chance to avoid Armageddon, how could one measure that against such amorphous terms as right and wrong? Nick had thought the world black and white; he'd been wrong. The world was gray, just as Carolyn said, and cold to the touch.

Nick pressed his eyelids tight; a feeling of isolation swept over him.

Carolyn's image came to him then, throwing open the drapes of her study. "It's such a beautiful night," she had said, "I don't want to miss a moment. The air . . . so clear. Look at the stars, the moon. So long since I even bothered to look."

*So long since I even bothered to look.*

*Don't make the same mistake.* Nick looked up—met the stars. They were beautiful.

As of tonight Nick's job was over for him; he would neither mourn it nor miss it. He had sought purpose through achievement—a chimera, a folly, he knew that now. And if that left only a void into which pain would flow, let it come. He had hid, and run, from pain all his life; perhaps he was now ready to face it.

In his mind's eye his father and mother appeared, and the familiar tumult of emotions squeezed him, but this time Nick did not hide. This time Nick did not run. What had Carolyn said, something about finally remembering her husband as the man he was, the man who had carried her lightly in his arms. Nick too looked past the anguish and remembered.

His father's large but quiet hands. Sandwiches wrapped in wax paper, smelling of his mother. Sharing the hammock with one or both. Fresh towels from the line smelling of ozone.

Nick's eyes filled.

Things to celebrate, why had he never seen that? Why had he thought them things to lock away to examine only rarely and only under the influence of alcohol?

Drives in the country in the pickup. His father's back, sturdy, as he split firewood. Card games, board games. His mother's voice, singing along with the radio.

The best times of his life and he was afraid to relive them. Why?

Nick wiped his face of tears; new ones took their place. And it felt good.

The cab continued to circle, passing to the north of the Washington Monument, a symbol of remembrance, tall, imposing, and lit for the world to see.

*Lit for the world to see.*

The cab driver cleared his throat. "Look, buddy, I can do this all night. . . . I mean that's fine with me, but if there's some reason—"

Nick shook his head and waved his hand, stopping

the cab driver in mid-sentence. Enough of circling, going nowhere, observing but not participating.

Where to? Where did he belong? He knew the answer. Had known it all along. "George Washington University Hospital," he said.

Visiting hours would be over, but he would talk his way in somehow. He would stop first at the rest rooms and clean the blood from his hair, the dirt from his trousers. The tuxedo would still show wrinkles, his shirt, stains, but he guessed Meg wouldn't care. And he would stay the night, if she'd let him, and watch over her from a chair so that on first light, when her eyes opened on a new day, he would be there.

As the cab driver left the road circling the Ellipse, Nick turned to look through the back window. The White House seemed to retreat, growing smaller and less significant. Then the cab turned a corner, and soon trees and buildings extinguished its glow entirely.

Dennis had claimed right and wrong were only labels invented by men. Perhaps they were. Perhaps, if the terms existed at all, they were for another power to judge. On the other hand, Nick thought, perhaps love was something very real. It was time, he decided, to find out.

Nick lowered the side window and let fresh air blow across his face. The streets of D.C. looked clean and wide and new.

# Epilogue

The small boy's legs churned furiously, carrying him down the path a few feet ahead of his pursuers. The moon, quarter full, dimly lit the faces of the trees, of the bushes, but of the path itself the boy saw nothing and could only trust that his feet, which dipped into the blackness below rhythmically, like pistons, would find soft sand and nothing more.

Something about the night air flushed the boy with excitement, raised goose bumps on his skin. Made him run faster, like an animal, a wild thing, impossible to catch.

The path ended, opening up on ten yards of lawn. The boy's lungs burned. He heard the footsteps behind him, gaining. Five yards now.

His bare feet moved from grass to wood—no one could catch him now. He lengthened his strides over the last few feet, then leapt high into the air, unleashing a victorious scream.

The pier was just wide enough for two, and Meg and Nick jogged its length hand in hand. They followed their son off its end, jumped into the warm, dark water. They bobbed to the surface and played then, the three of them, as children play. Their laughing continued as they stepped to shore minutes later. Three towels hung from a tree; Meg wrapped the boy in one and rubbed his back vigorously. "I won, Dad," the boy crowed between shivers.

Nick nodded, smiling, then draped an arm around the boy, another around Meg, and led the way up the path.